Infinite Reality
Daggerland Online Novel 1
A LitRPG Adventure
By Peter Meredith

I0598785

Fictional works by Peter Meredith:

A Perfect America
Infinite Reality: Daggerland Online Novel 1
The Sacrificial Daughter
The Apocalypse Crusade War of the Undead: Day One
The Apocalypse Crusade War of the Undead: Day Two
The Apocalypse Crusade War of the Undead Day Three
The Apocalypse Crusade War of the Undead Day Four
The Horror of the Shade: Trilogy of the Void 1
An Illusion of Hell: Trilogy of the Void 2
Hell Blade: Trilogy of the Void 3
The Punished
Sprite
The Blood Lure The Hidden Land Novel 1
The King's Trap The Hidden Land Novel 2
To Ensnare a Queen The Hidden Land Novel 3
The Apocalypse: The Undead World Novel 1
The Apocalypse Survivors: The Undead World Novel 2
The Apocalypse Outcasts: The Undead World Novel 3
The Apocalypse Fugitives: The Undead World Novel 4
The Apocalypse Renegades: The Undead World Novel 5
The Apocalypse Exile: The Undead World Novel 6
The Apocalypse War: The Undead World Novel 7
The Apocalypse Executioner: The Undead World Novel 8
The Apocalypse Revenge: The Undead World Novel 9
The Apocalypse Sacrifice: The Undead World 10
The Edge of Hell: Gods of the Undead Book One
The Edge of Temptation: Gods of the Undead Book Two
Pen(Novella)
A Sliver of Perfection (Novella)
The Haunting At Red Feathers(Short Story)
The Haunting On Colonel's Row(Short Story)
The Drawer(Short Story)
The Eyes in the Storm(Short Story)
The Witch: Jillybean in the Undead World

Greg Nelson stifled yet another yawn as he listened with half an ear to his chief financial officer go on and on. And Greg barely looked at the screen with its flow charts and pie charts and every manner of visual representation of statistical data forecasting the market trends of the blah, blah, concurrent with their blah and their blah, blah, blah.

He was having trouble staying awake, and yet, he couldn't simply disregard the capital side of his business. GN Industries, when it finally got off the ground, wasn't just going to create the perfect game world; it was also supposed to make gobs of money.

Not that he really needed the money. As one of the "Big Six" developers, Greg was already rich. He fit somewhere between: *Look at my yacht that I just paid for in cash* and *I'm building my own island the size of Connecticut.* He was comfortably rich, but in order to compete against his old company: Infinite Reality Gaming, he needed somewhere close to a billion dollars.

The very idea that his CFO was discussing ways to acquire said billion dollars should have been enough to focus Greg and keep him awake, however he had barely gotten four hours of sleep a night for the last month and hadn't seen the inside of a gym for, well, to be honest, he had never seen the inside of a gym.

In an effort to stay awake, he brought a pale hand up and began to gently smack his own round, soft cheek. He was in mid-smack when his smart watch vibrated with a message. Greg hated the vibrating mode because it felt like a wasp was landing on him and, as always, he fairly jumped in fright.

"Sorry about that. Go on," Greg said to his CFO, who had stopped at his odd twitch. The CFO smiled blandly and slipped straight back into "yawn speak" as Greg was beginning to categorize it. Surreptitiously, Greg took a peek at his watch: *There is a break-in occurring at Mendenome right now!*

"Shoot," Greg whispered. The timing couldn't have been worse. He brought the watch to his face and replied to the message, "Give me twenty minutes."

"Twenty minutes?" the CFO asked.

Greg hit the send button on his watch. "Sorry, a slight emergency. Will this take much longer?"

The CFO grimaced as he glanced at the forty slides he still had to go through. "I suppose I can speed things along."

"I'm all ears," Greg said. "Please, continue." The endlessly bland words began to flow once more from the finance officer. They washed like a breeze over Greg and were quickly forgotten. Another attempt at Mendenome? This made the third in only a week and the fifth in the last month. It was strange but not very worrisome. Most likely it was just another gang of thieves and, if so, they were going to find out that Greg Nelson was far more cutthroat than he appeared.

Of course, five break-ins in a month could mean it was a collaborated financed operation.

"If so, someone is spending a boatload of money on this," Greg muttered under his breath. "A lot of lives and a lot of money, for nothing." He couldn't understand what they thought they were going to get. Yes, there were expensive paintings at Mendenome, and gold-threaded carpets, and gems and jewels in abundance, but there were also guards and guard dogs and all manner of traps.

The risk to reward ratio was far out of proportion. It didn't make sense to Greg Nelson. He was a very concrete thinker— every action of his was reasoned and thought out, while these break-ins were a complete waste of someone's resources.

The remainder of the meeting seemed to go by quickly as Greg dwelled on what he would find when he got to Mendenome—more than likely, nothing but blood and hacked apart bodies.

Greg fairly jumped out of his chair when his CFO finally asked, "Are there any questions?"

"No, thank you. I'll make sure to review my notes and get back to you if I can think of anything," he said, ushering the man out through the crystal doors of his office.

His receptionist, a drop-dead gorgeous blonde who could barely answer the phones, but who never wore a bra, announced, "Mr. Tim Cole is here to see you." Her smile was more than a little crooked as she glanced Cole's way. He was a bruiser in a bad suit. As always, his jacket was rumpled, his hair was greasy and he leered openly at the receptionist.

"Okay, Cole, that's enough," Greg said, trying to sound stern. "You can take off, Brandee. It's getting late." She made it obvious that she didn't like being around Cole and was gone so quickly that she caught up with the CFO before he could make it to the elevators.

"Why don't you ever cinch your tie properly?" Greg groused, looking up at Cole, who towered over him.

"Because life is more fun with a loose tie," Cole said, looking down his bent nose at Greg and speaking as if he were either imparting wisdom to a twelve-year-old or reading from a fortune cookie.

The two stood watching through the glass outer door as Brandee swayed over to the elevator. She seemed to be flirting with the CFO as they waited. When the elevator door closed on them, Cole turned to Greg. "So? Are you going to Mendenome, or what? They've been inside for over an hour, now. I don't think the guard dogs are cutting it this time."

"I'm not too worried," Greg said, and he wasn't. Not in the least. "Make sure the building is locked down and then join me on the other side." Cole gave a nod and left. Greg went back into his office and locked the door behind him. Going to one of the oak wall panels, he pressed its top right corner and stood back as a portion of the panel slid to the side, revealing a retinal scanner.

He stared into the light and said as clearly as he could: "Greg Nelson." This activated a secret door that led to a small room that held nothing besides a soft bed and a wireless neural coupler. Like the other seventy-four million couplers created by his old company, his was a half circle of clear plastic, enclosing enough computing power to run a small city.

Taking off his suit coat and tie, Greg lay on the bed and placed the coupler across his forehead, just above his eyes. He took a deep breath and "thought" *INFINITE REALITY.*

This activated the neural coupler and with only the words: "Begin program," Greg's reality fell away. He was no longer in the secret room. He was no longer Greg Nelson. For the moment, he was only a singular consciousness among millions and before him were limitless possibilities. He entered a new world, where, if he wished, he could be a farmer on Mars, or a milkmaid in fifteenth century France, or a computer programmer in twenty-first century America.

These options were open to anyone, but of course no one ever chose them. There were sixty official games within the *Infinite Reality* world. They ran the gamut from World War Two strategy to first person zombie survival, to virtual sports which allowed the sickliest person the ability to play linebacker in the NFL. However, the most popular game by far was Daggerland.

Daggerland, the swords and sorcery brain child of Atticus Arching, another of the Big Six, was perfect in every way. It overflowed with rich detail, from the smell of a warrior's sweat, to the feel of a butterfly's wing, to the way a war hammer sounded when it crushed in an orc's skull.

The world of Daggerland was as utterly seamless as it was huge. Within the game, there were over two-hundred million square miles of mountains, rivers, forest and oceans. There were cities and towns of every size, some floated among the clouds where the views were breathtaking, and others were subterranean, buried deep beneath the earth where the dark things preyed upon each other and upon anyone foolish enough to delve too deep.

Unlike the real world, it was an endlessly exciting land where every imaginable beast, and many beasts that denied imagination, roamed freely. It was the home of mythological heroes, a place where gods ruled in majestic halls, and demons fought for souls deep in bloody charnel pits beneath the earth.

Daggerland was a mix of endless evil and miraculous good. There was magic and heroism and skulking thieves. And there were adventures. Tens of thousands of them, and there were quests, some of which were amazing sagas that could take years to finish and some that were epic in scale, involving armies of millions. Most of the adventures were programmed into the game, but there were many that sprang up among the players out of pure happenstance, or out of desperate need.

Before Daggerland there had been other virtual reality games, but none could compare; and they had all withered and died. In fact, Daggerland was such a wild success that the Supreme Court had declared it a monopoly, and now three of the Big Six developers, including Greg Nelson, had broken away and were designing their own virtual worlds.

In the meantime, Greg couldn't get enough of the lands he had helped to create.

With his coupler firmly fixed, his consciousness floated in an eternal darkness lit only by a glowing grid. Within the grid were the names of the sixty official games and at the top was…"Daggerland," he told the program. Immediately, the grid vanished and two doors took its place. Over one was the word *Gethahyme* and over the other was *New Character*.

Greg went to the door marked *Gethahyme*, opened it and walked through. At that moment, he ceased being Greg Nelson, game developer and all-around nerd. He was no longer soft and weak and pale. When he went through the door, he stepped out as a real man, tall and slim, and yet very strong. He had long, wavy black hair and eyes the color of emerald.

He became Gethahyme, Master of the Red Wizards, and he was no longer bound by the normal laws of physics. Yes, gravity held his feet to the floor and water froze at thirty-two degrees and if he were to strike a match, it would still create a flame. All of this was built into the game, but so too was incredible magic.

"Show me the intruders," Gethahyme commanded. He was on the very top floor of Mendenome, a citadel he had created out of stone, steel and sorcery. This was his lair/workshop/office, and as organized and tidy as he was in the real world, he was something of a slob in Daggerland. Books, papers, and scrolls littered every surface, magic swords had been tossed in a heap by the fireplace, and of the several arcane, amber potion bottles in a silver box on the hearth, at least one had broken open, so that the room smelled of sulphur and lilac.

His office was circular and windowless, lit by torches that burned endlessly. In the center of the room was a desk that had been carved from a single huge hunk of redwood and polished until it gleamed. Behind it was a comfortable leather chair that looked as though it belonged back in GN Industries, and, set just to the side of the desk was a full-length mirror on an elaborate stand.

It was to the mirror he had spoken. While before it had only reflected the mess of his office, now it displayed the adventurers; a group of eight people: six men, two women. Four of the men were encased, head to toe in heavy plate armor that was dented, scratched and bloody. They carried shields and swords, and these too were bloody. These were the tanks, the warriors who shouldered the burden of much of the fighting and who took the brunt of the damage.

Two of the others, a man and one of the women wore what was called "half plate." It consisted of plates of fitted metal, in this case steel, over supple leather. This made the armor much lighter and was usually worn by clerics and rangers, or by adventurers who couldn't afford the more expensive full plate. These two were clerics: healers who could fight and cast spells. The last two were shrouded in long, grey robes. One carried a staff of oak and the other a straight wand—they could only be spell casters.

"No rogues, that's strange. Show me the exterior grounds." The surface image of the mirror faded into a blur of colors that gradually reformed to show the area between the outer wall and his castle. It was strewn with butchered and burned bodies.

He'd had over a hundred men-at-arms and fifty war-dogs guarding his walls, and now there wasn't one left alive. From the scorched stonework, it was clear that the two spell casters had killed most of them. "Incineration spells, very much standard," Gethahyme commented. "And some chain-lightning, but no meteor swarms. Hmmm, mirror show me the audience chamber."

The image switched to a huge room with heavy stone columns stretching to a dome of burnished bronze; he had modeled the room after St. Paul's Cathedral in London. Instead of an altar, it had a wide dais and a bejeweled throne.

There had been a fight here as well. Flanking the dais had been two tremendous figures. Although they appeared to be only statues, they had been iron golems with orders to remain inanimate until certain circumstances occurred—trespassing being one of them.

As they were made of iron, magically imbued with great strength and immune to most spell work, they were very difficult to destroy. But there they were, broken and lifeless.

"So, I finally have a small challenge," Gethahyme said. "Show me the intruders, again. Good. Detect magic." He had worked certain spells into the mirror and now he saw different aspects of the six adventurers glow in a golden light: the staff and wand, which was expected, all four of the swords carried by the tanks, a few rings, a couple of shields and a cloak.

"Bog standard, as our English friends say," he murmured and then strode for the secret stair that led down. As he went to meet the group, he thought: *SPELLS*. The white marble stairs faded into the background of his vision as in front of him, glowing in neon green, there appeared a list of his spells, ordered by tiers from one to nine.

He began casting defensive spells on himself and, by the time he opened the door to the sixth floor, the air around him fairly crackled. The intruders were in one of his experimental laboratories, poking through a large cage in which a juvenile *shambler* had been housed. Gethahyme had been trying to domesticate the creature, but it had proven to be difficult and now was nothing more than a mass of rotting vegetation.

"It was a shambler, in case you didn't know," he said from the doorway. The adventurers leapt back, making him smile. "I'm going to give you one chance. If you tell me who sent you, I'll let you turn around right now and walk out of here alive."

The group glanced back and forth before one of the tanks said in a voice as deep as a troll's, "Maybe if you threw more of an incentive our way we might think about it," When he said "incentive" he meant gold, the only question was if he wanted actual gold or virtual gold. "Ten thousand dollars per person might do it."

Dollars it was, then. Ten thousand was nothing to Greg Nelson and yet it was an incredible sum to ask for. Gethahyme looked at the man closely. The tank was mostly covered in steel and only blue eyes shone out from his helmet. Despite that, he saw the man was perfectly serious.

"Ten thousand dollars?" Gethahyme asked. "Is that what you're getting paid to undertake this suicide mission?"

The tank didn't answer, he only smiled, his eyes crinkling behind the face-bars of his helmet.

"I'll give you a thousand," Gethahyme said. "And your lives." Again, the man said nothing, which was answer enough. Someone was bankrolling these goons. But why? It couldn't be to test Gethahyme's security arrangements since he could change them at any time. And it definitely wasn't an assassination attempt. Even six to one, they didn't stand a chance.

What was happening didn't make sense and, for the first time in this world, a worm of fear began to squiggle in Gethahyme's belly. For the first time, he felt like Greg Nelson—and he didn't like it. He had chosen this game and this world to get away from Greg Nelson. The fear made him angry.

"New offer," he said. "I'll give you one dollar *and* I'll let one of you live. Just tell me who sent you." The tank grunted a laugh, but otherwise neither answered nor moved. It almost seemed like they were waiting for him to attack first. It was a big mistake. At level forty-one, he was the most powerful wizard in Daggerland.

"Shiy-yevr-muk-mi!" Gethahyme hissed. In a blink, there was a thunderous noise followed by a sudden explosion of flame and in the midst of the flame stood a towering creature. It seemed to be either on fire or made of fire. It roared at the group, breathing out a huge cloud of superheated ash, blinding and burning them. It then rushed at the group, slashing with its huge burning claws.

One of the wizards dodged to the side and sent golden bolts ripping at Gethahyme, who didn't even blink as the bolts struck his magical protections and puffed out of existence. In response, he said only a simple word that was so full of magical energy that the wizard's eyes rolled up into his head and he collapsed, stunned as if he'd had a safe fall on him.

More attack spells came his way and they too fizzled against his barriers. Gethahyme reversed gravity for one of the fighters just by lifting a hand. The man "fell" twenty feet straight into the air to crash against the ceiling, where he was pinned.

As the man struggled against the new direction of his gravity, Gethahyme swept the room with magical flame, laughing as he did. He lived for this. He loved it and he was just getting started.

2—

As Gethahyme prepared to summon a second fiend, this one from an outer ring of hell, the body of Greg Nelson suddenly opened his eyes. With a jerk, he sat up and with a great deal of wobbling, he stood.

Walking was much more difficult than standing. Stumbling like a toddler, he made it to the door, but fell twice on the way to his desk. Thankfully, he managed to get into the leather-bound chair without marking up his face. He needed that face intact for the computer to recognize it. To the man inside Greg Nelson, the face felt like a rubber mask sitting over his own.

Opening a laptop, he sat as still as possible as red lights zeroed in on his eyes, scanning his retinas. Next, the facial recognition software gave him a once-over and passed him through to the voice analysis.

"G-G-reg Nelmson," he mumbled.

"Error," the machine said. "Please restate your name."

He cleared Greg's throat and tried again, "Greg Nelmson." He heard the mistake and yet, the software gave him access. Slurred or not, the voice was Greg's. "S-s-security," he said. Everyone who knew Greg, knew that he had always been one for both micromanagement and centralized control. The laptop was proof of that. He could monitor and adjust the security for the entire building from that one computer.

"Far controwl systems," he said.

"Please restate your command."

He worked his jaw around and tried again, "Fi-re contro-el systems." This time his lips barely tripped over the words. In a blink, the computer brought up the layout for the building's high-tech fire suppression system. "Turn off fi-re control on all floors." The computer gave him a: *Are you sure you want to do something so stupid?* prompt. When he repeated the order, the fire suppression system flashed: *Disabled.* Next, he commanded, "Access all files on the mainframe." He now sounded very close to Greg Nelson.

The computer responded by bringing up over ninety-six thousand files. "Delete all files... Yes, I understand. Delete all files." Just like that, three years of work disappeared. But he wasn't done yet. Working his legs with a little more dexterity, he made his way to the third floor custodial room where a middle-aged woman stood by a cleaning cart, looking at him in confusion.

"Mr. Nelson?"

He tried to smile but it didn't feel right and he didn't have a mirror in which to practice. "I want you to take the night off," he said, hoping it sounded like something Greg would say. He reached into his pocket and fumbled out a wad of twenties. "Take this and go have fun. The dirt will still be here tomorrow." Bewildered, she thanked him and left without looking back, her hand clutched around the money, which was probably close to a month's pay.

Once she was gone, he went through the storeroom and hauled out everything that read: *Caution Flammable!* It didn't take long before the cleaning cart was filled and tilting madly. He struggled the cart into the R & D team work area and began to splash gallon after gallon about.

Unfortunately, he couldn't destroy every last vestige of what he considered stolen proprietary information, but he sure as hell was going to try. Of course, most of that information was still locked up in Greg Nelson's brain—but it wouldn't be for long.

When the carpets, the walls and the computers were well saturated, he calmly rolled a chair to the center of the room, lit his fire and then sat down in the middle of it. He had a front row seat to the destruction of GN Industries. A smile cracked his face as his skin began to peel and his hair began to smolder.

In Daggerland, Gethahyme had just slaughtered the last of the tanks, cracking open his armor with a lightning bolt and half-cooking the man inside. He then turned to the one wizard left alive. She was out of spells and nearly out of hit points. Blood puddled around her feet—she should have conceded and clocked out but she seemed to be waiting for something. Perhaps for him to make her another offer?

"I'm just looking for a name," Gethahyme said. "You can say you tried to fight me. You can say that it felt too real and that you panicked. The money will be just between you and me."

"How…much?" she asked, around a sharp intake of breath. They were both playing *Extreme Mode* and the pain from her wounds had to be intense.

Money really wasn't a problem. Gethahyme literally had tons of gold and Greg Nelson had boatloads of cash. "Two thousand? What do you say?"

"Fifty thousand."

He could afford that much, but it was outrageous. He laughed and countered, "Five thousand."

"Forty-five thousand," she answered, seeming to gain strength, as if their haggling fueled something inside of her. "Though I might go as low assss…" She paused, drawing out the moment for so long that, in a cold fury, he touched her, sending electricity coursing through her flesh. It wasn't enough to kill her, just enough to hurt like a bitch.

"You aren't clocking out, so you must want money," Gethahyme said. "Give me your final price or I will keep frying you until you do, and you know what that means, all of this will have been for nothing."

"How do you know I want money?" she asked. "You're the one who keeps offering it. I could be just buying time."

This made him laugh. "Buying time for what? Are you waiting for the cavalry to show up and rescue you in the nick of time? Or do you actually believe…" In the middle of his sentence, Gethahyme's eyes suddenly rolled up in his head and he collapsed. He was very much dead because without Greg Nelson, who was burning away in the real world, there could be no Gethahyme, Master of the Red Wizards.

"I was buying time for that," the wizard said with a grin. Slowly, painfully she stood, her eyes seeming to gaze off into nothing. She wasn't staring at all the loot that would be hers, she was staring at the words in green neon that sat in the air in front of her face: *Congratulations, Kyra! You are now a level 14 Wizard!*

Seeing that was even better than the treasure that was hers alone. Of course, it wasn't nearly as good as the cash she was going to pocket in the real world. The wizard had fifty thousand dollars waiting for her when she clocked out. It was scary money for something so simple. Whoever Gethahyme was in the real world, he had enemies with lots of cash to throw around.

"Too bad for him," she murmured.

The building had been torched on purpose. Supervisory
Special Agent Daniel Roan could see that even before he rolled
down his window and flashed his badge to get through the
perimeter of the crime scene.

It took an effort to burn down a building of glass and steel,
especially when tech companies were involved. Generally
speaking, they didn't have much flammable material on the
premises and, what was more, they almost always had state of
the art fire suppression systems. Ninety-nine percent of the time,
they used dry chemicals to protect their acres of server farms.

Which begged the question: "What's with all the fire
trucks?" Roan asked. There had to be twenty fire trucks of all
shapes and sizes parked around the still smoking building.

"Probably to make sure the job was complete," Agent
Amanda Waterfall answered from the passenger seat. "Nothing
kills electronics faster than a jet of water fired from a high-pres-
sure cannon." She leaned over and hunched close to Roan's lap
to peer up at the building through his window. He was acutely
aware of her long, blonde hair spilling onto his thigh. She was
pale but pretty with soft features partially hidden behind black-
rimmed glasses.

From the back seat, Jarrod Maddox's caffeine-wired nerves
sent his left knee bouncing up and down. "What I want to know
is why we're here? Sure, it's a tech company, but unless I need a
new prescription for my glasses, that right there is arson. Or
maybe not. Maybe it was an actual accident. I would never know
and do you know why?"

"Because you're not an arson investigator?" Roan asked the
obligatory question, rolling his ice-blue eyes.

"That's right. I am *not* an arson investigator, I am a computer forensic examiner and we...us right here, we are not one of
the CAT teams. We belong in the lab where there's air-condition-
ing and where a building won't fall on us if the wind blows. And
you know what? I read that arsonists like to come back and

watch their handiwork. He's probably one of those people back there. Or maybe it's one of the firemen."

Amanda made a face, her pert nose wrinkling. "A fireman, please. You're being ridiculous."

The fourth person in the car, Marshall Mutch, who was also a forensic examiner, said, "I agree with Jarrod. I read there is actually a disturbing and growing trend among firemen to light fires. Like in *Fahrenheit 451*."

Jarrod started snapping his spindly fingers rapidly. To Roan they looked like dancing white spiders. Where Amanda was pale, Jarrod was sickly in his lack of color. "That's right," Jarrod said. "Or like *Backdraft*. It was a fireman who was setting all the fires, only you didn't find that out until the end, except I knew it long, long before."

"Of course, you knew it, because Hollywood sucks," Marshall said, pulling Jarrod back. In his excitement, Jarrod had practically crawled into the front seat. He was so skinny that he could fit between the chairs with ease. Marshall was Jarrod's physical opposite. He was overweight, but not grossly so, and looked bigger than he was because of the way he was always so *relaxed*. The way he lounged at every opportunity made it look as though he took up more space than he really did.

"Forget the firemen," Amanda said. "Jarrod is right about the CAT teams. Why aren't they here?"

The FBI's CAT—Cyber Action Team—provided rapid response when a major computer intrusion occurred or when there was a cyber-related emergency, which happened far more frequently than people realized. There were approximately fifty agents all told within the Cyber Action Team and they were spread out in field offices around the country. It was an overworked group.

"They're busy and we were on deck, so live with it," Roan said, getting out of the car and raking a hand through his short dark hair.

Behind him, Jarrod muttered, "On deck? I thought he'd been in the army, not in the navy."

Amanda groaned. "It's a baseball term, idiot. Now get your gear and try not to embarrass us." They each carried a stainless steel case about the size of an airplane carry-on. All save Roan. He was new, both to the New York Field Office and to the Cyber Division. He only had a basic knowledge of computers. His real expertise lay in his knowledge of people. He could spot a scumbag from fifty yards and sniff out a lie like a bloodhound could sniff out a rotting corpse.

What he was doing in the Cyber Division was not just anyone's guess, it was *everyone's* guess; rumors flew all around him, mostly behind his back, though some asked him point blank. When that happened, he almost always just shrugged his brawny shoulders and changed the subject. But this was the FBI where the people were not just trained to snoop, they were paid to do so.

They found out that trouble seemed to follow Roan wherever he went. In his twelve years with the Bureau, he'd had more firearm incidents than any other agent, and not just during the previous twelve years, but in any period in the Bureau's history. His jacket read that he was "violently effective."

Still, violence from its agents was not the image the FBI wished to present and so Roan had been promoted and shuttled to the Cyber Division where most of the detective work was done outside the public eye and the opportunity for violence of any sort was almost zero.

Being in the computer lab kept Roan out of trouble, but it also bored him to death. He had spent the last two months staring at a computer screen and he was starting to lose his tan. Soon he'd be as pasty-white as Jarrod, and the thought bothered him.

"I'm looking for Special Agent in Charge, Mike Caron," he said to the first uniform he came to. Roan was pointed to a Ford Taurus where an aging FBI agent with thin blonde hair sat with his long legs jutting out of the driver's side door, a laptop open across his thighs.

Caron glanced up and snorted. "Roan! Look at you. I never thought I'd see you with the nerd patrol."

On one hand, it was an odd thing to say since half the FBI was made up of scientists and analysts who never saw the light of day while they were on the clock. On the other hand, the Cyber Division seemed to be the place where the geek factor was off the charts. There was no getting around it or pretending otherwise.

Roan only grunted though what the grunt could mean was anyone's guess. Caron glanced at Roan's team, his eyes hanging on Amanda a second too long. "He's the only agent they've booted from the Violent Crime Division for being too violent," he said as if speaking only to her. "Hi, my name is Tim Caron."

He had his hand out to her. She took it, saying, "I'm Agent Waterfall and these are forensic examiners Jarrod Maddox and Marshall Mutch. Why are we here, Agent Caron?"

"Because we need your particular expertise, of course, Agent Waterfall."

Roan didn't like Caron's smile or the lies he was spinning. "You need our help to solve an arson case?" Roan asked. "Alright, let me narrow it down for you: it's either the owner hoping to collect on the insurance money, a disgruntled employee, or someone looking to cover up a crime."

Caron tut-tutted him. "Don't be too hasty, Roan." He turned to Amanda and said, "He's always too quick to jump to conclusions. I told him that when he was just a pup right out of Quantico. You should have seen him back then; you never saw a more eager beaver."

Roan ignored his old mentor's badgering and concentrated on the case. He knew there were only two other possibilities when it came to arsonists, but both were highly unlikely. "A serial?" He gave the building a second look. "No way a serial arsonist did this. I can see from here that the fire started on the inside and barely made its way out. No, serials like the big show and this one was dull."

"And that leaves?" Caron asked.

"A corporate hit," Roan answered, his face screwed up as if he knew the answer was obviously wrong. "That's extremely rare in the white-collar world, even more rare than a serial arsonist. There's too much downside. From what I can tell about these suit-wearing criminals, they'll gamble with money, but not with hard prison time."

Amanda spoke up. "Anyone desperate enough to resort to arson is going to leave a trail. If you wish, we can start checking into GN's competition. We can also look into their employees to see if anyone unexpectedly came into a little extra cash. Maybe check their bank records and phone logs…of course, we could have done that back at the office. There's something else, isn't there?"

"Oh, she's a smart one, Roan. Keep her close." Caron turned his laptop around and showed it to Roan's team. "This is security footage taken yesterday evening, just after six." They watched Greg Nelson in his R&D lab splashing around gallons of carpet cleaner. "That's the owner and CEO of GN Industries," Caron explained.

"So, it was an inside job." Roan squinted at the screen. "Is he drunk? The way he's acting he looks like he's...What the hell?" Greg had just started the fire and instead of running away, he calmly sat down. Within a minute, fire and smoke had engulfed him.

Marshall was a light shade of green as he said, "Suicide is not under the FBI's purview. Unless you're suggesting that he was coerced or controlled in some way."

Jarrod looked excited by the idea. "Is this an *Area 51* deal? Or, you know, an *X Factor* situation? Or is this sort of like in that movie where the girl..."

Roan glared him into silence. "As messed up as that video is, it still looks like suicide. Do you want our AV guys to check the footage to see if it was tampered with?"

Before Caron could answer, Jarrod said, "I know what it is. Did you see that thing on his head? That was a neural coupler. I'd bet any one of you a dollar that he was in Daggerland." Marshall and Jarrod shared a look that mingled horror and excitement.

"That is actually a possibility we're checking into," Caron said. "We contacted someone over at *Infinite Reality* to get this guy's login information, but it turns out, because of privacy laws, that sort of information is not stored. They don't keep any of it. When a person logs on and what he does and where he goes in the virtual world can't be tracked."

Total immersion virtual reality had been around for eleven years and Roan had never tried it. He liked his mind securely locked away in his own brain. Virtual reality was supposed to be perfectly safe and yet there was Greg Nelson burning himself alive.

Marshall and Jarrod were whispering in excitement about another case involving Daggerland when a long, black limousine pulled through the police tape. "You want to know why you're here," Caron said. "This is it." Caron walked to the limo and opened one of the doors, gesturing for Roan's team to climb in.

In the very back of the limo was an older man, grey haired and round in both the face and the belly. He sat with his hands resting on the head of a cane that stood propped between his wide-splayed legs.

"You're Greyson Fulbright," Jarrod said, his voice filled with awe. "You're like the seventh richest guy in the world."

"Fifth, actually," Fulbright corrected. He then looked long at Special Agent Caron. "Now do you believe me? Now do you believe that Arching is behind this? Suicide by fire? It's extremely apropos, considering."

Caron drummed his fingers for a few seconds on the gleaming wood of the vehicle's wet bar. "I'm not even going to ask how you know about Nelson's death, but yes, it's starting to look like a possibility. I don't know how, though. Every expert in the field keeps telling me it's impossible."

Fulbright thumped his cane. "That's because it should be impossible, damn it!" Seeing Roan's team glancing back and forth at the two of them in confusion, Fulbright explained, "This isn't an isolated event. There were six developers who designed the Infinite Reality worlds, you know, Daggerland and all the rest. Of those six, only two are still alive: Christine Carson and Atticus Arching, who some people call the Father of Virtual Reality."

He paused to let that sink in, before going on, "Three months ago, Lane Gorman walked out of his house one night without saying a word to his wife or kids. He walked away and no one has seen or heard from him since."

Caron nodded. "We've been monitoring his accounts, his phone, everything, but he's in the wind."

"He's not in the wind, he's dead," Fulbright announced. "Probably six feet under, just like Kriesse and DeAngelo. They were homos, not that I care. But two months ago, they were in Kriesse's home, online…"

"You don't know that," Caron said.

Fulbright made a humph sort of noise and thudded his cane a second time. "They were found in his 'reality room' so it follows. Either way, Kriesse stabbed DeAngelo to death and then *slit his own throat*." The old man sounded to Roan as though he were telling tales around a campfire, trying to scare little kids. "And now this. Greg Nelson burns down his own building with himself in it. There is only one explanation if you ask me."

Agent Waterfall surprised Roan by saying, "As much as we appreciate your input, Mr. Fulbright, the investigation is only twelve hours old. We don't like to jump to conclusions so quickly."

Fulbright smiled, showing overly-perfect teeth. They were the kind of teeth that only lots of money could buy. "I like you. You have guts. You'll do well on the other side."

"The other side of what?" she asked.

Fulbright's smile dimmed. "This isn't the team you're sending into Daggerland?"

"We haven't decided anything. As Agent Waterfall pointed out, this aspect of the investigation is just beginning. We haven't even interviewed Mr. Arching, yet."

"I can tell you right now that you won't be able to," Fulbright said. "If anyone is in the wind, it's Arching. In fact, he is the wind." He reached out with his cane and tapped the limo's door. It was their cue to leave. "Call me when your investigation hits its inevitable dead end."

2—

"How did he know about Nelson's death before us?" Amanda asked Caron. "He had to have seen that video. Either he has a mole in the Bureau or he's illegally hacking security feeds. And, what's more, you didn't do a thing about it. Don't you care about the law?"

Caron glanced her way and then yawned, widely. "Sure, I do, but I'm not going to waste our time and the taxpayers' money trying to prosecute him. Fulbright's got to be worth like fifty billion. When you have that sort of money, laws become, let's say, pliable, and all those looks of righteous indignation aren't going to mean a damn thing."

Her current look of righteous indignation turned fiery. Roan put out a hand. "Okay, okay. I've got a dead guy in there, some more dead guys in the ground, and some missing guys. What I don't have is a reason for my team to be here."

"You're here because you're a damned FBI agent, that's a crime scene, and I'm your superior." Caron had turned on Roan and the two were now almost nose to nose. Roan was younger, stronger and faster. Only the law kept him from stomping the piss out of Caron. The law wasn't pliable for him, at least not with witnesses around.

After a deep breath, Roan took a step back. "What are your orders, mein Fuhrer?"

Caron laughed easily as if the moment before hadn't happened. "Number one: stop being a dick. Number two: there's a possible witness in that white van. Go talk to him. Find out what he knows."

Once more this was a job for pretty much any other team in the FBI. As far as Roan knew, there was only one reason that he, in particular was being asked to talk to a witness. "When you say talk, what exactly do you mean?"

"It means I want you to talk to him. That's it, just talk. Now, if you'll excuse me, I need to get a warrant to get us onto Arching's properties." Caron waved a dismissive hand and, abruptly, Roan turned for the white van, forcing his team to jog to keep up.

Amanda did so wearing a scowl which did a number on her soft midwestern features. "What did he mean by 'just talk?' What else were you going to do?"

"As far as I know, nothing," Roan answered. "I don't know who this guy is. He could be just some schmuck."

"Tell me, would it be different if he was a criminal?" She added an arched eyebrow to her scowl. The answer depended on what sort of criminal he was—Roan was easily triggered when children's lives were involved. He gave her a half-shrug in answer. She stopped just feet from the van. "Listen, sir, I can't be a part of illegalities. I joined the FBI in order…"

"We're just going to talk," he said, interrupting. He tapped on the sliding door of the van. "Hello in there, you decent?" Roan didn't wait for an answer and slid back the door.

Tim Cole, his hair still greasy, his teeth unbrushed, and wearing the same ill-fitting and rumpled suit he had worn the night before, sat on the back bench of the van. He was a big man who took up the entire bench, and then some. He looked at Roan, blearily. "You ain't my lawyer and since you ain't my lawyer, you can shut that door and let me sleep."

"In my world only a criminal asks for a lawyer right off the bat," Roan said. "Are you a criminal?" Cole didn't say a word. Roan turned to Amanda. "You went to law school, right? Make a note every time he obstructs justice by refusing to answer. Okay let's start. What's your name, sir?"

Cole's eyes slid over to Amanda, who had pulled out a small notebook and had a pen poised, ready to write down his first obstruction charge. He groaned, "Timothy Cole, but call me Cole; *don't* call me Timothy."

"Sure, Cole," Roan said, agreeably. "Why don't you tell me what got you stuck in this van? I'm guessing that since you were so quick to demand a lawyer, you weren't simply walking by and saw the fire."

"No, I wasn't." Another glance at Amanda. She only gave him a slight shrug. It seemed to confuse him. "I was in my room in the basement. I worked for Mr. Nelson. I did, like odd jobs for him. Like private investigator work, you could say. One of the French benefits was that I got to live here rent free."

Jarrod snorted in mocking laughter, Roan guessed that he found "French benefits" funny. Roan turned his hard blue eyes on him and glared the laughter out of him before he addressed Cole again. "See? That wasn't so hard, was it? You don't need a lawyer for this sort of thing. We would have found all this out simply by taking your fingerprints. Licensed P.I.s have to be fingerprinted...you are a licensed investigator, right?"

"I don't need a license. I worked for him on the other side."

"I don't get it," Roan said. "The other side of what? In Jersey?"

Jarrod laughed. "Jersey, that's a good one. No, he's talking about in Daggerland. You act like you've never been there." Roan hadn't been. So far, his life had been exciting enough that he didn't need to escape into a fantasy world to get his kicks. It was obvious on his face and Jarrod grinned. "We've got a virtual virgin in our midst."

"Shut up," Roan growled at him and then faced Cole. "Explain how this worked. You live in Nelson's R&D building and you get paid for P.I. work done in a game?"

Cole bristled at the description. "It's more than a game. It's life, but better than life. And yes, I make a living working in Daggerland for Mr. Nelson. I would keep an eye on his rival4s, I would watch over his castle. I would kill his enemies—virtually kill them that is."

Roan was having trouble wrapping his mind around the concept. "And you got paid in real money? Real American currency?"

An ugly grin crossed Cole's face. "Yeah, probably a lot more than you. I raked in six figures last year. What did you make?"

A whole lot less than a hundred thousand dollars, Roan thought. "This isn't about me. This is about you and Mr. Nelson. So, you get paid to help him in Daggerland. Did anything happen there last night?"

"Yeah, there was a break in. He's got this castle. Over there he is...I mean he was, Gethahyme, Master of the Red Wizards. He lives in a place called Mendenome and it has all these guards, but they're only NPCs. It means they ain't real. They're part of the program, but they fight for him. Either way, this group of adventurers comes up and tears into the guards. I clocked out and told Mr. Nelson. That was the last time I saw him."

"Not even in the virtual world?" Amanda asked.

Cole gave her a long up and down look. "Naw, I made a sandwich and the next thing I knew the building is on fire. That's all I know. So, can I go?"

Roan didn't like his answers, they were too…odd.

3—

The next day they were in Fulbright's limousine, again, only this time it was whispering southwest. To Jarrod's endless amusement, they were heading to New Jersey. The headquarters of Infinite Reality was situated on twenty acres in what appeared to be a fifteen-story cube of pure black glass.

Although it was midday on a Wednesday, the parking lot was completely empty. "It's been like this for the last three weeks," Fulbright said. "The lot has been thinning out for a year now. Arching has been laying off his staff by the dozen, but who's taking their place, no one knows."

"He shipping the jobs overseas?" Caron asked.

Fulbright shrugged and began to once more tap his cane; he'd been doing it for the entire ride. It was driving Roan nuts. "I'm missing your connection to all of this, Mr. Fulbright. Were you a partner of Nelson's? An investor or what?"

"I am part of a consortium that owns the majority share of Infinite Reality and I am a minority owner of GN Industries. I stand to lose billions so you might say that I have a vested interest in the virtual world."

"You also stand to gain billions," Amanda said. "Isn't that true?"

Fulbright chuckled and thumped his cane harder; his way of clapping. "Yes, my dear, I do, but only if the balance is maintained and Arching is not one for balance. He's been the driving force behind the virtual world for over twenty years and no matter what the other developers say, Daggerland is his baby. I get the feeling that he's like an actual mother in that regard. He'll do anything to protect it."

"And that includes killing off his competition," Caron said, speaking as if it were a fact and not a hypothesis. Fulbright answered by nodding and thumping his cane quietly. Then Caron asked a question that was on Roan's mind, "Are you afraid that he'll come after you?"

"On this side? No. He thinks of me as just one of the 'money guys.' To him we simply supply an item he needs. Possibly, in his mind, we are no more important than the people who supply the keys to his keyboards or the tiny screws that hold the sidewall of his computers on. No, he won't kill me, but I believe he doesn't need me any longer. We'll see when we open those doors."

The six of them exited the limo and went to the black glass doors. Caron thumped on the doors with his fist. When no one answered, he gave the handles a pull. They didn't budge. With a grunt, he took out a collapsible steel baton, gave his wrist a flick in order to extend it and then smashed in the glass. Although Caron made no attempt to stifle the sound, no one came to investigate the crash. The building was dark and silent.

"Mr. Arching!" Caron yelled at the top of his lungs as he stepped across the threshold. Heavy silence greeted them. "I guess we'll go floor by floor."

"Why bother?" Roan asked. "We won't find anything, will we?" Fulbright shook his head, his jowls swinging. Roan felt the glare creep onto his face as he asked, "So, what was the real point of coming here? My guess is that you are hoping that we come to a conclusion concerning Arching on our own, but let's cut out the baby steps. Just tell us."

"Hold on," Amanda interjected. "As far as we know, Atticus Arching hasn't committed a single unlawful act. We don't have a shred of evidence that points to him. All we have is Mr. Fulbright's word."

"That's not all we have," Caron said. "We have three dead developers, each of whom died under suspicious circumstances and each linked to Mr. Arching. I didn't want to believe it before, but every time I watch that video of Nelson lighting himself up, I can only come to the conclusion that it's not him. You know how he appeared to be drunk? Tox came back on his blood. It was completely clean."

Fulbright thumped his cane on the sidewalk and sighed. "Of course it was clean. Nelson acted the way he did because the person who was walking in his body had never been in it before. I suspect it takes some getting used to."

"That's only more conjecture," Amanda said. "You have no proof. If we intend to go forward with a case against Mr. Arching we're going to need real, tangible proof."

"That's too bad," Fulbright said. "Because the only proof you're going to find is virtual. The proof you need for a conviction can only be found in Daggerland."

Amanda planted her hands on her hips and looked at Fulbright as though he were crazy. "You can't be serious. Virtual evidence can never be corroborated. Nothing we get in Daggerland will ever stand up in court."

"Don't listen to her," Jarrod said, pushing Amanda behind him. "Count me in." He stood in front of Fulbright softly clapping his hands together like a child who'd been told he was going to go see Santa.

Marshall came to stand shoulder to shoulder with his friend. "Yeah, me too. I'm in. We'll probably need stipends to outfit our party properly. I have an idea for matching cloaks. They're dark blue with..."

"Enough," Roan said, quietly, but forcefully. "We're not going anywhere. You don't solve crimes by prancing around in a make believe world. Perhaps, maybe, once we've exhausted all the leads here, we can see what there is in Daggerland. Until then, we have to check out Cole's alibi. There's also Nelson's secretary to interview and there was the cleaning lady...what?"

Caron was shaking his head. "I have agents working on those leads already. What I don't have, is someone in Daggerland asking questions."

Roan couldn't believe what he was hearing. Caron had been his supervising agent when he was fresh out of Quantico. Caron knew that Roan wasn't just another badge putting in the hours. Roan lived for the hunt. He balled his fists and was about to get in Caron's face when Fulbright poked him with that annoying cane.

"I don't see what the issue is," the old man said. "If anyone will break the case, it's going to be you four. You'll fit right in." He turned his cane and pointed it at each of them in turn. "Nerd, nerd, girl nerd, and enforcer. You'll blend."

Neither Jarrod nor Marshall seemed to care that they'd been called nerds, but Amanda glared, although not as hard as Roan. "So, we've been auditioning?" he demanded.

"You should be happy that you passed," Caron said, with a cold as ice look which told Roan he wasn't going to listen to another word on the subject. Caron turned on his heel and walked out of the building, heading for the limo, saying over his shoulder, "You'll go under back at the field office. I've got some cots set up in the basement."

Fulbright seemed appalled at the idea. "A basement? With spiders and old boxes of whatnot? Please! I have plenty of space in my home where the agents will be perfectly comfortable. They'll each have their own room, and I have a pool for when they come back from Daggerland. It's very relaxing."

Jarrod and Marshall shared a look of excitement, but Caron dashed their hopes. "No. You are very generous, Mr. Fulbright, but that would be too much. It'll spoil them and we wouldn't want that. Besides, we're going to monitor their bodies while they're gone, just in case."

The words "just in case" put a damper on things, especially with Jarrod and Marshall, who sobered up quickly, remembering this wasn't just an online romp. There could very well be danger.

Amanda seemed especially nervous as she found a spot in the limousine. "We're going to be monitored?" she asked, her tongue flicking out to wet her lips. "Will you be able to see what we do online? I've never done this before. It sounded like fun, but it's always so expensive and I heard it could become addictive. You know, like gambling. And now people can get hacked? I don't know about this."

Fulbright waited until the limo was whisking along again before he thumped his cane. "My dear, do not be afraid. The security for the system is top notch. In fact, it's so good that what happened to poor Mr. Nelson is utterly inexplicable. The designers, all six of them, foresaw this sort of mind control as a possibility and built protections into the system, starting with the *neural coupler*. How can I put this? You've been to a concert before, yes?"

"Yes, of course, but this is…"

He held up a finger. "Picture a concert with general seating. Now picture the concert in a football stadium with ten million people in attendance. It's like that. The game knows you've walked through the door, but after that it has no idea where you are because what is happening is only happening in your mind. To continue the analogy, the game doesn't know where you parked, either. In other words, there's no way for the game to know where you logged in from."

"What about your neural print?" Jarrod asked. "Shouldn't that be unhackable?"

Instead of an immediate, *of course!* Fulbright shrugged. "That's sort of a grey area. Your neural print is very much like your fingerprint. It's perfectly singular. And again, just like a fingerprint or your DNA, it's not exactly secret. Everywhere you go you leave fingerprints and bits of DNA, and as you sit there, Mr. Maddox, your neural print is radiating from your mind."

Subconsciously, Amanda touched her blonde hair. "And it can be picked up?"

"Sure. It's simple. You've seen an electroencephalogram? Where people have electrodes hooked up to their skulls? With a very subtle machine, a person can be 'read' without all the electrodes."

"But even if they could take your neural print, the most they can do is take over your character," Jarrod said. "That's how the game knows who is who. Those neural couplers are receivers only. They can't send out brainwaves. And even if they could, it would probably just give someone a conniption fit."

"Exactly," Fulbright said with a final thump of his cane. "The game is perfectly safe."

"Except it isn't," Roan said, softly. "Otherwise we wouldn't be in this limo and Greg Nelson would still be alive."

2—

The basement of the Manhattan FBI field office was as dark and spider-filled as Fulbright had supposed. Four moldy-smelling cots had been arranged and set side by side with only a few feet in between. The pillows were new, Roan noted and the neural couplers were still in their original packaging.

"This is going to be awesome," Jarrod said, kicking off his dingy sneakers and sitting on the first cot. "Look out world! Mad Max, King of the mountain city of Agmire is back."

"No, he's not," Caron said. "You'll go in as new characters. Call it a precaution, but I don't want you to go in as someone you've played before. The one developer who's still alive says she had been playing a series of first level characters."

The whole thing felt like nonsense to Roan, especially the ridiculous names. "And don't for a second think I'll be calling any one of you king this or queen that. Your name will be Jarrod. And your name will be Marshall. You can pick a goofy last name if you wish."

"Sure, sure, that's cool," Jarrod said. "I have to warn you that once we're in the game it'll take off points if you break character."

Roan had been untying the laces on one of his shoes, but he paused just long enough to glare at Jarrod. "We're not going there for points, whatever those are," Roan said. "Our job is to find Arching and see what he knows about what's going on. It's as straight forward as that."

Marshall was already on the far bunk, spilling into the area between his and Amanda's cot. "It might be a little more in depth than that. We're going to need a rogue—not it!"

"Not…" began Jarrod, but then he saw Amanda's confused look and Roan's glare, which had intensified. "Oh, fine, I'll be the rogue. Marshall will be the cleric, Amanda will be the wizard, and Supervisory Special Agent Roan will be the fighter. Hopefully, you'll let me call you Roan when we're in Daggerland?"

Roan was slow to answer. He was still trying to wrap his head around all of this: cleric, wizards, and what the hell was a rogue? "Yeah, call me Roan. We'll keep this simple."

"If you want simple, then you should play as yourself," Marshall said, propping himself up on one elbow. "You too, Amanda. You get a choice to either play as yourself, a random generation, or as a build. I always do a build because all of your attributes start at twelve and then you have nine points to divide among them. You can't make any one attribute higher than a sixteen, still it's pretty good. I don't play as myself because although I'm pretty smart, I have only an eight dexterity and a nine in both constitution and charisma. That's pretty sucky."

"I should go as myself? Really?" Amanda asked. "I'm not very strong."

Jarrod gave her an extra close look. "You work out, right? And you're smart and pretty. I'd say you have at least a sixteen intelligence, and a fifteen charisma. Maybe a fifteen dexterity. It's hard to judge wisdom, but you're at least average and probably higher. Yeah, I'd go as yourself, you'll make a good level 1 wizard."

"Anything else?" Roan asked.

"Yeah, there's a million things," Jarrod said, stretching his arms out. "At first, it'll be sort of like going to a foreign country as a toddler, but you'll catch on. Just follow the prompts. We'll meet in the middle of town. Just use the party name of, hmmm, how about mystic gorilla?"

"Mystic gorilla?" Roan asked. "It's going to be like this the entire time, isn't it?"

Jarrod grinned. "Yeah, cool, huh?"

3—

Roan settled onto his cot, placed the coupler across his forehead and closed his eyes. Completely on their own, they popped open, but it wasn't the ceiling of the basement that he saw. He found himself in a dark alley, but it was no alley that he had ever seen before in his life.

It was paved in damp cobblestones, moss growing between the stones. The way was narrow with odd buildings looming on either side. The structures were absolutely haphazard, no two were alike in height or construction. Some were made of what looked like homemade kiln-fired bricks, and others were of wood planks that had knots poked out, or were warped, letting light and noise filter out.

Some had iron bars across their windows while others had wood shutters that were flung wide. A few had gutters and downspouts and most had wood-shingled roofs.

The alley was empty except for an oily-looking rat that sat, hunkered down next to one of the buildings. It had its beady eyes turned to Roan as if it had been surprised by his sudden appearance and didn't know which way to run.

Roan turned away from it, ignoring it. He wasn't there for a rat, at least, not this sort of rat. With a quick and very surprising, move, he leapt up onto the wall to his left where the bricks were uneven, set by an amateur. To his amazement, he climbed right up the wall as if it were a ladder, aiming for a window that was partially closed.

"Is this part of the game?" he asked. His voice was only an echo in his head. In the game, he was soundless as he peered into the window. The room beyond the rickety shutters was dark, filled with shadows, however, he could just make out a bed and upon it was what seemed to be a man.

Roan's head nodded and a real word slid from between his clenched teeth: "Yes." His right hand let go of the sill and reached into a pouch that dangled from his belt. From it, he produced a stoppered vial. Roan thought it was a potion of some sort, however he didn't drink it. Instead, he lifted it to the hinges of the shutters and dribbled some on them.

It was oil. Now, the shutters opened soundlessly. Like a giant spider, he crawled into the room making barely a whisper of sound. When he pulled his dagger, it came out of its sheath with a tiny scrape and when he plunged it into his sleeping victim— Roan jumped in shock as the image froze and a woman's voice, soft and silky spoke: "Welcome to Infinite Reality."

The image broke into thousands of points of light that evaporated leaving behind only darkness. Roan was no longer in his body or in the body of the *rogue*—the idea behind the word had suddenly popped into his head—Roan was part of the darkness, which didn't last for more than a second and then there was a glowing grid in front of him.

"What is your desire?" the woman asked.

Daggerland was the first game on the grid. "Uh, Dagger…" Even before he had finished the word, the grid vanished and was replaced by an image of a red dragon that towered over his head. From its gaping jaws fire poured out, looking as though it were about to incinerate a knight in armor and a buxom woman in what appeared to be some sort of bikini.

Why would she be wearing a bikini? Roan thought. It didn't make any sense. Next to the woman's bikinied right breast were the words: *New Game* and beneath that in darker print was: *Resume Game*.

"New game."

The image of the dragon disappeared and was replaced by what felt like a movie. A scroll unraveled before him and upon it was a map with the word *Daggerland* etched in looping letters across the top. "Many thousands of years ago when the world was young and mankind was still filled with hope and vigor, there was a land where magic ruled and creatures of every sort made their home…" It was an old man's voice. He spoke as if telling a story—a long story.

"Can I skip this?" Roan asked. He didn't need or want to hear about the made-up history of a made-up world.

The voice cut away as did the image. What replaced it was a picture of himself, standing in the darkness, completely naked. Next to his body were three choices: Play as yourself—Random Generation—Build.

"I'll play as myself," he said, thinking that this would be the quickest way to get into the game.

"Please pick up the barbell, and lift it over your head," the woman said. In front of him was a simple metal bar with what looked like a twenty-five pound weight on either side. Fifty pounds was nothing to him. He reached down and jerked the bar to his chin, but as he pressed the weight over his head, the weights on either end began to grow bigger and heavier with every inch he lifted the bar until he was straining with every muscle in his body.

At a certain point, he just couldn't lift the bar any further and the weight disappeared. "Strength 16, Modifier +3."

Now a series of boxes filled his vision. At first, he thought it was a game of tic-tac-toe, however the first block on the upper left contained a square, the middle block had a circle and the last had a square within a circle. On the next row appeared a triangle, then a circle and then a triangle within the circle. Before the last row could be filled in, Roan asked, "What is this?"

"Your intelligence is being rated," the woman said. "Intelligence is an important trait for wizards. It is also used to…"

"Can we skip all of this?"

The tic-tac-toe box disappeared and he found himself back at the screen with his body and the choices: Play as yourself—Random Generation—Build.

"Random Generation, please," he said, hoping to speed up the process. There was a blur and then he saw that he had changed, and not for the better. He seemed skinnier and instead of the sharp look in his blue eyes, he thought that they were somewhat dull, perhaps even dim. And although he still recognized himself, his dark hair was clingy and greasy and his teeth were crooked and his forehead seemed larger than usual.

Next to his body was another grid which read:
Character Name: Roan

Strength – Dexterity – Constitution
S: **12(+1)**   D: **12(+1)**   C: **14(+2)**

Intelligence – Wisdom – Charisma
I: 8(-1) W: 14(+2) C: 10(+0)

Now he understood. His strength had dropped four points, which accounted for his small size, and he supposed that his natural charisma was significantly higher than a 10. He curled his lip at the image and the stats, but hit the *accept* button nonetheless.

After this, he was inundated with more choices and he buzzed as quickly as he could through them. He was asked his character's name and that was simple enough, Roan. Next came his sex, which was another easy one, male.

Then came a question of class. Now things grew muddled. Fighter was what Jarrod, Marshall, and Fulbright had suggested and yet it seemed so limited. As far as he could tell, as a fighter he would only be able to kill, crush, maim!

"Why do I even care?" he asked. He wasn't there to play, he was there to learn about a possible suspect. With this in mind, he chose the first fighting style that was offered: Archery. He was about to click through the race options just as quickly—he was human, after all, but paused when he saw the elf choice.

It called to him, but only for a second. Quickly he chose: human. Next came alignment which was basically a person's moral position. That was easy. He was an FBI agent and lawful good was a natural fit.

Next came character traits. "Skip," he said. Did he wish to change his appearance? No. Did he wish to add background information? No. Did he wish to add credit card information to purchase extra starting gold? Hell no.

Are you playing with a party? "Yes. Uh, it's called Mystic Gorilla." It sounded stupid just saying it.

The final question concerned the difficulty level of the game. "Whatever's easiest."

"Do you accept the character, Roan?" the woman asked.

There was a surreal wedding feel to his answer, "I do." It was almost as if he was marrying his real life to this fake one. The second he accepted his character, a door appeared in front of him—it was made of rusted iron and looked as though it belonged in a dungeon. The old hinges screamed at him as he opened the door and walked through into a different world.

His first reaction was one of shock. He had assumed that the game would be "lifelike" or close to real, but maybe just a little off, so that'd be able to pick out the fake clouds or see that the grass was just a little too green.

But the game was as real as reality. It was so unexpectedly real that for a moment he felt dizzy. When he reached back for the door, he found that it was gone.

"This is crazy," he whispered, tasting the clean air as it passed over his tongue. Bending down, he touched the hard-packed dirt at his feet. It was gritty and rough. He picked up a handful and stared hard at the individual pebbles and the tiny pieces of earth. It was all perfect, right down to the smallest detail and he was sure that if he put the dirt under a microscope it would be indistinguishable from any other dirt.

Standing, he looked past the minutia and saw that there were some differences in this world. He was on the edge of what appeared to be a medieval town square. It was a perfect example of a town right out of merry old England, except there were dwarves in the square. Not dwarves that would be found on earth but dwarves out of Middle-earth. They were Tolkienesque.

Three walked right past him, chatting in deep voices. They were short, not quite four feet in height, but they were incredibly thick through the shoulders, arms and thighs. They wore armor made of metal rings sown over hard leather. Two carried battle axes that had short handles but very wide blades, while the third carried a war-hammer with a steel head. It was nicked, pitted and bloody.

Roan didn't realize he was staring until one of the dwarves stopped and stared right back. "Jarrod?" Roan asked.

"Pfff," the dwarf answered. "You got the wrong dwarf, noob. And if you keep staring like that, someone's gonna knock your teeth in for you."

"Sorry, it's my first time. I've never been in a reality game before. It's a little disconcerting and…uh…" He was distracted as a light tone sounded in his head and words appeared in his vision just to the right of the dwarf: *EXP -0.* "What the hell is that?"

The dwarves pushed on by, one muttering, "Next time read the manual, moron."

Roan wasn't used to people or dwarves calling him names, but just as he was about to respond, an elf walked by and once more he found himself staring. "It's so real," he whispered.

It was a female elf, just an inch or so over five-foot and slender as a willow. She wore soft leather armor that had been dyed green and had been cut and stitched in such a way so as to exactly resemble leaves. Her face was thin and sharp with angular cheekbones and dramatically pointed ears; they had to be four-inches high.

The elf gave him a glance and he quickly turned away, not wanting to be offensive. When he did, he saw two people who didn't seem to belong in the crowd. They were humans and were dressed oddly compared to everyone else. They both wore plain brown pants and white shirts, spun from some coarse material.

Only when Roan noticed their outfits did he realize that he was wearing the same exact thing. "Noob clothes," he murmured, guessing that this was the standard starting gear.

He walked to the pair. It was Jarrod and Marshall, both looking strangely *average* in appearance, which was, to be honest, a boost. Jarrod was slightly taller and slightly thicker. He was no longer as pale, and the pouches were gone from beneath his eyes. Marshall was slimmer and much more muscular. His brown hair was thicker and hung to his shoulders.

Marshall was the first to notice Roan. "What did you do? You were supposed to play as yourself."

"That took too long so I chose, uh, uh…" For some reason he couldn't remember what he had chosen when he had started the game. There had been, what? Build yourself? That didn't seem right. It was build something and maybe being somewhere? Frustrated, he snapped, "It doesn't matter. We have a job to do. Where is Miranda?"

"Do you mean A-manda?" Jarrod asked. "My god what's your intelligence? Like a five or something?"

"It's a eight and it'll be good enough."

Marshall sighed. "No, it won't but I get the feeling you're going to have to learn your lesson the hard way." He gave his friend a significant look, an obvious one, one that Roan should have been able to deduce a meaning from, but it was lost on him. Marshall went on, "Jarrod, wait here for Amanda. I'm going to get us outfitted and we'll see what happens from there. Hey, Roan," Marshall said speaking loudly and slowly. "Did Caron give you any extra gold?"

Roan couldn't remember. The conversation he'd had with Caron was slipping away like smoke that he couldn't grab. As he was standing there, Marshall reached out and shook a pouch that Roan only just noticed. The pouch was tied to a short length of twine that was acting as a belt. The pouch clinked softly and seemed as deflated as a balloon.

"Damn it," Marshall swore. "We only have the minimum. Ten gold apiece. It's not much but it'll get us armor and a weapon."

That sounded promising enough since everyone else was walking about in plate or chainmail or leather. Around the town square were a number of vendors selling all sorts of items from candles to what were supposedly dragon ears. Marshall clucked at them as they walked by. "Fakes, you can tell by the scales. Here we go, armor."

Roan didn't know which to stare at first, the suits of finely wrought armor or the little creature who was selling them. He knew what dwarves and elves were, but this thing was neither. It was as small as a dwarf, but much slimmer. It had long fingers and sharp eyes.

It caught Roan staring and raised an eyebrow at him. "Yes?" the creature said in a creaky voice.

Roan's wisdom was high enough not to ask the obvious question: *what the hell are you?* Instead he pulled out his gold and asked, "What can I get for this?" It seemed like a lot of money and he was sure he could score at least some chainmail, but the creature only pointed at a suit of dull brown leather armor and an odd set of clothes that looked like it was made out of quilted cloth over pillow foam. Football players had better armor. He started to shake his head, however Marshall pointed at the padded armor.

"We'll take that. Five gold, right?" Roan started to protest and Marshall gripped his arm and hissed, "It's all we can afford for now. It's why we need more gold from Caron."

Roan felt it best to rely on Marshall, who seemed to know what was going on. The armor was paid for and Marshall said, "Think the armor onto you. When you're not in combat, you can 'think' armor on and off. It saves time in the game."

It was simple and, in a snap, the padded armor was nestled all around him. He made a face. It was light enough, however it was also oddly thick and he felt "puffed up." They moved onto weapons. With the last of his gold, Marshall bought him a war-pick. Not a sword or a battle axe or a bow, but a war-pick, which was exactly like a mining tool. It had a blunt end for hammering and a pointy end— for stabbing, Roan supposed.

"It's really not that bad," Marshall said.

"Then why aren't you getting one?" Roan had just noticed that Marshall had neither armor nor weapon.

Marshall clapped him on his padded shoulder. "Because I am saving my money to buy you a drink. You know, while we wait for Amanda." He led them away from the vendors and to a tavern.

Roan had been in his fair share of seedy, puke-smelling dumps in his time but this beat them all. There were all manner of people and creatures inside though the place was so dark and smoke-filled that it was hard to get a good look at any of them. Arching could've been in one of the many little alcoves and Roan wouldn't have had a clue.

The clientele was diverse and so were the employees. There were three bartenders and only one was human. "What is that?" Roan asked, under his breath and jerking his head towards a hulking, pig-nosed, tusked, off-green bartender.

"It's a half-orc," Marshall told him. "They're usually unpleasant, but since he has the shortest line, let's get you a drink." Marshall shouldered his way over to the bar and ordered two house meads.

The half-orc grunted and grabbed two rusty iron chalices from a dripping pile. He wiped the chalices with a filthy towel and proceeded to pour in an amber liquid. Roan watched in disgust as drool slid from one of his tusks and dropped into one of the cups, the same cup that he pushed towards Roan.

"Four coppers," the half-orc growled, wiping his chin with the back of his hand.

"There's drool in this," Roan said, pushing it back. "And the cup is dirty. Try again." He didn't need to be a genius or even very smart to know that it wasn't good to drink drool, especially from this sort of creature. It was not something he would allow in the real world and it wasn't something he would put up with here.

"Oh boy," Marshall said, taking his chalice and stepping back as the half-orc reached beneath the bar and picked up a scimitar. The sword was three feet of curved, razor-sharp metal.

Using his filthy thumb, the half-orc tested the edge and said to Roan, "Now it's eight coppers."

Roan shook his head, taking up his war-pick. He had never used one, but it felt natural in his hands. "No. Four coppers and a fresh, clean glass. There's no reason to threaten…"

The half-orc leapt over the bar and still Roan did not really think the creature would attack him. Why would he? No one did that in the real world, not over a glass of weird looking beer. He was still in denial when the bartender slashed in a downward stroke with the scimitar.

Roan was too slow in bringing up his war-pick and the scimitar tore through the padded armor and went deep into the sloping muscle between his neck and shoulder. There was a strange dull pain in his now severed trapezius muscle.

He wasn't close to recovering from the shock of the attack when he noticed that in the upper right side of his vision were words etched in a red: (*Damage -8)* and beneath it was a bar graph that was more than half gone. Was that his life? Was he already half-dead?

Instead of using his war-pick to attack, Roan bellowed, "Hey, stop!" The half-orc did not stop. He drove his sword under Roan's useless pick. The tip curved up through his diaphragm and into his heart. Roan knew he was going to die a second before his heart was slit in half. When the realization of it struck him, there was nothing virtual in the horror that gripped him.

He started to fall just as more of the bright red words flashed in his vision:

(*Damage-Critical Hit -14*) Beneath it, the bar graph was completely empty.

Chapter 4
—Morin, Kingdom of Ellisbar

With a gasp, Roan sat up on his cot, clutching his chest; he could still feel where the scimitar had slid deep into him. There was even a grinding echo where the blade had gouged into his spinal column after it had torn through his heart.

"W-What the hell?" he asked in a whisper. "What kind of game is that? Who would actually pay money to play that?"

Marshall sat up as well. He seemed completely fine. "It's actually a lot of fun if you play it right, which you didn't."

Roan thought the game had been interesting and the graphics, if that's what they were even called, were without parallel, but fun? No, it was definitely not fun. "Did you die, too?"

"Naw, I just clocked out. That half-orc hadn't done anything to…"

The door to the basement opened and down came Caron, followed closely by Fulbright. Caron looked disgusted. "Damn it, Roan, what did you do?"

He shrugged, feeling disjointed and lost. His chest felt uncomfortable, the echo of his wound still there. Marshall answered for him. "He did everything, everything, everything wrong. He didn't play as himself. He didn't go through the tutorial. He picked a fight right off the bat for no reason."

Roan looked at Marshall in amazement and then began to sputter in indignation, Caron didn't want to hear it. "Shut up, Roan. What you just did cost the bureau and the taxpayer's money. And it cost me money as well." Roan watched, puzzled as Caron took out his wallet, counted out five twenties and gave them to Fulbright.

"I didn't think you'd last fifteen minutes," Fulbright explained. "For reasons that are inexplicable, Agent Caron had more faith in you, Mr. Roan."

A curse began to form behind Roan's lips and Marshall quickly said, "It's cool, no great loss. We're just going to call that a practice run. The game takes time to master, Roan."

"Unfortunately, we don't have a lot of time," Fulbright said. "The intervals between each of the incidents have picked up, meaning that Arching is hitting his stride. It won't be long before he begins to wield his power here."

"If you and that last developer are that worried, just don't go into the game," Roan suggested. "You'll be fine."

Fulbright lifted his cane and pointed it at Roan, saying, "Your problem is that you still see Infinite Reality as a game. In Arching's mind, it's not. It is life and it's just as real to him as this life is to you. And he is just as dangerous in this world as he is in the other. Think about it. Think about what sort of power he controls. He can take anyone and turn them into an assassin."

"Anyone in the game," Roan said. "The answer is pretty simple, we can just shut it off. But you don't want to do that, do you, Fulbright? You are afraid of dying but you're also afraid of losing your billions."

"You want to turn it off?" Fulbright shot back. "Sure, just tell me where the 'off' switch is and I'll do it. You saw IR head-quarters. That's where the game used to be run from. IR hosts its own websites and has its own servers and…" He paused and glanced at Caron before saying, "It has its own protocols and they're *entwined* in the normal TCP/IP protocols."

Caron eyes narrowed. "Meaning what, exactly."

Fulbright took a deep breath before answering. Roan guessed that it was the sort of breath heard frequently in confessionals. "Meaning, you can't just shut down Infinite Reality. It is coded within the protocols. At their most basic level, protocols establish the rules for how information passes through the Internet. They're how one computer can 'talk' to any other computer. We thought it was a good idea to, uh, work the game into them to stop potential threats from foreign governments."

"And your own government?" Roan asked. "You wished to be able to thwart them as well, if you wanted."

"No, not at all. Before today, I assumed that you Feds could shut us down anytime simply by seizing our servers and our hardware, but where Arching is running IR from is anyone's guess."

Caron ran a hand through his thinning blonde hair. "So where does that leave us? Shutting down the Internet?"

Fulbright laughed in a short bark. "Eighty percent of all commerce is tied in some way to the Internet. That's eighty percent of the *world's* commerce. No. Our choices are few: find Arching, or find where on this planet he's set up his platform, or rewrite the IPv6, which happens to be a 128-bit address system protocol. To change it out would take at least five years to implement."

The room was quiet as each thought over their predicament. Finally, Roan said, "I'll look for him on the other side. If he's there, I'll find him."

2—

"Play as myself," Roan told the game. He then whispered, "It's not a game, it's life." It was a concept that he had to instill within his own mind.

"Please repeat your command," the female voice said. "Life is not one of your choices."

"Play as myself," Roan repeated. As before, he was put through a series of tests. He lifted the heavy bar to measure his strength, and went through a series of increasingly difficult puzzles so that his intelligence could be quantified.

Wisdom was all about perception, intuition and understanding. He was asked to find items in pictures before going through a series of questions where the answers were always ambiguous: *Corinna Troost, who is three, accidentally drinks poison and at same time Kariann Morgan, who is twelve, is dangling from a rain gutter after trying to rescue a cat from a roof, who would you attempt to save first?*

His dexterity tests were "ball" oriented. A rubber ball was thrown to him and he was asked to catch it. Then two balls were thrown, two seconds apart, then three and so on. After that, he was asked to dodge the balls which came at him faster and faster. Finally, he was supposed to throw the balls at different targets.

Next came a constitution challenge in which he ran sprint after sprint, before running through an obstacle course where the obstacles would sometimes suddenly come alive and smash into him. He was bruised and bloodied by the time the test was over —a second later, he was utterly whole again.

Last, came a charisma test, which was the hardest challenge for him since it felt the most like playacting. He found himself in different scenarios: *A pretty girl across from you makes eye contact; ask her to an up-coming dance. You have five coppers but the turkey dinner costs six, talk the waiter into lowering the price. You are facing an ogre and your party is considering running away...*

When he had completed the last of his tasks he was shown his stats:

Character Name: Roan

Strength – Dexterity – Constitution
S: 16(+3)   D: 15(+2)   C: 17(+3)

Intelligence – Wisdom – Charisma
I: 16(+3)   W: 16(+3)   C: 16(+3)

"That is a lot better," he said to himself, remembering how awful the "8" intelligence felt. "So far so good. I'm ready for the next part." The woman then began asking him questions concerning his character in Daggerland and this time he went through the questions with far more care:

-What is the character's name? Roan.

-What race do you wish to be? Human.

-What sex do you wish to be? Male.

-What age do you wish to be? After a moment's hesitation, he said: "36."

-Do you wish to add character traits: No.

-Do you wish to change your appearance: No.

-What class of character do you want to be? Again, he paused over the options,

some of which were intriguing, but he finally went with: Fighter.

-Choose a fighting style: Defense.

-What alignment do you wish to be: Lawful Good.

-Do you wish to add background information: No.

-Purchase extra starting gold: Yes. 1,000 gold.

-Are you playing with a party: Yes; Mystic Gorilla.

-Difficulty Level: Roan went back and forth for a long time before he

chose: Extreme.
-Accept: Yes.

Once more he walked through the door with his name above it and again he found himself in the town square. It felt different. It felt better this time. He was in this world looking at it through his own eyes and hearing it with his own ears.

Marshall, the new and improved, slimmer and stronger, Marshall was there waiting for him. "Now, that's what I'm talking about," he said. "Let me see your stats. All you have to do is think: *show stats to party members* and we'll be able to see them." Roan thought the request and Marshall whistled.

"What?"

"Oh, those are some killer stats," Marshall said. "No wonder you kick ass in the real world. But don't let it go to your head. Right now, you are, forgive me for saying this, you're a chump. You're cannon fodder. Probably half the people here can make you their bitch. So be cool and try not to get into any fights until you level up."

This was a little perplexing to Roan. "Don't you have to fight in order to level up?"

Marshall shrugged. "Yeah, but you have to pick your battles. That half-orc was probably a third level fighter, while you're just first level. You get the difference, right?"

"I think so, for the most part." With as much patience as he could muster, Roan had watched the tutorial, though he still had not been able to get through the "history" of Daggerland. "Each time I level up I get more hit points and usually some sort of bonus that has to do with fighting."

"And there are feats, like two weapon fighting or sword mastery. Stuff like that. You'll get the hang of it pretty soon, but now let's go find Amanda and Jarrod." The two of them pushed through the crowd, however their teammates weren't at the fountain in the middle of the square as had been expected. "Don't worry," Marshall said. "We're all in the same party. If you ever get separated, just think: *Find party members* and you'll see an arrow. Do you see it?"

Roan thought: *Find party members*, but nothing happened. He tried it again with his eyes shut, but when he opened them there still wasn't an arrow. "I think I'm doing something wrong, I don't see anything."

"Huh? That doesn't make sense. You don't have to close your eyes. You should be able to just see…wait, what level are you playing on? Are you playing on extreme? Oh, crap. Why on earth would you play on extreme? You'll feel *everything!*"

He had chosen the extreme level because it had offered a +20% experience point advantage, which meant he would level up faster. Leveling up meant that he'd be harder to kill and he would have more in the game to catch Arching. Unfortunately, there were disadvantages in playing the game on the Extreme level. He wouldn't have access to certain game mechanics and he would feel all the pain associated with actual combat. After being stabbed with the scimitar while playing on easy, it hadn't been an simple decision.

"I know," Roan told him, "but they wanted me to play as if this were real. This is as real as it gets."

"I played on the hard setting *once* and that was enough for me. I stick to normal or easy. The game is supposed to be fun, right?"

"That's what I keep hearing," Roan said. He looked around at the crowds, searching for two people dressed in the dull noob clothes. "So, where are they?"

Marshall led the way to one of the carts, where the odd-looking Jarrod was leaning against a stall, wearing a bored expression on his face. Amanda, dressed in the coarse clothes but otherwise herself, was inspecting herbs.

"Oh, thank the heavens!" Jarrod cried when he caught sight of the two of them. "Where the hell have you guys been? You weren't on the map…Oh, I see. You died, didn't you Roan? Ha! I knew it."

"Shut up," Roan growled. He might have been a noob compared to most of the people there, but he could still wipe the floor with Jarrod.

"Of course, oh exalted leader," Jarrod said. He glanced back at Amanda, who was still looking over the items in the cart. Leaning in close, he whispered, "Have you ever been shopping with a girl before? Let me tell you they can't even make that fun in a fantasy world. I never thought I'd be bored gearing up for an adventure. Hey, speaking of which, did we get anything extra from Caron?"

After Roan, Marshall, and Fulbright had explained the nature of things in Daggerland, Caron had given Roan permission to charge the FBI Accounting Office an extra thousand dollars for armor, weapons, and necessities. Roan knew there were going to be some eyebrows raised when he got back to the real world and turned in his receipts.

He divvied out two-hundred and fifty gold apiece and his little crew went shopping. With receipts in mind, he told them to keep track of their spending. It was an odd request, especially when he finished gearing up and opened his *items* menu:

Scale mail—50 Gold
Round shield—10 Gold
Long sword— 15 Gold
Long bow— 25 Gold
Dagger—2 Gold
Quiver—1 Gold
Arrows x 20—1 Gold
Backpack—2 Gold
Bedroll—1 Gold
50' rope—1 Gold
Potion of Healing—50 Gold
Flask of Holy Water—25 Gold
Green cloak—1 Gold
Rations x 3—15 Silver
Tinderbox—5 Silver
Waterskin—2 Silver
Torches x3—5 Copper

"Potion of Healing," Roan whispered, shaking his head as he picked up the red vial. "They're going to make me pay all this back, I know it." He still had a heavy pouch filled with eighty-one tiny gold pieces, each about the size of a dime.

Marshall finished with twenty-one in gold, Amanda with forty and Jarrod with negative eighteen—he had borrowed heavily from Amanda to purchase a fine hat with a matching cloak, both in the deepest of purples.

Roan wanted to snatch the hat off his head and smack him with it and would have forced him to return it, only Marshall explained that they wouldn't get nearly half of what Jarrod had paid for it.

"Then you owe her," Roan said.

"Of course. No problem, but you'll see that this sort of finery is well worth the money. My outfit screams success, while yours…" He waggled a hand back and forth at Roan. "Not so much."

Roan looked down at himself and secretly had to agree. He had on what the merchant had called scale mail. It was basically a suit of thick leather on which little metal plates had been sewn. They overlapped, giving him somewhat of a fish-like appearance. The armor was so ugly that he had bought a green cloak, which hung down to mid-thigh to hide it as best as he could.

"The guy said it was pretty good armor for the money," Roan said, defensively.

"Yeah, but you look like a common soldier. You don't have any flair. And you Miss Amanda of Water Fell, what's with all the grey?"

She had on knee-high, grey leather boots, grey pants, a white shirt and a grey cloak. Roan had to agree that the outfit was a bit dull. She touched the collar of the cloak self-consciously, saying, "Camouflage, I guess. I thought we'd be out adventuring. There were some very nice dresses but what good would they do out there with all the monsters?"

"Speaking of which," Roan interjected, "Where are we going? Neither Caron nor Fulbright gave me any clue."

Marshall, who had on scale mail as well, shrugged and said, "Not very many people use their real names in the game, so it'll be a waste of time asking around for someone named Atticus Arching. But, I think we can safely assume someone like Arching is one of the big dogs out there. The Wizard of Ontair, maybe. Or perhaps the Witch-King of Adon."

"Why would you think he's a wizard?" Amanda asked. "It's not all that great if you ask me. I have two spell slots to use, per day. Two! That's it. After that I'm screwed. I can't wear armor and all I have for a weapon is a one-shot crossbow, a few darts and a big stick."

"Once you level up, you'll put us all to shame, trust me," Jarrod said. "Once you reach fifth level, you'll be fine. You just have to live that long."

She looked ill at the thought. "We won't let anything happen to you," Roan told her. "I say we head towards the closest of these big dogs. Who would that be?"

"We're in Ellisbar," Marshall answered. "And I'm pretty sure the king is a real person. This land used to be called Naturn, or something like that. Generally, the game doesn't change out the names of places without cause, so the king here must be very powerful. We should head to the capital and see what there is to see."

Jarrod stared off into space, looking blankly at nothing. He even pointed at nothing, saying, "It's about thirty miles. We have enough gold to rent a cart and horse."

Roan guessed that he was looking at a game map and so he thought: *show me game map*. When that didn't work he thought: *show map*. Still no map. With a sigh, he asked, "How much would it be to rent a cart?"

"Fifteen, twenty gold, somewhere in there," Jarrod said, as if the price was nothing. "That's a better deal than trying to buy horses. With all the crap you have to buy with them, it'll run a hundred per person, easy."

"We could walk," Roan suggested. He was very conscious of their money situation. They had blown through most of a thousand gold pieces in no time and he didn't think he could keep going back to Caron every few hours to beg.

Jarrod laughed high and loud. "Have you ever walked in that much gear? What's your encumbrance? Seventy pounds?" It was more than that. With his armor, shield, pack and all the rest, Roan was lugging around seventy-six pounds.

"I saw donkeys for sale," Amanda suggested. As Jarrod groaned, she went on. "We could buy a couple and load them up with most of our stuff. It would make the walk a little easier."

Roan jumped at the idea and marched straight away for the stables, only to find a bunch of empty stalls and six raggedy boys lying in the hay. "They all gone, but we'll get more a-morrow," one of the boys said.

"You had, like fifty animals here not more than an hour ago," Amanda said. "What happened to them all?"

The same boy repeated, "They all gone, but we'll get more a-morrow."

Amanda looked confused until Marshall whispered, "He's a non-player character, an NPC. Some are better than others. We can always go see who bought all the animals and see if he's willing to let us buy one off of him."

It was a woman who had purchased the animals and she wasn't hard to find. They followed a trail of hoof prints and dung to where thirty or forty people were loading thick linen bags onto the different sorts of animals. The smell of cinnamon was so heavy that it overpowered the unpleasant musk of donkey urine.

The woman, red-headed and green-eyed, was garbed in a silk cloak that hung over finely wrought plate armor. She was nearly as tall as Roan and gave him a quick appraising eye as the four came up. "Looking for work? I can always use a couple more mercs on the trail."

Roan blinked in confusion. Was this another NPC or was this a real person? And when she said mercs, did she mean mercenaries? And if so, what did mercenaries have to do with cinnamon?

"Possibly," he said, guardedly. "It depends on the pay, the work involved, and the destination."

"We're heading to Riverport by way of Thornwall. It's straight up guard work at ten gold a day, for three days, but you'll have to see it straight through, except for thirty-minute breaks three times a day."

Roan glanced back at the others. He had no idea where Riverport or Thornwall were or if ten gold a day was a good price. Amanda was trying not to look as lost as Roan; Jarrod, his lip turned up in disgust was staring at the closest mule; Marshall gave one of his little shrugs, suggesting that the offer was fair but that he didn't want to speak for everyone.

"We'll take it," Roan said. "What are the usual arrangements? Half up front and half when get to Riverport?"

"You must be American by birth," the woman said.

The way she said it suggested that she wasn't. "Yes, actually, and you?"

"Ukraine."

This was very surprising. "My name is Roan, and this is Amanda, Marshall and Jarrod. By the way, your English is flawless," he said, and was surprised when she laughed at him.

"He's new," Marshall said. "It's his first day, but he's very solid."

"Hmm," she said, appraising Roan. "He looks it. He looks very solid. Very, very solid. I can tell you're not a build and I like that as well. You're hired. Clock out for twenty and get back here as soon as possible. I want to get some miles behind us before the sun goes down. Oh, and you can call me Korrin of Mirrorton"

In the dank basement of the FBI, Jarrod sat up laughing. He was no longer the above average looking rake with the fine purple cloak. He was back to being sickly pale with buggy eyes. "Your English is flawless! Holy crap! I thought I was going to bust a gut trying to hold back laughing."

Roan glared but Jarrod only fell back in a state of girlish giggling. Roan had to resist the urge to punch him. "I don't understand what's so funny. Do you think I was hitting on her? It was just a compliment."

"No, you're not getting it," Marshall said, and then took two tries to heave his now soft looking body off the cot. "She wasn't speaking English and neither were you. The game takes all languages and translates them into what's called 'common.'"

"It's really not that funny," Amanda said, standing and stretching. "It could have happened to any…" She was just thrusting out her breasts in an attempt to crack her back when she saw a man sitting in the dark staring at her.

With a cry, she leapt back, just as Roan jumped forward, pulling his gun. The man's eyes bugged at the sight of the barrel. He put out his hands. "Hey, hold on. My name is Agent DeMott. I'm just babysitting you guys. Caron sent me, okay?"

"Oh, sorry," Roan said, holstering his piece. He was embarrassed over his reaction, but at the same time he was tired of being embarrassed over every little thing. Turning from the man, he barked, "Let's hit the bathrooms, asap. If you're hungry I'm afraid we only have time for whatever they have in the vending machines."

Jarrod grumbled at the idea. "You know what? We should have some sandwiches on hand and, like a mini-fridge with some 'Dew and some diet whatever, you know that stuff Amanda drinks."

"And we need an elliptical," Amanda added. "I can't just lie here for three days without any exercise."

"And some weights," Roan said. "And some comfortable clothes. Sweats or scrubs. Can you take care of this for us, De-Mott? Thanks."

DeMott had a smirk on his face. "Uh, you guys are playing a game. It's not like it's a real case."

Roan stopped in the doorway. "Murder, kidnapping, arson, corporate espionage, etcetera, etcetera, etcetera. You don't think that equals a real case? Really? Is that compared to what you're doing, babysitting four sleeping people?" That wiped the smirk off of DeMott's face.

Five minutes and an empty bladder later, Roan stopped by the vending machine. "It all looks like crap," he said to Amanda. She nodded, a dollar in her hand.

Marshall bought two *Snickers* bars. "Wait until you dig into those iron rations we bought in Morin. Man, you can get some good meals in Daggerland, but rations aren't them. They're like jerky without the flavor. It'll keep you going, though."

"And if you don't eat on the other side?" Roan asked. "Will your character die?" Marshall mumbled a 'yes' around three-quarters of a *Snickers* bar he had stuffed into his mouth. This still wasn't an inducement for Roan to buy anything from the machine. He didn't exactly treat his body as a temple, but it wasn't a crack-house either.

He went back down to the basement, followed by Amanda and Marshall. DeMott wasn't in sight. Jarrod was sitting on his cot, craning Doritos into his mouth. His fingers and lips were orange.

"Finish up," Roan said, taking up his neural coupler—in seconds, he was back in Daggerland where the weight of his armor and pack settled once more onto his broad shoulders. He shrugged and stretched, accepting the weight, but not liking it. All the adventuring gear slowed him down, made him less nimble on his feet.

A second later, Amanda appeared next to him. Immediately her lip curled and she dropped her pack to the ground with a thud. "Man, that's heavy."

Marshall had also returned to the game and he was as loaded down as Roan. He rolled his eyes at her tiny pack. There was already sweat in his hairline. Jarrod came last, the orange of the Doritos nowhere to be found, his hair clean and toppled easily across his forehead, his eyes clearer.

He was so different that Roan had to ask, "How many points did you give to your charisma?"

"That's none of your business," Jarrod said, almost forgetting to add, "Sir."

"Actually, it is my business," Roan shot back. "This isn't a game, not for us. And we're definitely not here to indulge your fantasies. Let me see your stats." When Jarrod hesitated, Roan leaned in close and added, "There are a dozen guys back in the office who would take your place in a second, so when I give an order, you hop to, got it?"

Reluctantly, Jarrod nodded. "Show stats," he mumbled.

Character Name: **Jarrod The Dark Adder**

Strength – Dexterity – Constitution
S: **14(+2)**   D: **16(+3)**   C: **14(+2)**

Intelligence – Wisdom – Charisma
I: **12(+1)**   W: **12(+1)**   C: **14(+2)**

"Oh, boy," Marshall said, seeing that Jarrod's charisma had been bumped two slots up.

"I don't understand this at all," Roan said. "You're a rogue. You could've had an eighteen dexterity. You could've been stronger or tougher. This is…this is unacceptable. I'm going to need you to start your character over. Put those two points any-where but charisma."

"He doesn't have time," Amanda said, pointing to where Korrin was directing her pack animals into place. "We're going to be leaving soon. And besides, he'd lose all of his armor and gear. The game does not allow first or second level characters or any of their party members to retain any initial gear or gold. It prevents people from cheating."

Jarrod looked relieved. "We wouldn't want to cheat, right? We are the good guys after all, ha-ha." He quickly started for-ward, the white feather in his deep purple hat bouncing along. The rest followed him to where Korrin was talking to the other guards. Including his group, there were twenty-six in her com-pany. Roan did not know whether that was a good number or one that was pitifully weak.

"On time, that's good," Korrin said, to Roan and his team. She stood, rubbing her hands together as she gazed at her company. A few appeared to Roan to be rogues, one might have been a cleric, but the rest looked like fighters. Unfortunately, almost all of them wore only leather armor and those that didn't had on ring mail, which Roan now knew was only a few steps up from leather.

Korrin pointed to Roan. "I want your team in front with me. Mitera, take four of the townies and watch the left. Janis take four and watch the right. The rest of you are the rear guard. Mages and clerics, you are now on my time and that means no spell work without my express permission. I can and will dock your wages. Let's mount up, people!"

At the front of the train were two water buffalos hitched to a blue wagon. The wagon's paint was flaking off and as Roan climbed up the side, he received his first wound while playing on extreme mode: a splinter poked up under a fingernail on his right ring finger.

"Son of a bitch," he hissed as he tried to dig out the splinter.

"Did widdums get an owie?" Korrin joked. "I know you are new so I should tell you that you cannot sue me for damages. Or pain and suffering." She laughed at her own joke as she stood on the first bench and looked back at the train of carts and loaded-down mules. It was strung out for about two hundred feet. She waved an arm to someone at the very back and then sat down next to Roan, sitting so closely that their armor scraped together.

There were two benches in the front of the wagon. Roan, Korrin and a teenage boy sat in the front. Amanda, Jarrod, and Marshall sat on the next one. In the back were mounds of bagged cinnamon and two fighters in ring mail who almost never spoke and when they did, they tended to repeat themselves.

Roan didn't need it explained that they were NPCs, but what he did need to know was why the wagon with its fading paint and its splinters and its bumpy ride was so utterly perfect in its realism while the NPCs were only so-so.

When he asked Korrin, she shook her head. "I don't mean to be rude, but maybe that is something for one of your friends to explain to you."

It actually did seem rude and he was already in mid-scowl when Jarrod tapped his armored shoulder. "She just doesn't want to explain because the game subtracts experience points when you break character. Talking about the game instead of playing it is something that'll get you every time."

"That's right," Roan said. "I remember seeing the red negative sign last time. Does it work in extreme? I haven't seen..."

"Wait," Korrin said, talking over him. "What mode are you in? Extreme?" When he nodded, she made a noise in her throat that sounded like disappointment or disgust. She explained, "You're new and on the toughest level. It's not a good match. I don't even know why they have it even for old campaigners. No one ever uses extreme and, oh, crap! I just lost ten points, thank you very much."

Jarrod chuckled and said, "I don't have points to lose so I can talk all I want. I've only heard of one person ever playing on extreme before. It was a friend of a friend. By some miracle, he got to sixth level and then found himself in the middle of this huge war. I'm talking army against army. Supposedly, after half an hour he just walked away in the middle of the fight, clocked out and started over."

"Starting over at sixth level," Marshall said with a wistful shake of his head. "What a waste."

"I take it that's bad?" Amanda asked.

"Of course it's bad," Jarrod answered. "I read that it takes the average player a year to get to level six. Could you imagine taking a year to build a character and then just walk away from it?"

Korrin turned to look at Jarrod. "Could you imagine getting stabbed in the gut for real? It's hard enough, you know, like this."

"Hard enough on the normal setting, you mean?" Jarrod asked. She wasn't about to lose any more points and only nodded.

"Well, you're making me feel great about my choice, thanks," Roan said. "So, Korrin, when can I expect my first stabbing? Is this a dangerous trip?"

She was quiet for a while, watching the scenery slowly passing by. They rode southeast on a rutted dirt road crossing an open prairie while above them, the sky was a pretty blue. Eventually, she said, "I take a different route every time to keep the bandits guessing. We have a pretty good chance of getting through without any problem."

"You do this a lot?" Amanda asked, perplexed. "This is how you play the game? It's sort of strange if you ask me."

Korrin gave Amanda a hard look. "This is how I live my life. We can't all be born in rich America, fat and happy. In the land of the Ukraine, the people are very poor. This pays my bills. I take a load every week from different cities out to Riverport and I get a cut of the profits. I might get two-thousand in gold on this run alone."

"And how much does that equal on the other side?" Roan asked.

"By itself? Nothing. But I can use it to buy a magic weapon or a fine suit of armor. The Japanese players will pay big Yen for traditional samurai armor, especially if it's magical. All in all, I probably make about five-hundred of your, uh, currency a week."

Roan found it amazing how people were so adaptable. Here was a woman from the Ukraine, shipping pretend cinnamon from the made-up city of Morin to the equally imaginary city of Riverport so that she could purchase a "magical" suit of imaginary armor to sell to a Japanese man halfway around the real world.

He dwelled on this as the miles trundled under the wheels of the cart. Eventually, however, his mind went other places and he found himself staring at the scenery which was as real as anything he had ever experienced, which brought his thoughts back to the two NPC fighters in the back of the wagon.

They looked and sounded and spoke like average men, but were perhaps a little too average. They were dull and Roan enjoyed everyone else's company—even Jarrod's—over theirs. He guessed that this was on purpose, that the creators of the game wanted people to interact with people whenever possible.

There was plenty of time to interact and Roan spent most of the day chatting with Korrin. She wanted to know all about this "rich American," while he wanted to know all about the game world including the current king of Ellisbar. She knew very little. "Though he must be powerful since he controls Morin. Its mines are very rich. I hear he makes two-thousand a week in tin, alone. But enough about him. When are you going to visit me on the other side?"

"It's time for our break!" Amanda announced all of sudden. "We'll go in shifts. Roan and I will go first and then Jarrod and Marshall. Good. We'll be back in half an hour."

2—

"What a hussy!" Amanda declared as she sat up in the basement of the field office. "Can you believe her? Ooooh, I am just poor Ukrainian girl. Can you believe that story?"

Roan shrugged. "I do, actually. I don't see why she would lie. How long do you think we were under?"

"Six hours and eight minutes," a woman said. She'd been sitting on the stairs with a book on her knees. "Hi, I'm Joanna Niederer, your babysitter."

"I don't know if I like the term 'babysitter,' exactly," Roan said, hoping to change the subject away from Korrin. "Maybe body-sitter?"

Amanda was still steaming and the subject wasn't going to be changed so easily. "Didn't we just leave a body-sitter back there?"

"Hmmm, you're right, body-sitter sounds weird," Roan agreed, sort of. "How about we call you our security detail, Joanna." It was much better sounding, only Joanna looked more like a school teacher than an FBI agent. "Are you with the bureau?"

"In a manner of speaking," she acknowledged with a wide smile. "I'm Agent Caron's administrative assistant."

This brought Amanda around. "You're his secretary?" She asked in a tone of complete disbelief.

Joanna's bright smile dimmed. "I prefer 'administrative assistant.' It really is a more thoughtful term, if you don't mind. Now, while you were away I took care of some of the things that were requested. Each of you has a little locker with clean underwear and sweat suits. We're getting the refrigerator tomorrow, but for now we have a cooler filled with deli meats and cheeses. I could make each of you a sandwich if you wish."

Roan was still stuck on the fact that Caron had his secretary watching over them. He blinked at her and then gazed around the room at the new additions. One thing she had failed to mention were the weights. On the ground next to Marshall's out flung hand were a tiny pair of barbells, each stamped with 2.5 and each looking like they belonged at a senior rec center.

"What the hell?" he whispered.

"Oh, I brought those from home," Joanna said.

He felt the heat of anger rising in him, but Amanda caught his eye. He swallowed his outburst. "I would like something a bit bigger. And if Agent Caron is going to have you guarding us,

I would suggest that you get a lock on the basement door and maybe hold onto the key. It could be a dangerous job he's given you."

Conscious of their time limit, Amanda and Roan cleaned up, ate sandwiches prepared by Joanna and then reentered the game.

Not much had changed except Korrin had walked down the line of beasts to check things out. The water-buffalo were still plodding along as before with the boy lazily flicking his whip every minute or so. Marshall and Jarrod were dozing on the cinnamon.

"Your turn," Roan told them after he had kicked them both awake. They were gone their allotted time and the afternoon wore on easily. They each told stories, or day dreamed, or sharpened their swords, something Roan was surprised to find that he already knew how to do.

Toward evening the rutted path wound down a series of hills and into a thick forest. Where before the trip had been a lazy spring outing, now tension ran high as they began to hear secretive sounds coming from the dense undergrowth. Korrin packed the animals and carts as closely as she could get them so that as they trudged through the forest the air was dense with a sour combination of cinnamon, barn animal, and dung.

"Bows at the ready," Korrin ordered. It was the least necessary order ever given. Only eight of the guards had bows or crossbows and they were all at the ready. They traveled for an hour into the forest and despite the increasing fear among the company, nothing untoward occurred. When the light started to dwindle, Korrin found a wide spot where the trees around the road weren't as dense. She unhitched the animals from the wagons and carts and formed a rudimentary defensive perimeter.

In the middle of the perimeter was barely enough room for a bonfire and the twenty-six guards and rovers.

Watches were set: four people per hour, each person standing at one of the cardinal points of the compass. Roan volunteered his crew for the first watch. When Jarrod started in with his grumbling, Roan explained in a whisper, "This way your sleep isn't broken and a lot of these guys will be up anyway."

Their watch went by quickly and when they were relieved, they tiptoed to their bedrolls and tried to sleep. Because he had never slept in scale mail before, it took Roan a full hour to fall asleep. Five minutes into his snooze, the howl of wolves woke him.

He glanced over at Amanda. She was just as wide awake, her eyes shining like newly minted nickels in the dark. Korrin rolled over, saying, "There's only a few of them. Go back to sleep."

Two watches later, Roan's light doze was again interrupted when there came loud crashing noises from the forest. The eastern guard came rushing over to Korrin, but she was already on her feet, nocking an arrow.

"Everyone up!" she hissed and then kicked Jarrod, who was snoring. The noises in the forest came closer and closer until there seemed to be a huge shadow among the shadows. "Get me a light spell up there," she ordered and it was a moment before Amanda realized that Korrin was talking to her.

"Uh, Monhi-rho-ghs," she said, drawing a quick pattern in the air. A ball of white light about the size of a cantaloupe blinked into being right in front of her. In the new light, Roan could see Amanda marveling over this creation.

"Up there!" Korrin yelled

Amanda pointed and the light whisked away to the shadows revealing three tremendous creatures. They were humanoid in shape, except that their muscular arms hung past their knees. They were eleven-feet tall, tinged green, had long, tusk-like teeth and sharp claws.

Roan took a step back in shock, regretting once more having chosen extreme mode, he would get to feel exactly what it would be like to have those jaws bite his head off.

"Get away, troll!" Korrin yelled at them. "We have fire and magic. We have swords and bows!"

"Cow," the largest of them said, pointing at one of the water buffalo and then at its own gaping mouth.

"No cow! We have fire. We have magic!" The trolls stood for over a minute grunting at each other in their language until at last they yelled nonsense words at Korrin and then slowly trudged away, making even more noise as they left, breaking branches and uprooting small trees in their anger.

Wearing a smile, Korrin unstrung her bow and laid back down. "The whole forest had to have heard that. It's a good thing. If the trolls didn't want to mess with us, then the gnolls won't either and the goblins will keep far, far away. Sleep tight."

Gnolls? Goblins? Roan wasn't reassured in the least, while next to him Amanda was shivering in fright. "It'll be okay," he told her. It felt very much like a lie, but for reasons that were completely inexplicable to him, Amanda seemed to be comforted by this and when she laid down next to him, she fell asleep long before he did.

3—

Korrin was a slave driver, at least according to Jarrod, who had to be kicked awake for a second time. "The sun's not even up yet," he grumbled, trying to roll up his bedding in the gloom of the predawn.

"You're getting paid and soon we're going to get la…" Marshall stopped, sneaking a quick peek at Amanda. "I mean, it's all cool man. We'll have a good time in the capital when this is over. I just wish we had taken on those trolls. Think about the loot those guys would've had."

"And think about how many of us would have been killed," Amanda said, chastising him. She paused and looked down at her hands. "But I did do magic. That was awesome."

"It was a basic light spell," Korrin snapped. "A cantrip is something any neophyte can do. Now give me a hand getting this damned wagon turned around." With a lot of grunting and cursing, they managed to turn the cart around so that it pointed south again. Next, the two water buffalo were hitched in front and they were ready to go.

"We're going to take turns clocking out now," Korrin said. "We won't be able to again for a good six or seven hours. Things are probably going to get a little dicey. Sometimes rumors fly faster than the wind."

By twos, the characters clocked out and spent a very quick thirty minutes back in the real world. When it was Roan's turn, it felt like ten minutes of his time was wasted simply urinating. He then spent twenty minutes doing pushup and dips. With about a minute left he shoveled one of Joanna's sandwiches down his gullet. She grinned as he ate.

"I have two grown children," she remarked, as he washed the sandwich down. "My son could put it away just like you. He plays linebacker for Michigan State. You look like you played football."

"I was a linebacker in college, too," Roan told her, "but that feels like a million years ago."

When he got back to what was beginning to feel like his actual life, he found Amanda with an inch-thick book set on her knees. When he asked about it, she said, "It's my spell book and I don't care what Korrin says, I think what I did last night was very cool. I'll admit that I was skeptical about all of this and then that spell just came out of me. I could feel it come out of my, my soul I think."

They were on the back bench of the wagon and she leaned in close enough for Roan to feel her breath on his neck. "I want to do it again."

He laughed loudly and forgot himself, saying, "You're too cute." She smiled briefly and then he saw the "rules" kick in and her smiled became strained. It was against FBI regulations for one agent to have a romantic relationship with another when working in the same field office and it was especially egregious that he was her superior.

"I'm sure you'll get the chance," he said, slipping down from the wagon. "I'm going to stretch my legs." It was a good excuse to get away and clear his head. He had been within an ace of sliding his hand along her back as if she were just another girl he was trying to pick up.

As he walked toward the back of the train, he thought about Amanda's magic. She was right, it had been breathtaking to see that ball of light suddenly appear—and that had been the very simplest magic. Korrin had called it a cantrip and he remembered that it was a zero level spell. It was a spell for rookies.

"And what do I have?" He pulled his long sword from its sheath. Both the sword and the sheath were unadorned. "Maybe if I die, I'll come back as a wizard. It seems I can rent a fighter if I need one." Sullenly, he gave the sword a flick; it did feel good in his hand, almost natural, which was strange since he had never used a sword in his life.

For once Jarrod was back before Marshall, and Roan mentioned the way his sword felt to him. "It's all about the game mechanics," Jarrod explained. "It's a level based game as opposed to a skill based game." When Roan gave him a blank look he went on, "It's like this, a skill based game is sorta like real life. You know, practice makes perfect."

Roan thought he understood. "Like if you want to learn how to throw a curve ball you have to just go do it every single day." He blinked when he saw *EXP -0* cross his vision. Curve balls were a no-no in Daggerland, it seemed.

Jarrod nodded. "Exactly, but when you're in a full immersion RPG like this, it's tedious as hell. Back before the virtual reality gaming systems, people would build their characters by constantly using their skills. You would have guys jumping everywhere they went to increase their jump skills. Could you imagine that here? People bopping about like bunnies?"

"There's a lot of weird stuff around here already."

"Not weirder than ten paladins in platemail hopping down a road. It's probably why IR is so successful. Swordsman don't have to spend all day hacking at dummies and wizards, don't have to go blind popping out frog eyes to make a potion. The game assumes that you train in your spare time that way when you level up you automatically get the bonuses. It frees you up for more fun."

"And you think this is fun? We really haven't done much and, I don't mean to be a dick, but you complain a lot."

Jarrod grinned sheepishly, suddenly looking more like himself on the other side. "Yeah, well that's just who I am. But I do think this is fun and we haven't even done any of the cool stuff yet. It's fun because we're *doing* something. You know what I'd be doing back in the office? Looking through some idiot's computer files, trying to see where he defrauded the government out of two hundred dollars or whatever. And I have a cool job. Just think if you were an accountant or a lawyer. Everyday you'd drag your ass to work and sit in front of a computer all day. On Tuesday nights you stoink the wife when the kids are at cub scouts. On Friday you order a pizza as the high point of your day and then on Monday you do it all over again. Here, you can do anything. Think about it. I have no clue what's going to happen in ten minutes or in ten hours."

"Or in ten seconds," Roan said. Movement in the forest had caught his attention. All he saw was a shadow, but he knew that it was a person or something close to a person, like that half-orc. He or she had been trying to be stealthy, but Roan hadn't been fooled. "Korrin!" He pointed and as he did the shadow raised something to its lips and blew a loud note.

Trouble had come early.

Chapter 6
—The Down Forest Road, Kingdom of Ellisbar

The single horn was answered by another, deeper in the forest. Roan felt a spike in his chest and he immediately searched out Amanda, but she had clocked out, as had at least five of the other guards.

"Form up on me!" Korrin yelled. Sixteen first level fighters, a few rogues and a single cleric wouldn't be much of a formation and certainly wouldn't instill much fear in another party unless it was significantly smaller and Roan guessed that the single horn blast hadn't been the signal to run away.

"Roan, anchor the left," Korrin said. "Mitera take the right. Everyone else, fall in around them, all except you, cleric. You stay in the back and heal those who fall. Bloody hell, where is Janis and that stupid witch?"

Jarrod, who had twitchy eyes and a bobbing Adams apple, said, "She clocked out. I could go get her if you want." When she hesitated, he added, "I'm not running away."

She snapped her fingers. "Go, before we're engaged and you can't. Everyone else, bows at the ready!" Now they were down to nineteen. The rovers didn't count. The boys were standing in a group, ready to bolt if things went bad for Korrin.

Against them were thirty or forty raggedly looking individuals, almost all of whom wore the god-awful padded armor and carried clubs. They came down through the trees flitting from one to another, and although they were wary of the crossbows and longbows carried by Roan and a few others, they came on eagerly, looking for blood and treasure.

Roan nocked an arrow when they were fifty yards away, though he knew better than to attempt a shot; there were still too many trees in the way. He was ready to fire the moment they got a little closer, however they stopped, as one of them called out, "Korrin! Walk away and you and all your men can keep your lives. We promise not to hurt you."

"Screw you, Algar," was her reply. She then half-turned toward Roan and spoke out of the corner of her mouth, "Go for the ones in metal armor first."

"G-Got it," he said, surprised that there was a tremor in his voice. Though why he should be surprised didn't make sense. He was seconds from being in actual hand to hand combat where the chances were very good that he would be bludgeoned to death. It made his stomach roll over.

He thought he'd see the same sort of nervousness when he glanced down the thin line to his right, but he was astonished to see that of all the people in Korrin's group, only the NPCs appeared nervous. How was that possible? How were Marshall and the others cool and steeled against the coming battle, when Roan, who had always considered himself a hard guy, was sweating so badly he could feel it trickling down his back in little rivulets?

"You guys ready?" Algar called to his men. They yelled back that they were and the few that had shields smashed their clubs against them for effect.

Roan thought that they would charge in a screaming frenzy as they always did in the movies, however, they were for the most part quiet, conserving their energy. They ran down the hill and through the last of the trees and there was one second there where Roan realized why everyone was so cool over this fight and why he was freaking out. He was the only one there who was actually going to die. On the *extreme* setting, his death would be as real as it got.

He had been in sticky situations before, plenty of them in fact, but he had never felt so weak. He was first level. He was nothing. Feeling desperation well up, he did the only thing he could think of: "Halt!" he bellowed at the top of his lungs. "Daniel Roan, Special Agent FBI! You are interfering with a federal investigation. Leave the area immediately."

In the upper right hand corner of his vision the red words flashed (*EXP -0*), only he didn't even notice. His attention was on the charging men who came to a faltering stop.

"Is that for real?" someone asked.

"The FBI? Here in Daggerland? Why?"

Everyone was murmuring to each other and staring at Roan, and for just a moment he thought that he had thwarted his imminent death, only just then Jarrod reappeared yelling, "Sorry! Amanda was in the shower and Mrs Niederer had locked the door…"

His sudden appearance was like a signal for the battle to recommence. Algar and his men charged again as if Roan had never shouted to the world that there was an FBI investigation going on in Daggerland. Roan knew that it had been a mistake and his only hope was that what he'd said would be laughed off and forgotten.

The break in the action had one advantage for Roan: his embarrassment was now even greater than his fear of dying. It allowed him to ignore his fear and concentrate on killing. Bending back his bow, he centered it on one of the men wearing the bulky ring mail who was lumbering at him.

The tutorial Roan had watched made combat appear simple in terms of game mechanics. An unarmored opponent has a base armor class of 10. When a player attacks him, the game randomly generates a number between 1 and 20, meaning that the attacker has a simple fifty-fifty chance of striking him.

Things are never quite that simple, however. The man charging at Roan had on ring mail which was thick and tough, giving him an armor class (AC) of fourteen, meaning that Roan only had a six in twenty chance of hitting the man.

BUT, and in combat there is always a but, Roan was a first level fighter and was proficient with the long bow and so a +1 was added to his randomly generated attack score. He was also dexterous(Dexterity 15 +2) and he got to add another +2 to his attack.

In this instance, Roan was almost back to a fifty-fifty chance of hitting the man with an arrow. It was a coin toss and it came up heads for Roan.

None of this filtered into Roan's consciousness. He only knew that he let the arrow fly and it hit the man in the leg. He had hurt his enemy but he wasn't dead.

As if he had practiced the move a thousand times, Roan pulled a second arrow from his quiver in a fluid motion. He aimed once again at the man in ring mail, only just then a bolt from Marshall's crossbow whipped through the air and pierced the man's chest.

When he fell, Roan quickly adjusted his aim and shot at another of the armored men. This time the arrow hit dead center only it bounced off the tough armor and flicked away. Roan didn't have time to curse. He threw down his bow and with one hand ripped out his sword and with the other he took up his round shield.

The shield was barely on his arm when another man in ring mail hacked at him with a sword that seemed oddly short. The sword clanged off his shield and Roan felt a moment of panic when words flashed across the bottom of his screen:

Class Ability Unlocked: Fighting Style-Defender—While wearing armor, the Defender gains a bonus of +1 to AC.

"Not now!" Roan snapped. He had chosen the fighting style of *Defender* while building his character. It had seemed to be one of the better perks of being a fighter, though "unlocking" it in the middle of a fight was terrible timing. He swung his long sword through the white lettering and into the neck of his opponent. The man grunted as blood flowed.

Roan was slightly better with the sword than the bow. His level gave him a +1 to hit, but with his strength of sixteen he was able to add +3 to both his chance at hitting the man as well as to the damage done by the sword.

The man had taken terrible damage and, since he was likely first level, Roan figured he was close to dying. It seemed like a perfectly natural response when he choked on his blood and backed away.

Algar didn't see it that way. "What the hell, Tiki? Get in there!"

Tiki didn't have the heart and he lurched back, giving room for one of the club-wielding, padded armor guys to take a hack at Roan, only Roan was quicker and slashed in with his long sword. The man's padded armor, combined with his dexterity gave him an AC of 13. With Roan's +4 attack, he had an eleven in twenty chance of hitting and he did for eight points of damage. It wasn't enough to either kill his enemy or deter him and he swung the club, going up against Roan's 19 AC.

The club thudded off of Roan's sword arm but he didn't even feel it as he drew back his sword for the killing stroke. He lunged forward, the long sword splitting the built-up cloth as if it were tissue paper and driving into the man's chest. He died and for a moment, he hung there on the end of Roan's sword as Roan realized something: killing a man like that was beastly and barbaric, and…and it was horribly natural and strangely fulfilling and, in a sick way, exhilarating.

Somehow the game had managed to capture this inhuman side of humanity to perfection.

Civilization tried to smother this insidious aspect that infected mankind, but it remained. Hunters had just a taste of it when they stalked their prey, while serial killers wallowed in it, thinking that taking lives was what made their life worth living.

Roan found himself somewhere in the middle. On one level, he knew that it was wrong to take a life, while at the same time it was right to defend himself. Yet on still another level, he rationalized that he was just playing a game and that he had faced an opponent in a fair trial of arms and had won.

He didn't know what to think of the exhilaration—either way, it didn't last. The game stole a portion of it as neon green words floated momentarily in the air near the body of the man (*EXP +40*). Just like that, the life of a man had been boiled down to just a number. The next thing that happened, which kept the death of one man in perspective, was that Roan was bashed in the head.

The reality of the game was exact. It felt precisely like getting hit with a baseball bat. His head rang from the blow, his legs wobbled beneath him and everything went out of focus—well, almost everything. In the upper right side of his vision he saw with painful clarity: (*Damage -7*) and beneath that, the bar graph was slightly half used up.

Before he could recover, a different bat-wielding smashed him in the leg: (*Damage -3*). Now the bar graph had only a millimeter left. Roan was now so close to death that a cat's scratch would send him over the edge. He reeled backwards, wondering whether he'd be allowed to walk away as Tiki had done. With the two aiming more blows at him, Roan guessed not.

He was trying to collect himself when a soft voice spoke from behind him: "Basia-rah." Bright red bolts of energy flew through the air faster than Roan could follow and struck one of Roan's enemies, throwing him backwards. Amanda had clocked back in and had used one of her spells.

There was still one of the clubbers left, and although he was practically dead, Roan put himself between him and Amanda, who was staring wide-eyed at the person she had killed.

Roan flailed with his sword and missed, and the clubber pressed in so fast that Roan fell. There was no telling if he would have died right then, but Jarrod suddenly appeared, stabbing the man from behind and killing him in one blow.

"Marshall!" Jarrod yelled and then aimed his hand-crossbow into the melee. It was a wild fight. Initially, Algar's men had an overwhelming advantage, but as more and more of Korrin's people clocked back in, things evened out. Algar had more fighters, however they were terribly armored and easily hurt. They were there for experience and loot, not to die gloriously for a cause and so frequently the wounded backed away as Tiki had. Korrin's people didn't have that option and fought tenaciously.

Marshall rushed over, digging in a pouch. "I'm out of spells!" He pulled a Potion of Healing from his pouch and poured the red liquid into Roan's mouth—(*Heal +8*). Only then did Roan remember that he had a potion of his own.

He wasn't fully healed—his head ached and there was a dull pain in his leg, but he leapt up nonetheless. "I forgot I had one of those," he said. "I'll give it to you when this is over. But for now…" There was no time for any more discussion. The fight had swayed away from them, but now it came roaring back.

Roan met it head on, hacking left and right with his long sword. Marshall stood on his right, swinging his mace back and forth. The mace was a mean looking metal club with a spiked head. The two, with their heavy armor and shields, seemed impervious to the wooden clubs of their foes.

Behind them, Amanda sent out bolts of fire and more of the magical red missiles and when her spells ran dry, she used her light crossbow. Jarrod was cut off from the others as five men came at him. He cursed long and loud as he ran with them chasing.

To Roan this was a plus; it was five fewer people to kill. Slowly, Korrin's crew came together to form a circle that crumbled inwards whenever one of the guards went down under the hammering blows. Eventually they formed a hard nub, against which the bandits dashed themselves to pieces.

As the battle went on, their opponent's weaknesses became more and more apparent: they were ill-led and utterly self-serving. Although Korrin challenged, their leader, Algar, to a one-on-one battle, he refused to fight her, and when half of his men were either dead or injured, the rest slowly backed away, mumbling threats.

The battle had been won. Roan stood huffing and puffing, feeling a surge within him—he had leveled up! A notification ran across the bottom of his vision: *Congratulations! You are now a Level Two Fighter and have gained the following bonuses:*

Increased Hit Points(+9)

Attack +2

Second Strike: Once per day, following a missed attack, you can use your momentum to make one additional attack.

"Better than a stick in the eye," he said, blinking the notification away. Now that he could focus on the world around him, he saw that instead of celebrating their victory, Korrin's people were staring at him.

"You're with the FBI!" she demanded.

An excuse was just forming on his lips, but it froze there as he saw Marshall staring down at one of the corpses. It was Amanda. She hadn't just been killed, someone had cruelly abused her, bashing in her pretty face even after she had died. The sight was more painful than any injury he had ever had.

2—

Korrin demanded an answer, but Roan only said, "I have to check on Amanda. I'll be back in ten minutes."

He found her in the real world sitting on her bunk, looking down at the neural coupler. When she saw him stir, she said, "They were evil. They were evil and they were real people. That's what I don't understand. I-I fell and I said: 'I give up' but they kept hitting me over and over."

"I'm sorry. I wish I could have protected you, but there were too many of them."

She wouldn't look up from the coupler. "I don't get people. Sometimes I hate them."

What could he say to that? He often felt the same way. "Hate the evil in them, that's what I do. I hate the evil and love the good." He stood up and placed both of his balled fists into his back and stretched. "I'm going to take a leak before I go back. Maybe you can meet us in the next town. I'll ask Marshall what the rules are."

"You didn't die?" she asked.

"No, we won the battle, but I might have screwed up." She finally looked up; her eyes were rimmed red. There was an agent seated on a chair about ten feet away, a man Roan had seen a few times. Embarrassed, he whispered to Amanda, "I sort of let on that I was an FBI agent. I'm going to tell Korrin that I was just making up stories."

Amanda managed to smile. "And I thought I had problems. If it gets out that you blew our cover, Caron is going to be pissed. Let's hope that red-headed hussy believes you."

Whether Korrin believed him or not, Roan couldn't tell. Not that it mattered. She was now shorthanded and afraid of a second attack. After stripping the bodies of anything of value, she had the rovers drive the pack animals as fast as they could. They were headed to Thornwall, a town on the southern edge of the Kingdom of Ellisbar. Without a game generated map in his head, Roan really had no clue as to where he was in this huge world.

In order to change the subject of him being an FBI agent, he had tried to ask Korrin where the borders were.

"Walk in any direction, when you run up against the mountains, then you've hit the borders. Ellisbar is shaped like an eye with mountains all around and the Great Blackfen River running right along the eastern edge of it. If Ellisbar were a clock, Morin would be at the twelve o'clock position. Thornwall is southeast of it, sitting right up against the beginning of the Orc-back Mountains."

"Orc-back?" Roan asked with a shiver, remembering the first time he'd died.

She cast a quick eye at him. "Don't tell me a big time FBI agent is afraid of a few orcs?"

"I was just trying to buy us time and I did, so let's drop it, okay? I don't want to get a reputation." But it was too late for that. They pushed into Thornwall just before sunset. Just as Korrin had said, it sat right up against the towering walls of the Orc-back Mountains. It was a small town, surrounded by two moats and two walls and, like Morin, the roads were made of a combination of hard-packed dirt with a layer of trod-down manure covering them.

For the most part, the people were peasants and merchants, wearing local homespun clothes. The women wore conservatively cut dresses and seemed to like the many variations of purple, from lavender, to nearly pink to royal purple. The men wore sturdy work outfits almost exclusively in brown or black.

Of course, there were adventurers among them, coming and going, buying and selling goods. These all seemed more energetic and full of life compared to the townies. Their armor ran the gamut from dull padded to richly detailed platemail.

As the light began to fade, Korrin went about trying to recruit more guards for the next part of her trip, while Roan, Jarrod and Marshall went in search of Amanda. With the *Find party member* game mechanic, they tracked her to one of the quieter taverns in town.

She was sitting by herself, making faces every time she took a sip of the "house" wine which she said tasted like vinegar. "Meet the new me. I am now Lady Amanda of Water Fell."

"New?" Roan asked. "You had to make a new character? She doesn't get to reincarnate?"

Jarrod laughed. "That's how the corporate owners make their money. It's fifty bucks to start a new character and then you have to 'buy' gold so you aren't like those guys we fought with their stupid padded armor. It's a scam, alright."

"I thought you loved it," Amanda asked, quietly. She wasn't herself. Although she clearly didn't like the sour wine, she kept sipping at it.

"I do. It's just a rich man's world even on this side. But, you know what?" he asked, grinning. "There's nothing to stop us from getting rich, too. Korrin is doing it wrong. Five hundred a week for hauling cinnamon around? No, the big money is in adventuring. I heard about a dragon hoard, once, worth two million in gold and gems and magic. Think about…"

Just then a very buxom barmaid came over and stopped Jarrod's mouth cold. She had on a flaring blue skirt and a simple button up white shirt that she had failed to button all the way up. She was practically falling out of her top and although Jarrod was dumbstruck, Roan couldn't help thinking that if the woman was real then her breasts were fake, but if her breasts were real then *she* was fake.

"Would you boys like a drink?" she purred.

"A bottle of your best white wine," Jarrod told her.

She arched an eyebrow. "Ooh, a big spender, my favorite sort of customer. What's your name, cutie?"

"They call me Jarrod, the Dark Adder. I've just come from slaying foes by the score and I am thirsty, so be quick." He gave her a slap on the bottom and, to Roan's complete shock, she didn't turn around and smack his face. In fact, she giggled and hurried off.

Roan was still staring after her when, Amanda said, "Your eyes are going to pop out of your head, Roan."

With a guilty flush creeping up into his cheeks, he turned back. "I'm sorry but I couldn't tell if she was real. You know, a real person on the other side. I find it hard to believe that someone would come here to sling drinks and get hit on by sweaty adventurers, but at the same time, she's so much more vibrant than other, uh, non-people."

"Oh, she's not from the other side," Jarrod said, "but you would never be able to tell the diff once you get her in bed."

"Or she could be a dude from the other side," Marshall said. "He could be here playing up a fantasy."

Jarrod made a face, similar to the one that Amanda made every time she took a drink of wine. "Why would you say that? Are you trying to ruin Daggerland for me or…"

The door to the tavern opened and all conversation ceased. A man in black entered. He wore platemail of such deep ebony that it seemed to suck in the light around him. Across his shoulders, he had on a cloak with the cowl thrown over his head, hiding his face, increasing the aura of danger that emanated from him.

Slowly, confidently, he came towards the table and as he reached up to pull back his hood, he drawled, "Why if it isn't the FBI." When the light struck his greasy features, Roan saw that it was Tim Cole, the man who had worked for Greg Nelson. "Hey, Law-dog. It looks like you're out of your jurisdiction."

"What do you want, Cole?" Roan asked. "You couldn't be here by happenstance. You got a new boss?"

"What I have is a strong desire to slit your throat." His hand, covered in the same dark steel, went to his hip, where he carried a sword, the pommel and hilts of which were also black. "But first, why don't you tell me what you are doing in my world?"

Roan wasn't about to divulge the nature of his investigation to the likes of Tim Cole. And he wasn't afraid of him, either. "We were intrigued by the game and decided to check it out. Everyone says it's fun."

"Intrigued? What a big word."

"Nine letters isn't especially big," Roan answered. "Listen, Cole, maybe you should move on and let us eat our dinner in peace. We wouldn't want anyone to think you were *interfering*."

The threat was obvious and yet, Cole only laughed. "You don't want me interfering with an investigation? Is that what you mean? You want to keep it a secret, is that it? It's a little late for that, don't you think? You spend half the day quizzing people about the King of Ellisbar and then you go and announce to the whole world that you are Daniel Roan Special Agent FBI! Ha! And you worry about me blowing your cover?"

"I'm warning you, Cole, turn around and…wait. How did you know about Ellisbar?"

In answer, Cole reached into his cloak and pulled out one of the smaller bags of cinnamon that Korrin had been shipping to Riverport. There was blood on the bag. "You're not the only one who can conduct an investigation, moron. And you're not the only one who can issue a warning. Stay out of Daggerland. The FBI is not welcome here."

Roan tore his eyes from the bloodstained bag and glared up at Cole. "I'll go where I want and there's nothing you can do to stop me."

"Is that right?" Cole asked drawing the black sword.

"Son of a bitch!" Roan roared, sitting up in his cot, his hands clutching at his throat. A second earlier, Cole had taken his head clean off his shoulders and the pain and horror was still with him.

Jarrod woke up next, his orange lips, still with their film of Dorito dust, curled in pain. Then came Marshall, who moaned, "Aw, crap. He killed me." Last was Amanda. She lay in her cot, blinking back tears.

"I'm sorry about that," Roan said. "Maybe I shouldn't have lost my temper. But who knew that he would go to such extremes?"

"Everyone," Jarrod answered. "Everyone knew it. Cole is a bad guy, okay? That's what they do. They kill people for fun."

Amanda shook her head. "It wasn't for fun. You heard the way he spoke. It wasn't natural. He was 'conducting' an investigation? And he was 'issuing' a warning to say out of Daggerland." She sat up, looking down at the neural coupler in her hand. Roan thought she would throw the thing across the room, but she only placed it neatly on her pillow. "Someone doesn't want the FBI there and I think we can safely assume that it's Arching."

"Yes," Roan agreed. He stood and looked around. "What time is it? Where's my watch?"

Joanna Niederer answered from her spot near the stairs. "It's just after nine in the morning, dear. And I took the liberty of removing any watches and jewelry. I read that it wasn't good to wear such things while in the game. It really is fascinating technology. Do you know that NASA is looking into it? They want to adapt it so that the astronauts can hibernate while traveling between the stars."

"I have no doubt it'll work," Jarrod said. "The Infinite Reality guys conducted an experiment and they found that you can be on the other side for eight days before there is any muscular breakdown. The mind is a powerful thing, you know. If you're running around battling monsters on the other side, it kind of thinks you're doing it here."

Roan couldn't have cared less about space travel just then. He had screwed up badly. If he hadn't opened his mouth, they wouldn't have died and they would still be on Arching's trail. He was in the middle of a solid brood when the basement door opened, but no one came down.

Amanda glanced over at Roan, who slid his hand beneath the cot's slim mattress, grabbing his pistol. He had taken the grip in hand when there came a thumping noise—it was a cane.

"I hope you don't expect me to navigate these stairs," Fulbright said. "We'll talk in Caron's office."

"Oh boy," Jarrod whispered. "They're going to pull us off the case. I know it. I can feel the doom in my bones. What do you think, Marsh? Are we screwed?" Marshall only shrugged and heaved himself up.

Roan led the way to Caron's office. Fulbright sat on a couch that could sit three, however, he was a wide man and with his legs splayed the way they were, it didn't leave much room for anyone else. Mike Caron sat behind his desk, looking at Roan as if he were a bug.

"Word is that there's an FBI team in Daggerland," he said, softly. Roan kept silent, knowing that Caron would just lay into him even harder if he tried to defend himself. His boss didn't want excuses; he hated them. "Have you forgotten what being undercover is all about? Do you need to go back to Quantico to learn that the first rule is not to break cover?"

"Now, now," Fulbright said. "The game is not easy, especially at first level and especially on extreme mode. I applaud you for that, by the way."

Caron glared at the financier. "Don't…just don't. These are my agents and I'll handle them. Roan! I don't care if this is a game or not. You put people's lives in danger. Their real lives."

"I understand. It won't happen again."

"Damn right it won't," he said, slamming his hand down on his desk. "I shouldn't even send you back. You've been *made*."

Fulbright tapped his cane a number of times. "Oh, let's not be hasty. They aren't as made as you seem to think. They can change their appearances with ease. In fact, I think they should go in this next time as elves. How does that sound?" He was beaming at Amanda as if he were conferring some sort of boon.

Her eyes flicked to Roan's and he read the hesitancy in them. "Really, how does it sound?" Roan asked her, honestly. "Do you even want to go back?"

"I think I have to, for the sake of the team and the mission, but I don't want to go back as a wizard. I liked the magic at first but it's not strong enough or maybe I'm not strong enough. I can't face someone with a sword when all I have on is a robe. The fact that you can't wear armor is ridiculous. You-you just die so easily and it's sort of awful."

"Would you go back as a cleric?" Roan asked. "If you went as a cleric, you'd be able to wear armor and you would have healing spells. If you ever got hurt, you'd be able to fix yourself in a snap." Jarrod opened his mouth to say something but Roan shot him a look. The group's cleric was supposed to use her powers to heal everyone, not just herself.

She nodded without any sign of eagerness. "Then it's settled," Fulbright said, thumping the cane exuberantly. "Our Amanda will be the cleric. Roan will take over as the spell caster. I would suggest the sorcerer class. And Marshall shall be our fighter. Maybe a paladin to add a touch more healing to the group."

Jarrod raised his hand. "I'm going too, right."

"Of course," Fulbright said, ignoring Caron, who was turning red. "There is a spawn point in the Ash Forest and I know the head of the council there. He owes me a gob of money. He'll outfit you properly this time. Just remind him…"

"Hold on!" Caron snapped. "You're moving a little too quickly. I need to know exactly what Cole said to you on the other side."

Roan explained, word for word, while Caron drummed his fingers. When he was done, Caron asked, "And is this Ash Forest place near Ellisbar?"

Fulbright held two pudgy fingers an inch apart. "Twenty miles. Not even a day's ride. I thought it was odd as well that Cole would mention Ellisbar. The king there is a low twenty-level fighter. Seems like a nice of guy, but I suppose it's the sort of disguise that Arching would approve of."

"Then we're going back in?" Jarrod asked, grinning his orange grin. He still had Dorito crumbs on his lips.

"Not just yet," Roan said. "Two things. I need Cole picked up ASAP and I need to know what's going on with the investigation on this side?"

Both Caron and Fulbright sat back as if their lack of progress was a weight that was difficult to hold up. "For the most part, dead ends," Caron admitted. "There's no sign of Arching anywhere, and we've managed to discover some very strange happenings around Infinite Reality." He lifted his chin to Fulbright who looked pained.

"We had three service centers in Bangladesh. *Had* being the key word. They were closed down months ago. But here's the strange part: the service number is still receiving calls."

"How?" Roan asked, though he was afraid he knew.

Fulbright shook his head. "Either Arching set them up in another country where his investors can't reach him or…or he's set them up on the other side."

2—The Ash Forest

This was Roan's third time creating a character and he hoped that it would fly along a little quicker than the previous two times. It did not.

-What is the character's name? Roan.

-What sex do you wish to be? Male.

-What race do you wish to be? High Elf. (*STR-1, CON-1, DEX+1, INT+1*)

-What age do you wish to be? 100-Elves aged far slower than humans.

-Do you want to add character traits: No.

-Do you want to change appearance: No.

-What class of character do you wish to be? This took the longest to decide. There were many variations of spell casters with perplexing differences: Warlocks received their powers from some otherworld entity, the Magi got theirs from the earth. Necromancers were strong in death spells. Sorcerers were limited in the number of spells they could learn but had more freedom to use them.

Wizards seemed dull in comparison to all of them. They were all-purpose spell casters but powerful at higher levels. Although he didn't think he would get that far, Roan decided: "I'll be a Wizard."

-Special Abilities: Spell Casting.

-What alignment do you wish to be: Chaotic Good.

-Do you wish to add background information: No.

-Purchase extra starting gold: No.

-Are you playing with a party: Yes; Mystic Gorilla.

-Difficulty Level: Roan's stomach went through a slow roll at the question and he wondered briefly if he could throw up in this strange in-between world. When he said, "Extreme," it came out of his lips as a whisper.

-Accept: He paused again and looked at, not a character, but himself:

Character Name: Roan
Class & Level: Wizard - Level 1
Race: High Elf
Alignment: Chaotic Good

Experience Points: **0**   XP To Next Level: **300**

Strength – Dexterity – Constitution
S: **15(+2)**   D: **16(+3)**   C: **16(+3)**

Intelligence – Wisdom – Charisma
I: **17(+3)**   W: **16(+3)**   C: **16(+3)**

Armor: 10(13)   Hit Points: 9
Initiative: +3   Speed: 13
SAVING THROWS: Will: 5   Fortitude: 3   Reflex: 3

GOLD: 10

-EQUIPMENT-

Weapons
None

Armor
None

Magic	Misc
None	**None**

† Spells Known †

Cantrips:
Tier 1 Spells:
Tier 2 Spells:
Tier 3 Spells:

† Spells Prepared †

Cantrips:
Tier 1 Spells:
Tier 2 Spells:
Tier 3 Spells:

Attacks

Name	ATK Bonus	Damage
Weaponless/Fist	0	1-2

Abilities
Spell Casting

Skills
Listen: +6, Spot: +6, Knowledge: +6, Search: +6, Spell Craft: +6

The disembodied voice of the woman guiding him through the tutorial asked a second time: "Do you accept, Roan?"

"Yes."

When he went through the door, Roan felt a moment of disconnect and for once the game did not feel exactly real. Everything was a bit off. Then he realized that the game hadn't changed, he had.

He was seeing the world not through the eyes of a human, but through the eyes of an elf. Everything was sharper, the colors brighter, the smells more engaging, the little things that he normally took for granted were more present in his mind. He could feel his own pulse, he could feel the way the cloth of his shirt rubbed against his collarbone.

Roan could sense himself. He was slightly smaller and weaker than he had been, and yet, he felt he could leap higher and run faster.

And then there was his magic—

Class Ability Unlocked: Spell casting. At first level choose 3(+2) cantrips and 6(+1) spells from the Tier 1 list.

"Ugh, more choices," he whispered. In front of his vision in glowing green script were dozens of spells. He could mentally "click" on each and a description would open in a separate information box.

The cantrips were all minor league spells; simple things like the *Fire Bolts* that Amanda had used on one of the bandits, or minor illusions that lasted less than a minute. He chose: *Simple Illusion, Fire Bolt, Ray of Ice, Electric Hand,* and *Acid Spray.* Other than the illusion spell, they were all attack spells.

The first level spells were much harder to choose from. He could charm people, or fall from great heights without getting hurt. He could call a Familiar, like a witch's cat or an owl to be his companion. He could shield himself in magical armor or send stronger bolts of energy from his fingers. And there were a lot more to choose from.

But at first level, he could only hold two of the spells in his head at a time. In order to change them out, he would have to spend time pouring over his spell book, memorizing the minute details involved with each spell, which was something that couldn't be done in the heat of battle.

With the recent fight against the bandits still fresh in his mind, he chose a sleeping spell which could affect multiple people, a flame blast spell for the same reason, a spell to summon lightning, and a thunder spell that could not only damage opponents but also throw them back.

He figured that was enough in the way of offensive spells and added a few situational spells, as he thought of them. The first was *Summon Familiar*. The idea of having a pet that would act as scout, spy, servant, and friend was too good to pass up. To that he added a charming spell and lastly, he chose a stronger illusion spell than the cantrip.

Roan was a little surprised that he liked his spell choices as much as he did. Hadn't Amanda been given the same choices?

"Hey, Roan?" Jarrod asked. "What the hell? Make a choice for goodness sakes. The locals are staring."

"Huh?" He looked past the words floating in the air and saw a strange sight: Jarrod as an elf. He was still a 'build' so he wasn't a geeky elf, but he didn't look as though he had added any of his extra points to charisma this time. Marshall was equally odd looking. He usually had such a relaxed way about him that the slow look in his eyes clashed with his sharp elfin features.

Amanda with her long, golden blonde hair and smooth skin was a natural elf. She was willowy and beautiful, with huge, intelligent blue eyes that lacked whites completely. They stared at each other until she broke into a smile. "You look, I don't know, different," she said.

"Yeah," Jarrod said. "For the first time since I've met you, you don't look like you're ready to tear someone's arm off and shove it down their throat."

That struck Roan as harsh but as Marshall was nodding along, Roan had to wonder if he really looked like that. He certainly felt like that half the time. He had been neck-deep battling evil in the real world for the last twelve years. It seemed to have left its mark on his face.

"Then I'm glad for the change," he said. "Speaking of change, there were some pretty good spells, Amanda. Maybe you missed them before. Did you see the one about the familiar?"

"Yes, I did, but I didn't know if we were going to have time for it." Her elfin features drew down, including the points of her ears. "I was freaked about coming to Daggerland. I-I didn't know what to expect and it's a long spell."

This is my fault, Roan thought. "I rushed us out too quickly. I didn't give you a chance. But, but, if you want, we can clock out and change back."

She shook her head. "No, thank you. I like this better. The cleric spells are more my style, healing and protection are better than fire and lightning. And I'll be happy once I get some armor. I feel naked with only a bit of silk between me and a sword."

"Okay good," Roan said. He then glanced over at Jarrod. "I'll be a rogue if you want to switch."

"Naw, naw. I'm with her. After getting hacked apart by that Cole guy, I get the feeling we have a target painted on us. I'd rather be a fighter, but, hey I'm a team player. I'll stay as a rogue. So, who are we supposed to meet? Some council guy?"

They hadn't been given a name, just a title. "He'll probably find us." After everything they had been through, Roan wasn't eager to start his time as an elf snooping around asking questions. "I'd rather slow things down just a little this time. Let's explore this…this town, I guess you'd call it."

The elves didn't live like humans, exactly. They had roads, but they were neither cobblestone nor dirt, they were covered in soft grass. It was like walking on a putting green. And their homes and businesses were not ordered in any obvious way. Instead of lining the streets on either side, they were found down little paths that branched from the main road. Frequently the paths were hidden from sight by the many trees that had apparently sprouted at random.

In front of them was a towering sequoia that split the road in two. Further on, they found another that had such a massive girth that the road went through the trunk of the tree. As they were walking through it, they saw that a door had been set right into the core of the tree and looked to be made from the wood itself.

It was open and from it they could hear the chatter of a hundred voices. The door led to a spiraling stair that had been carved with loving hands. The fine detailing—leaves and vines and flowers—etched into the bannister made it a piece of art that would have been worth thousands of dollars on the other side, but here it was just a bannister.

The walls and steps were soft and glossy as if the tree had never known a splinter in its long life.

After a dozen steps, the stairway opened on their left into a room that, had it not been for the same glossy walls, Roan would never have believed was part of the tree. The room was carpeted in a plush burgundy that elegantly set off the richness of the polished cherry furniture.

It seemed at first to be a sitting room. There were chairs and small tables set here and there, some even in carved alcoves. It wasn't a crowded place. Only six others were there. Four elven men in the garb of adventures sat around one small table, while at a window that overlooked the town sat two women in long robes. All six gave Roan and his team a cursory glance before nodding in their direction.

"We should bow to them," Marshall whispered. "It's how the elves greet each other."

Roan bowed clumsily, partially from lack of practice and partially because he was an American and found bowing to be a mark of a servant and not of a free man. It didn't seem to matter, the bows were perfunctory and the four in their noob elf clothes were quickly forgotten.

Movement on the stairs above him had Roan stepping into the room to let a woman in a dress of brightest yellow and whitest white sweep down. She had dark hair that fell in curls around her shoulders. "My lords, my lady," she said, bowing with the upper part of her body. "You appear new to the forest. Are you in need of guidance? A place to rest?"

"We are just exploring, my lady," Roan answered. "Hopefully we're not trespassing in any way."

She laughed, high and sweet. "Of course not. My home is your home. My name is Reasa-mila. Call for me if you need anything at all."

With that she breezed past them to chat with the men at the table. "Well, that was nice of her," Roan remarked.

Marshall grunted out a laugh. "She's an NPC and this is the elven equivalent of an inn. I played an elf once for a few weeks. It's not the easiest thing in the world, let me tell you. For one, it's very expensive. They guilt the crap out of you if you're not generous enough."

"Generous?" Jarrod asked. "Are they looking for charity or something?"

"No, it's just how they conduct business. Instead of stating a price upfront, they offer everything as a gift, only it's expected that you offer a gift in return. Sometimes if you 'over pay' they'll say something like 'you are being too generous' or that sort of thing."

Once more, the American in Roan reared up. There was a reason why capitalism was the best monetary system in a corrupt world. It was based on freedom and a clearly stated pact between individuals. This elven system, although pleasant sounding, had waste built into its very concept.

And yet, Roan was now an elf. He took a deep breath and said, "While in Rome, do as the Romans do. Let's go see what other sorts of oddities there are."

"And maybe we should summon your familiar while we have time," Amanda suggested. "If we'd had a crow scouting for us, that fight with the bandits might have been avoidable. We would have been in Riverport by now and one step closer to our goal."

They decided to make that their first priority. Reasa-mila gave them directions to a man who "dabbled in that sort of thing." His name was Amiriah and he wasn't far. Roan was expecting to find a shop where he could browse over goods, instead he was surprised to find that Reasa-mila had directed them to Amiriah's home.

For some reason Roan was also surprised to find the elf's home to be as elegant as everything else in the Ash Forest. It was small, no more than a cottage, and set in a glade where the sun was able to slip between the boughs of the trees and light it in just such a way as to add a fairy glow around the eaves.

Amiriah, an old elf with white flowing hair that matched perfectly with sky-blue robes, offered them tea and cookies and chatted with them about dull pleasantries until Roan was about to pull his hair out—but he didn't want to be impolite, however that was defined in the elfin world.

Jarrod was finally blunt enough to spit out, "We need some spell stuff."

"Of course," the old elf said. The materials for Roan's *Summoning Familiar* spell: exotic herbs and plants, a brass brazier, and a filament of pure silver, cost them half the gold they had between them, though if that was a fair price none of them knew.

Their "gift" seemed to please Amiriah, who decided to help Roan with the summoning rites. The old elf guided Roan into his garden where they sat among the clover. As talkative as Amiriah was inside, the elf was nearly silent once they stepped from the threshold of his home.

"A summoning such as this is different from many spells," he said quietly. "It is a bonding ritual. The brazier, first if you please. Place it here among the clover and light it."

Roan set it down between them and lit the charcoal. It flared for a brief second before settling in to smolder. "The *Acrhera*, next," Amiriah said, indicating the golden flower. Roan knew this, already. He knew all the ingredients and rituals involved with the spells he had chosen. The game had instilled them into his mind, just as it had instilled his ability to wield a sword when he was a fighter.

So why was Amiriah helping him? A real player would have known that it wasn't needed and would not have bothered. Roan assumed that he was an NPC and simply programmed in this fashion, but then Amiriah said this, "The Jasseve, next. There are many eyes upon you, my lord Roan."

Roan jerked just as he was about to put the Jasseve in the brazier, spilling some into the clover. "What's that?"

"There are eyes searching for you. I can feel them. Some were aware when you crossed over. Now, pick up the Jasseve."

He picked the Jasseve out of the clover and threw the stems of the plant one by one into the brazier, all the while staring at Amiriah. The elf stared back, placidly, not offering any more information. They went through most of the incantation before Roan asked, "Who was aware?"

Amiriah stared straight ahead until Roan asked a second question, "Who are you?"

"I am Amiriah the Warlock of Ash Forest, but I've already told you that. We were introduced earlier. I see that your ritual is nearly complete. You must wrap the silver filament around the token of your familiar."

"Who are you on the other side?" Roan demanded.

The elf looked confused. "I am the same inside and out. Please, the token. You have chosen the feather of the raven. A fine choice."

Roan had the filament in one hand and the blue-black feather of the raven in the other, but they sat forgotten in his hands. "Who do you work for? Arching?"

"I don't know who Arching is," Amiriah replied. "I work for the good of my people and for the betterment of the world as a whole."

Accidentally, Roan crushed the feather in his right hand. "What about Fulbright?" Amiriah's confused expression only infuriated Roan even more than he had been.

"Be careful, my lord, Roan. Anger in spell casting creates not just mistakes, but volatility as well. Your feather."

"What about my…oh, crap!" The feather was crushed and the green flame in the brazier had reached its peak. He only had seconds to entwine the filament around the feather, lift it to the sky and say: "Eram, de-el, fereye. I open the gate and summon thee."

When the words were out of his mouth, he was supposed to place the filament and the feather in the fire, only the fire was dying and when he hurried the last action, the feather fell out of the filament and spun in a lazy circle until it landed in the clover.

"Crap," Roan muttered, again, thinking that he had just wasted twenty gold pieces, only just then there was a high hissing sound, like air escaping from a balloon. A second later, the brazier exploded, sending out glowing hunks of ash. Both Roan and Amiriah fell back, swatting themselves where the ash burned. There was a white smoke in the air and when he breathed it in, the smoke filled his chest with a heat that seemed to creep up his throat. Only gradually did it taper away.

After some time, when Roan could breathe normally again, he said. "Well, that sucked."

"You are strange to me, my lord Roan," Amiriah said, standing and smoothing down his sky-blue robes; they were pocked with dozens of burn marks. "Your words and your mind are unlike anything I have yet experienced. May I suggest that in the future you more fully embrace the concept of gratitude. I wish you and your familiar the best."

Roan didn't know what to say to this, other than a feeble: "I'm sorry." When the elf left, Roan stood and glanced down at the brazier. It was still smoldering, little wisps of smoke lifting from it. "I don't want to burn down his backyard. He'll blame me for that as well."

As he set the brazier up right, he thought about what Amiriah had told him about being watched. "Was that a real warning? Or was it part of some in-game quest?" The old elf was almost certainly an NPC. Maybe he had been programmed to be purposefully cryptic as part of a quest?

"Or maybe it was a glitch."

If Arching had been watching him, what was stopping him from showing up and killing him right that second? And Amiriah had said there were *many* eyes on him. "Arching might know we're here, Fulbright definitely does, but he's on the other side. Who else? Cole? The elf friend of Fulbright's?" That didn't sound like "many" in Roan's book.

Roan turned to go back to the others when he jumped slightly. Something sat in the air, two feet from his head. It was as if the air was *curled* in on itself. It shifted the light from the sun slightly. Slowly, Roan put out a hand to touch the little spot and discovered that it was cool on his flesh.

"Huh, it's a glitch," he said. Here was a little programming error. "So, the game isn't perfect, after all." Strangely, this had a comforting effect on him. If the game wasn't perfect, then maybe Arching wasn't perfect, either. He started walking toward the home and saw the glitch following him. "Maybe that explains things a little."

Entering the home of Amiriah, he bowed to the elf, who was back on the soft couch, sipping from a tea cup. Amanda, Marshall, and Jarrod all looked at him expectedly.

"So, where is it?" Jarrod asked. "Are you letting it stretch its wings, or what?"

Before he could explain the nature of his latest screw up, Amanda asked. "What did you name it?"

"Glitch," Roan answered with a snort, deciding to blame the game instead of himself. "Right in the middle of the casting Lord Amiriah, here says that I'm being watched." At this the old elf raised an eyebrow and Roan amended his statement. "He told me that there are eyes searching for me and that he could feel them. He also said that some were aware when we crossed over. My guess is that there's a glitch in the game. Look."

He pointed at the strange twerk that still hung in the air. Jarrod came closer, his lips pulled down as he touched it. Marshall was next, saying, "That's pretty funky."

"I beg your pardon," Amiriah said, "but that is not 'funky' if I understand the word correctly. That is an air elemental."

"An air elemental?" Roan asked. "Do you mean this thing is alive?" He put out his hand and the little glitch floated to it and settled on his palm.

Amiriah bowed his head. "Life and death are not always applicable to all beings. This being is made of air and thus can't be destroyed in the same manner as flesh and blood beings can be. Still, as a summoned creature, it can be sent back to its home plane with certain spells."

So, it wasn't a glitch, Roan realized. And that meant... "What you told me about the eyes searching for me is true, isn't it?" Amiriah nodded. "And do you know who it is searching for me?"

Amiriah cast his eyes down. "No, I do not. I only know that they are powerful. The question that I have, is why would they be searching for you? What about you draws them? Perhaps the answer to your question can be discovered in the answer to mine."

"It's Arching," Marshall said. "It has to be. He's the most powerful, right? He probably has a bunch of wizards hunting you. Hell, hunting *us,* I should say."

"Yeah, case closed," Jarrod agreed. "And if they are looking for us maybe we should get our gear and get our asses out of town. No offense, your lordship." Amiriah had raised an eyebrow at his uncouth tongue.

This was agreed upon and, after getting directions from the warlock, they hurried through the elf town to another of the tremendous trees, this one had untold numbers of branches that sprouted golden leaves and instead of its trunk being burrowed into, there were steps cut into its outer bark somewhat like a spiraling staircase.

After they were four or five stories up into the tree, the lattice of branches gave way to an open area, an atrium of sorts many hundreds of feet high. The branch of the tree that they were on reached out to others of its kind and formed interlocking pathways. There was an entire second village high above the first.

The houses and buildings here were not built into the trees, but rather set upon their branches or constructed around the trunks themselves. It was an amazing sight and Roan whispered, "Wow." A second later came an echo: *Wow*. He jumped and reached to his hip for either his gun or his sword, only he had neither.

"Did you hear that?" he asked Amanda, who was closest to him.

"Hear what?"

"I think my familiar said something. I think it repeated what I just said, but I couldn't tell if it was in my head or what."

"Maybe you should talk to it," Amanda suggested. "You'd talk to a pet, wouldn't you? And maybe you should name it. I feel weird calling it an it. Oh, wait. Maybe it already has a name. Ask it."

It seemed like a good idea and yet, as it was just a knuckle of air, Roan felt very strange asking, "What's your name?" It seemed as though he were talking to himself.

Glitch. The word popped into Roan's head, sounding like an airy whisper.

"No, what's your real…" He paused as he spied more words at the bottom of his vision:

Familiar: Glitch
Type: Air Elemental
Size: Tiny
Hit Points: 4
Armor Class: 28
Attack: N/A
Damage: N/A
Special Attacks: *Haze*
Special Defense: Impervious to standard weapons
Special Abilities: Gaseous Form, Greater Invisibility
Alignment: Neutral
XP Rating: 1
Abilities:
Str-1, Int-8, Wis-4, Dex-20, Con-6, Chr-10
Skills: Search +8, Spot +3, Move Silently +25
Feats:N/A
Spell-like Abilities: *Haze*: Familiar may temporarily disrupt the vision of a single opponent. Attacks are made at -4.

After reading through all of this, Roan was fairly impressed, except on one point: "Your name is really Glitch?"
Glitch.

"Oh boy," Roan whispered, realizing that he had accidentally given him a very poor name. "I think his name is now Glitch. In the backyard, I said, 'That's a Glitch,' and he must have thought it was his name."

Jarrod tried to touch it again, saying, "It's not a bad name. It looks like a glitch to me. What do you think, Marshall?"

Marshall shrugged though it was more of a sullen move as compared to his usual lazy response. "I don't like it. I mean he's cool and I bet he'll come in handy, but it doesn't feel right. You screw up the spell but still get a better than average familiar? That's not right."

"In what way?" Jarrod demanded. "You know the game has random factors built into it. It's like playing the slots at Vegas, someone's got to win the jackpot eventually. You know what I think, Marsh? I think you're jealous."

"I'm not. I'm just nervous. By itself it could be just a glitch or random factors aligning, but if you take it into account with everything else, it's more proof that someone's been tampering with the game. It sorta makes me feel, I don't know, a little vulnerable."

Roan wasn't nearly as worried. "We might not be safe in the game, but we're safe in real life, and that's what counts. If Arching wants to come for us here, that's fine by me. He'll give away more and more information every time he does. Like with Cole. He went from being a witness to a wanted man because of what he did here. And, if you think about it, the more we keep Arching's attention on us, the easier it'll be for Caron to snatch him up on the other side and end this."

This seemed to put a little more steel in Marshall's spine and with his head held a little higher, he followed Roan along the wide path through the trees. They all seemed in good spirits until they came to the council chambers, the doors of which were twenty feet high and intricately carved with birds and butterflies. The doors were also locked.

Roan balled a fist and thumped them. They felt as solid as rock and, as he was massaging his hand, Glitch sent a vision into his mind: someone was coming up behind them. Roan spun around ready to fight, bare-handed if needed. It was only an elf clad in platemail, a sheathed sword at his side and a cloak of canary yellow across his shoulders which perfectly matched the color of his eyes. "My lord, Roan?" he asked.

"Yes?" Roan answered, cautiously, his mind somewhat tilted by the fact that Glitch had been able to enter it the way it had. Before, when Glitch had said its name, Roan actually thought that he had heard the word just like he could hear anything else. But he was wrong. The word had originated inside of him.

"You are looking for Leomagnus, the Golden? I've been sent to give his apologies. Matters elsewhere have detained him. He'll be back in the morning. In the meantime, I have set you up with fine rooms. If you'll follow me."

The elf led them up to an even higher pathway where the drop was a hundred feet at least. Despite their elven dexterity, the group moved in towards each other, none wishing to get too close to the rounded edges of the branches.

Their rooms were simple and at the same time beautiful and sumptuous. There was little in the way of furniture in each: a sitting chair set by a wide window, a bureau of polished wood and a bed with pure white sheets and a mattress that was as soft as down.

"Man, this is the life," Jarrod said, reclining on his bed. He hadn't bothered to take off his shoes and there were smudges of dirt on the sheet. It annoyed the elf in Roan.

"Clock out for an hour," he told Jarrod. "Get some exercise and some real food in your belly. If you see Caron on the other side give him an update and if Mrs. Niederer is still there, ask her *politely* if she wouldn't mind leaving me a roast beef on rye."

Jarrod mumbled, "I'm polite," before clocking back into the real world. He was gone for his hour and then Marshall went next. By then evening had come to the Ash Forest. Roan was lying on his bed as darkness began to descend. Above him, Glitch was playing with a spider that had come sliding down on a silken thread.

It seemed to Roan that Glitch was just as new to this world as he was. He could feel a curiosity brewing in the knuckle of air as it explored the room and the spider. The poor arachnid was being buffeted by little puffs of air, which was all that Glitch could manage just then.

He was about to get up and save the spider from what had to be a dizzying torture when Amanda burst into his room. "You have to see this!" She reached down, took him by the hand and yanked him outside to the path. Their view of the arboreal atrium was fantastic, but it was nothing compared to what was happening above them.

The great leafy canopy had seemed thick and green as they had come up the spiraling stairs. Now, white flowers of immense size were opening, thrusting back the heavy leaves. Within the flowers were what appeared to be golden orbs. Some began to fall, though they did so very slowly, dropping languidly like soap bubbles.

Gently, they settled about the vast open area, lighting the interior of the trees with a soft, golden radiance.

"Wow," Roan said. In his head, Glitch echoed, *Wow*.

Amanda watched the falling globes, standing so close to Roan that they were touching. In fact, they were still holding hands, something Roan was just beginning to realize.

She looked up at him, the lights reflected in her giant, blue eyes. "I have to say this makes everything else worth it."

The view beyond her was stunning and yet, he couldn't seem to drag his eyes from hers. Slowly, he leaned in until the tips of their noses touched. Her nose was small, pert, soft as a rose petal and he could only wonder what her lips would be like.

Behind, Glitch spoke suddenly into his head.

He jumped away from her just as Marshall stepped from his room. "That's pretty cool," he said, looking down at the lights and the wonderful world that the elves had created. He didn't see the flush in Roan's cheeks or Amanda's chest heaving.

"I-I should clock out," Roan said, quickly. "I'll be back." With a thought, the heart-breakingly beautiful image in front of him disappeared, only to be replaced by the basement ceiling of the FBI field office.

"What am I doing?" he whispered, sitting up and looking at Amanda in human form. She was just as pretty, lying there in her cot, her features unmarred by fear or stress.

He reached a hand out to touch hers just as Mrs. Niederer said, "I have that roast beef on rye you asked for."

Once more, Roan jerked in surprise, snatching his hand away as if he had touched a lit stove. "Oh, thanks," he said, hoping he didn't look as guilty as he felt. He had no right to touch Amanda's hand, or to be as close to her as he had been. And he certainly shouldn't have entertained the idea of kissing her. He was her superior officer. It was wrong.

He stood and accepted the sandwich from Mrs. Niederer. Taking a hearty bite, he headed for the stairs but the woman stopped him. "Do you like it there?"

He had to wait until he swallowed before he could answer. "Yes, I guess I do. I didn't think I would, but it's…I guess interesting is the right word. We saw trolls the other night and just now we're in an elfin village and everything was…" He paused, picturing Amanda painted against the golden light. "Everything was breathtaking."

"Oh, good," Joanna said. "My daughter was kind enough to send me one of those headset things, but I haven't even taken it out of the package yet. I didn't know if it would be right for me. I'm not much of a game person."

"I say give it a try. It's not all about killing, you'll see. Some adventures are different. Some are personal."

2—The Ash Forest

"Glitch missed you," Amanda said. She was sitting on his bed, while Glitch had been on his pillow. The second Roan materialized, the air elemental sped at him, blowing back his dark hair. Strangely, it was only then that he realized his hair was as long as Amanda's.

He took a deep breath and blew on the familiar. Glitch was as light as air and flew across the room. It came zipping back for more, finding the game fun.

Fun, it said into his mind.

Roan blew it a second time and then glanced at Amanda who was watching with a smile on her face. In only a blink, he found himself staring at her. "You're going to need to clock out, too," he told her, turning away and going to the window. "You'll be happy to know that Caron got you the elliptical you asked for."

"Is that right?"

"Yeah, it's nice, I guess," he said, talking to her reflection in the glass. He felt it was safer this way. "When you get back, you're going to need to hit the hay. Isn't it weird that you have to sleep here, but not there?"

She went to the door and cast a last look back. Roan knew the look and knew that if he had been allowed to act on his feelings, he could have stopped her from leaving, but he said nothing.

"It is weird," she eventually said. "I guess that's how it is. They're two different worlds with two different rules to live by. Don't you think so, Roan?"

"They're not completely different. There are some things that carry over from one to another." Didn't she see that? There was no way they could have a relationship in one world and not the other.

Perhaps it finally sunk in as she sighed. "Goodnight, Roan." She shut the door and clocked out. Glitch zipped under the door and then came back a moment later.

???

"We'll see her in the morning," he answered, climbing into the bed.

Morning?

"It's when the sun comes back." He pictured a sunrise and Glitch made a noise inside of Roan's head that seemed to be one of understanding. "But now, it's time to sleep."

???

"Rest. It means it's time to rest." He pictured a person sleeping and when that didn't help Glitch understand, Roan pictured a cartoon moon with closed eyes sitting in a bed of clouds. He fell asleep to the image and woke hours later with Glitch in his mind, screaming: *!!!*

"What is it?" he asked, coming instantly awake. Glitch put a picture in his head: the same platemail clad elf from the day before was a second from knocking on Roan's door. When he did, Roan slid softly out of bed. "Come in."

The elf bowed and announced, "Leomagnus the Golden requests your presence as quickly as possible."

Roan glanced at the window. It was still dark. "What time is it?" he asked, brusquely.

"Just after four. I'm sorry for the inconvenience, however there is an emergency. An orc army from the Pits of the Black Hand is fast approaching and there is much to attend to. Can you find your way down to the council hall?"

"Yes, thank you," Roan said, snatching up his shoes and heading for the door at a quick pace. There was only one reason an attack would be happening just then: the searching eyes had found him. "Glitch, wake up Jarrod and Marshall."

As Glitch zipped away, he went to Amanda's door, tapped softly and then stepped in. He could see her eyes gleaming in the dark. "An attack is imminent and Fulbright's friend wants to see us," he told her.

She leapt up and nearly forgot her shoes. He stopped her and they sat side by side on her bed as she slipped them on. "They're attacking, now?" she asked. "You know who's behind it."

"Arching," he said and as he did, Glitch came through the door. The familiar was utterly invisible in the dark and only his growing presence in Roan's mind clued him in. "Like I said before, he's putting his neck out, maybe the elves are strong enough to take his head off. If his character dies in this world, we'll have a lot easier time moving about."

Roan strode out to the branching path and saw that the entire tree-village was awake and moving. Elves, some geared for war, others prepared for travel, were everywhere and when Roan's little team joined them, they stood out because of their simple tunics and because Jarrod kept yawning in a very human-like manner.

Leomagnus the Golden, a tall gold and green-clad elf with yellow eyes, was in the council chamber, having five conversations at once. The room reminded Roan of a cathedral right down to the stained-glass windows. However, there were no pews and instead of an altar, there was a raised dais with five empty thrones.

It was an easy guess that the council members were too busy to sit languidly upon them. Leomagnus spotted Rona's team as soon as they came through the doors and barked in a very un-elf manner, "Get down to the armory. You have been gifted up to a thousand gold pieces. Gear up and be out of the gates by sunrise."

"I don't understand," Roan said, coming forward and offering an abbreviated bow. It was so quick that it could only be taken as rude and Leomagnus's yellow eyes flared in anger, but Roan didn't care. "First off," Roan said to the elf lord, "a thousand gold was not what Fulbright said. He said…"

Leomagnus made a gagging noise as he pulled Roan away from the other elves. He sounded as if he were stifling a long string of expletives. "Look, a thousand is plenty for what you need. See this? See everything going on? That's because of you and my bastard cousin."

"Fulbright's your cousin?" Amanda asked. "You wouldn't think he would hold money over your head."

"Well, you don't know him as well as you think. I declared bankruptcy last year and he seized all of my assets and now he wants my stuff in this world, too! But you know what? If those orcs attack, I'll be broke here as well. Not to mention, all of this will be destroyed. I know it's a game, but I love the beauty here and I love the people."

Roan looked at Amanda and saw her squaring her shoulders and summoning her courage. She nodded to him and Roan told Leomagnus, "We won't leave you. We'll stay to help fight."

It was strange to see an elf lord roll his eyes. "Ugh, no. First off, four level one noobs won't make a nickel's worth of difference and second, I'm hoping that if you leave the orcs will chase after you."

They were being kicked out, so they could be bait? Jarrod and Marshall began cursing loud enough to draw stares from the other elves, while Amanda could only shake her head in disbelief. Roan felt a sharp sense of betrayal but at the same time, he too felt a need to preserve the beauty and innocence of the elf village. "If you're kicking us out, then you should set us up properly," he said. "For your own sake, at least. If you send us out there with crap for armor and we die, I doubt your cousin will see this as exactly helpful on your part."

"Okay, two-thousand, but with everything going on, tell him that we're even. Promise me."

Roan made the promise and in no time, they were being rushed into the catacombs beneath the council chamber. All around them, roots as big around as their bodies twisted like giant snakes sinking into and out of the dark soil. Here and there were not tombs, but "resting" places of elven dead. It seemed they didn't believe in coffins, so the bodies were simply lying out. Roan had never seen so many grinning skeletons in his life.

Glitch was nervous being so close to them and wobbled the air around it as it shook in fear. Thankfully, the group took a separate passage away from the catacombs. It ran straight and true for a hundred yards before coming to an underground storage facility which was bustling with dozens of elves.

There seemed to be a separate room for everything. One for weapons, one for armor, another simply stacked with arrows. The order to it as well as the abundance was a quartermaster's dream. But who the quartermaster was, Roan couldn't tell and it took a few minutes to find who was in charge. It turned out to be a young female elf, who wore a leather apron and had soot on her cheeks.

"We need gear," Roan told her. "Not just armor and weapons, but adventuring gear."

She looked at Roan in disgust. "You are the ones who brought this on us, aren't you?" she demanded.

Roan glared, ready to snap, however Amanda put a calming hand on his arm and spoke to the woman, saying, "Place the blame on those who perpetuate evil, not on us. We are looking to rid this world of a demon of a man. It's a noble pursuit."

"Forgive me," the woman said. "You are correct. Soon, however, it'll be you who are pursued. That is the hope, at least."

Amanda blanched at this truth, while Jarrod and Marshall looked sick in the torch light. Roan was sure he looked the same. Deep down, it felt as though they were only hours away from dying, yet again. It would be his third time in four days and unlike them, his pain and death would be once again extremely real. Roan had to strain to keep the fear of it from registering on his face. To buoy their spirits as well as his own, he said, "They'll get more than they bargained for if they catch us."

A sword lay upon a table in front of them. Roan picked it up, thinking that having a weapon in his hands would make him feel better in some way. At first the blade was clumsy in his hand, but then he saw lettering at the bottom of his vision.

Racial Ability Unlock: Elves are naturally proficient with the longsword, rapier, longbow and short bow.

"Well, that's something," he said. He had been secretly dreading having to walk about with a quarterstaff, which was usually a wizard's best option when it came to weapons. "If you please," he said to the elf woman, "I will need a long sword, a longbow, a spell book..." Roan went on to list everything he thought he would need and as he spoke, the items began to pile up in his inventory list:

    Long sword
    Long bow
    Dagger
    Quiver
    Arrows x 20
    Backpack
    Bedroll

50' rope
Potion of Healing
Flask of Holy Water
Green Cloak
Rations x 3
Tinderbox
Waterskin
Torches x3
Spell Book
Pouches x3

It was a good start. He felt a little better having a sword strapped to his hip and a longbow across his back—and yet he didn't have armor. Armor interfered with a wizard's magic. In spite of his tunic and the emerald green cloak across his wide shoulders, he felt naked.

This confused Glitch, who said, *???*

"Just a weird feeling, don't worry about it. What do you say we look at the spell book?" Although he knew only five cantrips and seven tier one spells, his head felt oddly crammed with information. It was jumbled and broken and somehow, he knew that the only way to make any sense of it was to get it out and on paper.

Grabbing his gear, he searched around in the low-ceilinged armory until he found a forgotten corner. He figured that while the others were being fitted into their armor and picking out their gear, he would begin scribing the spells into the book. Ten minutes earlier, he wouldn't have had a clue how to do it, but the moment he cracked the leather-bound spell book, the knowledge just seemed to appear in his mind as if he had overturned a rock and there it was.

He was also thrilled to see that there were spells written onto the pages of the book. He read the first; it was a cantrip that he already knew: *Simple Illusion.* The writing was amazing. It was a combination of engraving and calligraphy, and whoever had scribed the words had been an artist of the highest caliber.

The appearance of the words was stylish and beautiful, the meaning much less so. There were lists of the odd and exotic material components needed for the spell, as well as the manner in which they had to be harvested and stored for the best effect. There was also a lengthy description of the very precise and intricate hand motions needed to produce the desired spell effects and finally, at the bottom of the page were written the strange, mystical words that not only tied the components of the spell together, but also released its power.

He thought it was fortunate that one of his cantrips was in the book, but then he turned page after page and saw that the book contained all of his cantrips: *Simple Illusion, Fire Bolt, Ray of Ice, Electric Hand, and Acid Spray.* After that were his level one spells: *Summon Familiar, Flame Blast, Lightning Summoning, Thunderous Wave, Illusion(Minor), Charm(Minor), and Instant Slumber.*

It was a game mechanic and an obvious one at that, but he didn't care. He only hoped that when he picked up spells later, they would "magically" appear in his book. If not, he would do the work himself, despite the fact that he had the sloppy penmanship of a third-grader.

"We'll worry about that if we ever get there," Roan mumbled. "We have orcs to worry about, right Glitch?"

!!!

"Don't fret too much. With you scouting for us, we have a shot at making it through." But through to where? And what would be waiting to kill them when they got there? "All in good time," he told himself. "For now, I'll get my spells ready."

At first level, he could only cast a few spells per day: three cantrips and two level one spells.

He started with the cantrip *Fire Bolt* because it did the most damage. He concentrated on absorbing the spell, moving it from the book and into himself. The most interesting aspect of this was the "breathing" in of both the material *and* the words. The *Fire Bolt* spell needed simple ingredients: charcoal, copper dust and what seemed like a string of nonsense words, but when he spoke over the charcoal and copper mixture, a light gas lifted into the air. It snaked up into his nose and down into his chest where he could feel its power simply waiting for him to speak the "trigger" word to release it.

All of this was something he simply "knew" how to do. The game mechanic allowed him to skip twenty years of magical schooling. It was a serious cheat and at the same time, the reality of the spell within him was shocking. It was one thing to pick up a sword as a level one fighter and swing it around with a touch more expertise than he normally would have in the real world, but this was different. He was a wizard—a real wizard, but not the most powerful one.

"Maybe adding the other spells will help," he said.

He could store two more cantrips inside of him and decided to see whether it was possible to absorb the *Fire Bolt* spell a second time and quickly discovered that he could. He chose *Fire Bolt* for the third slot as well and then moved onto the first level slots. Since *Thunderous Wave* worked well against multiple opponents, and he expected to face who knew how many orcs, he filled both of his tier one slots with it.

Roan felt a little stronger, but nothing compared to what Marshall must have been feeling.

The new paladin found Roan and asked, "What do you think?" Marshall turned this way and that, showing off his new armor. Across his shoulders and chest were large plates of shining metal, while along his arms and legs there were narrower plates over a chainmail mesh. To top it off, he had on a gorgeous electric blue cloak.

"I'm jealous," Roan answered with a fake smile—he really was jealous. In comparison, he felt like a pauper.

"With the shield, I have a 19 armor class," Marshall went on. "And let me tell you that is awesome. Paladin's are a little too goody-goody for my tastes, but you have to admit we look damn good." He was right, he had never looked so dashing. "It's the charisma," he admitted. "Paladins need it in order to work their healing."

"Don't rub it in," Amanda said coming from behind one of the huge roots. Her armor was lighter and it had to be since she was so small. She had on a breast plate of gleaming metal that covered her torso. Her arms and legs were covered with thinner strips of the same metal. Finally, she wore knee high boots and a cape that was somewhere between a rose and a soft pink. Somehow, she made the armor feminine, sexy and practical.

Roan tried not to stare. "It-it's alright."

"It's not alright," Jarrod groused. "These two took up practically all of our gold and look at me!" He wore studded leather armor, boots and a grey cloak. "I look like an NPC."

Annoyed by his whining, Roan snapped, "I don't think the orcs will care what you look like." He climbed to his feet and, after tucking his spell book into his pack, he led them back up to the surface where the village was even busier. Most of the elves were racing around preparing their defenses as best as they could. Others, women and children with heavy packs on their backs, were already fleeing towards the Ash Forest where they would hide from the coming battle which was rushing down upon them, quicker than anyone could have foreseen.

In the distance, ugly, blatting horns could be heard. The orcs were coming.

Along with the orc horns, they could hear howling wolves. The sound seemed to burrow straight into some primitive part of Roan and he felt a shiver go up his spine. He wasn't the only one who felt it either. Amanda was pale, while Jarrod cursed. Close to them, a little pixie-eared child let out a whimper.

"I can't believe we're running away," Marshall said. "It's embarrassing. This place looks like it would be easy to defend. Think about how many arrows they could rain down."

Roan glanced up and saw that Marshall was both right and wrong. The rain of arrows would be horrific, but limited. It was an elven village, not an elven city. There were probably not more than four hundred elves there. How would they fare against two thousand orcs? Or three thousand? Or five?

Not well in his opinion, especially as their defenses were extremely limited. It seemed as though the elves were putting too much faith in their trees, perhaps forgetting that trees could be put to the torch or hacked down. But even if they had taken such considerations into place, Roan doubted that they would be able to deal with Atticus Arching. What sort of powers would the founder of this world possess? Could he cause an earthquake to tear apart the forest? Could he summon flying demons or perhaps even a dragon?

Was he invincible?

"Swallow your pride, Marshall. Keep our mission in mind. One of the reasons we're here is to keep Arching busy on this side and if that means running, then so be it." He led them down one of the grass roads to a gap in the great trees that ringed the town.

There was no telling what they would find beyond the village. All he knew was that they were somewhere in the Ash Forest, which, according to Fulbright, was a day's march to Riverport, the capital of Ellisbar. It was supposed to be their destination, but now he had second thoughts. What if it was as small as this elf village? It would be destroyed if the orc army followed them.

"Does anyone know anything about Riverport?" he asked as they paused at a set of gleaming silver gates that had been mounted between two towering trees. The Ash Forest beyond the gates seemed exceptionally gloomy and despite the howling of the wolves growing louder and louder, he wasn't looking forward to venturing away from the minimal safety of the town.

"What about it?" an elf in padded armor asked. He had a club resting on one shoulder; he had to be an adventurer who had just started a new character.

Roan immediately became suspicious. Was the man a spy, or was he just terribly unlucky, spawning in the face of an invasion? "I just wanted to know how big it is and what sort of defenses they have."

"I've been there a few times with a different character. It's pretty big. Maybe, uh, five or six thousand people. If you're going there, I'd love to join up with you. I'm a fighter and not even a build."

Marshall frowned at the idea. Amanda cleared her throat, pointedly, while Jarrod wasn't nearly as subtle. "Hell no. Hit the road, Jack."

The fighter flipped Jarrod the bird and left, jogging towards another party of adventurers. "Nice job, Jarrod," Amanda said. "I didn't trust him either, but he did have information. We don't even know which way Riverport is."

A sharp-eared elf overheard her. "It's almost due northwest." She was a young elven woman, with hair like spun silver. She wore traveling clothes and on her back was a pack nearly as big as she was. Attached to each hand was a child, both with silver eyes and hair.

Roan thanked her and started off, heading north. She jogged next to them as they left the village. "I could show you the way. We wouldn't be any trouble, I promise."

"I'm sorry," Roan told her. "We can't. I would if I could."

"But you can," she said, breathless under the weight of her pack. She and her children did their best to keep up as Roan marched along. They were now in the Ash Forest itself and Roan momentarily forgot the woman. He was more than a little stunned by the state of the forest. The trees of the elf village had been towering and beautiful. Outside of it, however, the trees were twisted and ugly...and grey. As he walked, he reached out to touch a drooping leaf and found that it was covered in ash.

"What the hell?" he muttered. "Did a volcano erupt, or was it always like this?"

The elven woman hurried around to put herself in front of Roan. She bowed low even as she walked backwards, saying,

"No, my lord. It's the orcs of the Orc-back Mountains. About ten years ago, they began digging in the Black Pits and have released something that is causing this. We all agree it is an affront to nature, my lord. No one knows what to do about it, not even Lord Leomagnus. He has…"

A new howl, a close one caused her to freeze during its duration. When it was over, she dropped to her knees and grabbed the hem of Roan's green cloak. "I humbly beg you, my lord. We are defenseless and will die without your aide. I can pay you… anything. Any price you wish, I will pay it to save my children."

"We will not take payment," Marshall stated, helping the woman up. "It would be an affront to our honor."

"What honor?" Jarrod asked, walking around them and heading deeper into the forest. "I really don't like this new you, Marshall. You aren't thinking straight. We can't help this lady. Have you forgotten that we can barely help ourselves?"

A pained look swept Marshall's new elven features. "He may be right. My lady, those wolves are after us, not you. You'll be in more danger being with us than being alone. I would suggest striking a path north and then cutting west later this afternoon. That way you'd…"

The forest had been quiet but now there was a terrifying scream that went on and on, and along with it they could hear the snapping of teeth and the frightful growls of the wolves as they fought over their victim.

"I think it's too late to worry about who's in more danger," Roan said. "We have to move! Glitch, can you find out how close they are?" The puff of air shot away as Roan hurried off to his right where the forest was a little more open. They wouldn't be able to hide once the wolves got their scent, if they didn't have it already.

Glitch was back in a minute, filling Roan's head with terrible, bloody images of elves being torn apart. "Yes, but how far away are they?" It wasn't a question the air elemental could answer easily. It tried showing Roan the different trees it had passed, but that was not only confusing, it also made him dizzy. "Stop! Give me an aerial view. Can you do that?"

"Who is he talking to, Mummy?" the smaller of the two elf children asked.

"Never mind that," the lady answered, as she hurried them along. "Just keep going and don't look back."

It was impossible not to look back, especially when a new scream erupted. Roan wanted to tell himself that it was all just a game, only he couldn't. It was too real. The fear, the screams, the howls, the blatting horns, the air rushing in and out of his chest. Even the pictures that Glitch was sending into his head were real.

There were at least a hundred wolves in the forest behind them. Most were miles away chasing down the fleeing elves, but there was a pack that was very close. He counted twenty wolves within a mile. Half of them had their bloody snouts buried in the bodies of two elves and were tearing into them. The other half were spread out, scurrying around with their noses to the ground, hunting down others—perhaps even hunting Roan and his small group. The closest of the beasts was just a little over a hundred yards away.

Roan put his finger to his lips and veered the group back to true north. He sent out a telepathic question: *What's ahead of us, Glitch?* A second later, he heard a light whirring sound as Glitch swept by.

What they needed was a cliff to scale or a river to float down. Unfortunately, the answer to his question was miles and miles of this terrible forest. As far as Glitch could see there were only gently rolling hills, foul, stinking air and trees that were barely holding on to life.

They had barely made it another mile when behind them, a new howl went up. The shrill cry was very close. The nearest wolf had caught their scent.

2—

"Bows at the ready," Roan said, before recalling Glitch. "We'll keep moving as long as we can. If one of us goes down, the rest will keep going. There will be no giving up, understood?"

Only Jarrod failed to nod. He looked at the elf woman un-happily. Roan knew what he was thinking: if it wasn't for her, they could have clocked out and started over. Jarrod was wrong in his assessment of the situation. They couldn't keep starting over. A few more times and Caron would pull the plug on this part of the investigation. From an accounting point of view, it certainly had to seem like a colossal waste of taxpayers' money.

"One of us will get through to Riverport," Roan said, "and the rest will join them there. It's the only way to keep the pressure on Arching."

!!! Glitch screamed into his mind. Roan "saw" the closest two wolves break left, while the next two went right. It was perfect pack mentality. They would surround Roan's team and then attack from all sides.

Of course, they didn't have aerial reconnaissance. "This way," Roan said, breaking *towards* the first two wolves. The team wasn't being exactly quiet and when the wolves heard them coming, they slunk down, looking for an opportunity to spring an ambush.

"Right there," Roan said, using his drawn arrow to point at the wolves. A second later, all four bows were in firing position. The wolves had a natural armor class of 14, but that was with their dexterity taken into account. Just then they were sitting targets and had an armor class of only 12.

Because of his wizard class, Roan was technically the worst fighter among them, but even he had a +3 dexterity bonus when shooting an arrow—still, he missed, his arrow zipped an inch over the wolf's head. Amanda and Jarrod both scored hits and the wolves yelped.

Normal wolves would have slunk away to lick their wounds, but these were Daggerland wolves. They both broke from cover and charged, and both died seconds later as Roan's team let off another flight of arrows. This time Roan's arrow went four inches deep into a wolf's chest*(XP +40)*.

!Behind!

"Turn about!" Roan cried. Two more wolves were heading in at a full charge. Arrows were nocked and fired. Again, Roan missed, as did Amanda. There was no time for a second round. Marshall threw down his bow and out leapt his sword. With one swing, he cleaved the triangular head of a wolf in half. The second one was on him in a flash, its teeth crushing down on the steel leggings he wore, but with a nineteen armor class, it wasn't going to be easy to get past that much tempered steel.

Amanda tried to hack into the wolf with her sword, only it jumped away too quickly and all she cut was a tuft of fur. Jarrod started to move to the left to get his own shot in, but Roan stopped him. "There's more coming!" Glitch was a hundred feet above them with a perfect view. Marshall was their strongest fighter. He would have to take care of the wolf on his own.

Amanda pulled her shield from her back and braced herself for the assault. Her shield was small and circular, her sword long but slim. She was a match for any one of the wolves but there were four coming, their tongues lolling out of their gaping, hungry mouths, the unnatural evil in their eyes shining out.

Jarrod shot one with his bow and Roan shot another, though this was actually by accident. He missed high on the one he'd been aiming at and struck another of the wolves only because it leapt over a low branch at just the right moment.

Then the wolves were on Amanda, almost barreling her over. One got a hold of her boot and half spun her around, but a slash from her sword across its snout had it howling in pain and jumping away. A second one drew her blood, darting in to sink its teeth into her shield arm.

She tried to stab it, however the angle was wrong. The first wolf had already half-turned her and now with this one on her she was in danger of falling where she'd be almost defenseless. It was then that Marshall bellowed a cry and brought his sword crashing down.

Almost at the same time, Jarrod shot the wolf that had Amanda's boot. It died with its teeth still clamped around her ankle. The last wolf tried to run away, only Roan shot it in the hind quarters and the most it could manage was a cringing limp into the bushes.

!!! Glitch sent a new picture into Roan's head.

Roan sighed. "We're not done. In thirty seconds, we're going to have three in front and two on the side. Amanda, heal yourself. Marsh…"

The elf woman startled him by hurrying up and picking up the bow Marshall had dropped. She held out a hand to Marshall and he gave up his quiver. As she was doing this, her two children scampered around the battlefield pulling arrows from the slain wolves or from the dirt in the case of the missed shots. They only had seconds, but each grabbed a handful and retreated back behind the fighters.

As he was unarmored, Roan tried to stay behind them as well, however the wolves went right for him this time in a move that didn't make any sense. So far, he had been the least effective of them. His main role had been as a go between, shuttling information from Glitch to the others.

It seemed to him that the only reason they were coming for him was that they were being *directed*. The thought sent a shudder down his back just as he fired his long bow. He missed again! It was terribly annoying being such a poor fighter, but he didn't have time to complain beyond biting back on a curse.

His cloak was snatched in a pair of powerful jaws and he was yanked forward, but he was no ordinary wizard who would have been killed in seconds. Roan was stronger than the wolf. He planted his feet and hauled back with one hand as he pulled his sword with the other. It only came out half way before jaws snapped onto his elbow.

The pain was sharp as tendons ripped and muscles tore—the words in his vision were back (*Damage -3*) and beneath that, his health bar was already a third depleted—through gritted teeth, he sucked in a sharp breath, gave up the sword and pulled his dagger with his left hand. He drove it into the wolf's eye. The wolf seemed to scream and Roan yanked his arm away.

While this was going on, Marshall and Amanda were swinging their swords up and down like axes, chopping at the wolves, and Jarrod and the elf woman were shooting as fast as they could.

Blood was flying everywhere and the wolves were beginning to pile at their feet as more joined the fight.

Roan's green cloak tore—he tumbled back, as did the wolf. Before he could get up, gaping jaws with inch-long fangs were on him, clamping down on his shoulder and his neck. His collar bone snapped and his left arm went limp while at the same time he felt a vessel burst in his neck.

(*Damage-Critical Hit -14*) His health bar swung to the left, further, further, further, until there was nothing left. With his eyes growing dim, he saw Jarrod's bloody blade hack into the wolf's back. It fell away and as if by magic, it seemed to morph into Amanda. She was on her knees, leaning over him, her hands out and already they were glowing blue. Through the light, two drops fell, one sweat and one blood. They landed on his cheeks like tear drops.

He saw that she was hurt and yet, she was healing him (*Heal +8*). "No," he whispered, but it was too late. She had brought him back from the precipice of death instead of healing herself. "You shouldn't…" She was gone before he could finish his sentence.

There were too many wolves for words. Roan stood, his shoulder, neck and elbow healed. He picked up his long sword and slashed its clean edge at a wolf that was just attacking. The strike was heavy, sending jarring vibrations into the palms his hands. Still the wolf was a tough one and shook off the blow and went for Roan's unprotected side.

!!! Glitch dropped out of the sky "attacking" with its *Haze*. It landed on the wolf's face, spinning the air with all its might, temporarily disrupting its vision. As the wolf snapped uselessly at the air elemental, Roan stuck his sword right down its throat.

He pulled the sword out as the wolf went limp. "That one!" Roan cried as another of the beasts threatened the elf woman. Glitch sped to it and again the wolf reacted as any animal would; it twisted, trying to rip the air. It met only Roan's steel.

Roan spun, looking for the next set of jaws that were hungry for his blood, but the remaining wolves were backing away, most limping and leaving a trail of blood. "We're alive," he said in awe.

"Speak for yourself," Jarrod said. The rogue was on one knee, breathing heavily, blood trickling down his neck from a face wound. "I feel like someone tried to make me into a hamburger. Why didn't you…"

(*XP +200*) crossed Roan's vision. Jarrod must have been given the same message. "That's it?" he complained. "I was hoping to get at least to second level. I mean that was a hard fight."

"And it's not over. Look." Roan pointed back the way they had come. Black smoke was drifting into the early morning air; it was coming from the direction of the elf village. "Who's in need of healing? I'm eight of nine, so I'm good."

Jarrod raised a hand. "Two of nine."

"Six of thirteen," Marshall said. "As a paladin, I have a bit of minor healing. I can take care of myself."

Roan looked towards Amanda. She was shaking and barely able to stand. Her cloak was ripped in half and her armor was dented and bloody. "One of eight," she answered. "But I only have two very minor healing spells left."

"Heal yourself," Roan ordered. "Jarrod and I will use a healing potion. You two kids, let's police up those arrows. Glitch get upstairs and tell me what's coming next." In a minute, his banged-up team was ready to move out again. For the time being, most of the wolves were feasting on some of the stray elves they had caught, while the rest were off licking their wounds.

"I don't get you," Jarrod said. "You know you're a wizard, right? Why the hell didn't you use any spells?"

"Because it's only eight in the morning and we still have an army after us." Glitch had shown him the bad news. At least a thousand orcs had turned aside from the elf village and were pressing on, heading like a spear right for them.

2—

With Glitch above, Roan led them northwest at a terrific pace that soon had everyone flagging. The heat began to rise and sweat ran like rivers. The ash clung to them, turning them grey inside and out, or so it seemed. Roan kept coughing up grey phlegm.

It wasn't even an hour into their flight when Glitch called out, *!!!* and showed him an image of the orcs coming ever nearer.

"Damn…I mean thanks, Glitch." Knowing that they weren't going to get away at this rate, Roan turned to the elf woman. "You're going to have to leave that stuff behind. Please, drop your pack."

"But it's full of irreplaceable family heirlooms. Some are thousands of years old. You have no idea what you're asking!"

The argument was lost on Roan mainly because the game was only eleven years old, but he couldn't exactly say that or he'd be penalized. He tried a different route. "Which are easier to replace? Knickknacks or your children?" She bowed her head and quietly laid the pack aside. "Good. Now, Amanda, let's have your pack." She started to argue, saying something about pulling her own weight, however since she was gasping for breath, her words were hard to follow. "Look, since I'm not wearing armor, I'll carry it." After the hard fight, the blood loss and the march, she was so tired that she didn't need any more convincing than that.

Jarrod watched with a lip curled. "When I die, I'm coming back as a girl."

"You mean you're not one already?" Marshall joked.

"Ha-ha, very funny. I'm just saying there is a double standard here."

Roan glared Jarrod into silence before squatting down to look into Amanda's pack. "I don't think we'll need all this," he said, throwing out the torches, rope, and most of the rations. He went through his own pack, tossing away unneeded items and had the others do the same with theirs.

With their burdens lighter, they were able to stay just ahead of the orcs, who braved the sunlight in a way that wasn't natural for them. Hours went by and still they came on without let up or rest. Twice, small packs of wolves attempted to cut the team off by looping far around them, but with Glitch's help they were able to drive them off, killing a few and gaining a little more experience.

Then they left the forest behind them and marched onto an open plain. As much as they had hated the Ash Forest, being on the plain made them feel exposed and naked. The sun directly overhead was oppressive and seemed to cook Marshall and Amanda in their metal armor.

"Arching must be whipping the flesh off of them to get them to come out of the forest," Marshall said not long after. Roan gave him a questioning look and he explained, "Orcs hate the sun. It makes them feel sick, I guess."

"And that doesn't?" Amanda asked, gesturing to the mountains that bordered the forest. One of the closer peaks belched out an endless dark cloud which was swept over the Ash Forest by the wind.

Marshall shook his head. "They seem to thrive on poison." He was about to turn back to the march when he asked the elf woman, "What mountains are those?"

She looked at him strangely. "Those are the Orc-backs, of course. Where do you think the orcs came from?"

With that simple explanation, Roan finally knew where he was. Most of the eye-shaped Kingdom of Ellisbar lay to the northwest with Riverport being almost straight north. When he squinted in that direction, his sharp elven vision could make out a smudge on the horizon. It seemed far away, especially compared to how close the orcs were.

The filthy beasts looked like a swarm of locusts covering the plain behind them. The closest of them was little more than two miles away. "Let's go," Roan ordered. Seeing the orcs so close was frightening and that fear pushed them on despite the blisters that were forming on their feet, and the pain from their injuries.

The proximity spurred the orcs as well and gradually, as the minutes ticked away, they drew closer. Roan pushed his team harder in response until they were practically jogging.

An hour of the hellish pace went before they saw Riverport. It was a cramped city that sat on an island in the middle of a broad river. It had wooden walls that went right to the water's edge. Beyond the walls, it looked like a fine city, a pretty one, even. There were boats on the river placidly going about their business and people moving on the four bridges, some with teams of oxen, some, from a distance looking as though they were just out for a stroll.

Roan feared that the city would be caught unaware however, when they were a mile away, the first of the signal trumpets blared. The desperate sound was a call to arms and the boats were no longer placid and the people no longer strolled. They ran around preparing what defenses they could in the short time before the orcs were upon them.

Above the city, the silver and blue pendants flying from the towers were hauled down and switched out for black ones, perhaps denoting a city under siege. Roan didn't know and couldn't spare a breath to ask. The orcs had redoubled their efforts and now his team was running. Laden down with armor and weapons, Marshall sounded like a garbage can filled with pots and pans being rolled down a hill.

"We're going to make it!" Amanda cried a minute later. The first of the two western bridges was very near. Soldiers were hurrying from the city while civilians were running towards it. Roan figured they would be counted among the latter, however the soldiers stopped them.

"She can go on," said the sergeant in charge, pointing his spear at the elf woman. "The rest of you have to fight."

"Look at us!" Jarrod cried. "We're covered in wolf blood! We've been fighting plenty in case you haven't noticed."

The sergeant had such a thick mustache that it covered both of his lips when he wasn't speaking. When he scowled at Jarrod, the mustache seemed to scowl along with his eyes. "Those who can fight, will fight. If not, you're just another mouth to feed and you can go take a hike."

Since they didn't have a choice, the four of them unslung their packs, letting them thud to the ground.

"This is ridiculous," Jarrod grumbled under his breath.

"It is what it is," Roan said. "We roll with it. Let's get our bows ready." He was just nocking an arrow when movement at his elbow caused him to jump. It was the elf woman grabbing the two packs he had dropped. Her children were dragging away Marshall's and Jarrod's pack as well.

"We are in your debt, Lord Roan," the woman said, bowing once and then pulling the packs away.

"You think she'll sell all our stuff?" Jarrod asked, looking back. "Hey! What are those guys doing?" Halfway down the bridge, men and women wielding saws and hammers were attacking the supports holding up the middle span of the bridge.

The sergeant cast a nervous a look back. "What do you think? They're cutting the bridge. Our job is to give them the time to do it." It was a job for a hundred soldiers and they had only eleven. Yes, they were well armed and armored with their spears and chainmail, but they were not going to be able to stand up to the orc army for more than half a minute.

It wasn't going to be long enough, but they were now out of options. "Amanda with me on the left," Roan ordered. "Marshall and Jarrod on the right. Soldiers in the middle. Arrows first."

They had their backs to the bridge as the orcs rushed down on them. The orcs were grinning, their pig-like tusks showing right down to their yellowed roots. A battle lust was on them, they were practically mad with it. Roan saw all of this from a hundred yards as he aimed his bow. At this distance, he could not miss, especially if he aimed high.

It was like shooting at an ocean from the beach and this wasn't even the full army. How many more orcs were still in the elf village, raping and pillaging and feasting on fresh blood?

"You ready?" he whispered to Amanda. She couldn't hear him. The workers were hammering and sawing like mad, the orcs were screaming, and the soldiers were praying.

Roan looked into her huge blue eyes and knew she wasn't ready. This wasn't her world. Even as a cleric, she wasn't made for Daggerland. He knew it as fact in that moment, just as he knew that he was.

Roan knew the reason for the sudden feeling of belonging in this magical land and it was exactly as Jarrod had said: they were doing things, seemingly important things. Even if it was just a game, their lives and their deaths had meaning.

All of which made this strange life very real to Roan. The elf woman and her children had been real to him, and the frightened men-at-arms who were slowly backing onto the bridge were real to him. And their situation was very real.

Somehow Arching had discovered exactly where they had crossed over into this world and while Roan had been foolishly wrestling with his feelings for Amanda, Arching had set the orcs marching from the Pits of the Black Hand. Roan was the target, but it was an untold number of beautiful elves who had paid the price. And now the orcs were at Riverport lighting a panic in the population and poising Roan once more on the precipice of failure.

In spite of this, Roan knew his duty. Unlike Amanda, he had been made for this world. It wasn't just his heavily muscled body or the easy brutality in which he fought, it was in the simple way his mind worked. In any world in which he walked, he knew that the strong protected the weak and that good people stood against evil, no matter the cost.

It was obvious to him that the bridge had to be defended or the city would fall in one furious attack.

Calmly, he waited until the mass of orcs was in range of his bow, before saying, "Fire." Four arrows arced through the air and even before they struck home, the group was readying a second strike. *(XP +30)* flashed across the bottom of his vision. He ignored the words saying, "Fire for effect."

Because of his high dexterity, he was able to shoot three more arrows to Marshall's and Amanda's two. Of the first eight, he hit six times and saw: *(XP +30) (XP +30) (XP +30) (XP +30) Congratulations! You are now a Level Two Wizard and have gained the following bonuses:*

Increased Hit Points(+7)
Attack +1
You can fill +1 Cantrips per day
You can fill +1 Tier one spells per day

You have +6 skill points to allocate

It was too bad that he didn't have the time to fill those spell slots just then. He needed every spell he could get his hands on just then. The orcs were bearing down on them in a vast mob. "Hurry!" the sergeant cried to the workers behind them—there were maybe twenty of them and as their courage slowly failed them, they began to run back to the city a few at a time.

This had a cascading effect and now the soldiers were on the verge of deserting wholesale. They had yet to strike a blow and already they had retreated thirty feet onto the wooden bridge. "Stand fast!" Roan cried, sweeping out his long sword. The soldiers paused, their spears out towards the running orcs. Many of the men were terrified, and for good reason, it was obvious that they were going to be nothing but a speed bump for the orcs on their way to the city walls.

"Eda-eram gdiy!" Roan yelled, feeling the magic inside of him come out in a shockwave of sound. The *Thunderous Wave* blasted from him like an unseen explosion and hurtled into the first line of orcs, throwing them back. One was killed outright by the spell (*XP +30*) while six others fell and were trampled (*XP +175*).

The bodies of the seven were turned into grey jelly by the rest of the orcs pressing in. The spell had been unexpected and the momentum of the orc army was checked just enough to keep the soldiers from being swept away in the first assault. In fact, their bristling spears managed to kill a number of the beasts while Marshall and Amanda took down two as well.

Roan had more room to fight compared to the others. The orcs were frightened of his magic and with good reason. He sent two bolts of fire into the faces of a pair of orcs, who threw themselves, screaming into the river (*XP +60*).

The fight swayed back and forth on the bridge for a full minute before the weight of the orcs pushed the soldiers back into the workers, who picked up and ran, leaving the job of destroying the bridge only half complete.

With so many people battling back and forth, one of the supports gave way beneath them. The span of bridge they were on yawed far to the left, throwing Jarrod and another spearman into the water.

Jarrod came up gasping, his sword lost, his leather armor sticking to him like a second skin. The soldier, weighed down by fifty pounds of metal, was not so lucky. He slipped beneath the surface and was never seen again. Seven or eight orcs also fell in and drowned in a surprisingly noisy manner, screaming loudly in their croaking voices.

Then the bridge began to swing back. Amanda started to fall, her arms pinwheeling, her sword nearly taking a chunk from the top of Roan's head as it swished past. Like a sailor, he had his feet splayed and as she went over, he grabbed the edge of her ragged cloak and reeled her in to him. They collapsed onto the wood planks, holding on with desperate strength.

"Back! Everyone back to the walls!" cried the sergeant. In his eyes their only option was retreat or death.

The remaining soldiers backed away, however Roan's team was not in the position to run away just yet. Marshall was hauling a spluttering Jarrod out of the water, while Amanda and Roan were only just getting to their feet.

"Go," Roan said, pushing Amanda towards the soldiers. She wobbled back and forth as the bridge swung. Thirty feet away, a gulf of uncertain swaying wood between them, the orcs were hesitant, but seeing her go was enough to get them moving again.

Roan stepped to the center of the bridge, standing solo against the orcs, none of whom could have known just how weak he was. To stop a thousand of them he had a single *Fire Bolt* spell and his last *Thunderous Wave*.

"Stop!" he bellowed. His voice carried over the noise and it was heard as a challenge by one of the largest and meanest of the beasts. The huge orc chieftain wore steel armor taken from his victims and wielded a steel axe with an edge like a razor.

It roared something guttural in reply and swung the axe over its head. Roan said: "Maya-gitch-gummee, rum-a tum-tum tug-ga, hurry, damn it!" It was nonsense, not just designed to play on the orc's fear of magic, but also to give Marshall enough time to pull Jarrod to safety. The orc paused, looking at Roan with piggy eyes, waiting to see what magic would come blasting from his hands.

"Hola mi amigo. Rala tigo, sun walla-walla wigo!" Roan went on just long enough for the orc to decide that Roan wasn't casting a spell and for Jarrod to climb onto the bridge with Marshall's help. The near drowning left him gasping and so exhausted that he could only crawl away.

The orcs laughed at him, thinking that he was a fool or a jester. Jarrod didn't seem to care, he just kept crawling with

Marshall walking backwards towards the city and Roan left standing alone.

"I have gold," Roan lied to the orc. "I'll give you a thousand in gold if you let us go."

"Coward," the orc croaked, to the increased laughter of the others. "You cannot buy life. Get on your hands and knees and beg Gurak for your worthless life. Beg Gurak and worship Gurak!"

Roan needed two more seconds. "And who is Gurak?" Roan was not an expert in orcs and thus was a little shocked when Gurak the orc flew into a rage and charged. "Eda-eram gdiy!" Roan yelled when the orc hit the point of no return. He was square in the middle of the bridge, as were a hundred others with the rest pressing forward.

The *Thunderous Wave* spell, a sonic boom that could be heard for miles struck, not Gurak or any of the orcs, but one of the last bridge supports. Roan needed the bridge to come down and the shock of the spell combined with the weight of a hundred orcs and all their gear finally did the trick.

A series of loud snapping noises could be heard coming from beneath the bridge as a vibration swept along the wood. Roan turned and ran just as the supports let go. His first two steps were fine, but the next one hit nothing but air and he fell along with the front edge of the orcs. In a desperate attempt to catch a hold of the remains of the bridge, he flung out his arms, his fingers catching the last board.

He swayed for a moment, ten feet above the water, however the moment, dependent upon a few bent nails, did not last. His weight pulled the nails right out of their sockets and he and the board dropped with a splash. All around him were orcs flailing around. They were subterranean creatures and generally feared the water as much as they hated the sun. They could not swim.

Once he had jettisoned the green cloak and the soft elf shoes, Roan had no problem swimming to the edge of the bridge that was still standing. He had lost his sword, which was nothing compared to what he had gained. (*XP +30*), (*XP +30*), (*XP +30*)
…

The orcs were drowning by the dozens, and in a minute, he saw these words scrolling at the bottom of his vision:

Congratulations! You are now a Level Three Wizard and have gained the following bonuses:
Increased Hit Points(+7)

You can fill +1 Tier two spells per day
You have +6 skill points to allocate
And still the experience kept piling up: (*XP +30*), (*XP +30*), (*XP +30*)…he had even gained a thousand experience point bonus for destroying the bridge. "That's got to put me into fourth level for sure," he said as he brought up his stats:

Character Name: Roan
Class & Level: Wizard - Level 3
Race: High Elf
Alignment: Chaotic Good
Experience Points: **5,999**   XP To Next Level: **1**

Strength – Dexterity – Constitution
S: **15(+2)**   D: **16(+3)**   C: **16(+3)**

Intelligence – Wisdom – Charisma
I: **17(+3)**   W: **16(+3)**   C: **16(+3)**

Armor: 10(13)   **Hit Points: 23**
Initiative: +3   Speed: 13
SAVING THROWS: Will: 6   Fortitude: 4   Reflex: 4

GOLD: 22

-EQUIPMENT-

Weapons
Longbow

Armor
None

Magic
Spell Book
Flask of Holy Water

Misc
Quiver * Arrows x6
Backpack * Rations x1
Tinder Box * Waterskin
Pouches x2

† Spells Known †

Cantrips: Minor Illusion, Fire Bolt, Ray of Ice, Electric Hand, Acid Spray
Tier 1 Spells: Summon Familiar, Flame Blast, Lightning Summoning(lesser), Instant Slumber, Thunderous Wave, Illusion(minor), Charm(minor)
Tier 2 Spells:
Tier 3 Spells:

† Spells Prepared †

Cantrips: Fire Bolt x1
Tier 1 Spells:
Tier 2 Spells:
Tier 3 Spells:

Attacks
Name - ATK Bonus – Damage
Longbow   +5   1-8

Abilities
Spell Casting

Skills
Listen: +6, Spot: +6, Knowledge: +6, Search: +6, Spell Craft: +6

2—Riverport, Ellisbar

"That was awesome!" Marshall said, as he helped Roan onto the remains of the bridge.

"It was kind of cool," Roan agreed. "And I made it to the third level, but you want to hear something that's cheap? I need one point to get to the next level. One point!"

Jarrod, looking like a bedraggled rat with pointy ears, said, "Oh, boo-hoo. I barely got to second level and I lost my sword and I never got a hat, and I bet that elf chick sold all of our stuff."

"Don't be like that," Marshall said, clapping his game-enlarged hand on Jarrod's shoulder. "We'll probably be counted as heroes. We saved the city…for now." Across from them on the far bank of the river, the remaining orcs—thousands of them—milled about uncertainly, blinking hard against the late afternoon sun.

"Of course, we were the ones who endangered the city to begin with," Amanda said, coming back to join them on the edge of the bridge. "Perhaps we shouldn't mention that. It can be our little secret." When she said this, she tipped Roan a little wink, making him think about their moment from the day before when he could have kissed her. It seemed like that had been a long time ago.

The wink made him stiffen slightly. He still couldn't touch her or kiss her, and he really shouldn't even be thinking about her in such a…

A sudden blast of air in his face made him jump. It was Glitch making high piercing noises in his head: **!!** and blowing air into his face. He tried to shoo the elemental away, but it dodged his hand, easily. At first, Roan thought that it was trying to distract him from Amanda, but then he realized that it was trying to blow dry him.

And that was okay. The water had been bracingly cold, only he had been so focused on survival that he was only just realizing it.

"Let's move to the wall," Roan said. "Remember that the king here is still a suspect. Based on the little we know about what's going on over here, he's still possibly connected."

They turned their backs on the orcs and marched four abreast and in Roan's mind, they were heading to a hero's welcome. Reality did not live up to his vision. At the end of the bridge was a heavy portcullis that was partially lowered so that they had to duck to get under.

"Move yer asses!" barked a guard captain as Roan paused just past the gate. "Let's go, yer Majesty. And you, ya' dumb elf can shove that look up your ass."

Amanda had been staring in astonishment. Now, she blinked and looked away. No one seemed to have heard or noticed the sergeant's rude behavior, except for Roan, who had to be restrained. "Now's not the time," Jarrod said. "You can slit his throat later."

This let the air out of Roan's anger. He looked at Jarrod in amazement and with more than just a little embarrassment. Not that anyone else noticed that either. There was too much going on all around them to pay attention to one man snapping in anger.

As he stood there, Roan was jostled by the hundreds of people cramming the streets. Most were heading west, hauling carts or lugging packs that seemed as big as themselves. Most were peasants, some were of the merchant class, and sprinkled in with them were adventurers in leather or metal armor, carrying swords and bows. The rarest among them were spell casters, who would lock eyes with Roan as they passed, whether in challenge or respect, he couldn't tell.

There was so much going on and so many people treading the narrow streets that Roan didn't see the one person who was actually congratulating him on his victory. It wasn't until he felt a tug on his wet tunic that he noticed the elf woman and her two children. They were bowing so that their chins almost touched the ground.

"I thank you again, my lord, and acknowledge your victory over the orcs. Say the word and I am at your service."

Roan had never heard such an offer before and, in confusion and worry that he was about to screw up again, he looked to

Amanda. Her face was clouded over in doubt. Trust was no longer her default setting. She shrugged, no more at ease with whatever the offer suggested than he.

Marshall was looking away, while Jarrod had a cold, calculating look in his eyes that Roan wasn't comfortable with. One way or another, Roan couldn't have this woman and her children tagging along with them. "Miss, I release you from any debt that lies between us. You are free to go as you please."

The woman bowed even lower and then left them much to Roan's delight. In his mind, he had fulfilled his duty, he had delivered them to safety and his commitment ended there.

(Escorting Seriah and her children to Riverport: XP +300)

Roan stared at the words, a scowl back on his face. He had honestly tried to help the woman and to find out that she had been planted there by the game made him feel very much used.

"So how do we know when we're being good for the sake of being good?" he asked, mostly speaking to himself.

Everyone had received the same message. Amanda must have been thinking the same thing. She was looking back towards the woman. "I don't know. I was just about to go and give her some gold, but now I know it would be a waste."

"You can't look at the game that way," Marshall told her. "If you are a good person on the other side then be a good person here, and just like in life, sometimes you get rewarded for being good, but most of the time the satisfaction of knowing you are good will be your only reward. I think you should give her some money."

Jarrod rolled his large elven eyes. "I hate it when you play a paladin. You always give till it hurts. Do I have to remind you that I don't have a sword? And it's not just me. Roan's is missing, and both you and Amanda have lost your shields. And look at my quiver. I got like four arrows left."

They were in a sorry state, it was true, still, the woman was worse off and part of that was Roan's fault for making her get rid of her heirlooms. "Amanda, go give her ten gold. We'll have Caron give us a little extra when we get back to the other side, and if he doesn't, I'll pay out of pocket."

"And that's how the game makes its money," Jarrod snorted as Amanda ducked through the crowd. "They get you coming and going. They're always trying…"

"Shut up," Roan snapped. He didn't like hearing someone criticize his orders in any world. Jarrod started to mumble under his breath as Roan checked his stats. Right away he saw that something was wrong. He had fulfilled a quest and had supposedly received 300 experience points, but for some reason he was still one experience point away from fourth level, just as he had been earlier.

Was this a real glitch? Or was he doing something wrong? Marshall had the simple answer: "You can't level up more than twice a day. It's to keep balance in Daggerland and believe me, everything here is all about balance. It's a good thing if you ask me."

"No way," Jarrod said. "It's another game cheat…aw, nuts, I just got dinged for negative ten. Sheesh! Either way, that whole last man standing stuff should be allowed, if you ask me. It's like hitting the l-o-t-t-o. You don't know what I'm talking about, do you Roan?"

He shook his head and Jarrod said, "Let's say there's like fifty players going after a dragon and one is this complete noob. You know, like a first level guy who's got himself a sword and is just along for the ride. And let's say that he hangs back as the other forty-nine guys fight the dragon until they're all dead and the dragon is clinging to life with one hit point. Out pops the noob and stabs the dragon in the back and bam, it's dead. Technically, all the experience points should go to the last person still alive, right?"

Roan didn't see why it should. "If he hadn't done anything to warrant the experience, then why should he get it? But this is different. I helped that lady just like the rest of you, but I didn't get the experience."

"It is what it is," Marshall said, just as Amanda came back. "And there's nothing you can do but go on. Speaking of which, where are we going now?"

Although their conversation had not been loud, an adventurer walking past heard the question and decided to throw his two cents in. "That depends on if you plan on fighting or running. If I was you, I'd run."

Was he a game plant, Roan wondered, or maybe he was one of Arching's agents? Roan grabbed his arm and stared into his eyes hoping to be able to read the answer. The man only glared until Roan let go of his arm. "Sorry, I, uh, thought you were someone I knew," Roan said. "So, you think we should take off? Why? The river won't stop the orcs?"

The man made a show of straightening his sleeve saying, "No. Why would it? You never heard of a pontoon before? I was going to see if you wanted to go on an excursion with me, but I think I'll pass."

Roan waited until he was out of earshot before saying, "We're not running away. We still have to check out the king of this city and see if he's connected in any way to Arching. So, step one is to find an inn as a base of operations and go from there. Agreed?"

It was a sound enough plan and one that was quickly implemented. As the orcs gathered on the far bank looking more like a mob than an army, Roan and his team wound through the narrow and very crowded streets, looking for an inn. There were many and most were clearing out quickly. Since a very pure form of capitalism was in effect, the team secured two very nice rooms at what Jarrod said was a steal of a price.

Amanda had her own room, which made her nervous. She didn't want to sleep alone, while Roan was afraid to sleep in the same room with her. They both knew Jarrod would be weird about it and Marshall looked like he had been hit by a club when the subject was broached.

"You should be fine," Jarrod said, glancing at her simple room. It held nothing besides a dresser made from some dark wood, a desk and chair, again made with the same wood, and a heavy wooden bed, upon which were gnome-woven sheets. Jarrod went to the shuttered window and checked the hinges and lock. "Yeah, you should be fine."

Roan didn't like "should be fine" when it came to protecting Amanda. There was a simple solution. "Glitch can stay with you."

"Can he?" she asked. "That would be perfect." She put out her hand and the little puff of air, which didn't seem quite as little as it had, came to land on her palm, where it alternated between pulsing and spinning.

As they had so very little in the way of luggage, they were able to settle into their rooms in minutes. "Now what?" Amanda asked when her meager belongings were set out. After the day they'd had, she looked tired and filthy. "I could use a shower. Do they even have those here?"

"Oh, yeah," Marshall answered. "This place is sort of like a normal hotel, only different." It turned out to be a lot different. Dinner was a goose that was even then being chased around the courtyard by one of the owner's children. They were offered rentable clothes while theirs were being cleaned—a simple blue dress for Amanda, and dull homespun woolen shirt and pants for the men.

A drawn bath was free, however fresh water could only be had at an extra charge.

Amanda, with Glitch in attendance, bathed first in a wide copper tub that could have fit two of her. The steam and the soap was endlessly intriguing to Glitch, who made hundreds and hundreds of bubbles, and then chased them around the ceiling like a hyperactive flying kitten.

Since she was in good hands, Roan clocked out, hoping to talk to Caron, only it turned out to be the dead of night in the real world. A sleepy-eyed FBI agent sitting at the bottom of the stairs jerked in surprise when Roan suddenly sat up.

"Hey," Roan said. Compared to the danger they had been embroiled in, catching their babysitter scraping up a few Zs seemed like a minor affair. Roan stood and stretched, feeling very strange to be back in his own human body. His injuries were completely healed and his fatigue dispelled. Honestly, he felt like a new and different person.

"You guys almost done?" the agent asked.

Roan glared, a look that was at home on his face in both worlds. "Not yet," was his terse answer. He didn't feel the need to explain himself to this low-level peon who would never understand that on the other side they didn't have access to banking records, IRS files, fingerprints, DNA analysis, or any of the usual crime fighting tools.

He was operating blindly and yet he felt he was getting closer. "A few more days, probably," Roan said. "Could you tell Caron that? And tell him I'm going to need to dip into the old wallet, again."

"Sure, but he won't be happy."

"When is he ever happy?" Roan asked. The agent grunted out a laugh, mentioned something about having to take a leak and then stomped upstairs. While he was gone, Roan ate one of Mrs. Niederer's sandwiches and drank a Mountain Dew because he felt both awake and asleep and didn't know which way to turn.

Next, he took up the weights and pumped iron until his arms, chest, and shoulders were burning. Then he took a turn on the elliptical, spinning the chains until they were a blur—subconsciously, he was trying to find some sort of equilibrium, matching the pain and exhaustion that his virtual body was feeling on the other side with his real body here.

Consciously, he never stopped worrying about what was happening in Daggerland. He was supposed to have an hour break, but he clocked back in after only fifty minutes.

When Roan returned to Daggerland, he found a fresh and very hot bath just sitting ready to go in the bathroom. He didn't know whose turn it was to bathe and he didn't care. His virtual body was aching from everything he had gone through and a bath sounded perfect. He only paused long enough to gaze out an east-facing window towards where the orcs were still gathering. They had yet to begin constructing a way to bridge the river, which he assumed would take a few days.

He slid into the near scalding water and sat there relaxing until his slim elven fingers were pruney and the water's temperature had dipped below warm and had turned tepid. With the succulent scent of goose on the air, he dried off, dressed quickly in the simple woolen trousers and shirt and hurried to find his friends.

There was no official dining room within the inn. There was a common area, where smoke from a crackling fire mingled with the grey puffs coming from the dozen or so pipe smokers to drift lazily along the ceiling.

At the far end of the room was a wide bar where a few beer-swilling patrons tilted back what appeared to be pewter mugs. Along the sides were booths with seat-backs that were so high that they created an alcove effect. The people in them were shadowy and reclusive.

Finally, there were long, communal tables in the middle of the room where people of all sorts sat: stone-grey dwarves, peasants from the countryside who were taking refuge from the orcs, a smattering of adventurers and even a family of halflings whose children were amazingly small and utterly adorable with their piping voices.

It was a somber group compared to the last tavern Roan had been in. For the most part, the patrons ate without talking. There was one exception: Jarrod.

"You wouldn't be sitting here if it weresn't for us," he was saying as Roan came up. "We were the ones who stopped the orcsess on the bridge. That was a fight 'n a half let me tell you. It was us, four peoples against ten thousand orcsess. We shotted our bows and there was this big…oh, hey, Roan! Our fearless leader-er is back an' all cleaned up!"

"Are you drunk?" Roan asked.

Jarrod held up a finger as he considered his state of drunkenness. He finally concluded: "Yes, but only a little. Martian is even more drunkerer than me and Amanda is...Amanda is only a little drunk, but don't tell Roan because she likes you."

Marshall was slumped across the table, snoring, while Amanda had been sitting with her hands clasped and a bleary look on her face, but now her huge elven eyes went even wider. She turned and punched Jarrod in the arm.

Wearing a hurt look, Jarrod explained, "I tolded him it was a secret, dang."

"That's not the point," she snapped at him. Turning to Roan, she said, "I didn't say I liked you. I said you were a good leader and that we were lucky to have you. That's about it." Jarrod began to open his mouth again, but she raised a fist and he shut it.

Roan wanted this aspect of the conversation to end as quickly as possible and so tried to change it. "I can't believe you three got drunk so fast. How long was I gone?" Time was a tricky thing jumping between the two worlds. Sometimes things ran parallel, an hour there equaled an hour here, but other times the minutes seemed to stretch out or shrink so that it felt like no time had elapsed.

"I think an hour," Amanda said, holding up three fingers. "But it's not our fault. These drinks are strong. It looks like normal beer but it isn't. It's super strong. And we have the right to a drink. We been on the clock for days and days and days."

She patted his arm once each time she said the word "days." Then she left her hand there as she smiled vacantly up at him. He could tell things were about to get weird between them again and so he asked, "Where is Glitch? Isn't he supposed to be watching you?"

"That's him," she said, pointing to where the halflings were sitting. The puff of air was tickling the nose of the children, making them squeal with laughter. Roan smiled at this right up until Amanda stuck her arm in his and whispered. "They are so cute that I want to take one home. Do you think they'll care? America is a great place. There are no orcs or nothing. We could adopt them, you know?"

She was soft and warm, and so beautiful that it took a tremendous act of willpower to disconnect their arms. "As nice as that sounds, I think they will mind. Kids belong with their parents, don't you think?"

"Yeah," she said, sounding disappointed that she wouldn't be able to steal a child. She was still staring at the halfling children when a tall, red-headed woman in platemail walked in. Across her shoulders she wore a blue silk cloak. Amanda's eyes went to slits. It was Korrin, the adventurer/trader they had traveled with a few days before.

Roan turned away. "Maybe we should finish up in our rooms. We wouldn't want to call attention to ourselves now that we're in…"

"Korrin!" Jarrod shouted, raising his pewter mug. "Hey, it's Jarrod. You remember us, right?"

As they were now elves, it took her a moment to place their faces, but when she did, she practically growled, "You're behind this aren't you? You are a plague! You've screwed me yet again!"

"No, it wasn't us," Jarrod said. "It's Arching or the king who's behind all this orc stuff, not us. We are only like a little, teeny bit to blame for the attack. We're the good guys, remember?" He slunk low and put a hand over his mouth to whisper, "F-B-I."

A low groan slipped from Roan, while Amanda had a more direct method of showing her displeasure: she punched Jarrod in the arm again. While he cursed and rubbed the spot, she turned her fierce gaze towards Korrin. "What happened to you before was not our fault. We couldn't have known we were being tracked."

"And what about now?" Korrin demanded. "This is the second shipment you've screwed up for me. There are no barges. They've all zipped out of here and I have five tons of witch grass sitting in a warehouse down by the docks. Do you know what happens to witch grass when it's bagged up? It gets hot and begins to decompose. Every day that I have to wait for a boat, it loses about twenty percent of its value. Are you going to reimburse me, or will the goat-humper?"

"Goat-humper!" Amanda cried, standing up. "Are you calling me a goat? Of all the crap I've heard in my time, that…"

Roan put his hand on her shoulder and gently lowered her back down. "This is all a misunderstanding. How much have you lost, Korrin? Maybe the, uh, Bureau will reimburse you."

"Including all of my gear? Seventeen hundred from last time and a thousand this time and that's in dollars."

"Twenty-seven hundred dollars?" Roan asked, shocked. "Okay, okay, Caron might be talked into that amount. We can see if we can expense that. Amanda, will you please clock out and talk to Caron?" He worried that if he left, the two women would come to blows.

Wearing a glare, Amanda clocked out and while she was gone, the four of them sat in a very uncomfortable stony silence. When Amanda clocked back in a few minutes later, she was cool as she said, "Caron was not in and the duty agent couldn't authorize the amount."

Korrin stood, seething. "Just what I thought." She stormed out of the inn, but not before picking up Jarrod's mug and splashing the contents into Roan's face to the general laughter of the room.

"That is one hot filly," Jarrod muttered. "What I wouldn't give to take a ride on that."

"Go take a bath," Roan ordered, wiping beer from his face with his sleeve. He was angry with Jarrod, but knew it was misplaced. Korrin had a right to be upset. She was innocent in all of this and twenty-seven hundred was a lot of money to lose, especially for someone from the Ukraine.

Roan sat down to eat and found the goose to be excellent and the heavy beer relaxing. Amanda continued to glare at the door as if she knew that Korrin would be back—and she was right.

Just after Jarrod came down, somewhat clean, and Marshall slowly hauled himself to his feet, the Ukrainian woman walked in, a small grin on her face. Behind her came eight soldiers.

Too late, Glitch cried a warning *!!!* The elemental was about to go at them with its Haze attack, but Roan stopped him.

"Hide yourself for now," he whispered to Glitch. To the soldiers, he calmly asked, "May I help you?"

"You can come with me peacefully," the leader of the group said. "Or you can come with me in pieces. You are under arrest on the charge of spying and conspiring with the orcs."

2—

They were hustled away and marched through the nearly empty town to a grey bricked building where they were pushed and shoved down a steep stair leading to the dungeons. Roan demanded to see the king, but was laughed at by the guards who shut the men into one large communal jail. Amanda was given her own cell.

"I'll know if something happens to her," Roan said to the guards, a warning in his voice. When they had left, Roan whispered to Glitch, "Keep an eye on her, but stay out of sight." When Glitch wanted to, it could remain perfectly still and only someone with an astronomically high "spot" skill level could see it. With the dungeons lit only by a few widely scattered torches set into the walls, Roan doubted that anyone would be able to see Glitch.

"Well, this sucks," Jarrod said as soon as the guards left. "I swear, Roan, you are a jinx. I've never had this much trouble in the game, ever. It's one thing to run into a stray pack of ogres and get clubbed to death like a seal pup, but this is bad luck over and over and over."

Tired of Jarrod already, Roan leaned against a damp rock wall. "Didn't we already go through this? I can get someone to replace you in a second. I'm pretty sure that half the CAT team would jump at the chance. So stop your whining."

Jarrod scoffed at the idea of using someone from the CAT team. "You wouldn't want any of those nerds, trust me. Talk about Screech-central!" Marshall snorted laughter in agreement, while Roan just shook his head, not having a clue as to what Jarrod was talking about. "You don't know Screech? Screech Powers from that TV show, *Saved by the Bell*? He was the king of the nerds."

"Oh, right. That's, that's…just quit your bellyaching, got it?" Roan turned away from the rogue to study the bars. They were black iron, grimy, foul and unmovable. "Any ideas on how to get out of here?"

Marshall rapped one of the bars with his fist and shook his head. Jarrod put his back to them and peered into the dark cell. A second later, a deep growly voice demanded, "What the hell are you looking at?"

"Nothing," Jarrod said, quickly, his voice unnaturally high.

Roan turned and stared into the dank, dark cell, and at first all he saw were a few shadowy figures, but then things began to firm up. He saw outlines and color and before he knew it, he saw with perfect clarity a hulking man relaxing on a bench meant for four people while two smaller men sat on the floor.

Everything was so clear that it was a little perplexing until he noticed the words at the bottom of his vision: *Racial Ability*

Unlock: Elves have natural low-light vision and can see in the dark up to ninety feet.

Hoping that this new ability would show him something previously overlooked, he looked at the cell closer, but there wasn't much more to see beyond heavy stone walls, the sad-looking prisoners and a bucket that was half-filled with urine.

"Don't look at my bucket," the big man said.

"I'll look anywhere I damn please," Roan answered. He wasn't afraid, but when the man stood up and nearly scraped his head on the ceiling, Roan definitely reevaluated things. *Glitch! Get in here, quick!* he thought. Aloud, he said to the man, "If you mess with me, you mess with all of us."

The threat didn't faze the man a bit. He cracked knuckles the size of walnuts and grinned. Thankfully, Glitch arrived just then and went right at the man's eyes, blurring his vision and whipping his long hair around. The man tried to swipe at Glitch, but since it couldn't be hurt by nonmagical people or weapons, his hands closed on nothing but air.

"What the hell?" he shouted in frustration.

"That is an air elemental and my familiar," Roan explained. "And if I order him to go down your throat, he can choke you from the inside and there won't be a damn thing you can do about it." Roan didn't know if this was true or not, but he suspected that it wasn't.

The man believed him, however. "No way, really?" he asked, backing up until he hit the bench, where he sat down.

"Yeah way," Jarrod said. "Now push over." He gave Roan a quick wink and went to sit on the bench next to the giant of a man as if they had won a victory when all they had won was the right to piss in a bucket.

Whoopee, Roan thought. "Glitch, can you go back to Amanda, please. Try to tell her that everything is okay."

???

"I don't know, purr or something."

???

"It means making soothing noises." Glitch made a soft hum and Roan said, "Yes, do that." When he was gone, Roan paced the room, stepping over the two other prisoners who hadn't budged from the floor. They were both so similar in size and appearance—small, greasy black hair and dark hooded eyes—that they could have been brothers. Neither said a word as Roan looked them over.

"You're like a sorcerer," the big man said. "Can you whip up some magic to get us out of here?"

"No. I don't think I have anything that'll do more than scorch this metal. And they have my spell book." Glumly, he went to sit down next to Jarrod. At the moment, he was out of ideas. Glancing over, he saw the hulking man, sitting calmly with his long legs stretched out in front of him. He seemed at home in the jail…as this wasn't his first time in one.

Roan asked him, "Do you think they'll keep us here long?"

The man shrugged beefy shoulders before saying, "It depends, what did you do?"

"We didn't do anything," Jarrod answered. "You see, we've got this guy after us. He's sort of a big shot in the real…" Roan elbowed him. "Right, sorry. It's a long story. What about you? What did you do?"

"I just killed some guys," he said with another shrug as if it was no big deal. "They had it coming, though. They looked at me all weird. You know what I'm saying, right? You mess with the bull you will get the horns and that's a promise."

Roan put aside the very casual way he discussed murder and said, "You don't seem too concerned. Can you get out of here by clocking out or something?"

The man laughed, a great ringing sound. "I wish. That would make things a lot simpler. I mean, yeah, you can clock out, but when you clock back in, you'd be right back here. The only way to get out of here is to start your character completely over, but I'm seventh level and it took me a long time to get here. I don't want to throw that all away. No, you just have to wait and hope that they need you for something."

"Like what?"

"Like I heard the horns and all the running around. There's a battle coming and they'll need someone to do their fighting for them. The king here is a real pussy. He barely keeps any fighters on the payroll. He thinks his river will keep him safe, but he's about to learn a lesson if you ask me. Hey, maybe I can spring you guys when they come for me."

Roan gave Marshall a look. He shrugged one shoulder. "I guess that would work," Roan said. "Hey, do you happen to know anything about the king? Where he's from or what his name is?"

"I don't know. It's Salazar something. Like Salazar the Conqueror or something. But where he's from? Are you talking like where he's from on the other side?" Roan nodded and the big man gave him a hard look. "Trying to find out about who people are on the other side isn't cool, man. That's some crap if you ask me."

And this was coming from an admitted murderer! Once more, this new world threw Roan for a loop.

The question killed the conversation and the men in the cell sat in a mind-dulling silence for over an hour before they heard the creak of a door opening and the odd crunch of metal covered boots striding on stone. A man in shining platemail was preceded by three soldiers bearing torches. The man in the fancy armor was tall and broad with piercing black eyes and grey in his hair. The fact that he wasn't a young man made Roan think that he was playing as himself.

"I hear you are asking a bunch of questions concerning me," the man said, speaking softly as his eyes took in his prisoners.

"Are you King Salazar?" Roan asked. When the man nodded, Roan answered, honestly, "Yes, we have. And we have more questions for you."

Salazar's dark eyes went to squints. "And what pray tell would compel me to answer these questions?"

Roan stood and came right up to the bars and said in a whisper, "Because you're being investigated as a person of interest in a number of murders."

"What? What are you talking about? What murders?"

"Does Greg Nelson ring a bell?" Salazar knew the name. Roan could see it register on his face. "How do you know him?"

"I-I don't know him," Salazar said. "I read about his suicide…wait that was a suicide. What the hell are you trying to pull here?"

Before Roan could answer, the hulking man leapt up. "They were asking about you, your highness," he said, pushing Roan aside and grabbing the bars with both of his huge hands. "They wanted to know where you're from, in the real world, but I wouldn't tell them anything."

"This is…this is…" Salazar looked lost and was blinking rapidly. "This is messed up. I don't know who you are, but you might as well clock out now, because you will never get out of that cage."

He turned and started striding away. "Stop!" Roan demanded, sounding not like an elf but like an FBI agent. The King of Ellisbar paused and glanced over his shoulder as Roan went on, speaking to him as though their positions were reversed, as though he was the one with all the power and Salazar was the prisoner.

"This is an FBI investigation and you will be charged with obstruction if you walk away. If you leave us here, I will clock out and when I clock back in, you will be the focus of more than just one agent. You will have the full force of the US Government on your ass and we'll make that little orc army look like a bunch of children playing in a sandbox. Trust me."

(*XP -10*) Roan ignored the words floating in his vision and stared hard at the king until the man threw his hands in the air and cried, "But I didn't do anything."

"We'll decide that. If you wish to verify our credentials, please call the New York field office and ask for Special Agent in Charge Mike Caron. He'll confirm our identities. I am Supervisory Special Agent, Daniel Roan. These two gentlemen are Forensic Examiners Jarrod Maddox and Marshall Mutch, and the woman you have in custody is Agent Amanda Waterfall."

"But…this is ridiculous. Do I need a lawyer?"

Roan shook his head. "Not to verify our real identities. After that it's up to you. If you keep us locked up, you will definitely need a lawyer, and I will advise you that lying to the FBI in either world is a crime."

"Son of a bi…" the king said, clocking out in mid-curse.

Roan clocked out a second later, waking up in the basement of the FBI field office and jumping to his feet, startling Mrs. Niederer. "Hi. Can't talk," he said, racing past her and rushing up the stairs. His first stop was the front desk where the incoming calls were taken.

He had no idea what he looked like with the neural coupler still on his head, but the receptionist raised an eyebrow as he breathlessly demanded, "If Agent Caron gets a call, I need you set up a trace on it." She gave him a curt nod and he was off running again, heading to Caron's office.

When Caron saw him, he began shaking his head. "No. Twenty-seven hundred dollars for what? For some imaginary cinnamon? I can't authorize that."

"Oh, right, Korrin." Roan didn't know what to do about her just then. He had hurt her livelihood, but at the same time, she was the reason they were jailed. "Let's put a pin in that for now. We've managed to score an interview of sorts with the King of

Ellisbar. He should be calling you any minute and I've asked the front desk to start a trace."

"I can't believe my job has come to this," Caron said, sighing. "But, hell, we don't have any other leads. Cole is off the radar, Arching is a ghost and *Infinite Reality* is basically untouchable. We've come up with zilch on the company. So, I guess I have to talk to some guy who thinks he's a king. Should I call him 'Your Highness?' or..."

His intercom buzzed. "Mr. Caron? We have Agent Roan's call on the line. Trace says they need another minute."

Caron thanked her, waited thirty seconds, and then picked up the phone. "This is Special Agent in Charge Caron, how may I help...hold on, who is this? Max Canez. Okay Max, what can I do for you?"

They spoke for a few minutes and as they did, Caron turned his computer monitor towards Roan and clicked over to a display of the trace. Max's address came up in a San Diego suburb. A second later they had his driver's license pulled up, his social security number, his place of employment and more. None of it seemed in the least bit out of place—but they would still look.

"Here's what's going to happen, Max. I want you to release my people and accommodate them in any way possible. Then I'm going to send a few agents to interview you...no, I can't discuss the nature of the investigation. Yes, you can have a lawyer present. No, that's okay we have your address already."

Caron hung up and said, "For a king, he seems very high strung."

"I'm going to need some money," Roan said. "And not for that woman."

"First off, no. Second, I thought there were dragons on the other side," Caron said. "From what I know about dragons, they have all the gold you will ever need. Take it from them."

Chapter 12
—Riverport, Daggerland

Roan and Salazar returned at about the same time and the king immediately began to pace back and forth. "I can't believe this is happening. I didn't do anything wrong."

"Perhaps," Roan said. "Now, if you'll release us."

Salazar gestured to one of the guards and as the man worked the key in the lock, Salazar said, "You have to tell me what's going on. Because, I really didn't do anything. I mean I'm just playing the game here."

"Do you know Atticus Arching?"

His dark eyes bulged. "*The* Atticus Arching, wow, no. I only know what I've seen on TV."

"Do you know what name he uses here?" Salazar shook his head and Roan followed up with, "Okay, what about a man named Tim Cole? Greg Nelson, Christine Carson?" He shook his head to each name. "What about Gethahyme, Master of the Red Wizards?"

"I've heard of him," Salazar said, speaking quickly. "He has a citadel called Mendenome. It's about three days' ride south of here beyond the Orc-back Mountains. If you want to know about Gethahyme that's the place to go."

Jarrod groaned. "Back south? Tell me we've got some cash for some horses, and other gear?"

"It all depends on how accommodating our host will to be," Roan said, looking pointedly at Salazar.

The king jumped a little and then nodded, agreeably. "Of course, anything I can do. I just want this cleared up as fast as possible."

He made good on his word and had them released in no time, and, as it was the middle of the night in Daggerland, he set them up with rooms in his home. It wasn't exactly a grand castle and it couldn't compare to the artistry found in the elven village, but it was a fine stone home with wide staircases and soft beds and warm breezes that were marred only by the sound of the orcs. They were on the other side of the river, hammering and sawing away at some sort of project. Every once in a while, they would scream a curse across the water

When Amanda entered her room, she went right to the window and gazed out into the night. The eastern portion of the river was just visible. "When will they attack? Do you think it'll be tonight?" Roan had followed her in and came to stand beside her. He had to fight the urge to put his arm around her.

"I really don't know much about this sort of medieval warfare. I think the best I can give you is a definitive maybe. If I were them, I'd attack as soon as possible and I'd attack at night."

She looked up at him. "Shouldn't we get out of here, then? We've talked with the king and I'm pretty sure he's not Arching in disguise. We don't really have much more reason to hang around."

"I think we should stay. The orcs have been on the move longer than we have, and they had to have lost quite a number going against the elves. Salazar can't be too much of a pushover or they would've attacked him long before now. I'm betting that things will go badly for the orcs, forcing Arching to put in an appearance. He'll probably beat us, but at least we'll have a face and maybe a name. Once we have that, we'll be able to move on him no matter where he is in Daggerland."

"I guess that makes sense…I just don't want to die again if I can help it." She shivered at the thought and now Roan did put his arm around her. It was wrong and stupid, and he couldn't help it. And he couldn't help the first kiss or the second one.

!!!

Glitch's warning came just in time. Jarrod walked in a second later just as the two separated. The rogue walked to the window and pointed. Roan cut him off before he could start to complain. "We're staying for now, but I do want our bags packed and ready to go. Figure out who's in charge and make sure we have all of our adventuring gear ready. We'll need new swords, more arrows and horses. Got it?"

"You want all that done tonight?"

"Yes. Have Marshall help you if you need it." Before he left, Jarrod looked in Amanda's direction as if to ask *what about her?* "We have spells to prepare," Roan said in reply to the look. They actually couldn't. They were both too exhausted to make the attempt.

Once more Glitch stayed in Amanda's room while Roan slept alone next door. He slept deeply despite the drums that began pounding just after one in the morning. They were incessant, however he was so tired that they lulled him into an even deeper sleep than he had been in.

Amazingly, he was able to sleep until almost seven in the morning before Glitch woke him in frightened excitement, flashing and wobbling in the air. "Let's see what's got you all crazy," Roan said. The elemental showed him a picture of a strange crude house sitting on roughly hewn wooden wheels. There was what looked like a tree trunk slung on thick hemp rope under its roof. "What is that? Is that a ram?" Glitch spun once, meaning: *Yes!*

Roan went to the window but the river was hidden by an impenetrable smoky haze; it stank of rot, as if the orcs were burning corpses pulled from a cemetery. "You saw the ram yourself?" Glitch spun once more. "Okay. What about the bridge? Did they make a new span, or repair it in anyway?" Glitch wobbled in air. "You don't know...okay, are they still working, now?" One more spin. "Then we still have a little time. Are the others awake?"

Glitch showed an image of Amanda sitting in the middle of her bed with her eyes closed and her hands clasped. She was mediating or praying, or doing whatever it was clerics did to gain their spells on a daily basis.

"And the others?"

??? Glitch replied and then puffed out of the room.

While it was gone, Roan went to the door of his room and looked out, hoping to see anyone associated with the castle. As a wizard, he couldn't simply pray for his spells, he had to study them and he couldn't do that without his spell book and the last time he had seen his spell book, it was in his room at the inn the night before.

"Well, there you go, Jarrod," he said as he saw his pack sitting just to the side of the door. Propped up next to it were his longbow and quiver. There were only three arrows rattling around in it. "Almost," he sighed. "But as long as I have my book, we'll be in business."

It was with an addict's eagerness that he opened the pack, pushed aside his newly cleaned outfit and saw his spell book. Grabbing it, he dug for the odd ingredients for the various spells and rushed to the desk—without his spells, he felt empty and weak, and as the magic flooded into him, filling his mind with their power, he found himself grinning.

He prepared four cantrips, all of which were *Fire Bolts.* He had two tier one slots, both of which he filled with *Thunderous Wave* spells. And now that he was a third level wizard, he could prepare a tier two spell. There was only one problem—he didn't know any. Instead, he prepared another tier one spell: *Lightning Summoning(lesser)*.

At some point Glitch came back and sat in the air above Roan and it was some time before he realized that the little creature was there. "Are Jarrod and Marshall ready?" One quick spin was followed by an odd wobble. "Are you saying they're sort of ready?" Glitch spun once.

Roan stood and stretched, facing the window once more, but this time facing the world as a real wizard.

The smoke on the water was thicker than it had been, and the sun was only a silver disk that could barely be seen through it all. Gradually, the smoke slipped towards them. "Rrrrrr," Glitch said.

"You can speak?" It answered in a wobble. "Okay, can you speak a little?"

It spun and hissed like a snake, "Sssss."

"What? Did you just say, yes?"

Glitch spun again, once more hissing, "Sssss."

"Well, that's pretty cool," Roan said. Glitch agreed, spinning. It was a quick spin, however. The ugly smoke across the water drew their attention. "I don't like it either. I wish I knew a spell that would blow it back. Hey, you're an elemental, can you blow it back?"

Glitch puffed up as large as it could and blew into Roan's face with all the force of a child blowing out the candles on a birthday cake. "I guess not," Roan said.

"You guess not what?" Amanda asked, from the doorway. She was dressed for battle: beneath the tattered remains of her cloak, she wore her breast plate and across her back were her long bow and quiver. Although she was dressed for war, there was fear in her wide elven eyes.

"Glitch isn't strong enough to blow away the smoke. It was just an idea."

"Hey, speaking of a good idea," Jarrod said, coming up behind Amanda and tapping on the door. He had on his metal-studded leather armor, while behind him stood Marshall looking very thick in his mail. Jarrod went on, "The bridges are still intact on the west side. Sooooo, if we wanted to we could take off."

Roan shook his head. "No. We knew going against Arching on this side was going to be tough, and we weren't wrong. Let's go find Salazar and see what sort of help he can give us." Roan expected to find him in much the same mood as he had left him the night before, however Salazar was every bit the king with his imperious look, his shining mail, and his sable cloak.

He stood at the wall overlooking the remains of his two eastern bridges. Around him were soldiers in chainmail and adventurers who were obvious in their fine cloaks, their tall boots, their gilded scabbards and embossed shields. Compared to them, Roan's group looked like low-rent noobs.

Salazar ignored them as he and the other more experienced adventurers discussed how they thought the battle would unwind. It seemed straightforward to Roan: the orcs would bring bridging equipment up to the walls, then they would use the rams to try to bash down the gates and, if they had the equipment, they would try to scale the walls with ladders and ropes.

The key to victory on both sides would be to have more force at the point of attack than their enemy.

"Excuse me, Salazar?"

"It's *King* Salazar," he answered, glaring. He asked the adventurers to give him a moment before he pulled Roan aside. "Look, I have talked with my lawyer. From what he tells me, you and those other agents are on a fishing expedition. Let me save you some time: I didn't do anything wrong either here or on the other side and there's no way an obstruction charge on this side will stand up in court, so why don't you and your friends get the hell out of here. I don't need the hassle."

He started to turn away when Roan grabbed him. "Look, we're not fishing. There have been four murders associated with the game. Real life murders of people who were playing the game when they were killed."

"That's just an urban myth. It can't happen."

"Oh, yeah it can," Jarrod said, bobbing his head up and down. "We have it on video. It's authentic, trust me, and it's sick. This one guy killed himself by burning down his…" When he saw Roan's look, Jarrod shut his mouth with a click.

Salazar didn't notice. His focus was on something else entirely. "That's real? So, does that mean the government is thinking of shutting down the game?"

"That's what you're worried about?" Amanda asked. "There are more important things than just a game. I'm sorry to say, but your life may be in danger Mr. Canez."

Unexpectedly, he laughed aloud. "I'm not afraid of death, my lady. I've played this game on extreme for eleven years and in that time, I have died twenty-three times. I've been stabbed, poisoned, bludgeoned and eaten alive by a cave troll. So, no, I'm not afraid. The only thing I'm afraid of losing is the game. Tell me what I can do to keep that from happening."

"I need to know who's behind this attack," Roan said. "And if it is at all possible, I want to take that person alive."

"I don't know who it is," Salazar said. "I consulted my court seer early this morning and he picked up only fragments of information. The orcs are from the Pits of the Black Hand, that was easy, but who is controlling them, was more difficult. All he got was that someone with a lot of juice has come up from the south. He said he could feel his power without even trying, like it was radiating out of him."

Roan closed his eyes but couldn't feel a thing. "I take it that's not normal."

Salazar looked at Roan as if he were looking at a touched-in-the-head five-year-old. "No, it's not normal. It's very far from normal. It's *singular* if you ask me. That's what scares me, my lady. Trolls, ogres, hordes of orcs, all of these can be killed." He patted the hilt of his sword as he said this. "But there are beings in this world that defy the imagination. Gods and demon princes and creatures so strange that you would think they were alien. Those scare me."

"So, we run away, right?" Amanda asked. Roan looked to Salazar, who shook his head.

"This is my land and these are my people. I'm fighting and if you want answers, then you should as well."

2—

Although Roan suggested that Amanda ride west with Glitch, she wouldn't leave. She set her jaw and became so quietly focused that it was unnerving. Jarrod and Roan were given new swords and they all received more arrows than they could carry.

A soldier guided them to a place on the wall, though with the smoke lying like a choking fog covering everything, it was hard to tell where they stood in relationship to the two downed bridges. The only thing Roan knew for certain was that the action started around midday, and he only knew that because the sun, that little silver disc, was directly overhead.

On the wall itself, he could barely make out the men and women to their left and right.

The fight started when the drums went dead silent and the only thing that could be heard was the soft sigh of the smoke rolling across the river.

For a long minute, the soldiers on the wall held their breath, waiting to see what would happen and what was coming. Roan did not like the idea of waiting to be attacked. He sent Glitch across to the other side of the river to see what was coming. The little creature was the only being there not affected by the smoke. It naturally repelled the smoke, so that it was visible after a fashion as a moving pocket of clean air.

Glitch was back quickly, screaming in Roan's head *!!! !!!* Along with the scream came a picture of orcs massed on wide, flat-bottomed boats, using long poles to heave themselves towards the wall.

"Boats in the water!" Roan yelled. "Dead ahead."

With the smoke so thick around them, he was about to set aside his bow and draw his sword when the smoke was suddenly blown back towards the far side of the river, exposing forty of the barges. It was a magical wind created by a wizard with silk black hair and long red robes. The man stood with his arms outstretched and wherever he faced, a powerful wind swept down from him.

Roan wasted no time firing his first arrow. His elven fingers seemed to know precisely how to shoot and after only his second shot he saw words at the bottom of his vision (*XP +30*)

Congratulations! You are now a Level Four Wizard and have gained the following bonuses:

Increased Hit Points(+6)

Attack +1

You can fill +1 Tier one spell per day

You can fill +1 Tier two spell per day

You have +6 skill points to allocate

You have +1 to add to any one ability score. In a flash, he took in his character:

Character Name: Roan
Class & Level: Wizard - Level 4
Race: High Elf

Alignment: Chaotic Good
Experience Points: **6,029**   XP To Next Level: **2,971**

Strength – Dexterity – Constitution
S: **15(+2)**   D: **16(+3)**   C: **16(+3)**

Intelligence – Wisdom – Charisma
I: **17(+3)**   W: **16(+3)**   C: **16(+3)**

Armor: 10(13)   **Hit Points: 29**
Initiative: +3   **Speed: 13**
SAVING THROWS: Will: 7   Fortitude: 4   Reflex: 4

GOLD: 10

-EQUIPMENT-

Weapons
Longbow
Long Sword

Armor
None

Magic

Spell Book
Flask of Holy Water

Misc
Quiver * Arrows x60
Backpack * Rations x1
Tinder Box * Waterskin
Pouches x2

† Spells Known †

Cantrips: Minor Illusion, Fire Bolt, Ray of Ice, Electric Hand, Acid Spray
Tier 1 Spells: Summon Familiar, Flame Blast, Lightning Summoning(lesser), Instant Slumber, Thunderous Wave, Illusion(minor), Charm(minor)
Tier 2 Spells:
Tier 3 Spells:

† Spells Prepared †

Cantrips: Fire Bolt x4
Tier 1 Spells: Thunderous Wave, Lightning Summoning(lesser)
Tier 2 Spells:
Tier 3 Spells:

Attacks

Name - ATK Bonus – Damage		
Longbow	+5	1-8
Long Sword	+4	1-8+2

Abilities
Spell Casting
Low-Light Vision
Skills
Listen: +6, Spot: +6, Knowledge: +6, Search: +6, Spell Craft: +6

Roan had twelve skill points to allocate as well as an attribute point, but with the orcs heading right at him, grunting or screaming, working the poles as fast as they could, he couldn't spare a second. "Go for the guys with the poles!" he yelled, letting loose another arrow. Along with his little squad, there were maybe twenty archers on that stretch of the wall. They raked the deck of the first boat, taking out the orcs propelling it along. They then turned their bows on the next boat. In minutes, the closest three barges lost steerage and faltered as the experience points rang up in Roan's vision like he was playing an arcade game.

In fact, the entire attack on that part of the wall seemed to stall before it even got started. Unfortunately, their defense hinged on the one sorcerer controlling the wind and there was no way he was going to go unchallenged for long.

Out of the smoking sky dropped an elf with velvet, ebony skin and eyes that glittered like a beetle's. He wore a robe of the deepest green that was etched in threads of gold. The dark elf landed on the nearest barge, the green cloak flaring all around him as he lifted his right hand and shot a huge gout of fire across the intervening river at the sorcerer who screamed and fell back, his red robes burning.

"Get him!" Roan yelled, aiming his bow at the green-robed wizard. Twenty arrows from up and down the wall flashed through the air, aimed at the one elf—all twenty arrows missed. "What the hell?" Roan asked, looking at his bow. He could swear that his arrow turned in mid-air and that meant… "It's a spell! Don't waste your arrows." Roan turned to his team. "We'll have to take him out."

Jarrod choked back a curse. "No way. He's at least ninth level. We'll get murdered out there. I know I'm not…"

Marshall put a steel-gloved hand on his shoulder. "Look. It doesn't matter, he's gone." The smoke was pouring back over the river covering the barge, which was barren except for the corpses of a few orcs.

There were more orcs and more boats coming. "Archers at the ready!" Roan bellowed. For about a minute, the smoke was light enough for them to be able to use their bows effectively and they poured in a deadly and effective fire from the walls—

then the smoke closed in and they couldn't see more than five feet in front of their faces.

They could hear the boats thump against the walls and the hammers and picks of the orcs as they attacked the wall. Some of the men shot blindly, while others slowly backed away. "We need another wizard!" someone yelled.

Roan looked around, hoping to see a wizard flying down to save them. When one didn't come, he realized that he would have to fill the void—somehow.

"Glitch, can you do anything?"

The air elemental spun in a little circle and was able to whip the smoke about clearing an area of about eight or nine feet. It would have to do. "To the boat, Glitch." He pointed and the familiar spun down, allowing them to see the orcs on the boat below them who became sitting ducks for their bows. Their arrows piled the bodies against the wall, but it couldn't last. Glitch was already tiring.

"Wait here," he said to his team. Laying aside his bow and quiver, he leapt from the wall. He dropped twelve feet down to the closest barge, which suddenly lifted beneath him as more orcs jumped over to the boat he was on, changing the center of gravity.

"Eda-eram gdiy!" Roan roared, sending out a shockwave of sound from his hand. The noise was like a bomb blast and the power of the spell sent eleven orcs tumbling into the river and temporarily cleared the area around Roan of smoke. As the weight fell from the other side of the boat, his side dropped, nearly sending him into the churning, corpse-filled water.

He was on his hands and knees trying to find his footing when the boat lifted yet again. There were more orcs coming. It seemed to Roan as if there was an endless number of them, as if the earth was vomiting them up just across the river. He tried to stand, but the boat was tipping too far and instead, he found himself clinging to the edge as the boat gradually went vertical.

Across from him, the orcs were panicking, crawling all over themselves to find a hold on the boat, but their weight was too much and the wooden platform flipped. Roan was thrown amongst the heavily weighed down orcs, who could not swim in their armor.

With the smoke and the screams and blood and the flailing arms, panic had Roan in its firm grip until he found a hold on the edge of a boat. Next to him was a panting orc, red water running from its bedraggled head. It had lost its sword, however it had a dagger, the hilt of which was inches away.

Before the orc even knew that an elf was next to it, Roan grabbed the dagger and stabbed it in the base of the skull(*XP +35*). He had seen so many of these little words that he had lost track, and with an orc standing above him, he ignored these ones as well.

He tried to stab it in the foot, only the blade turned on the metal of its boot. For a moment, the orc didn't know what had banged into its foot, but when it saw Roan it let out a cry and swung a rusted scimitar. Roan pushed back from the boat and the sword missed. Unbalanced, the orc fell into the river and immediately began flailing.

Now that Roan had room to swim, he wasn't frightened in the least. He swam up to the orc and stuck the dagger in its neck and then moved away again as the thing bubbled below the surface. Unexpectedly a mailed hand grabbed his shirt and heaved him up. He was mostly out of the water and scrambling for his sword when he realized that it was Marshall!

His team had jumped down from the wall onto one of the barges. They were strange and ghostly figures in the smoke. As they swung their swords, there would be a flash of silver and then the clouds would swirl again hiding them. Amanda nearly took his head off as he got too close.

"Get to the corners!" Roan yelled. "And keep up the chatter. If things get too hot, I want to hear about it."

"Things have been way too hot from the get-go!" Jarrod cried. "Why the hell did we come down here?"

This section of the river was starting to get clogged with boats and now the braver orcs could leap from one boat to the next. There weren't too many who were brave enough to leap to a boat with elves swinging swords all about. When they landed on the shifting platform, they were at a distinct disadvantage and eight were killed before one of them saw a pole floating in the water. He started to heave an overloaded boat closer to Roan's, where the orcs would have a five to one advantage.

"Eda-eram gdiy!" Roan said, speaking the magic out of his soul. The sound wave sent half of them spinning into the water and concussed the other half, who were dazed as Roan, followed by Marshall and Amanda, jumped across and began hacking into them. So fierce was their attack that a few of the orcs chose the water to a certain death from their blades(*XP +35*), (*XP +35*), (*XP +35*)...

Roan was just about to congratulate his team when Amanda said, "You're bleeding."

He looked down and saw that he had a hunk of rusted metal sticking out of his leg. "Huh? When did that happen?"

"It doesn't matter," she said, unceremoniously yanking it out. Although he hadn't felt it before, it hurt like a bitch coming out. "Stop your whining," she said and then said a word that seemed to slip past his ears without sticking in his mind. A moment later her hand glowed blue and the pain was gone.

"Where is everyone else..." she started to ask when a huge thudding noise, followed by a spray of water stopped her. The river and the corpses and the floating arrows lifted in a swell. Even the smoke broke around what was coming—to Roan, it seemed as though a giant was coming for them.

It was over nine feet tall with a chest as wide as Roan could stretch. It was had huge sloping shoulders, long arms and was grey fleshed with pustules and sores covering it except where unkempt tufts of patchy greasy hair grew. Even more than its height and girth, what struck Roan with horror was its huge maw. Its lower jaw was the size of a bucket and the tusks within it were disproportionately huge.

"Ogre," Marshall whispered as it leapt across to the next closest raft. When it landed, its weight was so great that water rushed across the rough boards to cover his feet.

As shocked as he was by the creature, Roan saw his chance. He raised a hand: "Buda-aya-tien!" He had never used the spell: *Lightning Summoning(lesser)* before and jerked as the smoke surrounding them was rent with white flame, forked and hot. The air sizzled as the lightning slammed into the ogre. It flung out its long arms and stood frozen for a few seconds before it fell to its knees with a groan.

"Get him!" Marshall yelled and jumped to the next boat, hacking hard at the beast. Amanda followed right behind him, stabbing the thing and drawing sluggish black blood. It took a backhanded swipe at her and knocked her ten feet through the air.

Roan was moving even before the blow landed. He saw what was going to happen and even with his quick reactions, he nearly missed her as she sunk beneath the surface of the river. With Glitch screaming in his ear, he dove in after her and saw in the murk only a bit of her flowing golden hair and a glint from her armor. Flailing after her, he managed to snag the edge of her buckler.

He hauled her up by it until she was sputtering above the surface and trying to get onto the boat.

Once safe, he took in his little section of the battle. On the plus side, the ogre was dead and the orcs were holding back. On the negative side, his team was practically exhausted, his spells mostly spent, and worse, the orcs were holding back for a reason. The smoke was breaking up and in the light mists that lingered they saw a figure in black mail stepping lightly from boat to boat. When he got close, they saw it was Tim Cole.

"What a coincidence running into you here, Law-dog," Cole said.

Roan scrambled back onto the flat-bottomed boat. "I don't believe it's a coincidence at all. I believe that you are working with Arching to keep the FBI out of Daggerland."

Cole shrugged his broad shoulders and then made a show of pulling his sword from its scabbard. The blade was huge, four inches wide at the hilt and easily five feet long. He swished the air with it as he said, "I guess it's not what you believe, but what you can prove and you can't prove nothing."

Cole wasn't wrong and they all knew it. "Oh, and before I kill you, *again*. I wanted to let you know that your interfering friend, Fulbright is dead."

Suddenly, Roan had something more to fear than being dismembered by Cole's giant sword. "What? Are you talking about in the real world?"

"Of course," Cole said. "After Nelson barbecued himself, Fulbright was too much of a chicken to come here, but it didn't save him from getting his head bashed in with a fire-poker. Oh, and before you ask, no, I don't have much of an alibi. I was here, chasing after you."

"No alibi and yet you don't seem too concerned, Cole, why is that?" Roan was afraid that he knew the answer already.

Again, Cole swished the sword back and forth, a grin on his face as he enjoyed the moment. "Because the mean ol' bad guy who did such an atrocious thing is already caught. Hell, he even turned himself in and confessed. You know him. It was that jack-wad of an elf, Leomagnus the Golden, only now we can call him Leomagnus the Felon or maybe Leomagnus the Murderer. Sad, isn't it? It sort of makes you want to pack it up and go back to the real world before someone comes after you as well."

"We won't be scared off so easily," Amanda said. Seeing an orc sword, she stooped to pick it up.

At the sight of her, Cole threw back his head and laughed. "You are a riot. Who's trying to scare you off? I'm going to kill you, here and now, and if you come back, *someone* is going to kill you on the other side. These are simple facts. They are not threats."

"Is it Arching?" Roan asked. Instead of answering, Cole only raised an eyebrow as if to say: maybe. "Do you know where he is?" Now he shrugged. "I don't get you," Roan said, his aggravation growing. "Don't you realize how much you have to lose on the other side?"

"It's nothing compared to what I have to gain here," Cole said, with a gesture at the town behind Roan. "Riverport is mine for the taking."

As if the words had summoned him, Salazar, King of Ellisbar appeared at the top of the wall. "I think I might have something to say about that," he said, before jumping from the wall, flying over two of the boats and landing on the one Marshall was on. Salazar's sword was even bigger than Cole's and when he pulled it out, it pulsed with light. "I have to say, I don't like your chances, Aderon."

Cole had been helmetless, but from somewhere he fished out a jet-black helmet that matched his armor. "We'll see. You little kiddies better scoot back to the other side. And, if you were smart, you'd stay there."

Roan started to look for a sword, but Jarrod shook his head. "This is beyond us." It sure seemed that way. Neither man was any bigger than Roan, at least on the other side, but here, they wore their sixty pounds of steel as if it were six ounces of feathers. And the way they swung their swords was nothing short of intimidating.

That intimidation grew worse, however when Cole suddenly jumped across to the next boat, coming down with a sword strike that sounded like a wrecking ball as it hit Salazar's shield. The king went to one knee, and yet, his shield was unmarred by the blow; he quickly righted himself and struck with his own sword.

The fight was terrific as well as horrifying. Roan quickly realized there was no way the four of them could have beaten Cole on their own. He was far too strong and amazingly fast, and he could take more punishment than three bulls put together.

Still, Salazar was better. He drew first blood and did not let up for a second. He harried and harassed Cole, nicking him over and over, driving him across the river, almost to the other side.

And yet, as good a fighter as he was, he was just one man and there was still most of the orc army left to fight. They covered the far bank, and there were other creatures besides the common orc. There were companies of ogres, a scattering of dark elves, and sixty strange baboon-looking beasts who wore armor but still chattered like apes. There was even an actual sixteen-foot giant wearing the skins of a dozen wildebeests, or so Roan supposed. The giant, a tree trunk-sized club resting on one shoulder, watched Cole lose the fight with a slack jaw.

Although he lost the fight, Cole was not killed. Grumbling, he retreated from boat to boat and then to the shore where he disappeared into his army who closed ranks around him. He was taller than the orcs and they could see him signal to something more horrid than all the rest combined. It was a monster that could only have come from the deepest pits in Hell. It was seven-foot tall and made only from bone and rotting flesh. There was a cancerous presence about it. Even from across the river, the sight of it made Roan's bones go cold right down to the marrow.

As they watched, the thing blew onto its skeletal fingers and as its breath passed over the bare bones, it turned into the same foul-smelling smoke they'd been dealing with all morning. In no time, the smoke had covered the ranks of orcs.

"Get back to the wall," Salazar ordered Roan and his team. They retreated before the oncoming smoke and climbed up ropes that had been thrown down from the battlements. At the top, Amanda saw that the king was injured and offered to heal him, only he turned her down, saying, "You will probably need your spells long before I do."

He turned from them and stared out at the smoke—the top of giant's head could be seen above it. "This is insane. People are really getting killed over a game? That's not what this is supposed to be about. Who was this guy, Fulbright? The name sounds familiar."

"Greyson Fulbright," Marshall said. "He was the fifth richest man in the world and an original investor in *Infinite Reality*."

"And *he* was murdered?" Salazar asked. "I don't understand people sometimes. I used to think that so many people played evil characters on this side so that they could experience the opposite of what they are on the other, but now, I don't know. Maybe people really are just evil."

They were quiet for a time as the smoke advanced. Roan was antsy and didn't like just standing there. "We should go after that bone creature. Without the smoke, we have a fighting chance. If you neutralize Cole and maybe send in some adventurers to deal with the giant and the dark elves, my team will go after that thing, whatever it was."

"No, you're still too weak. It would eat you alive, perhaps literally. And we're not leaving the walls again. Our only chance is to hold for as long as possible. Thankfully, the way west is still wide open. We have to buy time for the women and children to escape."

"But you beat Cole pretty handily," Amanda said, looking confused. "You don't think we have a chance?"

"None at all. That demon could only have been summoned by a very powerful wizard. At least twentieth level, but probably higher. Our true adversary has yet to show his face."

2—

Because of the ingenuity and the determination of the people of Riverport, the second part of the battle was slow to recommence. Desperate to save their town and their lives, every manner of fan and windmill was constructed. Sails were taken from the few remaining boats, sheets were pulled from beds, and tapestries were yanked down from walls.

With every single animal already encumbered with goods and being driven west along with the non-combatants, the working of the thrown-together fans was left to the humans who pushed and pulled and pedaled the fans into motion, slowly moving the air eastward where it was met by a gentle wind pushing the reeking smoke at them.

In places, the fans were less effective and that was where the heaviest fighting took place. The screams and explosions and the battle cries could be heard all over the city. Roan and Amanda, along with a couple of dozen other spell casters, were kept out of the fighting as they tried to recover their strength.

They were sent to an inn a hundred yards from the wall and each went to a room to lie down. As usual, Glitch went with Amanda. Although the bed was soft enough, Roan didn't think he would be able to rest. His nerves jangled ceaselessly as he worried over what the correct course of action was for them. Should they stay and fight or should they flee? And if they did run away, should they go to the west or did they go with Jarrod's suggestion: "We should clock the hell out of here!"

A part of Roan wanted to go back to the real world and be done with all of it, only that was exactly what Arching wanted them to do. And if they did, there was a good chance that when they went back to the real world, Caron would pull them from the assignment.

"Maybe not a *good* chance," Roan mumbled. "He is a stubborn son of a bitch. He might keep us here out of spite or out of…" A yawn gaped his mouth and, despite his worry over his teammates and what was going on in the real world, Roan somehow fell asleep seconds later. He slept so deeply that he didn't hear the fireballs exploding among the massed orcs, or the lightning bolts arcing into the defenders, or the booming crashes as the giant waded across the river and plied his club against the walls.

"Roan! Roan, get up. Part of the wall has fallen." It was Amanda, shaking him. Although he had slept for three hours, he sat up, coming instantly awake as if he hadn't been asleep at all. It was a strange sensation.

"Come on," Amanda said. "We have to go. We're falling back; the king is shortening his lines." When he was upright, she thrust his backpack, a new sword, his old bow, and a full quiver into his hands. She turned to go only to stop short. Thrusting a hand into her breastplate, she pulled out a sheath of rolled paper. "Oh, and take these. They're magic scrolls of some sort. Marshall got them off that ogre we killed right before Cole showed up."

He glanced down at the rolled papers, but didn't have time to look them over as Amanda was already hauling him along down a crowded hallway. They pushed their way out the back door of the inn, where they were joined by hundreds of others heading to the center of the island where a wide boulevard was being transformed into a defensive line.

Piles of wood and furniture, as well as garbage and uprooted trees were being heaved into the alleys and streets between the buildings to create a makeshift wall. Glitch zoomed ahead of them, finding a path through the mayhem, while behind them, coming closer and closer, was the sound of battle.

"Find an empty second floor room with a window that faces out this way, Glitch," Amanda yelled out to the little knuckle of air. It winked out of sight and then, seconds later, popped back into being right in front of them, spinning, excitedly, trying to get them to go south a block to a fine old building that dominated the street.

The two lower floors had been a marketplace where everything from ox balls to magic swords had been sold, while the upper floors were simple apartments. They raced up the main stairs to the third floor of the building where they found an east facing room that held only a rickety looking bed and a chest with its lid flung back, revealing only a single woolen sock.

"Glitch, find Marshall and Jarrod," Amanda ordered. "Tell them where we are." As it sped out the window, she turned to Roan. "Get going with those spells. We don't have a lot of time."

"Yes, ma'am," he said and saluted her as a joke. He had never seen her so stressed out. She barely cracked a smile and it didn't last as she turned to the window, where the view of the coming fight was a little too good. They could see the soldiers slowly retreating through the streets as the orcs continually tried to flank them by racing around or through the buildings. Roan could see that they were going to need all of his spells and then some.

First things first, however. "What are on these scrolls?" There were three of them and, just as Amanda had said, they were spells: *Summon Flame Elemental, Invisibility,* and *Hypnotic Flame.*

Instead of rejoicing at his luck, Roan looked at them with deepest suspicion. "Why would an ogre carry scrolls?" he muttered. "And why are they all second tier spells?" It seemed a little too on the nose for his liking. To see if the spells were legit, he opened his spell book thinking that he would compare these new spells with his old ones.

"What the hell?" he asked in astonishment. The three new spells were already in his book. "That's not how it's supposed to be." His game-acquired wizard knowledge told him that he was supposed to scribe these scrolls himself, and that it was the only way to learn them properly. Something strange was going on and he didn't like it. The smart thing to do was to ignore the new spells...

A horn sounded, blaring with brassy urgency. The lines holding back the horde were crumbling and the call for retreat was in the air. "Screw it!" Roan cried. He needed all the firepower he could get. Since he had his four cantrips ready to go, all *Fire Bolts*, he started on his on his three tier one spells, going with *Thunderous Wave* with each, breathing in the magical words as well as the ingredients.

Next, he looked at his new spells, quickly reading over each, deciding to go with *Summon Flame Elemental* and *Hypnotic Flame.* The only problem were the ingredients needed. "Where am I supposed to get poppy seeds and ash from a moonlit elm? Wait, the market. I'll be right back!" he yelled to Amanda who was already aiming her bow out the window.

He flew down the stairs, rushing right into Glitch who was coming up. "I need your help. We have to find poppy seeds and ash from a moonlit elm."

???

"Downstairs in the market, I hope. Look for any stall that sold herbs or has anything to do with magic."

A moment later, Glitch said: *!?!* into Roan's head. The marketplace was a complete mess. The venders had lit out of there with only a few minutes of notice to spare and had left behind almost as much as they had taken with them. There were piles of silk dresses and steel shields, gallons of paint and lead ingots.

There was a fortune of items just sitting there being ignored. It had virtually no value to the men and women fighting the invaders. Living past the next minute was all they cared about.

!!! Glitch said, puffing up as large as it could so Roan could see it. The elemental was hovering over an apothecary's table. Roan ran to it and saw a mess that made the rest of the place look neat. Spices, herbs, leaves, bark, earth, metal, ash, and dust was everywhere. Most of it was loose, though "wild" might have been a better word, however some was stored in tiny packets.

Since he would never be able to distinguish moonlit elm ash from any other ash, Roan concentrated on the little packets. The first two were labeled: *Birch Cinder* and *Ground Dwarf Tooth.* He tossed them aside, but then realized he was being foolish to leave the items behind. There was no telling what he would need next.

Among the refuse was a large pouch. He began filling it as he looked for his ingredients. A minute later, "Yes, here's the ash." He was about to go on looking, only a tremendous crash from the front of the building had him rethinking the idea. Instead, he grabbed two huge handfuls of the packets and stuffed them in the pouch before jumping up and running for the main stairs.

Just as he was about to zip out of there, he passed a display of hats and without breaking stride, he grabbed a forest green one that was made of very soft velvet.

"Jarrod! Catch!" he said, entering the third floor room and tossing the hat to the rogue, who was at one of the windows shooting his bow.

He snagged it, gave a glance and stuck it on his head, covering his sweat-slicked hair. "Thanks, but you want to know a better gift? Getting the hell out of Dodge. Look at it out there. We're not going to last much longer."

Roan went to the window and saw the streets were filled with roaring orcs, screaming trolls, bellowing soldiers and the strange, chattering baboon creatures. Even the giant was there. He had so many arrows poking out of him that he looked like a pin cushion.

Still, there didn't seem to be any quit in the people of Riverport. "Aim for the eyes on that giant," Roan said in answer.

Jarrod sighed and pulled back on his bow, letting it sing a moment later.

Amanda fired and then caught his eye, giving him a look and a little shake of her head. He understood—she was right there with Jarrod, it was time to consider an exit strategy. "Glitch, can you please check the western bridges? Tell me if they're still standing and what's beyond them."

The elemental sped out of there so fast that it caused Roan's long dark hair to flutter. With that, Roan went to his knees in front of his spell book and opened it to the second tier spells. Since he only had the ash, he could only prepare the *Summon Flame Elemental.* "I hope it's bigger than Glitch," he said, before opening the packet.

This spell was much more complex compared to the tier one spells and required him to draw a glyph onto his flesh using a paste made up of his saliva and the moonlit elm ash. Since he was using the same spell twice, he placed both glyphs on the inner aspect of his forearm and when he spoke the words that unleashed the spell there was an instant of agonizing, burning pain as the glyphs seared his flesh.

Not much smelled worse than burnt flesh and when the smoke lifted up in a nauseating haze, he almost gagged, but then the power of the spell filled him to such an extent that he felt like his eyes were going to pop out of his skull. "Damn," he whispered, when the preparations were done. "That was something. Okay, let's see about that giant."

3—

The giant had already been driven off by the archers and now they were going after the ogres, only just as the first few were riddled with arrows, the bone and flesh demon materialized in the very middle of the battle almost directly below their window.

A hundred arrows were fired at it and a hundred arrows riddled the ground all around it, leaving it untouched. Roan wondered what good were arrows against something that was already dead. Only magic could wound such a creature. He lifted his forearm and, touching the still smoldering glyph, he spoke foreign words. There was an instant of searing pain as flame rolled down his wrist and hand to fall with a shower of sparks at his feet.

Before him stood a creature from the elemental plane of fire. It came up to his knee and was as wide around as it was tall. In truth, it looked like a medium sized campfire, only without the logs beneath it.

"Kill," Roan said, pointing at the demon. Unlike Glitch, the fire elemental was either mindless or so alien that Roan couldn't understand its mind. However, it could understand him just fine. Without hesitation, the flame creature rushed to the window and leapt out. When it landed, sparks flew and the fire seemed to grow slightly.

With a crackling noise, it charged the demon, engulfing one of its legs. The demon growled more in anger than in pain and lifted one of its rotting hands. From its palm, a pure white mist blasted out. It was as though it had condensed a city-sized blizzard into a cone twenty feet long.

The mist swept over the elemental. There was a hissing sound and a high scream in Roan's head and then the elemental was gone. "That was quick," Roan muttered. "How the hell did…" His breath caught in his throat and his heart began to hammer in his chest as the demon turned its baleful gaze up at the building. That horrid gaze was enough to freeze him in place. It didn't need any more magic than that. The demon lifted a hand and from it shot a ball of flame as big as a Volkswagen Beetle.

It raced up to the building and Roan could do nothing but watch as it shot right at—the room next door. The ball of flame exploded with a tremendous THROOOM!

Although the flames incinerated the archers in the next room, the magical energy of the fireball wasn't like that of a bomb. The building shook, the walls cracked, and the room was blazing with an out of control fire. Despite all of this, Roan and his team were unhurt.

Jarrod had been dazed by the explosion, Amanda had been thrown from her feet and Marshall, in his heavy armor had been unmoved. They were all in shock and were slow to realize that the fire was spreading very quickly in the old building.

"Get your stuff!" Roan screamed to the others, trying to be heard over the roar of the flames. "We have to get out of here before we're trapped."

Roan lifted Amanda to her feet and began herding the others to the door where smoke was already billowing thick and black and the heat made their skin stretch across the bones of their faces. Even though a raging fire engulfed the hallway, giving a glow to the smoke, it was impossible to see anything beyond a few feet. "Glitch!" he yelled. "Where are you?"

"Sss," Glitch said in his ear.

"Oh, good, you're back. Find us a way out of here, will you? Keep us away from the fire." Roan didn't know if an air elemental could be hurt by flames or if it even knew what they were.

Spinning quickly so that Roan could see him, Glitch ducked to the left as soon as he entered the hall and then swished away into the smoke. In seconds, he had left Roan and the others behind. They were literally moving at a crawl. To keep from dying of smoke inhalation, they crawled down the hall. Still, they coughed and hacked.

Glitch came back, screaming urgently *!!!* The warning really wasn't necessary as just then something in the building gave way with a tremendous crash. Roan could feel the building groan beneath his hands. It wouldn't be long before the whole thing came down around their ears.

Thankfully, Glitch guided them straight and true to a back stairwell where they were able to get to their feet and run. They weren't the only ones who were running. It seemed as if everyone in the city was retreating west. The center hadn't held and the weak defensive line had fallen.

Chapter 14
—Riverport, Daggerland

"Was it clear across the river?" Roan asked Glitch as they fell back to King Salazar's walled-off mansion which sat on a small bluff. It had a commanding view of both the river and the last bridge across it. In his wisdom, the king had ordered the northern span demolished and now the remaining soldiers and adventurers were running for the last bridge, where some would make a last stand so that the rest could escape.

"Ssss," Glitch said, but did so with a wobble. He sent a picture into Roan's head of a dirt road that went straight west. On it were civilian stragglers: the old, the lame, and the decidedly foolish: people so loaded down with possessions that they struggled to keep up. Bringing up the rear were the wounded who limped along, leaving a trail of blood and bodies.

On either side of the road stood a thick forest that was shadowed and murky. It had been cut back so that an ambush would be less likely to succeed. The vision didn't last more than a few seconds.

"You didn't go too far?"

Glitch answered, "Oooh," which Roan took to mean: *No.*

Roan turned from the bridge, went up a short path and crossed through the gate of the king's mansion. Instead of manning the wall as many of the others were doing, Roan hurried into the building itself and ran up the stairs, searching for a west-facing window.

He found one with a pretty vine-covered balcony and went out on it. Jarrod came to stand beside him and drummed his fingers on the railing, theatrically. "Wow, what a great, great, great fricking view," Jarrod said. "Are we just going to stand here while the orcs batter down the gate or are we going to get out of here?"

"We're looking at a trap," Roan said, gesturing across the bridge at the one road. "If I were in charge of the orcs I would have concealed a force somewhere along that road. Instead of allowing us to escape, I would have turned this into a battle of annihilation. Cole might be too stupid to have thought of this, but whoever conjured that demon has to be smart enough to have seen the obvious."

"I don't know, Salazar seems pretty savvy," Jarrod said. "He's not going to walk into a trap. I bet he's got all of this scoped out somehow."

That seemed logical, but Roan had a gut reaction against taking that road. "Glitch, if there is an ambush, it'll be five to ten miles away. More than likely they'll be hiding most of their force behind a hill where they'll have the advantage of height and momentum. Find them."

"And what are we going to do while he's gone?" Jarrod asked, watching as Glitch sped away. The answer was obvious. Roan unslung his bow and moved to the opposite side of the house, where he barged into the king's own bedroom. He flung back the sash and opened a bay window—the view of the bridge and the river might have been beautiful at one time. Now, it was frightful; orcs were coming from every direction, converging on the mansion and the bridge.

"Jarrod, we're going to need more arrows," Roan said. Between them, they had maybe sixty, which would last all of three minutes. "Five thousand would be good, but I'll take any you can find. And don't dawdle."

Marshall and Amanda were already firing. From the window, it was a sixty yard shot to the bridge, but only twenty to the open grass hill in front of the wall. Roan paused before taking his shot. He had spells left, if he wanted to use them, and he still had the one ability point to add somewhere.

He stole a quick look at his character—though it was now strange to even think of himself as a "character." He had merged so completely into Daggerland that Roan the FBI agent seemed less real compared to Roan the Wizard.

Character Name: Roan
Class & Level: Wizard - Level 4
Race: High Elf
Alignment: Chaotic Good
Experience Points: **8,156**   XP To Next Level: **844**

Strength – Dexterity – Constitution
S: **15(+2)**   D: **16(+3)**   C: **16(+3)**

Intelligence – Wisdom – Charisma
I: **17(+3)**   W: **16(+3)**   C: **16(+3)**

Armor: 10(13)   Hit Points: 29
Initiative: +3   Speed: 13
SAVING THROWS: Will: 7   Fortitude: 4   Reflex: 4

GOLD: 10

-EQUIPMENT-

Weapons
Longbow
Long Sword

Armor
None

Magic
Spell Book
Flask of Holy Water

Misc
Quiver * Arrows x12
Backpack * Rations x1
Tinder Box * Waterskin
Pouches x2 * Birch Cinder
Moonlit Elm Ash * Ground Dwarf Tooth

† Spells Known †

Cantrips: Minor Illusion, Fire Bolt, Ray of Ice, Electric Hand, Acid Spray
Tier 1 Spells: Summon Familiar, Flame Blast, Lightning Summoning(lesser), Instant Slumber, Thunderous Wave, Illusion(minor), Charm(minor)
Tier 2 Spells:
Tier 3 Spells:

† Spells Prepared †

Cantrips: Fire Bolt x4
Tier 1 Spells: Thunderous Wave x3
Tier 2 Spells:
Tier 3 Spells:

Attacks
Name - ATK Bonus – Damage

Longbow   +5   1-8
Long Sword +4   1-8+2

Abilities
Spell Casting
Low-Light Vision

Skills
Listen: +6, Spot: +6, Knowledge: +6, Search: +6, Spell Craft: +6

Along with twelve skill points, he had one attribute point to place still and it made sense to either place it in strength, where he would have an immediate benefit of gaining +1 to both his attack and damage, or to intelligence where his modifier would jump to +4. This would make his spells do more damage and be harder to counter. As a further incentive to adding to his intelligence, the highest tiered wizard spells required at least an eighteen to master.

"But I will never live to get to a higher level unless I live through this moment," he reasoned. Strength would help that, however it would be of far less help later, and if he was ever going to face Arching he would need to be all the wizard he could be. "Intelligence it is," he said and used his one point to reach an 18 in intelligence.

The sensation of increased intelligence was strange and exhilarating. He had started the game with a real world IQ of 126, meaning he was highly intelligent, within the top 4% of all humans. Having chosen a High Elf as a character, his intelligence had immediately jumped to a 17. Measured as IQ, he had only moved to 130.

Now, he was an 18 intelligence and had an IQ within the game of 140 which meant he was in the top one half of 1%. In essence, he was now a genius. He paused for a moment to let his genius kick in so he could think of a way to get them out of a terrible situation.

He was still waiting when Amanda suddenly cried, "Roan! What are you doing? We have an army to fight, damn it."

Roan jumped, feeling foolish instead of brilliant. "Right, sorry. I was just…never mind." He picked up his bow, sighted it on an orc, making sure to choose one in the third rank to help ensure a hit regardless if he missed his actual target, and let the string go (*XP+25*).

With that, he began firing, moving rhythmically so that he repeated each step exactly as he had the one before. It cut down on errors and increased his effectiveness by 10%. He only stopped when the door banged open. Expecting Jarrod, he turned and saw the King Salazar, his beautiful armor dented and bloodied, his black hair dripping with sweat, his dark eyes haunted and downcast.

"I thought you were dead," he said to Roan.

"Soon enough," Roan replied. "We all will be, especially if we flee directly west. You know your people are heading into a trap, correct?"

Salazar untied his tattered cloak and, letting it fall, he strode upon it as he headed for his closet. "What are you, sixth level? Seventh?"

"Fourth."

This surprised Salazar, who turned to look back at Roan, giving him a quick, appraising eye. "Even worse," he said. "You don't even know enough to know you don't know anything. For your information, I have a fourteenth level seer working for me. He has scried the route from here to Morin and it is clear. But thanks for your concern."

"If he's so good, why didn't he see the attack coming in the first place?"

The king cringed slightly at the question. "That was my fault. The moment you arrived, I should have known trouble would follow you. A seer, particularly a paid seer, must be told where and when to use his talents and I didn't ask him anything. It was a mistake."

Salazar sighed, and, turning to his closet, whispered something. Without him having touched it, the door opened. Roan expected to see more fine cloaks and silken pants and woolen socks, however the closet was more of a mini armory than a normal closet. Swords and shields were set upon the wall, while coats of armor sat on stands. In a display case, there were potions and rings and wands and more. Roan could feel the magic emanating from the room and a part of him, the wizard part, wanted to explore each item in detail.

He was still standing there, uselessly gazing with a look of longing on his face, when Salazar took a backpack from a hook, opened it and produced a blue linen bag that wasn't much larger than a grocery bag. The king began to fill the bag with the different magical items. And he filled and he filled the bag, and he kept on filling it. He stuffed the shields inside and the swords and the suits of armor and the potions, and he just kept on going.

"An extra-dimensional bag?" Roan asked.

"It's called a Bag of Holding," Salazar replied. "You should pick one up when you can. Listen, don't get trapped here. I'm going to order a retreat soon. It'll be three blasts with the horn and then we're moving to the bridge. Don't be late."

Roan glanced out the window to where the horde was crushed up against the wall. It was a short wall, a dozen feet at the most. Thankfully, the orcs were without ladders or ropes and had to rely on boosting each other up. This wasn't easy to do when they were under fire. When they finally did reach the top, they were not too difficult to kill.

With each death, however, the mound of corpses built higher at the base of the wall, bringing more and more orcs to within reaching distance of the top.

Salazar left and soon after Jarrod showed up with two more quivers and in eight minutes, Roan's group had shot through them. By unanimous agreement, they decided they weren't going to wait for the retreat signal. Roan's sword had just slid from its sheath when they heard the first of the three horn blasts.

"That's our cue to make like a tree and get out of here," Jarrod said. They ran for the door only to have it burst open in their faces. Before them stood a grey, bearded man in silver robes—the robe had eyes of spun gold stitched into it. In the man's right hand, held much as a conductor would, was a wand of black wood. He looked as though he was one twitch away from casting a spell on Roan.

"Who are you?" he demanded. "Where's King Salazar?"

"He's gone," Roan said. "Everyone's retreating to the bridge."

The man…the seer more than likely, glanced towards the open closet before he grunted. Without a word, he spun in a swirl of robes and ran out of the room and down the stairs.

Roan and his team followed him and every time Roan glanced out of one the east-facing windows, his heart skipped a beat. The defenders of the wall were deserting wholesale and now the orcs were pouring onto the grounds. Leading them was Tim Cole in his black mail.

"To the back!" Roan was only guessing that there was a backdoor and in this he was wrong.

The seer shot him a look and said, "We'll go out through the north entrance. It's close to the bridge. Ah, your Highness!" Salazar appeared, racing down a corridor. "We only have minutes to…" A huge echoing crash from somewhere in the front of the building spun them all around.

"Salazar!" Tim Cole's voice boomed. "It's time to settle things and I've brought some friends to help out. Salazar! Stop hiding under your bed and come out."

"Don't do it, your Highness," the seer said, urgently pushing the king into the next room. It was a fancy drawing room with elegant couches, bookcases, polished desks and a harp of all things. There were three doors leading from the room, and as they were heading for the far door, the one to their right opened revealing a beaming Tim Cole.

"Always turning up like a bad penny, aren't you, Law-dog," Cole drawled to Roan. He stood in the doorway, filling it with his cold menace. "I think it's high time I put you down."

2—

Cole was about to step into the room when, with a swish of his delicate wand, the seer sent out a bolt of lightning as big around as Roan's arm. It crackled through the air straight at Cole, but did not strike him; the spell fizzled, losing its magic as it came up against an invisible force surrounding Cole's black armor. The seer tried again with the same effect and then, to Roan's great confusion, he tried a third time.

Roan was closest to the door and as he leapt at it, he yelled, "Try something else, damn it!"

Cole stepped back, bringing his sword up and Roan did the only thing that would make even the slightest bit of difference, he slammed the door in Cole's face and threw his weight against it. Jarrod and Marshall joined him a second later as Cole pounded on the door.

"Stand back," Salazar ordered. "I will deal with this."

"No, Your Highness," the seer said. "We will hold off Aderon so you can get away."

"We?" Jarrod cried. "Why are you dragging us into this? We didn't…"

!!!—!!! Glitch was suddenly back from its scouting mission, screaming an alarm, drowning out Jarrod and the ever-present sounds of battle. Glitch showed Roan a picture: thousands of orcs hiding beneath the shading trees overlooking the road west. The evil creatures watched as the women and children struggled on towards them. It was a trap after all!

Just like that, things clicked in Roan's head: the seer was a traitor. Roan didn't need his new genius ability to read the evidence. There was no way a fourteenth level seer could have missed the orcs hiding behind a bunch of trees, which meant he had lied to the king and there was only one reason to do that: he was really working for Cole.

And yet he had attacked Cole on sight—however, he had done so uselessly. If, as Roan guessed, the seer was working for Cole, then it followed that he knew Cole had some sort of immunity to lightning based spells, thus the attack had been solely for show. As was the seer's stated desire to sacrifice himself for Salazar. What hired gun would ever volunteer for that?

And was it a coincidence that the seer had suggested that Roan and his team join him in holding off Cole? There was no chance in hell. The man was guilty as sin and there was only one punishment for traitors of this magnitude, death.

"Follow my lead," he said to Marshall and then moved away from the door. In one long stride, he stepped up to the seer and, without any hesitation, he reached out and plucked the wand from his hands.

"Wh-what are you doing?" the seer demanded, angrily. At first his eyes were set in hard squints, but then they opened wide as Roan suddenly lunged forward and speared him on the end of his sword. The seer screamed in shock and surprise, and had this happened in the real world, he would have died right there. Here, things were different. Through some sort of magic or ability on the seer's part, the sword didn't strike nearly as deep or as true as Roan would have expected.

Spraying blood, the seer jumped back as Roan began to swing his long sword a second time. Before he could strike again, the seer spoke magic—sending thin jets of pulsing light shooting from his palm.

Roan was hit by four blasts (*Damage -18)* and stumbled, his body coursing all over with teeth-gritting pain. It was a pain like he had never experienced before and could only be described as magical and awful.

"What the hell?" King Salazar cried. "What is wrong with you?" Next to him, Jarrod gaped in confusion, while Amanda jerked her sword around, seemingly perplexed by who was attacking whom. Luckily for Roan, Marshall attacked a scant moment later, catching the seer in the shoulder with his sword.

"Stop, damn it!" Salazar ordered, but it was too late. Roan could see the look in the seer's eyes: he knew he had been caught and now killing Roan was his only option.

He opened his mouth to give voice to another spell, only just then Glitch used a new and very strange attack. Perhaps having picked up the idea from Roan's threat to the hulking prisoner they had shared a cell with, the creature shot right into the seer's open mouth and sunk into his lungs, causing him to gag and choke.

Ability Unlock: Stifle—Familiar may temporarily keep one opponent from speaking by inhibiting the passage of air in the subject's trachea—size limitations apply. Like an easily digested subtitle of a foreign movie, Roan read the message appearing in his vision while at the same time attacking with his sword.

Choking, unarmed and unarmored, the seer appeared defenseless, still *something* turned Roan's sword aside, causing him to miss, and Marshall's next attack only opened up a nick on his cheek.

Jarrod fared much better. As Salazar tried to push Roan back, the rogue darted forward and stabbed the seer through the back, severing his spine. The seer let out a choking cry and toppled over. The cumulative attacks had killed the man: (*XP +1,100*)

Congratulations! You are now a Level Five Wizard and have gained the following bonuses:

Increased Hit Points(+9)

You can fill +1 tier three spells per day

You have +6 skill points to allocate—*Warning* Player must allocate accumulated skill points within 24 hours to avoid a penalty.

Roan was still trying to read all of this when the king spun him around. Salazar looked on the verge of going berserk. A vein throbbed in his forehead and his eyes were wild. Before Salazar could say anything or, more importantly, kill anyone, Roan said, "He was a traitor. There's an orc army on the western road. My familiar saw it plain as day."

"What familiar?" Salazar asked, his voice icy. Glitch puffed up so he could be more readily seen. It spun the air in a cloud the size of a basketball—it was definitely bigger now, Roan saw. Salazar looked amazed. "That's an air elemental. How on earth did you get one of them as a familiar?"

"It was a glitch in the system, I think," Roan told him, brusquely, turning to the heavy sitting room door, which was still being battered at. The fact that it was still standing was more proof of the seer's true allegiance. With Cole's game-augmented strength, he probably could have broken through with one punch, which told Roan that Cole really didn't want to confront Salazar one on one in his own home.

"We killed your spy, Cole!" Roan yelled. Immediately, the pounding stopped. "And we know about your trap. Your orcs north of the road are about five minutes from being destroyed. We have more resources on the ground than you realize. Do yourself a favor and give up. Let's talk about Arching. That's all we're here for."

In and around the house, the sound of battle seemed to fall away and it was the silence on the other side of the door that seemed loud.

Long seconds passed before Cole finally said, "You don't know his power, Law-dog. I would never cross him."

"He'll be rotting in jail very soon and I doubt he'll show you the same curtesy. He'll turn on you in a snap, Cole. When the top level guys get caught they always do what they have to in order to reduce their sentences. He'll give you up for your part in Nelson's murder. You know it in your heart."

As Cole digested this, there was an even deeper silence from the other room. Roan was still waiting for an answer when Salazar touched his shoulder. The king put a finger to his lips and tugged Roan towards the far door. "Even if he gives up, the orcs won't," Salazar whispered. "You can clock out and deal with Aderon or Cole or whatever his name is, once we're out of danger."

The others were eagerly nodding and tip-toeing away as quietly as they could. They were right to want to leave. Roan had been working with little more than bluff and bluster, and even he didn't think that Cole would fold so easily.

The group went through the far door into what looked like a second sitting room. It had a fine view of the river and of the bridge, though both views were marred by battle. Corpses and body parts gently drifted down the river which was now an ugly maroon color. If anything, the view of the bridge was worse.

The soldiers who had been battling to keep the way to the bridge open had been driven back and now the bridge was clogged from end to end with soldiers and orcs, fighting in a great scrum.

"We're trapped," Amanda said, hollow-voiced.

Salazar locked the door behind them and then thrust a huge couch in front of it. He handed Amanda one of the cushions, saying: "You're not trapped. You can swim, can't you?" Like so many of the windows in the mansion, the window opened onto a small balcony. He stepped out, sighed in the general direction of the bridge and said, "I'd help you guys if I could, but my people need me. Tell that to your bosses at the FBI, will you?" Roan said that he would. The king nodded once and jumped up easily onto the railing, his mailed boots gouging the wood and paint. "Good luck out there."

Roan thought that he was about to jump in the river, however the king produced a vial that was filled with some sort of light blue liquid. He drank it in a gulp and then leapt into the air, and to Roan's amazement, flew off towards the bridge. It was a moment before he realized that Glitch had flown off with him and was spinning excited circles around his head as if the little elemental was some sort of satellite.

"Glitch! What are you doing? Get back here." The elemental came back, making a noise that sounded like a propeller running out of steam. "Stop whining," Roan groused. "At least you won't be getting wet."

"You want us to jump into the river?" Marshall asked, looking as though he'd rather fight Cole and whatever demons he had at his beck and call.

Roan understood; the man's armor would send him right to the bottom. "It'll be okay. Get the other side of that wardrobe." Against one wall, standing almost to the ceiling, was an intricately beveled, two door cabinet. Inside were cloaks and long robes set on hangers. Roan threw them onto the floor before he leaned the wardrobe onto its side.

Marshall heaved up one side and the two men waddled the big hunk of furniture to the balcony. As they could now hear voices on the other side of the door, they didn't have time for anything more subtle than simply pushing the wardrobe over the side. It fell fifteen feet, landing with a hollow *boom!*

Jarrod was first over the rail. "Last one in is a rotten egg!" He hopped nimbly over the side. When Marshall jumped, he made as nearly a big splash as had the wardrobe. He came up spluttering and fighting the weight of his armor, and when he clung to the wardrobe, he nearly turned it over.

Amanda went in next. In the air, she looked like a picture, her golden hair flowing, the metal of her armor glinting. Coming up out of the water, bedraggled and unhappy, was something else altogether. She looked utterly miserable, and disgusted—she had landed partially on one of the floating bodies and now looked ready to puke.

Roan went last, and as he was without armor or a heavy cloak, he splashed in neatly. The water was disagreeably warm. With the hundreds of corpses all around him, he felt as if he were floating in a giant's stew.

"This is disgusting," Amanda said. "I think I got some of the water in my mouth. I-I'm going to puke." Her breath started coming rapidly and her face was white.

"You're not going to puke," Roan told her. "Elves can't puke, right Jarrod?" Roan had been going to ask that of Marshall, only he didn't look that much better off than Amanda.

At first, Jarrod seemed confused at the question. It wasn't until Roan winked at him that Jarrod said, "Yes, right, no, we can't puke. It's too, uh, un-elfin-like. The game won't allow it. So, buck up."

Amanda's eyes, which had been half-lidded, now flared with a gold light. "Buck up? Is that all you have to say? Buck up? I'll buck you up you little weasel. If you…"

They had just rounded the far side of the island and there before them was the same giant from earlier. It was twenty feet into the river and up to its knees. As though it were at a grocery store, it was picking over the bodies floating past. Whenever it spied a human, it would grab it, bite off its head and toss the rest of the corpse onto the bank.

The crunching sound the giant made as it chewed the heads was enough to prove Jarrod a liar. Amanda puked loudly all over the side of the wardrobe.

"Crap! Get down!" Jarrod hissed, slipping as low into the water as he could go. Each of them dropped down so that just their eyes were above the water.

"Did it see us?" Amanda asked. She was on the far side of the wardrobe and couldn't see the giant's huge, misshapen head swing around to search the river. Its dull eyes were squinting mightily as it tried to pick out the details of each clump of flotsam and jetsam in the river.

"Quick! Everyone get into the wardrobe from underneath," Roan whispered. He took a breath and then slid beneath the surface. Under the water, the long doors of the wardrobe hung open; he ducked beneath the one on his side and came up into the air pocket that he had calculated would be there.

Amanda and Jarrod popped up next and then came Marshall, his brown elven eyes spinning wildly. "I l-lost my grip and I was halfway to the bottom in, like a second. Is there enough air in here? It doesn't feel like there's enough."

"Dude, calm yourself," Jarrod whispered, glaring.

But Marshall was almost hyperventilating by then. Roan could see the panic on his face. "We have Glitch with us, Marshall," he said. "He's filtering in good air through the cracks right now."

??? Glitch did not know what "filtering" meant. Glitch was floating on top of the wardrobe with fear running through whatever counted as its brain. It was afraid for Roan and, to a lesser extent, Amanda. It wasn't the giant leering at the wardrobe as it floated by that had Glitch nervous. As an air elemental, Glitch was naturally afraid of the water—mostly of being trapped beneath or inside of it.

Roan tried to calm the elemental, thinking: *We're fine. Go pester the giant, quick!* He could see through Glitch's vision: the giant was pondering over the wardrobe and it was only a matter of time before he reached out with a hand the size of a pickup truck and plucked up their only cover.

In fact, one of the giant's arms began to stretch even then. Glitch went straight for the giant's left eye, blurring it with a *haze* attack. The hand stopped above the wardrobe, blocking out the light of the sun.

"What is…" Jarrod started to say, only to be elbowed by Amanda. She put a finger to her lips as outside there came an angry bellow. It was Glitch doing everything it could to distract the beast. It sent jets of air into the giant's eyes and then was nearly sucked into the thing's huge nostrils which might have actually killed it.

Luckily, there were few things in Daggerland that could equal an air elemental when it came to flight, and it was just able to get away. A second later it was back, shooting into the giant's ear and down its auditory canal, dodging huge mounds of wax in which were the preserved remains of dozens of bats. Glitch went right to the giant's ear drum and screamed as loud as it could: *ZZZZZZ!*

"Gahhhhh!" yelled the giant, stabbing a finger into the ear. Glitch had been expecting it and shot out just before the bloody finger got there. It zipped around the gigantic head and went for the other ear.

In the wardrobe, Roan's group held their breath, listening to the odd sounds, expecting the giant to either pick up the wardrobe or to smash it at any moment. Only Roan knew what was happening and he kept up a whispered play-by-play as Glitch worked mightily to distract the giant.

Eventually, after several long minutes, they were swept around a bend. *Come back, Glitch*, Roan thought, *you did great.* Aloud, he said, "It's safe to get out of here now. Marshall, why don't you go first? Better yet, we'll go together."

"Yeah, that would be good," he said, gratefully. Taking a deep breath, they both ducked beneath the water, swimming under the hanging doors of the wardrobe. As Roan guessed he would, Marshall panicked, his hands flailing as the water poured into his armored suit. Roan had to grab his wrist and direct him to each handhold otherwise he would have sunk into the depths of the river.

When they broached the surface, Marshall laid his face on the side of the wardrobe and refused to look at anyone or anything for some time.

The others came up without nearly as much trouble. Amanda found Roan's long legs beneath the surface and used him as a ladder. "Hi," she said, smiling at him as she broke the surface. They were practically nose to nose. "We live again."

Although he was now a genius, with her so close to him, he found himself suddenly tongue-tied and he could only manage a weak, "Yeah, uh, we did."

She seemed to enjoy the effect she was having on him and moved even closer. Under the water, her hand found his hip. "Sorry," she said, but didn't move the hand. "So, where are we off to?"

"Uh, south," Roan said, pointing down river. "We should check out Nelson's citadel. Do any of you know how far down the river it lies?"

Marshall looked stricken by the question. "At least a hundred miles. We're not going to float all the way. I don't think I can. I weigh like, over three hundred pounds with all my gear."

"But floating is better than walking," Jarrod said. "And we need to conserve our strength if we can expect the entire orc army to come after us. Once we are past the Orc-backs, there are some towns we can stop in and pick up some horses or a cart or something. Does that sound better, Marshall?"

He still didn't sound happy, yet he grunted out, "I guess so. I just don't like the water and this…this thing we're on, it doesn't feel safe at all."

"Then you're in luck," Roan said. With its aversion to water even greater than Marshall's, Glitch had been floating twenty feet above their heads and through its eyes, Roan spied one of the rough-hewn platforms that the orcs had built. It bobbed in the water near the eastern bank, caught up in the drooping branches of a tremendous willow. The tree stood eighty feet in the air and had such a thick screen of drooping branches that another giant could have been hiding behind it and they would never have known.

Glitch must have heard the thought in Roan's head because it sped off to check if anything was in the tree. It discovered two of the odd baboon-like creatures that had attacked Riverport earlier in the day. One was injured and neither wanted anything to do with the four adventurers and fled high into the uppermost branches of the tree.

Roan and his team kicked laboriously, slowly moving the wardrobe across the river to the platform. For Marshall, getting to the platform was easy compared to getting on it. Without a ladder, or really any handholds, he failed time and again to lift his unwieldy bulk.

To get him on board, they had to push the heavy platform to shore, let him crawl on and then launch it back into the river. It was exhausting, muddy work and for some time, they were all too tired to do anything but lie on the platform and watch the sky pass by.

"This feels like the slowest getaway of all time," Jarrod remarked.

"I doubt anyone's even looking for us yet," Roan said. "I think Cole's main concern is killing Salazar and the orcs will be busy looting and raping for hours. Besides they have to be even more tired than we are. They began their march two nights ago, fought a morning battle with the elves, chased us all day yesterday and then fought today. There's a good chance that they'll be too done-in to even think about coming after us until tonight at the earliest."

Amanda, who had been running her fingers along the rough planks, said, "And I wonder if we were really the main focus of any of this. It's one thing for the orcs to attack the elves of Ash Forest at the drop of a hat, but the orcs came prepared to cross this river. Despite what Cole said, I think it might just have been a coincidence that we were in Riverport when it was attacked."

"Damn," Roan whispered. "The traitor that Cole had there suggests that you are correct. They've probably been planning this attack for months. Though, we could have been the trigger. Arching might have decided to kill two birds with one stone."

"I can't tell if that makes me happy or not," Jarrod said. "I just know that I am one tired pup." He stretched and yawned, then asked, "You guys don't mind if I rack-out, do you?"

"I do," Amanda said, looking at him with sudden suspicion. "What is that?" She pointed to Jarrod's hand where a silver ring glinted in the sun.

Quickly, he curled his hand inwards. "What is what?" he asked, forcing a look of innocence onto his features. She grabbed his wrist and held up his hand so they could all see the ring. "Oh, this? Right...it's nothing really, and I didn't steal it, I promise. It was that seer guy's, so I took it."

Roan felt his lip curl. "You robbed a corpse? That's pretty low, Jarrod, even for you."

"Don't be too hard on him," Marshall said, propping himself up on one elbow. "I know it sounds pretty uncivilized, but in Daggerland it's not just normal, it's expected."

Jarrod snapped his fingers quickly, saying, "Exactly. It's survival of the fittest here, and it's common sense. If I hadn't taken it, some orc would have and then we'd have an orc running around with a..." He stopped abruptly and began to struggle for words.

"With a what?" Marshall demanded. "The ring's magical, isn't it?" Jarrod sighed and lifted one shoulder. Marshall punched that shoulder, the blow going right to the bone. Jarrod made a face of ultimate pain and began rubbing his arm. Marshall ignored him. "He was right to take the ring, but he was wrong not to tell us."

"I was going to," Jarrod said, still massaging his arm. "But Cole was there and then Salazar left us...and I just forgot. Here." He took the ring off and handed it to Marshall who looked down at it, his brow furrowing in concentration.

He grunted and handed the ring to Roan, saying, "I keep forgetting that I'm not as smart here as I am on the other side."

At first, Roan didn't know why they would expect him to know what sort of ring it was, then his eyes caught the writing engraved on it. He had never seen such elegant lettering. "Eldritch," he whispered, picking out a word here and there that he somehow knew. Unfortunately, the entire meaning was lost on him.

But he knew where he could find out. He had eighteen skill points to use and now was as good a time as any to assign them. With a thought, he brought up his current skills:

Skills: Listen +6, Search +6, Spot +6, Spell Craft +6, Knowledge +6

Roan attempted to add five points to his *Knowledge* field, but was only able to add two. It made sense to him. The game seemed to have been created with a sense of balance in mind and thus a relatively low level wizard would not have the understanding of a sage.

With this in mind, he raised each of his skills to their maximum, but still had eight points left over. He added all eight points to *Decipher Script* since it seemed appropriate for the moment and he figured that the further they went on, the more they would run into odd writings. Now his skills were listed as:

Skills: Listen +8, Search +8, Spot +8, Spell Craft +8, Knowledge +8, Decipher Script +8

When he blinked away the words in his vision, he saw the ring in an entirely new light and the knowledge of what it was,

was just there in his head in the same way that the knowledge of the chemical composition of water was there. "It's an Asari Ring of Defense. It'll increase a person's armor class by three ranks." This explained how the seer had been able to turn aside his sword.

"If it's for defense, then you should hold onto it," Amanda said. "You don't have any armor at all. Does this make sense to the group?" Marshall, who was a walking tank, nodded, while Jarrod, who only wore stiff leather with metal plates attached at the shoulders and the chest, barely grunted.

Amanda gave him a hard look. "Maybe this will make you think twice about keeping things from the group. Now, let's see what else you took." He produced a pouch that was filled with two-hundred gold pieces, which they divided among themselves equally.

"I also have this," Roan said, holding up the wand he had taken from the seer. "It's a wand of lightning. It has eight uses left."

"You hold onto that," Amanda said. "Now, who needs healing?" At the question, all three men raised tired arms. She didn't have the power left to heal all three and, once more Roan received most of her attention which had Jarrod complaining again, and had Amanda getting defensive.

They began to bicker and Roan had to step in between them. "Let's try to cool down, you two. We're all just tired. I'll stand the first guard shift. You three lie down and try to sleep." They didn't argue with this and in a minute, they were snoring.

"Well, Glitch. It looks like it's just you and me." He smiled up at the knuckle of twisted air. Glitch replied in a soothing voice, but what it said, Roan didn't know. He was already asleep.

2—

It was deepest night when Glitch woke him with an anxious whispering that was partially in his head and partially in his ear.

Roan sat up, his hand reaching for his sword, but he did not draw it from its scabbard. That would make noise and just then, he felt the need to be very quiet. The air was dark with soot and it stank of sulphur. To the west were the rugged, black peaks of the Orc-backs. Dark clouds hid their very tops, while all around the base of the mountains was a greenish glow.

Glitch wobbled in fear at the sight. "It'll be okay, Glitch," Roan whispered and then tried to pet the air elemental, which was like trying to pet a cloud. Glitch was cool and somewhat damp to the touch, but was otherwise without substance.

"Are we okay?" Amanda asked. Her blue eyes were open wide, her hand on the hilt of her sword.

Roan held a finger out to her as he slowly stood to his full height and gazed around, letting his elven vision pierce the gloom. There wasn't much to see. The riverbanks were no longer lush and green, crowded by plants and trees. The only vegetation near the river was choking vines and sprawling, ugly bushes with thorns like daggers and poison in their leaves.

"For now," he told her, "go back to sleep. I had fallen asleep, but I'm good to keep watch." She nodded and rolled over, then rolled over again, and again. "Come here," he whispered. "That armor looks like a bitch to try to sleep in. You can rest your head on my legs."

As he leaned back on his backpack, she laid her head down across his thighs. They were in a land of harsh fumes and desolation, very close to the hole in the world from which the orcs spawned, and yet, all he could think about was how pretty Amanda's hair was. Irresistibly, he was drawn to touching it. He stroked her golden tresses and she didn't mind. It must have been soothing because she fell asleep again.

By first light, they had left the Orc-backs far behind them and were now miles into a forest of towering sequoia. "Amanda," Roan whispered. He wanted her to see the sunrise through the trees. It was strange. From his army days, he had seen more sunrises than he cared to count, but he had never seen one anywhere nearly as beautiful as this one.

Amanda sat up and put her head on his shoulder. Together they watched the golden light through the trees. Roan had never seen anything so magical, so wonderful, so...

"Can we pull over?" Jarrod asked, breaking in on his thoughts. "I gotta take a massive leak. I have this cousin from Boston; he's always saying: 'I gotta take a wicked pissah.' You ever hear of anything so stupid?"

"Yes," Amanda answered icily.

Jarrod started to get a hurt look on his face and Marshall threw an arm around his shoulders. "You have to feel the room, dude."

Hearing an elf say "dude" killed the last remnants of the moment and Roan ordered them to kick the platform to the river bank. Once there, they cleaned themselves up as best as possible and then went in search of suitable tree branches which could be used to pole the floating platform about.

They weren't hard to find and soon they were back on the river. Roan found himself disappointed and missing the touch of the forest. "I guess I'm an elf," he whispered and then jumped as a soft blue light covered him. It was Amanda finishing the healing he needed and bringing him back up to his full thirty-eight hit points. She then worked on Jarrod, while Marshall used his paladin skills to mostly heal himself.

All of this reminded Roan that he needed to prepare his spells for the day. He pulled his spell book from his still damp pack and was afraid that he would find the pages ruined, but they were bone dry, as were all of his spell components. Again, the idea of this being a "cheat" crossed his mind, but it was nothing compared to what he found when he turned past his Tier-2 spells and saw a new one sitting on the next page: *Incinerate*. It was a Tier-3 spell.

"Whoa," Roan said, reading the spell which, in essence, caused a fire storm to blast an area. The component to the spell was actual fire. "Who has matches or one of those tinderboxes?" Marshall handed a tinderbox over and Roan excitedly started to scrape together splinters and slivers from the platform. He then tore a strip out of his shirt and wrapped it loosely together.

In no time, he had the fire going and that was when his enthusiasm waned. The fire he had made was very small but it was still extremely hot. Hot enough to burn his flesh. "Damn, this is going to suck." Taking a deep breath, he began the spell, speaking the words of it directly into the dancing flames. They pulsed and grew as he spoke the syllables—then it was time to breathe in the flame.

Roan had to remind himself that he had never seen a wizard with their lips burned off. With another steadying breath, he dipped low and took in a lungful of the most intense heat he had ever felt. He sucked it into his lungs and held it until, gradually, it seemed to be absorbed into him.

"Are you alright?" Amanda asked. "You, you just put your face in that fire. And now your eyes…they're a little strange. You have flecks of gold or something in them."

"It's normal. I think." He hoped it was. The rest of his spells were far easier to prepare: Two elemental summonings, three Thunderous Waves, and a handful of Fire bolts. Once again, he felt oddly filled inside, as if he were swollen.

Amanda prepared her spells next, and then came six hours of boredom in which the river carried them slowly southeast. Only once was there the least bit of excitement.

A herd or a squad, Roan didn't know the nomenclature, of centaurs came down out of the forest to drink from the river. Roan had his group pole away from the bank and the two sides eyed each other warily.

"Hello," Roan said in elvish and raised a hand. One centaur raised a hand in return, but said nothing. "Could be worse," he said to the others. It could have been; all of the centaurs had been armed with very large bows, while Roan's team was out of arrows.

Thankfully, they encountered nothing further until they came to the town of Tir-Kahn that afternoon. It wasn't a pleasant place. It sat on the west bank of the river, on a very sharp hill. Not far from the edge of the hill were marshes with only a single path leading through them. The path, starting at a dozen empty docks where a few sullen-looking men made fast their floating platform, wound up the jagged hill. As the four went up, they were surprised to find homes and business either carved into the hill itself, perched precariously on rocks jutting from the hill, or sitting on platforms suspended from the rocks that jutted from the hill.

Many of the buildings creaked and swayed, alarmingly, looking as though a strong wind would send them crashing down, creating an avalanche.

The angle of the road was so sharp that when they came to the first inn along the road, Jarrod looked up at the twisting, turning path and said, "I'm good here."

Marshall, who was sweating up a storm from the short walk, quickly agreed. Amanda looked to Roan for a decision. He saw no reason to go any further, either—that is until he saw the condition of the place. Suffice to say: refuse, excrement, and other unspeakable matter ran down hill in Tir-Kahn. The inn and its grimy owner stank abysmally.

Roan turned them around and started heading upwards. They traveled up, avoiding the foul gutters on the side of the road as well as the occasional thrown bucket of excrement. As they walked, they met many glares and the occasional: "More elves from Ash Forest, bah!" One old geezer spat tobacco out of the corner of his mouth, saying, "Look, their leader is a beggar! Beg somewhere else, elf." Another man in leather armor and a sword hanging from his hip asked, "Any news of Riverport, that's what we care about."

Although he was shocked at the clear racism, Roan ordered his team to ignore them. "Hold your head high. You each deserve much more of an honor than this." Only when they reached the top of the hill where the finest inn stood next to the prince's palace, were they accorded proper respect—it cost them two gold pieces a night, per person for that respect.

Young boys in ill-fitting uniforms took their bags and the front desk woman pretended not to look shocked at the shoddy state of their armor, or of the rags that Roan was dressed in. "We have very fine tailors here in Tir-Khan," she said, after accepting their gold.

"For now, just the rooms, please," Roan replied. The inn was surprisingly busy, its narrow halls bustling with people, including a number of adventurers that eyed Roan and his team as they filed through the main hall. Judging by their armor, leather and hide, mostly, they seemed to be lower level players.

"Was it me, or was *everyone* down there staring at us?" Amanda asked when they got to the first of the rooms. The inn was a bit of a maze with corridors zigzagging oddly and doors opening unexpectedly on staircases or other halls. Amanda had taken the first room with Roan across from her.

"They were," Marshall said from the doorway. "But it's normal. You can't be too careful, you know? Remember when Cole got us back in Thornwall? I wish I had seen him coming."

Jarrod pushed into the room, giving it a quick glance. "I say we get some grub. Those rations we've been eating weren't good. I feel stopped up, if you know what I mean."

"You three eat," Roan said. "I'm going to clock out for an hour or two. When I get back, Amanda will go next, then Jarrod, then Marshall. You'll exercise when you go back. That's an order."

Roan gave Amanda a last look before clocking back into the real world. A second later, he sat up, feeling a moment of disorientation. It felt almost as if he had clocked back into the wrong body. He had to touch his face to reassure himself.

"Good morning, Agent Roan," Mrs. Niederer said from her chair. "I was told to send you up to Mr. Caron's office as soon as you woke up. It's urgent, I guess."

"Oh, yeah? Did they get Arching?"

"No, they captured that man Cole who's been troubling you."

Roan felt a surge of relief. "Thank God. I was afraid he was going to find us in that…" He stopped, realizing that he was about to go on about a game as if it were real. "Good. Thanks, Mrs. Niederer." He started to head up the stairs, but paused and turned back. "Did you start playing, yet?"

"I did, but I'm not sure how much I like it. There are good parts that's for sure. Like the elves and the fairies and all the beautiful sights. I just can't stomach the violence."

"It is a little too real at times," he admitted. "I bet there are calm places. If I hear about one, I'll let you know."

He gave her a wave and headed up the basement stairs, his legs feeling oddly "springy," until he remembered that he was stronger in the real world. He decided to take the stairs the rest of the way instead of the elevator and for reasons unknown to him, he sprinted up the three floors to Caron's office.

Caron's brow came down when he saw Roan sweating and out of breath. "What's wrong? Did you guys get killed again?"

"No. I just wanted to get in some exercise. So, I heard you captured Cole. Did he say anything about Arching?"

Caron's brows came down even further. "That was supposed to be a secret. We don't want him to know, so don't say anything." Roan started shaking his head in confusion and Caron explained, "We have his body but he's still in the game. He had a lawyer guarding over him, ready with a letter from a doctor saying that removing that neuro-thingy could cause brain damage. We took it to a judge, but the judge sided with the lawyer."

Roan almost gagged on his disappointment. "And Arching? Please tell me you have something on him."

"A thousand leads and they're all going nowhere, fast. And he has struck again. Fulbright's been murdered, supposedly by his cousin, but I'm not buying it. This guy comes right here and turns himself in. One moment he's confessing and the next he acts like he doesn't know what's going on. He says he was in the game."

"He was," Roan said, dropping down into a chair. "None of this is news. Cole told me on the other side. He thought ruining a man's life was funny." Roan went on to give his boss a situation report and then, fearing the inevitable asked, "So when are you pulling us?"

Caron's answer surprised him. "Not anytime soon. It sounds like you're putting the pressure on Arching, which is more than we can say. And given what you've said about Cole, I doubt he'll talk when he finally comes up for air. And Arching...I don't know what to say. Even if we find him, I can't imagine any charge will stick. Almost all of the evidence is in the game where we can't touch it. The most we can hope for is a confession. Do you think you could beat one out of him on the other side?"

By the grin he wore, Roan saw that this was a joke on Caron's part. "You may not be that far off," Roan said. "Arching may be one of those guys who care more about his game life than his real one. A real threat to his 'character' might get him to talk. The only problem is his character might be an insanely high level. I'd need an army to take him down."

"An army is not in the budget, sorry."

Roan stood. "If we want to catch this guy, it might just have to be." He left Caron's office and headed down to the basement, where he exercised for an hour straight until he could barely lift his arms. He was exhausted, but when he clocked back in, it felt as though he had just woken from a refreshing nap.

He stretched, enjoying the feel of having "his" body back, and was about to head down to the main hall when he saw something sitting on his bed. It was a brown paper package tied with twine. Roan gave it a prod with one finger and felt cloth beneath the paper. There was a note with it which simply read: *Get dressed, Amanda.*

Within the package was a set of clothes: boots, trousers, shirt and cloak. All were cobalt blue, trimmed with silver fur. Roan put the outfit on and admired himself in a mirror. "Not bad," he said. The cobalt and silver were colors that he would never have picked out himself, but they looked good on him.

Strapping his sword to his hip, he went downstairs where he found dinner in full swing. The main hall was busting at the seams with people eating, drinking, talking and in more than one case, singing. Waitresses rushed around carrying trays of meat and bread and green vegetables and beer by the gallon.

In all the hubbub, Roan had no clue where his team was. He stood in the doorway, peering through a haze of smoke until

Glitch came whistling up and guided him to an alcove where Amanda greeted him with a smile, Marshall gave him a greasy handed wave and Jarrod an arched eyebrow.

"So that's where you went off to," Jarrod said, picking up a pewter mug filled with beer and pointing it at Amanda, sloshing some over the side. "While Marshall and I were left gathering information, you were out shopping for your boyfriend. I see how it is."

"He's not my boyfriend," Amanda snapped, glaring across the table at him. "You heard what people were saying. They said you looked like a bum, Roan, so I bought some clothes for you. It's no big deal. You got that, Jarrod? It's no big deal."

Roan had to quash any talk of boyfriend and girlfriend. If it got back to Caron, he would be investigated and Amanda transferred to another division. The thought of that was surprisingly painful.

"I think it was a smart move on her part," Roan said, sitting down next to Amanda but not looking at her. "I stood out and when you're on a job, it's not smart to stand out and nor is it smart to get drunk. Put the beer down and tell me about the information you gathered."

Reluctantly, Jarrod set aside his mug and said, "We found out that we're really close to Nelson's citadel, Mendenome. It's only about fifteen miles away. And we started asking around about Aderon the Black, AKA Tim Cole. He used to come in here a lot. Usually arrived Friday afternoons on a big black charger and left on Saturday, generally at midday."

Marshall, fresh from licking his fingers one after another, chimed in. "What was strange was that he wasn't heavy on intimidation. He preferred spreading the gold about. He was always chatting up the adventurers, trying to find out what they were up to."

"Yeah," Jarrod agreed, bobbing his head. "You want to know what was also strange? Over the last few weeks, really high-powered groups began coming through here and Cole met with them all. They'd ride west and never come back. The last group came through on the day Nelson died. I think he was trying to take down his boss."

"Okay, anything else?"

"Just that this town may not last," Marshall said. "They relied on the river traffic from Riverport economically and on Nelson for protection. They say that there are a thousand bandits roaming all over these lands now that the wizard is gone."

"Bandits we can handle," Roan said. "We have Glitch to guide us and, so far we've been pretty kickass. Alright that was a good briefing, you two." He then went on to explain the bad news in the real world.

Amanda didn't see it as bad news at all. "They have a lead right in front of their faces: the lawyer helping Cole. I'd bet you that Arching is paying him. And I'm sure he has a game account. How else will he be able to contact his client? If we can track him, he might lead us to Arching. We need agents digging up everything they can on this guy."

"Including his online activity," Marshall said. "A lot of people have the same user name on the message boards as they do in games. And have them check past game names. Once we get his name, it'll only be a matter of time before we get him."

Roan thumped the table. "That's what I'm talking about! We'll get this guy, yet. Amanda, since it was your idea I want you to talk to Caron about it. Clock out, get some exercise and some food."

Grinning, she disappeared. Roan was still staring at her empty seat when Jarrod said, "Look, I was just joking about what I said earlier. If you guys have something going on, me and Marshall won't say anything. Everyone knows that what happens in Daggerland stays in Daggerland. It's the beauty of this place. You can have any sort of fantasy you want here."

"With an NPC?" Roan asked. "No thanks."

"No, with real girls," Jarrod insisted. "See that girl at the bar? The one with the proverbial watermelons?"

Roan could hardly miss her or her watermelons and to say she was fetching was a bit of an understatement. They made eye contact and she gave him a wink. He felt heat rising in his cheeks. Turning away, he said to Jarrod, "There's no way she's a real. Especially her…"

"Ix-nay, ix-nay," Marshall said, waving a hand beneath his chin. "She's coming. She's…oh, hi."

The woman had strode over, wearing a come-hither smile, black leather boots that went to mid-thigh, a black leather miniskirt that barely concealed what it was designed to conceal, and a shirt made of thin, see-through white fabric that was straining to hold in her breasts. "Hello," she purred. "See something that you like?"

"Uhhhh," was Roan's initial response. "Uh, no. I mean yes, but no. Look, I'm a little confused about something."

"Your sexual orientation?" she joked. "Because I can *straighten* you out on that subject, if you know what I mean."

She moved even closer, putting a hand on his shoulder. He leaned away and now the heat spread from his cheeks to his ears. "No, I'm good in that area. It's just that I'm new here and I was wondering," he stopped, not knowing how to proceed. Surely it was impolite, even in Daggerland, to ask if someone was a real hooker or a fake hooker.

Jarrod, blunt as always, said, "He wants to know if you're a real girl. You know back on the other side."

"Of course," she said. "You ever been with one of them NPC skanks they got running around here? Let's just say they lack imagination, enthusiasm and raw hunger. I've got all three burning in me. The game masters might be smart but they don't know much about sex. Probably a bunch of nerds, right? Not like you guys. I know real, tough guys when I see 'em." Marshall and Jarrod shared a quick look before they both nodded. Her smile broadened. "And you're looking to party?"

"Hold on," Roan said. "You are really real? A real person? Where are you from?"

Her smile dimmed. "Milan, why?"

Roan couldn't wrap his mind around this. "Italy? And you do this for a living? I-I guess I don't get it."

"What's there to get?" the hooker answered, crossing her arms, barely, in front of her heavy breasts. "This is a fantasy world and for the right price I can be your ultimate fantasy. You have no idea what you're missing. What do you think, five-hundred a piece? That's a discount of a hundred in gold. You can't beat that."

Roan could only shake his head. "I still don't get it. Why would you do that here? You could do anything here."

"And I choose to do this, so what? Listen, I can make a grand a day on my back. Not a thousand gold, but a thousand dollars. And the johns here are much better than on the other side. Everyone is a build, so I don't have to worry about having some ugly fatty slobbering all over me. And there's no disease that can't be cured by starting over. And I will never need a breast lift, feel."

Before Roan knew it, the woman had picked up his hand and placed it on her left breast. It wasn't silicone, that was for certain…and yet, whatever he was feeling, Roan knew was all in his head. No matter what she said, she wasn't real. There was no way she looked or felt like this on the other side. To him that meant she was…

"What the hell!"

Roan jumped, snatching his hand back. Amanda had materialized right next to the hooker and now there was fire in her eyes. She slammed an open hand into the woman's shoulder, knocking her back.

"Calm down, darling," the hooker drawled. "He was just sampling the merchandise, that was all. He seems like a good boy. I'd keep an eye on him if I were you." She turned to Jarrod and Marshall. "So, what about you two? You up for some fun?"

Amanda slid between the hooker and the table, her hand on the hilt of her sword. "They don't have the money, so take a hike."

The hooker did a little twirl before she walked away, saying over her shoulder, "When your mom goes to bed, you know where to find me if you are looking for a mind-blowing time."

Seething, Amanda turned to the rest of the team and hissed, "I leave you for two minutes and this is what I come back to?" She opened her mouth to spit out more acid, but then she closed it and a look of cold disappointment crossed her face. "You know, I just came back to tell you that Caron liked my idea. He liked it so much that he gave us an actual working budget."

She produced a leather pouch that was bursting at the seams and tossed it on the table, gold spilling across the table. "But if you want to spend it on hookers, don't let me stop you."

Before Roan could say anything, she clocked back to the real world. "Damn it," he muttered.

Jarrod smirked. "Boy, are you in the dog house?" Roan looked at him with such malice that Jarrod leaned back. "What? How was I to know she was going to put your hand on her booby? I didn't even call her over here."

He was right. "It's not your fault, it's mine," Roan said. "I shouldn't have…" *I shouldn't have, what?* he wondered. Not fallen for Amanda? That was the problem. Had she been any other agent, a conversation with a hooker would not have been all that out of the ordinary.

It was why the FBI didn't allow their agents to date one another. It made things complicated and could lead to a compromised investigation.

"I'm going to my room," he said, getting to his feet. He collected the pouch of gold. "Remember, you two are still on the job. Don't get drunk and do anything stupid. You can relax if you want or try to gather more info. It's up to you. Good night."

Roan worked his way through the crowd, heading for his room, where he paused in the doorway, staring at Amanda's door. No light filtered from beneath. She was either asleep or still in the real world. "Glitch?" he asked, looking for the little elemental. The corridor was dim, lit only by a couple of spaced lanterns.

???

"Watch over her. Don't take no for an answer." Roan started to close his door but then a thought occurred to him. "Hey, Glitch, do you sleep?"

??? Roan guessed that the concept of sleep was foreign to the creature. "Never mind. Thanks, Glitch."

"Sssss," Glitch replied.

2—

In the morning, Amanda offered a very stiff apology. "I was out of line and should not have spoken to a fellow agent in such a manner. I am sorry."

Roan, who also felt the need to apologize, despite not having done anything wrong, nodded once. Hoping to dismiss the entire thing, he said, "It happens when people work in such close proximity for so long. We forget our boundaries. Let's just chalk it up as a learning experience."

Amanda studied him closely before answering, "Fine." She had bought herself a green and gold cloak, and when she turned from him it flared in the sun.

"Fine?" Jarrod asked under his breath. "I don't know a lot about women, but I know when one of them says that something is fine, it's definitely not fine."

"No one asked you, Jarrod," Roan said, hitching his pack. They marched down the steep hill until they came to the markets. These were unlike anything Roan could have envisioned. A good portion of the hill had been hollowed out to form chambers and tunnels where any manner of goods could be bought, including livestock, which added an eye-watering aroma to the entire affair.

As they were passing the first of the stalls—a pen crammed with sheep in need of shearing—Jarrod said, "It'll be a long walk and poor Marshall has to lug all that armor...but I guess it is the cheaper alternative."

"We're not walking," Roan said, stepping over a chicken. They were surrounded by the birds, all of whom seemed intent on pecking at Marshall's metal encased legs. "If I had an idea about what sort of terrain is between here and Mendenome, it would make figuring..."

"Did you say Mendenome?" a cloaked and hooded man asked, appearing suddenly at Roan's elbow. Pretty much like everyone else around them, he was armed with sword and dagger. "I am putting together an expedition to Mendenome. Maybe we can join forces. What level are you guys?"

Jarrod shoved him away. "Like we would tell you. And besides our party has a rogue, so take a hike." Roan was a little surprised at Jarrod's behavior and it must have shown. "You can't trust most rogues, especially ones who look like that guy. He looks like the kind of guy who'll slit your throat while you sleep just for the fun of it."

Roan didn't see how anyone could find fun in hurting others. He gazed after the rogue and saw him whispering with two others, both of whom looked as disreputable as the first. Just the sight of them firmed up a thought that had been floating around in his head. "We'll ride horses, the fastest that we can afford. We haven't been exactly flying under the radar since we got here and I want to get to Mendenome as soon as possible."

He started walking again and nearly plowed into a young woman in a plain blue dress and scuffed black boots. "Good morning, milord. Did I hear you correctly? Did you say, Mendenome?"

"Didn't we just go through this?" Roan asked, throwing up his hands and trying to push past.

"Not so fast," Marshall said. "This could be an invitation for a quest. You never just want to brush them aside. What can we do for you, milady?"

The woman grabbed Marshall's arm with both hands and clung to him. "It's my brother, kind sir. He left four days ago with a band of men." She pulled Marshall closer, whispering, "He's gone to the wizard's keep to make his fortune."

"And you want us to find out what's become of him? That should be no problem."

She began to weep, saying, "Thank you," over and over, before giving them a general description: Taegus Estes: brown hair and eyes, average height and build. Last seen in worn leather armor and carrying a circular shield with a fading yellow flower painted on it. Distinguishing characteristics: missing the tip of left pinky and has a mole next to his nose.

Quest accepted! Discover the whereabouts of Taegus Estes and return to Tedra Estes. Roan wasn't exactly happy about seeing the words. Had this been a real person, he wouldn't have hesitated, but this was a NPC and for him the quest was just another stress that he didn't need.

"That was nice of you," Amanda said, bumping him with her armored shoulder and then moving on before he could say anything. He watched her as she walked to where the horses were being sold, and he found himself smiling as she began petting and talking to them.

"Do you know anything about horses?" Jarrod asked.

Roan had to think about it. There was no telling what the game had implanted in him. The answer turned out to be, "No, not at all. I know hay goes in one end and crap comes out the other. That's about it."

"We'll let Marshall do the talking," Jarrod said. "Paladin's are all about their warhorses. Do you know about them? They're kind of like a familiar for wizards, only you get to ride them. For me it doesn't balance out having to be so goody-goody all the time."

As much as Roan didn't want to, they split up; Marshall and Amanda picked out the horses and saddles, while he and Jarrod went to get the rest of the gear that they needed: arrows, food, torches, bedrolls, spell components and rope.

They went through half their gold in an hour. The next hour was spent preparing themselves and their horses. It should have been easy. Throughout his life, Roan had been gifted with an ability to acclimate easily to every possible mode of transportation. He could ski, surf, skate, bike, drive and fly a plane. He certainly expected that riding a horse would be just as easy for him.

It was not.

His horse, a large grey gelding named Jetta, did not like him and he didn't much like Jetta. They butted heads on who was in charge. If he wanted to turn right, Jetta would spin half-way around. If he wanted to go forward, Jetta would sprint and if he wanted to stop, Jetta acted as though he were about to hit a wall and would brake on a dime, frequently spilling Roan to the ground.

"It's defective," he said, picking himself up for the fourth time, much to the enjoyment of everyone watching, and it did seem like everyone in the town was there laughing at Jetta's antics.

"No, you just need to be more gentle," Marshall said. "You'd have the same problem with any horse."

"Then let's switch," Roan said to Marshall, who had a snowy white charger that had a stride as light as a rabbit's and pissed rainbows…or so it seemed to Roan who couldn't find anything positive about the fiery Jetta.

Marshall wouldn't switch. They had "bonded," he claimed. Seething, Roan tried again to mount the horse. He needed to have some idea of what he was doing before they left the protection of the city. Speed was quite literally their only ally and they wouldn't be all that speedy if he couldn't keep his ass on the horse's back.

Amanda tried whispering soothingly to Jetta, but that only made his ears go back and forth and the skin on his back twitch.

"Do you know any songs, milady?" one of the stable hands asked. "This one likes a good song."

"Maybe," she said, casting a glance up at Roan. Quietly, at first, she began to sing a song that had been popular in the real world thirty years before. As she sang, she pulled Jetta around by her harness. The song worked and not just on Jetta. Roan found himself lulled by Amanda's voice and the next time she looked back at him, he was caught staring.

"Tha-that was good," he said. "I think I have the hang of this, thanks." In truth he didn't. He and Jetta fought all the way down to the gates, where they found out that they weren't going to benefit all that much from speed. The road west ran as straight as a rattlesnake's back through miles of salt marshes and was so narrow that it was dangerous for anything larger than a handcart.

The four of them stared at the road feeling tired, even though the day had just begun. A mosquito landed on Jarrod's hand. He smacked it, saying, "I can deal with bandits, but bandits and mosquitoes? I have to draw the line somewhere. What do you think we'll find in Mendenome? Everything has to have been looted by now and I'm sure we won't find Arching taking up residence in the home of the man he murdered."

Marshall reached over and punched Jarrod in the arm. "Stop being a wimp. Gethahyme, Master of the Red Wizards had to be loaded. Oh, I bet there's still some goodies in Mendenome."

That helped Jarrod's state of mind. With fresh eagerness he led the way, cantering along. Roan took up the rear, feeling his spine compress further with every one of Jetta's strides. *At least I'm still on board,* he thought, seconds before a black fly as big as his knuckle landed on Jetta's neck and bit him.

The horse kicked and Roan felt two seconds of flight time before he landed on the side of the path.

Amanda fetched Jetta's bridle and pulled the errant horse back. "It seems like you lost something."

"Nothing I really need," he groused, picking himself up and dusting off his new clothes.

She tried to hide her smirk as she effortlessly turned both horses around, allowing him to mount once more. Amanda's horse, Rhi-adol, was dun colored and had a pleasant way about her. The two seemed perfectly matched in temperament. "Why can't you be more like Rhi-adol? She's very well mannered and…" Jetta wasn't listening. He dashed forward to catch up to the others, mindless of whether or not he had a rider on his back, which he did, barely.

The biting flies and the mosquitos were enough to drive a man and a horse mad. They became so bad that Roan actually began to feel sorry for Jetta as he shivered and shook from the endless torment. Roan laid his bedroll over the gelding's back to keep him from being bitten and waved nonstop at his ears, which began to bleed from all the bites.

The insects were irritating, but at least they weren't dangerous. What followed next was. Clouds had been building up, and after two hours of riding through the marsh, the dark sky opened up in a deluge. In seconds, they were all soaked from a grey rain. Roan slid from Jetta's back and tried to roll up his bedding, only now it was more of a long sponge than anything one would use to sleep on. It defied his attempts to get it back in its waterproof shell.

"As if that matters anymore," he grumbled.

He was still on his knees, fighting with the rain-sodden material, when the first arrow landed next to his hand. It was a strange arrow with a somewhat twisted shaft and a piece of flint for a point. He was still staring at it when a second hit his bedroll and stuck there.

"Incoming fire!" Roan hollered, leaving the bedroll. He tried climbing up onto Jetta's back, but managed to get only one foot in the stirrups as the horse danced in a full circle with him hopping along next to him, feeling not just idiotic, but also as vulnerable as hell as more arrows were shot into the group.

Unfortunately, one struck Jetta on the hindquarters. The horse let out a sound like a scream as it reared up, kicking nothing but rain with its front hooves. Roan knew the horse would bolt the second it came down and to prevent that, he made a last desperate attempt to get on its back.

He was only partially successful, and found himself in much the same position as the bedroll had been, draped over the horse as it raced away down the path, leaving the others. Jetta was in an all-out sprint and fairly flew as it put a hundred yards between them and the archers in seconds. Then the path took a sharp turn that the horse couldn't manage at the speed he was traveling. Roan was thrown into a bog, while Jetta slid on his side into the muck on the side of the road.

With its hurt leg, the horse couldn't free itself. Cursing the ill-fortune of having such a pain for a horse, Roan waded to Jetta and heaved against the horse's back end, his feet slipping in the bog, but slowly forcing the creature towards the road.

The others rode up as he was still struggling. "Jarrod, get in here and help me!" Roan ordered. "Marshall provide cover with your shield and Amanda, heal the horse. He's got an arrow in his leg."

"Can I heal a horse?" Amanda asked Marshall.

"Why not?" he answered. "Just hurry. I think those are troglodytes. They are bad news when you're in their territory."

Roan looked past the horse's rump at the troglodytes. They were bizarre creatures that seemed to be half-man, half-crocodile. They used their long tails to propel themselves through the bogs. "Damn," he whispered.

"You got that right," Jarrod said, making a face as he came up behind the horse and started pushing. "Where the hell is Glitch? Wasn't he supposed to scout the road?"

Roan tried to sense the little elemental but he felt nothing. This wasn't unusual; their telepathic communication had its limitations. It had a range to it much like actual speaking. "He's doing what I told him to do," Roan said. "I told him to scout out the road and this attack is not coming from the road. Now, shut up and push harder."

Together, they managed to get Jetta onto the road, just as Amanda healed him. "Alright! Everyone, mount up!" Roan cried. As the others leapt up into their saddles, Roan begged, "Please, Jetta, just let me get on."

Jetta's answer was a firm "no." Roan had never been more tempted to punch an animal in the face as it tried to dance away again, only to run into Amanda's horse. She had purposefully waited for Roan, positioning her horse perfectly. Quickly, Roan clambered up into the saddle and, as the troglodytes splashed from one muddy little island to the next, heading for the road, the two cantered away.

"Do you see how I'm holding the reins?" Amanda asked. "I'm not..." An arrow bounced off her armor, causing her to hesitate. There really wasn't much they could do about the arrows. Luckily, there weren't many archers among the troglodytes and the ones they did have weren't all that good. Amanda went on, "I'm not using the reins to hold on. They're simply for steering. See?"

Roan had been holding his in a death grip. He eased off and the horse immediately flicked his head as if to say: *Thank God, you were strangling me!*

"There you go," Amanda said, smiling despite the occasional swish of a passing arrow. "Now, let's try to pick up the pace. If you have to, hold onto the pommel, but what you really want to do is squeeze with your knees and trust in your horse. He's not going to buck you off on purpose."

"Have you met this horse, yet?" Roan asked. Her smile was infectious and in spite of his hammering heart over the prospect of yet another fall, he grinned at her. The grin didn't last as they began trotting. He found himself bouncing up and down, feeling as though he were working opposite of the horse.

Amanda saw it as well. "Find the rhythm. When he's going up, you should as well, and drop when he does. No…it's a small motion."

He was just starting to get it when they caught up with Marshall and Jarrod. Glitch was there as well and although it was an air elemental and didn't have real features that Roan could make out, it looked miserable nonetheless. Glitch had shrunk in on itself, seeming smaller, and it shivered as the heavy rain passed through it.

Glitch showed Roan a blurry image of the road ahead, empty except for the pouring rain. "How far did you go?" The image fast forwarded only a few miles. There wasn't much to see. The elemental had a real issue with water and surprised Roan by ducking up under his cloak.

"He doesn't like the rain," Roan explained to the others. "He can't see very well in it."

"Then there could be another ambush ahead?" Jarrod asked. "We're screwed. We can't go on and we can't go back."

"We can go on," Roan said. "There's no proof that there'll even be another ambush. And if there is, well, we'll deal with it. I don't see us having any other choice. Besides, this isn't exactly ambush weather. Those troglodytes might like it, but I bet the bandits are holed up somewhere, keeping warm."

No one believed this statement, not even Roan. If Arching had a spy in Tir-Kahn, then there'd be an ambush. The only question was whether or not they'd be able to slip past it or not. There were smaller paths that squiggled away from the main one heading out into the marshes, which were dotted with mud-islands, cattails, bulrushes and haunted looking alder trees.

When they came to the first of these trails, the four of them sat on their horses gazing off into the rain. The path ran north, but where it led to none of them wanted to find out.

A little while later they discovered that the marshes were home to things worse than troglodytes and bandits. They were passing a particularly nasty looking bog that came almost to the edge of the road when Amanda jumped in her saddle.

"Look," she said, breathlessly, pointing to where the bog met the road. As they watched, the bog itself surged onto the road, going for the hooves of the horses. "What the hell is that?"

"It's a bog slime," Marshall answered. "Think of it as a giant carnivorous hunk of snot that can swallow a horse. They're mostly dangerous at night or if you decide to go swimming in the wrong pond."

While Amanda calmly backed her horse away, Roan had to hold Jetta back from bolting. "Easy, it's just some snot. It's nothing to be afraid of." Jetta didn't believe it and shook until they had left the bog slime far behind.

The next oddity they discovered was a set of huge footprints, each over a yard in length. They came up out of the marsh on one side of the road, trailed across it in a diagonal, before they disappeared on the other side behind a copse of hoary, moss-covered sycamores.

"Those tracks are fresh," Roan said. The rain was only just beginning to wash them away. "Glitch? Do you mind checking out what's behind those trees?" Glitch peeked out from his cloak and shivered; still it left the warmth of the cloak, sped to the trees, and came back as quickly as it could. "He didn't see anything."

"Hold on, time out. That was a pretty quick check," Jarrod said. "If that had been me, you would have sent me back a second time. Maybe you should consider sending him one more time."

Roan had seen through Glitch's eyes, and knew another trip wouldn't clear up the mystery of what had made the tracks and where it had gone. "No, if it was invisible, another look won't do any good. We'll just hurry on by." They did so with their bows half-drawn back, but whatever had made the tracks either kept hidden, or was so far away that it was oblivious to them.

Although they were all hungry, no one wanted to stop any time soon after seeing those tracks, and it was another hour before they stopped to eat some of the rations they had bought in the hill town. The meal wasn't as bad as Roan had supposed it would be: hard, but flavorful cheeses, salted meats, and bread that had a very brittle crust but a soft core.

They ate under a willow where the rain barely touched them. Even Glitch came out to fly around for a bit. Once lunch was over, Roan sent Glitch out into the rain once more and it wasn't long before it returned with visions of dozens of bandits, both human and goblin, squatting in the rain, smack dab in the middle of the road. It was clear that they were waiting for Roan's little group.

2—

"Is there a way around?" Amanda asked. "Thirty against four is bad odds. I know we've gotten a little stronger, but still, I don't like it."

"What are your levels?" Jarrod asked. "I'm fourth." Amanda and Marshall admitted to being fourth as well, while Roan told them fifth. "I guess that's good, but I'm with Amanda. I think I'd rather take my chances with one of these side trails. How far back was the last one, I wasn't paying attention."

Amanda remembered passing one after seeing the giant muddy foot prints. That threw a damper on the idea of going back. "Maybe we could send Glitch?" she suggested, putting out a hand to the puff of air. "He's very tough and brave…and smart. He should be okay, right?"

It bothered Roan to send it out in the rain. For him it was like sending his child on a dangerous mission. Glitch left, but did so at full speed, rocketing away faster than any bird could fly. It was gone exactly four minutes and when it came back, it was in a wild state.

!!!—!!!—!!!

"What is it?" Roan asked, opening his mind and seeing the pictures: twelve adventurers were hastening up behind them. They were led by the rogue who had asked to join them in the attempt on Mendenome back in the market place of Tir-Kahn. What were the chances that the thief was just doing his own thing and bid them no ill will? "Zero," Roan said under his breath.

In spite of Roan's inexperience on horseback, the group had carried on at a pretty good clip—faster than walking that was for certain. This meant that either the rogue's group had to have jogged all the way, or they had left earlier and had been hiding on some side trail and were now coming to trap Roan's party between a rock and a hard place.

As the adventurers showed no sign of a ten mile run, Roan could only conclude that they were in deep trouble. He explained the situation and when Jarrod started to groan, Roan shoved him to the ground. "We don't have time for that! As far as I can tell, they have six fighters, two rogues, two spell casters and two clerics. The question is, do we fight them or the bandits? We can't do both."

"If we fight the adventures and win, we can at least make it back to Tir-Kahn," Amanda said. "But if we beat the bandits, we'll still have to face the adventurers, unless we plan to outrun them. Did they have horses?" Roan shook his head. She frowned, looking further down the road in the direction in which they had been traveling. "Then I say we go on."

"You're not still thinking of going to Mendenome, are you?" Jarrod asked, after he climbed to his feet. "I thought we came this way to look for clues. That'll take hours. They'll catch up. It'll be two fights in one day and I don't think we can do that. I say we go back. Could you tell what level they were?"

Roan wasn't an expert on that sort of thing. "Some of them were like the rogues, kind of dirty, but some of the fighters wore half plate. So, either they were financed at a low level or they fought enough to afford it. Either way isn't good for us." He turned to Marshall to get his input, however the paladin was as noncommittal as always, which left Roan once again deciding things.

"I say we attack the bandits in front of us. We're here for information and we're not going to get it back in Tir-Kahn. They don't have archers so we'll start with arrows at a hundred yards. Chances are they'll lock shields and charge, if so, we'll keep firing until they get close. I'll fire off a spell and then we'll blast straight through them. Since Marshall and Amanda have the best armor class, they'll go first. I don't know what the rules are in this world, but in the other, the secret to a cavalry charge is unstinting speed. It takes training to stand up to fifteen hundred pounds of charging horse."

He waited for questions and comments, but there were none. Glitch led the way, this time without complaint. Roan was able to see through its eyes as the bandits spotted them through the rain. They jumped up, grabbing their weapons, most of which were spears and clubs. The bandits with shields moved to the front and as expected, they attempted to form a phalanx.

It was a weak effort. Their shields were too small and it was obvious that they hadn't drilled.

"Ready—aim—fire!" Roan said, and let loose his first arrow. His skipped harmlessly off a shield, but Marshall's pierced an eye, killing one of the men. They drew back their bows a second time and fired. This time Roan's struck as did Amanda's. On their third flight, only Jarrod missed. He started cursing, however it was then that the bandits realized that sitting there taking hits every few seconds was a terrible battle plan.

They began to creep up, which made their phalanx even less effective and the arrows scored more and more. When they were at fifty yards, Roan threw his bow across his back and began the *Inferno* spell, not knowing exactly what it would do.

"Eida fa dwi!" he intoned and then blinked in amazement as what looked like a fiery missile shot from his palm. It even roared like a launched missile as it arced through the air, growing larger and larger until it was the size of an SUV on impact. When it exploded it tripled in size and was so blinding that Roan almost missed the words under his vision: (*XP +22*), (*XP +22*), (*XP +22*), (*XP +22*)…

"Holy crap," he whispered.

He was still staring when Marshall yelled, "Mount up! They're not all dead." Amanda was already on Rhi-adol and was holding Jetta's bridle—of course Jetta was not dancing around for her. Roan's adrenaline must have been pumping after the explosion because he practically leapt straight onto Jetta's back without touching the stirrup.

That was the easy part. A second later Amanda and Marshall were racing forward, their swords drawn and held high. They blasted through the remnants of the bandits, scattering them. Jarrod was right behind them, looking back as Roan and Jetta did their usual stupid dance. Jetta was turning in circles and every time Roan tried to correct him, Jetta would go too far the other way.

Round and round they went. *I'm going to die,* Roan thought. *This stupid horse is seriously going to kill me.* The thought seemed so utterly true in his mind that it was somewhat liberating. He even went so far as to stop fighting Jetta. *What will be, will be*, he thought and let go of the reins altogether.

What happened next was magic that no wizard could have conjured. Jetta spun around, gathered his legs beneath him and then launched himself at a full gallop, heading right down the path, racing to join the others, with Roan leaning over his back with his hands in the horse's mane.

Jarrod yelled, "Come on! Come on!"

The screams seemed to spur Jetta and he raced through the blast zone of Roan's *Inferno* spell. The remaining bandits, fifteen or sixteen of them, surged towards them. Jetta was going too fast for most of them, but not all. At least two were close enough to attack.

"Glitch!"

The air elemental went for the eyes of the first with its *Haze* attack. The bandit flinched as he swung his club and it whistled just in front of Jetta's nose. The next bandit wasn't going to miss such a large target. It was a big goblin wielding a notched sword. With Roan sitting so high, the goblin went for the horse's back leg.

Roan reacted instinctually. He couldn't draw his sword in time and so he could only protect the horse's leg by sacrificing his own. Dropping down, he placed his leg in the way of the swinging sword and when it struck bone, (*Damage-Critical Hit - 18*) the pain was so exquisite, he had to stifle a scream.

He fell forward across Jetta's back and was completely in the horse's power. Had Jetta wished, he could have bucked him off with little more than a flick of his tail, instead the ride became smooth. For once, the horse felt as though it were gliding on ice.

"Are you alright?" Marshall asked, as Jetta caught up with him. He eyed Roan's bloody leg with a queasy look on his face.

Roan was still struggling not to scream. He didn't think he was alright, but didn't want to chance seeing what his leg looked like, afraid that if he did, he'd faint. "I-I'm g-good," he was able to spit out.

"I don't think so." Marshall glanced back towards where the bandits were standing. The road was covered in steam and dead bodies. "Amanda! We need your help over here."

Marshall reached across the space between the two horses for Jetta's reins, sending a sudden panic into Roan. "No, don't." Touching the reins was the surest way to set Jetta off and just at that moment, it was the last thing that Roan wanted. "Whoa," he said to his horse. "Slow down, boy." Jetta's ears spun back—he was listening. Gradually, the horse slowed and then stopped half a mile from the ambush site.

Amanda had checked her steed and was now trotting back. "What's going…oh, lord! Roan, your leg!" She dropped from her horse even as she spoke the words to her healing spell. The effect was immediate and he groaned, not in pleasure, but in relief.

Flexing his foot up and down, he pushed up from Jetta's back so that he was sitting tall in the saddle, again. "Thank you. That was…that was bad." He passed a shaking hand across his face, wiping away the rain and the sweat.

Jarrod shook his head. "And that's why I never play the game on extreme. Only a masochist would do something like that. Hey, maybe Arching is a sadist? Maybe he gets his rocks off by hurting people? You ever think about that?"

"And how does that help us catch him?" Roan asked, slipping from Jetta's back. He tested his lower leg where the echo of pain still reverberated. It was good to go. He then turned to Jetta's harness, slipping the bit out of his mouth and tossing it aside. Next, he started to undo the straps holding the bridle in place.

"What are you doing?" Amanda asked. "You're not letting the horse go, are you? Roan, please, if you do that out here, he'll die."

Roan had been tracing the leather straps, trying to see where the reins connected. "I'm not releasing him. It's all of this extra stuff. He doesn't like it. Yes, I know its purpose is to control and direct the horse, but maybe not all horses are the same. This one certainly isn't. Are you boy?"

Jetta lifted his head, blowing out in a manner that was more of a grunt than a neigh.

"See?"

"I see you're gonna regret taking that off," Jarrod said. "But, hey, you're the boss."

Though she didn't say it aloud, it was obvious Amanda agreed with Jarrod. She picked up the bit and bridle, remarking, "They still cost money. Come on, we should go."

Roan let her canter ahead before he whispered into Jetta's ear. "You did well back there, but you are still one false step away from the glue factory, got it?" In answer, Jetta took a large bite of marsh grass. "I'm going to take that as a yes."

Carefully, he put one foot in the stirrup and then began hopping as Jetta started moving away. Jarrod started snorting laughter. Roan shot him an angry look and tried again, this time ignoring the stirrup altogether. With one hand on the pommel and the other on Jetta's rump, he simultaneously jumped and pushed up, then swung his leg over.

Jetta gave him a look before taking another bite of grass. "Okay, that's enough for now," Roan said, giving the horse a little kick in the side. He was pleasantly surprised when Jetta trotted to join the others.

With Glitch braving the rain to scout ahead, the four rode along the path at a quick clip, needing to put as much distance between them and the bandits. Jetta was extremely well behaved, so much so that Roan found himself, at first, actually enjoying the ride—then his ass began to ache.

It felt like blisters were starting to form in places they had no right to form. When he groaned once too often, Amanda asked what was wrong. He made the mistake of telling her; she almost fell out of her saddle laughing, but she was so cute that he couldn't stay mad at her.

"Just one more reason not to play on extreme," Jarrod said. "If you were as smart as your character, you'd know that, Roan."

"No, you're wrong, Jarrod. If I hadn't been playing on extreme, I'd still be fourth level and we wouldn't have gotten past those bandits. We'd be dead and starting over, and who knows how many people...how many *real* people would die because of that?"

"Oh," Jarrod said, quietly. "I didn't think of it that way."

The group fell silent, concentrating on riding through the muck. It wasn't easy, especially for Roan who could only steer Jetta, through subtle tugs on his mane. Anything else was ignored by the horse or resulted in him fighting back.

Still, the two made progress as rider and mount, so that when the marsh gave way to gentle rolling hills that ran with thousands of small, rain-swollen streams, Roan felt that he was close to being the one in control.

The cold, grey rain, which had been a drenching downpour for most of the day, turned into a soft drizzle and then, just around four in the afternoon, it turned to a fine mist. It was through a veil of this mist that they first caught sight of Mendenome, the citadel of Gethahyme, Master of the Red Wizards.

The castle, which sat on the tallest of the hills, seemed to Roan to be a testament to loneliness. It was fair to say that it was one of the finest castles he had ever seen. It dominated everything around it, the only problem, there wasn't anything around it except the empty hills.

Walls encircled the grounds to keep people out, only there weren't any people. There wasn't even a village. And there were tall spires which must have magnificent views, but who would see them?

It made no sense to Roan. Why had Greg Nelson gone to such great lengths to help build this wonderful world and then this fantastic castle, only to sit in it alone with only a few NPC servants around?

"Glitch, can you check it out, please?" Glitch was much happier now that the rain had stopped and it zoomed off. In no time, it was making an alarmed noise in Roan's head: *!!!—!!!* Although Mendenome had been built in the middle of nowhere, it had had a lot of visitors in the last week—and they all seemed just as dead as Greg Nelson.

There were crow-picked corpses all over the castle grounds; hundreds of them. Glitch flew around, looking for something or someone left alive, but only the crows moved, jumping and squawking as the elemental went here and there. The bodies made Glitch nervous and he came back without going into the citadel itself.

Roan turned to the others. "You know how Cole told us there had been a break-in? The battle was bigger than I expected. There's got to be two or three hundred bodies in there. But none are alive as far as Glitch could see." He gave Jetta a light tap on the hindquarters to get him moving towards the gate. It was as far as the horse would go and Roan didn't blame him, the smell of death and decay wafting from the courtyard was atrocious.

The bodies were piled three deep in the short tunnel that ran through the wall. The four of them dismounted and left the horses to graze. Drawing their swords, they moved slowly and carefully into the courtyard to see the horror first hand.

"What the hell? Why are they all naked?" Amanda asked. The corpses had been stripped down to their underwear, if they'd been wearing any.

"Sca...scavengers," Marshall said, hiding his face in his cloak. He began gulping air instead of breathing normally. When he vomited seconds later, he only added to the stench and complete foulness of the scene.

Jarrod, who had his undershirt pulled up from beneath his leather armor, was staring all around him, his eyes huge in their sockets, and when he spoke it was with difficulty. "Swords, armor, a-all of it has value. H-how are you two s-so a-all normal?"

"When you're in the field, you see a lot of death," Amanda said. "Though I've never seen this many corpses in one place. This wasn't one battle. Look at the dead on the bottom. Look how decomposed they are. Compare them to that orc. The birds haven't even touched that one."

"It's like they are stratified," Roan said. He stepped through the mess until he got to the orc and then put the back of his hand on its cheek. As expected, it was cool to the touch while unexpectedly, its flesh was soft and pliant. He rolled the orc onto its back and touched its throat. "It's still warm and lividity isn't yet fixed. Death might have been in the last four hours."

While Jarrod and Marshall looked up at the citadel as if expecting a storm of orcs to attack, Amanda only shrugged. "I don't think we know enough about orc anatomy and physiology to make any conclusions just yet. Unless you two...never mind."

It was clear that Jarrod and Marshall knew next to nothing concerning the science of pathology and even if they did, they couldn't stomach looking at the dead.

"Okay, I'll run it," Roan said, gesturing around. "We have the initial attack a week ago. After that, I see evidence of at least six different battles. Man versus man, orc versus man, orc versus orc, goblin versus orc and maybe a mixture of all three at once. The question is, who won? Who's in there?"

Everyone looked to Glitch for answers. Bravely, the elemental led the way into the citadel, however Roan wouldn't let him get too far in front. Glitch wasn't immortal or immune to magic.

And there was definitely magic in Mendenome. Roan could feel it the moment he walked into the front greeting room, which was wide and spacious, brightly lit with floating globes of golden light. It was wonderful. The stonework was beautiful, the etched tile amazing in its detail, the vaulted ceilings gave everything an airy feel, and it was all ruined by the bodies littering the ground, some old and bloated and others fresh and still bleeding.

Roan and Amanda were just inspecting them when, from somewhere above them, there was a crash of metal falling. The four froze, swords at the ready.

When the sound didn't repeat, Roan said, "It's just as we guessed, someone is home. We'll go through this place one room at a time. Marshall and I will take point and…" Amanda cleared her throat and shook her head, reminding him that in this world she had the better armor and was his equal when it came to sword work. "Right, sorry. Marshall and Amanda will take point and Jarrod will take up the rear. Got it?"

They all understood their roles, and with Glitch entering each room ahead of them, they moved deeper into the castle. As they went, they discovered fewer and fewer bodies, but that did not make them feel any less uneasy. More noises kept filtering down from above them. It sounded as if someone was taking a hammer to the walls.

Although the others kept glancing nervously upward, Roan considered the sound a blessing. It suggested that whoever was in the castle didn't know about them yet, which gave them the element of surprise. As well, the noise would cover the sound of their approach.

He hurried them through the rooms, all of which had been ransacked in one way or another: paintings had been pulled from the walls, silverware stolen from cupboards, jewels pried from a huge throne that sat in an audience chamber. The throne itself had been toppled and dragged halfway from the dais on which it had once sat. Roan thought the bandits must have given up when they realized that, although worth thousands in gold, there was no way to cart it all the way back to Tir-Kahn.

Along with the upended throne in the room, there were two tremendous stone statues. One was laid out on the floor on its side, its arms flung, while the other had fallen against the far wall and had partially crashed through. Both were oddly scored as if someone had tried hacking at them with swords. "That's strange," Amanda said. "Why would anyone do that?"

"They weren't just statues," Jarrod explained. He picked at a crack in one of them, saying, "They were stone golems, I bet. They could come alive and attack people and boy are they tough sons of bitches. Whoever came to take out Nelson was bad ass to get past these two. They're worthless now."

He started to go onto the next room, but Roan stopped him. "Could Cole have done this? Is he strong enough?"

"Not by himself," Marshall said. "There was a wizard or two with whoever did this. See all those scorch marks? That's magic. Either way, Cole wasn't here. He was back in the real world."

"So he says," Amanda remarked. "We have nothing but his word, which I do not value very highly. He was meeting with adventurers. Probably hiring them for Arching which I guess means that Arching wasn't as powerful as Nelson."

Roan shook his head. "That doesn't exactly add up. I don't think this was about who was stronger than who in this world. Nelson and the others died because he was trying to break Arching's monopoly, I think that is obvious. The question is, how did Arching do it? How did he use the magic in this world to kill in the other? Hopefully, we'll find the answers up there." He glanced to the ceiling of the throne room.

Roan wanted to head up right away, but he knew better. They had a few more rooms to clear before it would be safe to go up. Along with the main entrance to the throne room, there were two doors and he sent Glitch to the one on the left.

The elemental slipped beneath the crack of the door and immediately shrieked an alarm into Roan's head.

!!! Roan went stiff as Glitch showed him eight orcs crouched in the room. They had their swords at the ready. It was an ambush, which meant that for all his genius, Roan was standing in the middle of a trap.

2—

The hammering from above had lulled him into a sense of security, but it had been a ruse—and now it stopped.

"Don't," Roan whispered to Marshall, who had his hand out to the doorknob. Roan's team looked to him as he shook his head and put a finger to his lips. *Glitch,* he thought, *check out the other door.*

Glitch slipped out of the first room and into the second. There were more orcs here. Roan counted ten of them and one carried a circular shield. Under a splash of blood, he saw that there was a fading yellow flower painted on it. It had belonged Taegus Estes.

At the bottom of his vision were the words: *Taegus Estes quest requirements: return to Tedra Estes with the news of her brother's…* Angrily, Roan thought the words away. He had his own quest to worry about and just then it was balanced on a knife's edge.

With a low whistle, he recalled Glitch and turned. Now, there was only one exit from the throne room left to them, and he didn't need to be a genius to know that orcs would be coming from that direction as well.

"This way," he said to the others and ran for the one partially standing golem. When it had "died," it had fallen to the side, smashing in part of the wall. There was a gap ten feet up that a man could just fit through. Roan sheathed his sword and began climbing the golem. As he was without armor, he was both nimble and quiet. Amanda was more nimble than quiet, while Marshall was neither.

He fell from the golem's knee with a clatter of metal and a smattering of curses. For reasons that weren't obvious to Roan, this triggered the trap. The doors on either side of the room opened and the orcs came screaming into the throne room, which brought on the attack from the hall beyond the main doors.

!!!

"I know," Roan said, pulling his bow from his back and nocking an arrow. He aimed at the chest of the first orc that made its way around the downed throne. The orc, with its mottled yellow tusks, its greasy grey flesh and its vermin ridden leather armor was repellent to Roan on a visceral level, and it was with some joy that he stuck the feathered shaft into the heart of the beast. (*XP +22*)

"Jarrod, help Marshall," Roan ordered, pulling a second arrow. Other than *Incinerate*, he still had all of his spells available, but as he had no idea what would be coming next, he held them in reserve. He fired his next arrow and missed. "What the hell!" he snarled, reaching for another.

He knew that as a wizard, he had the worst combat progression of any class. Still, with his sixteen dexterity and his level, he was shooting with a (*+5*) against a thirteen armor class; he should have been hitting sixty percent of the time. Were the misses another glitch? He could only hope not since he needed to hit on every try.

Amanda was doing better and had hit three straight times, giving Jarrod just enough time to help Marshall up to the lap of the statue. By then a flood of orcs from the hall had joined the others—there were too many to count now.

It was time to escape while they still could. "Let's go!" Roan cried and climbed to the golem's shoulder. He ducked through the hole in the wall and found himself in a pitch-black room, the dimensions of which even his elven eyes couldn't make out. Stumbling forward, his outstretched hand hit something steel—a pole, with thin metal lines running in two directions, forming… "A shelf," he muttered.

Another step and he found what was probably a rack and then another. "Glitch! Can you find a door?"

"Ssss," Glitch said. A second later, he made more of the hissing noises. Roan followed them, knocking into who knew what in the dark. When he finally found the doorknob and pushed open the door into a kitchen, he turned and saw that he had been in a windowless pantry.

Amanda came out blinking against the new light. She was followed by Marshall and then Jarrod, who was pushing his friend along. "They're right behind me!" He slammed the door behind him as Roan and Amanda grabbed a stainless steel table and heaved it in front of the door.

It was all the time they had for a barricade. Roan raced for the door to the kitchen, calling once more on the elemental: "Glitch, find the stairs."

"The stairs?" Jarrod cried. "No, we need to find the freaking way out of here."

"The stairs, Glitch," Roan said, slamming through the door and finding himself in a hall that he recognized. They had been there fifteen minutes earlier and now he knew where he was. He didn't need Glitch to find the stairs, they were down the hall and around the corner.

He sprinted, accidentally leaving the others behind. The stairs to the second and third floors were set in a huge atrium. A dozen men could walk abreast up those stairs and Roan felt small as he stood on the third step up waiting for his team to catch up.

He also felt terribly exposed as he stood alone facing at least half the orcs who had run back through the main entrance of the throne room and were now charging him. A couple of arrows fired from a single bow wouldn't cut it this time.

"Eda-eram gdiy!" Roan yelled and then fell back, tripping as the force of the *Thunderous Wave* spell blasted out of him and struck the orcs (*XP +22*), (*XP +22*), (*XP +22*), (*XP +22*), (*XP +22*). Five were killed outright by the power behind the spell while others were stunned, some with blood dripping from their ears and noses.

The rest of his team rounded the corner. Jarrod was pointing towards the front of the building, hoping to get Roan to change his mind, but Roan only turned and ran up the stairs. He knew that he was trapping them once again, but it was the right thing. *At least, they would barely feel their deaths*, he thought. His would be horrible.

When he got to the third level, he turned and nocked another arrow, letting it fly at the orcs following close on Marshall's heels—Hit! (*XP +22*) The lead orc fell, causing a little pile up among the rest. Roan fired again—a miss. "Damn." One more arrow was a hit but didn't kill the orc.

By then Amanda was next to him. "How do we get up higher?" Roan didn't know, but thankfully, Glitch had been searching and was now hissing and sending images into Roan's mind.

"This way." The second floor was dedicated to culture: music rooms, art studios, salons, and libraries. The third floor was where the guests had their suites. Roan guessed that these floors had been built by Nelson and then completely ignored by him.

What mattered to the Nelson was what was above: the wizard's tower. It was here that Nelson experimented and practiced his spells. It was here that he crafted potions, wrote magic scrolls, and conjured all sorts of demons from the dark planes. It was here where he kept his secrets and his treasures.

"What did he have guarding it all?" Roan wondered as he opened a door and saw a set of much narrower stairs heading up. He supposed that there had been numerous traps and dangerous creatures along the way to the very top. It was a good guess that none were left. Whoever had taken out Nelson would have sprung the traps and killed the creatures—he hoped.

The stairs only went up a single flight, ending at a door. Glitch was already slipping between the cracks. He showed Roan an empty corridor that went left and right. There was a door straight across from the stairwell door. It was a perfect place for another trap, but with the orcs hot on their tail, Roan didn't have time to fret.

He burst through, an arrow half-pulled to his right ear. Amanda jostled him to the side as she took up a position facing down the opposite corridor. Two seconds later, Jarrod and then Marshall rushed through the door, out of breath.

"Jarrod and Marshall, hold the door shut," Roan ordered. "Glitch, find me the next set of stairs. Amanda and I will find something that we can use to block the door."

It was a good plan, but it failed in seconds. In his current form, Marshall was very strong and Jarrod was at least average, but there were just two of them trying to hold back twenty times their number. The door was pushed half-open before Amanda and Roan had taken more than ten steps.

"New plan!" Amanda yelled and loosed an arrow into the gap. Roan's arrow followed right after (*XP +22*).

Then they were all running down the corridor which ended at a sharp ninety-degree turn. They passed door after door until the corridor took another right turn. Glitch was there, spinning in frantic circles in front of a door set in the exact middle of the corridor. It was the door to the next set of stairs and Roan was sure that he would find the same setup at the top of this set of stairs as well.

"Up!" he ordered. They couldn't keep going up forever, but he knew that his *Thunderous Wave* spell would be more effective in a cramped space. He pushed Amanda and Jarrod ahead of him and then trailed along with Marshall, who was sucking wind. The weight of his armor combined with all the sprinting and the stairs was dragging him down.

Roan took a hold of the back of his armor and heaved him along, helping as best as he could. When they got to the top, he thrust Marshall through the door and spun around. Below him, the stairs were crammed with orcs and more were pressing in from the open door.

The orcs in front knew they were dealing with a wizard and blanched back, only to be pushed onward by the rest. Roan waited until they were almost within reach before he let loose with another of his *Thunderous Wave* spells.

In the cramped stairwell, the sound was not just focused, it was trapped. The BOOM blasted into the orcs and then came back in a mind-numbing echo that sent Roan to his knees. His world swam with images both real and unreal; there was the stairwell heaped with dead orcs, mixed with the neon words: (*Damage -8, Stunned +5 Rounds*) (*XP +22*), (*XP +22*), (*XP +22*), (*XP +22*)...His brain felt like grey jelly, sloshing in his head and he fell over, senseless.

The next thing he knew, hands encased in steel were pulling him up and hauling him along a corridor that kept tilting up and down in a sickening manner. He was on the verge of hurling up whatever was in his stomach when they hit another set of stairs. Marshall was reeling from exhaustion and Roan fell from his grip.

Amanda was suddenly kneeling on the stair next to Roan. She gave Marshall a push, saying, "I have this, Marshall, get up those stairs. You and Glitch find a way to block the door on the next level. Find something big to put in front of the door."

"We need to find a way down, not up," Jarrod cried. He had his back to the lower stairwell door, his feet braced, but had yet to be tested. After what happened in the last stairwell, the orcs were probably not eager to face Roan's power so quickly.

They wouldn't hold back for long. "Jarrod, just keep that door from opening!" Amanda cried, her voice high and shrill in her stress. "I don't care how, just do it." She then looked down on Roan—there were at least three of her in his vision and he couldn't decide which he was supposed to focus on. "And you," she whispered. "You're an idiot, you know that?"

As his head was so numb that he couldn't remember his middle name, he didn't argue. She put her hands on his chest and spoke strange, magical words and a blue light poured over him. The relief was immediate. His world stopped spinning and the ringing in his ear disappeared.

The feel of those hands on his chest remained. They were so warm and soft...and perhaps even loving, that he didn't want to move, no matter the danger. "I'm an idiot?" It hadn't sounded like a put down when she had said it.

She snatched her hands away. "Y-You heard that? Well, you are one." She was up and moving before he could blink.

He stood, feeling not just healed, but rested as well. "Hold that door as long as you can, Jarrod."

"But..."

Roan didn't have time for arguments. Ignoring Jarrod, he ran up the stairs after Amanda. Glitch had found something large and was spinning and pulsing in front of Marshall, trying to get him to understand where it was. Roan knew. "In the third room on the right! It's a cage."

In the vision Glitch had sent into his mind, it looked as though the cage was filled with rotting cabbage...but with arms. "What is that?" he asked Marshall as he caught up with the paladin in the room.

"It doesn't matter," Amanda answered for him. "Just move it. I can hear them coming."

Roan couldn't hear the orcs, but he could hear Jarrod screaming: "They're here! They're here!"

Marshall hurried to one side of the cage and heaved; it slid three inches and stopped. Roan was about to join him when something else in the room caught his attention. There were eight bodies in the room, all of which were naked. Seven of them seemed to have been burned and tortured and yet, they were lined up side by side, their hands clasped on their chests. Someone had taken the time to arrange them in a respectable manner.

The eighth corpse had not been given the same treatment. It was laying in a heap in the corner of the room, its arms akimbo, its mouth wide open, showing a hugely swollen black tongue. The corpses spoke to him. They told him a story. They pointed to a fantastic, but one-sided battle in which...

"Roan!" Marshall yelled. "Come on!"

"Sorry," Roan said, coming around the cage. Together they managed to slide the cage out of the room and into the corridor. At the same time, Jarrod raced up out of the stairwell and slammed the door behind him. "There's got to be at least a hundred of them," Jarrod cried in a fright. The door banged behind him and he strained against it.

Amanda joined him, pushing with all her might. Still the door began to open and Roan saw that he and Marshall wouldn't get the cage to it in time. Stepping back, he pulled back his sleeve where he had etched three glyphs into his skin; each letting off little wisps of smoke. He spoke his magic and suddenly felt an instant of searing pain as flame rolled down his wrist to fall with a shower of sparks at his feet.

He had summoned a fire elemental and with a thought, Roan sent it leaping past Jarrod and Amanda and into the stairwell. An orc screamed and there was the sound of swords ringing against cement and the whoosh of flames. Jarrod and Amanda were able to heave the door shut and, seconds later, Roan and Marshall pushed the cage in front of it.

"Great," Jarrod said. "Now we're really trapped."

"We're here for a reason, Jarrod," Roan said. "We're here to find Greg Nelson and we have."

Chapter 19
—Mendenome, Daggerland

Roan was about to explain where Greg's body was when words appeared in his vision: *Quest Completed! Discover the whereabouts of Greg Nelson +1200 XP.*

"Are you guys seeing this?" he asked. "How is this a game quest?"

"What?" Jarrod demanded, his eyes bugging more than usual. "That's what's on your mind just now? There are a buttload of orcs right on the other side of that door and there's no way out of this tower."

"That we know of," Marshall said.

Jarrod shrugged. "Yeah, I guess, but all I'm saying is that quests and XP and all the rest should be put on the back-burner until we can figure a way out of here."

"That's not our main concern," Amanda replied. "We're here to find out how and why Greg Nelson was murdered. I take it he was one of those bodies in the other room?"

"He was. Let me show you." As the two of them hurried down the corridor, Roan looked back over his shoulder, saying, "One of you watch the door, the other find more stuff to block it up. I don't care which of you does which."

Roan pushed Jarrod and Marshall, as well as the orcs out of his mind. He needed to concentrate. He and Amanda stepped through the third door on the right and now that he had more time to take in the room, he saw all sorts of oddities beyond the strange arrangement of the bodies. There were other cages filled with mystical but very dead beasts; their bones and flesh charred. In fact, there were burn marks everywhere. The seven arranged bodies were particularly scorched. As well, there were patches of oily looking blood that was only now becoming tacky. The smell of it sent the hackles lifting on the back of Roan's neck and caused Glitch to wobble.

"This blood...it's otherworldly," Roan noted in disgust. "I mean, it's hellish. Perhaps even demonic."

"Yeah, I get that feeling as well," Amanda said, gazing around. "Quite a battle was fought here and yet look at him." She pointed at the eighth body. "You think that was Nelson? It doesn't look like him." She squatted next to the body, slipping into FBI mode as if she weren't wearing a cloak and armor. "No insect activity whatsoever. Hmmm. The body has been moved at some point after death. Judging by the lividity, it had been on its side. Hmmm. No tattoos, no piercings, no scars and no obvious cause of death."

"Exactly," Roan said. "It's why I think it's Nelson. He was a powerful wizard. So powerful that he mopped the floor with these guys…the same guys who took on those golems. They were good, but he was better. Much better. A hell of a lot better. They had to have known they didn't stand a chance and Cole had to have known. So, why did they throw away everything they had worked for? Money? It's understandable why they would make the attempt for cash on the other side, but from a certain point of view, it would seem to be a waste of Arching's money."

Amanda stood, her armor creaking. "Maybe Arching wanted Nelson occupied so he could enter his earthbound body and kill him, something Fulbright had insisted wasn't possible."

Roan had been thinking the same thing. "Only, it wasn't their first attempt. Cole had hired a number of parties before this one. Were they practice runs? Did they have to get their timing perfect or was there something else we're…" He stopped as he heard a sound drift in from faraway.

"The horses!" Amanda said and rushed out of the room. The two of them went to a front facing room that had a window. The four horses were racing away from a pair of humans who had been trying to grab their reins. "It's those adventurers and the bandits. Maybe they'll fight the orcs. If the two sides can kill each other, we might be able to escape."

"At the least it will give us more time to investigate. I think we are done with Nelson's body. What's relevant is that he, or more accurately, his mind was here when he died. If he had clocked back, we wouldn't have a body. I say we go higher in the tower and see if there are any more clues."

Jarrod and Marshall were more than happy to leave. The orcs had been hammering on the door which, although extremely stout was beginning to come apart.

There were four more floors and at each, they raced around looking for items to brace the doors with. The tenth floor held nothing whatsoever. The stairs opened up on a room that was a perfect square. The walls were flat and white, windowless and, other than the one, doorless.

"There's gotta be a secret door," Jarrod said, going to the wall on his left and placing his cheek to it so that he could look down its length. He began running his hands across it. Marshall went to the far wall and, after a shrug, Amanda went to the right and began looking for a hidden door.

"Okay," Roan said to himself and started feeling a wall which seemed utterly seamless and completely flat. After a minute of this useless activity, he began tapping here and there, hoping to hear a hollow spot. Soon, everyone was drumming on the walls.

They were getting nowhere while the orcs were getting closer. "Glitch? Can you help us? We're looking for a door. It might be hidden by illusion, but it probably isn't completely airtight. All we need is a crack."

The air elemental went to a wall and flattened out, spreading itself so thinly that it could only be seen from certain angles. It went along the wall and then the next and then the third and fourth. Without being told to, it flowed onto the floor and rippled along until it suddenly came together forming a little pulsing cloud.

"There's something on the floor," Roan said, dropping down to one knee and blowing Glitch out of the way. Barely visible was the outline of a circle about the size of a can of peas. He pressed it with his thumb and then jerked as a sound came from above. A portion of the ceiling gently lowered until it came in contact with the floor, revealing a spiral stair.

"Yes! Glitch, you are the man," Jarrod said. He started for the stairs and then thought better about it. "You first, Glitch."

The elemental spun up the stairs just as if it were climbing them. At the top of the stairs was another room; unlike the empty tenth-floor room, this one wasn't just cluttered, it was trashed.

Roan went up next, his eyes falling on a seven-foot tall mirror in its stand. It was the most obvious thing of value that was still there and in one piece. A beautiful desk had been chopped into pieces, a chair had been ripped apart, a chest broken apart, shelves had been torn from the walls, and even the fireplace had been partially dismantled.

"Someone ransacked this place," Roan said, as the others came up, "but for some reason, they left the mirror." Briefly, he gazed at his elven self, before looking at the rest of the mess. It was all rather mundane: a broken ink well, a silk shirt, a cracked plate with dried egg yolk fused to it. He had been hoping for a diary of some sort, one that would give him a hint as to where Arching was.

"Hey!" Jarrod cried. "The mirror changed."

Roan was straight in front of it and instead of seeing himself, the surface of the mirror held a picture of a slowly rotating planet, one that he didn't recognize. Roan reached out a hand and carefully touched the mirror; it felt just like glass, but with a slight tremor to it.

"It's magic," he said.

Unexpectedly, Jarrod and Marshall took a step back. "Ask it if it knows where the treasure is in this place," Jarrod suggested.

Jarrod hadn't been quiet and yet, the picture had not changed as Roan had expected. Roan cleared his throat and asked, "Can you please show us the treasure in Mendenome?" The glass shimmered and Roan found himself staring at his own reflection once more. "Okay, that didn't work. How about, can you show us a safe way out of Mendenome?"

The shimmer again and then it showed the front gates.

"Ah, that's just great!" Jarrod said, throwing up his hands. "It's broken." He kicked a pewter mug and it bounced off a wall with a thud. The sound seemed to give him an idea. "Hey, maybe there's a secret door in this place. You know, to like a treasure room. Get Glitch to look for one."

"Ssss," Glitch said before Roan could ask it. The elemental spread out and started looking again.

While it did, Amanda stepped in front of Roan and said, "Show me where Atticus Arching is in the real world." The mirror shimmered again, but when the picture formed, it showed only Amanda with Roan standing behind her. "Maybe it doesn't know anything about the real world," she said, going to the mirror and touching the polished wood frame, inspecting it.

"Or it's broken like Jarrod said," Roan answered. "Show me Tim Cole...I mean Aderon the Black."

The image changed, showing a military camp, a slovenly one where the tents were poorly stitched animal hides and where the ground was littered with feces, small bones and trash. It was an orc camp and in the middle of it was a white tent. Its flaps were closed, but the mirror was able to see into it and there was Aderon the Black, sleeping on a cot, with two soldiers guarding over him.

"Can you pull back?" The image pulled back slowly until Roan could see a town a mile or so distant. "Hey, that's Morin.

That's the first town we were in. You know the one where that bartender killed me?"

"It's under siege," Marshall said. "And it doesn't look good. Have it show a better view of the town. Their walls were…"

"Why bother?" Jarrod asked. "It won't help us get out of here. You know what I think? I think that mirror is Arching's or was programmed by him. Case in point: Aderon. The mirror wouldn't show us where Arching is, but shazam, it just gave us Aderon without a problem, almost as if Arching is trying to get us to tie up his loose ends. I think it's highly, highly suspect."

2—

They were all quiet for a time, considering this. Roan didn't know what to think about the mirror. What he did know for certain was that their trip to Mendenome had been a waste of time. There was nothing in the tower that pointed to Arching.

Disappointed, he was poking through the trash when he realized the sound of the orcs hammering on the door had changed, becoming monotonous…a single heavy, repetitive thudding noise.

"I think they're setting up a new ambush," Roan said. He turned to Glitch, who had been frustrated in his search for a secret vault, and asked, "Can you go find out what's happening? Just be very careful." It turned translucent and drifted down the stairs which Jarrod raised behind it by touching a button on the wall.

The second Glitch was gone, Roan regretted sending it down there alone. "Show me the intruders," he said to the mirror. The scene shifted from Morin and showed Roan and his team standing around Nelson's office. "No, the new intruders."

Now, he saw the bandits creeping around in the lower halls. He counted twenty-three of them, a mixture of human adventurers and goblin bandits. Roan directed the mirror to show him the orcs who had been after his team. They were sneaking into position, getting ready to attack from all sides.

A new plan sprang to mind. "Show me the stairs down, starting with the tenth floor!" The scene shifted and showed the tenth floor was still untouched, but at the ninth there were only five orcs and none below that. "The way out is practically clear! We can slip out when the fighting starts."

Jarrod hit the button, lowering the stairs down to the tenth floor and started for them. Amanda stopped him. "Shouldn't we wait until the fighting starts?"

"We can at least get in position," Roan said. They trooped down the stairs and as they did, he recalled Glitch and had him take up a position behind the orcs who were hammering on the ninth-floor door. Then it was just a matter of waiting and listening.

When the first cry came echoing up from below, Roan and Jarrod thrust back the desk that had been barring the door. When Marshall opened it, the orcs were scrambling for their weapons. He waded into them swinging his long sword with grim efficiency. Roan didn't know what his attack bonuses were, but it didn't look as if he could miss.

Two died in as many swings and the rest fled down the stairs. Glitch watched them as they ran onto the eighth floor. One hid himself behind a door to a bathroom, while the other two kept going. As the others ran around the corridors to the next set of stairs, Roan went after the lone orc.

He didn't want it sneaking down behind them. It was an easy kill. With a heavy kick, he hammered the bathroom door into the orc's face and, before it could react, Roan ran it through with his sword (*XP +22*).

For a brief moment, he considered going through the orc's pockets, however the creature was hideous and stank to high heaven. He left it lying there and ran to join the others, catching them just as they got to the fourth level. They were standing over the two orcs as Jarrod rifled their pockets and pouches.

"There you are!" Amanda cried. "I thought you were right behind me. I was just about to go look for you."

"There was another orc," he explained. "Jarrod, that's enough. It's not going to have anything. Come on." With Glitch showing the way, they ran down to the main atrium. From high up, they were able to look down on the first floor, where the battle was in full swing. It had started in the throne room, but the adventurers had formed a square and had forced their way out into the center of the main floor, almost right in front of the stairs.

The only good news was that, as of that moment, no one had noticed them. The bad news was there were far more orcs than he had counted on. They were swarming all over the bandits and for a moment, he considered heading back upstairs, only he knew that such a move would gain them nothing and lose them time.

Their one option was to attempt to slip past while the orcs were focused away. He charged down the stairs, sword drawn, with his team behind him. Marshall made a rattling noise as he went. Thankfully, the din of battle covered the sound. It wasn't until they were halfway between the first and second floors when one of the orcs saw them.

"Glitch!" Roan cried.

Glitch knew what to do. As the orc opened its mouth to scream a warning, the elemental went right down its throat. The orc choked on air and was then shot through the chest as Jarrod loosed an arrow at it.

This gained them fifteen seconds and by then Roan was racing past the very edge of the mob, followed by Amanda and Jarrod. Marshall was the slowest and was attacked by eight or nine orcs at once. He swung his sword in wide arcs, trying to disengage, but they pressed in from all sides.

Roan summoned his last fire elemental and had it charge at the orcs while Jarrod and Amanda fired arrows into them from the rear. Marshall killed one and cut the hand off another. The rest fled, yelling to their friends. Quite a few of the orcs turned from the battle with the bandits, but when they saw the fire elemental leaping on orc after orc, most backed away, not wanting to be next.

While this was happening, the team rushed down into the courtyard and ran for the tunnel. Glitch was excited to be free and even though the mist had grown into a drizzle, it shot into the sky and raced away. Roan felt a moment of sadness as he wondered if Glitch would just keep going, heading back to whatever strange air world it had come from. Roan wouldn't blame it if it did.

But Glitch was not leaving. As always, it was looking out for Roan's interests. It had flown high enough to spot the horses and was now relaying the information straight into Roan's mind.

The horses had not gone very far. They were a mile from the citadel, grazing on the tall grasses. When Roan told them where the horses were, Marshall groaned. The paladin could not run in his armor. The best he could manage was an ugly, unwieldy shuffling jog.

A dozen or so orcs came through the wall after them. "Go on," Roan said to Marshall, as he unslung his bow and faced the orcs. He got off two shots, hitting with one, while Jarrod hit with two out of three. Amanda was on fire and killed three of them, one after another.

They then ripped out their swords and rushed to attack. Roan took a scratch on the cheek as he sunk his sword deep into the guts of a big brute of an orc. It let out a curse and staggered away (*XP +22*). Another of the beasts made an obvious lunge that Roan dodged easily. He was not the best swordsman, but he should have been able to whack the head off the orc with ease. Instead, his sword clipped off the thing's leather shoulder without cutting through the armor. The orc lunged again and Roan parried, following it up with a great riposte, but again had his blade stopped by the armor.

"Son of a…" His curse was interrupted as Amanda stepped in and stabbed the orc through the eye.

"You're welcome," she said, before jogging away after Marshall.

All of the orcs who had come out after them were dead and Roan had only managed to kill one of them. It didn't sit right with him. "I think that one had magic armor," he said to Jarrod, who was busy looking for treasure on the bodies.

The rogue went to the last orc that Amanda had killed, took a quick look at its armor and said, "No way. It's got holes all over it. And mold, gross." He wiped his hand in the grass. "I think you have to face the fact that a girl is a better fighter than you. It happens over here."

Roan grumbled at this, but didn't have time for the stern reply that had jumped to his lips. More orcs were coming through the wall. The two men turned and began a ground-eating jog. They quickly caught up to Amanda, who was puffing along, her armor, although lighter than Marshall's, was still heavy on her.

"Hey," she said, between breaths.

"Hey," he answered, biting back the question on his mind: *What are your plusses?* Although he meant it in a game sense, it didn't seem like a polite question. Still, he felt he had to know. Was the game cheating, or was she just better than him? He had been letting her go first and take risks because of her armor. With her shield and her dexterity, she had to have at least a nineteen armor class and against orcs and bandits that was almost untouchable. But, one on one, could she beat him?

Jarrod must have read the look on Roan's face correctly. He nudged Roan, saying, "Let's get in some target practice." Stopping, the two unslung their bows and snatched arrows from their quivers. Orcs were not fast runners and even though the team hadn't been running full out, they had opened up a fifty-yard lead.

"You got to chill about this fighting business," Jarrod said, sending an arrow into the orcs. "She may not be really better than you right now, but she will be pretty soon, just like you will get stronger in magic. It's the way of things."

Roan let off an arrow (*XP +22*). "Yes! That's a hit." He nocked a second arrow but paused before shooting. "You're probably right. I think my main problem is that it feels like we're still spinning our wheels. We aren't any closer to catching Arching than when we first started." He fired and saw this one plunk off a shield.

"You're wrong." Jarrod fired, killing one of the orcs. "Not only have we discovered that Nelson really did die while he was playing..." He paused to fire again, this time at almost point-blank range. Roan fired at the same time and was satisfied to see the (*XP +22*) drift into his vision.

They both turned and ran with the orcs hot on their heels. "He died playing the game," Jarrod went on when they had put a little distance between them and the orcs. "That tells us we're on the right path."

"How far are they going to chase us?" Roan asked, after a look back.

Jarrod glanced up at the dark sky. "With this weather? Could be for miles, but once we get to the horses, they'll give it up."

The horses weren't far now, only a few hundred yards. Seeing Jetta reminded Roan of the trouble he'd had with the horse. He wouldn't have time for playing around.

Jetta turned out to be in an obedient mood. He tossed his head and danced in a circle around Roan in what could only be called a prance. "I missed you, too," Roan told him. He petted the horse's cheek as he stuck a foot in the stirrup and, with Glitch slowly orbiting his head, he vaulted up in one smooth action.

This time it was Marshall who had trouble with his horse. When he was building his paladin character, he had obviously put more of his ability points into strength than constitution, and the mile-long run had left him gassed. Jarrod had to boost him into his saddle before the orcs could swarm him.

"Holy crap!" Jarrod exclaimed, his face red. "You weigh a freaking ton."

Roan was just about to climb down to help when Marshall finally managed to get up. The four immediately set their horses galloping away, while behind them the orcs cursed and yelled insults. They were all too tired to respond.

Amanda spurred her horse along next to Jetta. "So, that was a bust," she said, with a long sigh. "So, where to now? Hopefully not east back through that swamp. That place gave me the willies."

"No, the swamp is out of the question," Roan said. "And so is north; the Orc-back Mountains are in that direction. I say we go south for a while and then head back east to the river. After that, I don't know. Maybe by then Caron will have found out who the lawyer is on this side."

This was met with two grunts from the men and another sigh from Amanda. "Hey! We're not out of the fight just yet," Roan told them. "If Arching programmed that mirror, it's because we're getting close."

"I just need an inn with a bath and a good house ale," Marshall said. "Then I'll be back in it with you, Roan."

"Yeah," agreed Jarrod. "I could use all that and maybe some loose barmaids. Then I'll be raring to go." Amanda rolled her eyes. "What? A man has needs."

Amanda cocked an eyebrow at this. "Yes, but an FBI agent has a duty and obligation that supersede these so-called needs, right Roan?"

"Normally, I would agree with you, however we all need a break. We've been at this for days, and a beer and a bath sound wonderful right now. Glitch can you find us a town?"

The elemental shot straight up and it was only then that Roan realized that the sun was beginning to wester behind the clouds. Glitch was gone just long enough for Roan to think he wasn't going to sleep in a bed that night. Luckily, the elemental had seen smoke trailing up into the sky and had gone to investigate.

"Glitch saw a town eight miles southeast of here," Roan told the others when Glitch had relayed what it had seen. As tired as they were, eight miles sounded like a long way. Roan worried that it wasn't far enough. There had been at least two hundred orcs in Mendenome, and there was no telling if there were more deeper in the hills. What if the town walls were weak? What if they were poorly defended?

He worried right up until he saw that the town walls were both weak and undermanned. By then, he was too tired to care all that much. Their near endless adventuring had worn him down and they entered the trashed-out town of Carthia running on fumes.

The entire town was as foul and stinking as the lower parts of Tir-Khan. It was so bad that when Jarrod asked a gate guard where the best inn was located, all he received was laughter in response. They were forced to follow the crooked streets until they discovered the Real Macara Tavern—three stories of warped wood siding, dirty windows and strange shrieking laughter.

A painted lady sat behind the counter smoking a long pipe. Roan wanted to ask her what a "macara" was, only he didn't have the energy. "Four rooms and dinner, please," he said.

"Please? You must be a lordly elf," she said, with a cackle. When she laughed, her age showed beneath the thick make-up. Roan just stared at her until she quoted him six silvers a piece for the rooms, two more for dinner and two for stabling the horses.

He pushed four gold at her and she happily yanked a purse from her bodice to stash the gold in. "This way, *milord*." She cackled again and showed them to rooms on the third floor. "Dinner's been on the board for an hour. I'd get to it before the roaches do."

The moment she was out of earshot, Amanda groaned. "This place is disgusting. I'm going to sleep on my bedroll. Hey, can you get bedbugs here?" She groaned again when Jarrod nodded.

They each claimed a room, none any better than the rest, and once their packs were stowed, they went down for dinner. Like the rest of the tavern, the main room was only about half-filled, with people sitting evenly around the place. Most were adventurers and not a very friendly lot. There were cold stares as the team found an empty table as far from the bar as they could get—there were three half-orcs sitting with a couple of shaggy-looking dwarves at the bar. One of the half-orcs made a snide comment concerning Amanda.

"Just ignore them," she said, grabbing Roan by the arm. They ordered dinner and drinks. When their food came, Roan expected something disgusting, yet he hid his fear better than Amanda who leaned away from the plate that was set in front of her as if expecting the roast duck to come alive and attack her.

The meal was surprisingly good, if not a little cold. It was the opposite with the beer. It was warm, had flecks of mold floating on the surface and was so bitter that it was undrinkable in Roan's opinion.

Marshall proposed ordering a bottle of wine, which caused more snide remarks from the party at the bar. "I think we can take them," Jarrod said, sneaking a long look at them. "Ratty hide armor and a few wood shields? Who do they think they are?"

"I'm with Amanda," Roan said. "I'm really not in the mood to fight and my spells are nearly used up. Ahh, the wine." The waitress, an indifferent commoner, set a dusty bottle in front of them and left without saying a word. She hadn't brought glasses with the bottle.

"Are we supposed to drink straight from the bottle?" Amanda asked.

"I wouldn't if I were you," a stranger at the next table said. "The bottle has been poisoned."

Chapter 20
—Carthia, Daggerland

Roan turned to take in the man who was hooded and cloaked in ranger green. Other than the gleam of his eyes, his features were hidden by the shadows. "And how would you know that?" Roan asked.

"That doesn't matter at the moment. If you drink the wine, you'll die and if you don't, you'll be attacked."

"Or," Roan said and reached for the bottle, "accidentally" knocking it to the floor. "Shoot! Well, I guess I wasn't all that thirsty, anyway." Although the party at the bar laughed even louder, they hadn't made any move for their weapons. It wasn't true of some of the other patrons. At least eight of them were gazing at Roan and his team without the least bit of mirth in their eyes.

There was a moment of odd tension in the air and the next thing Roan knew, swords were being drawn, his own included. Then came a wild melee filled with flashing blades and shouts. Tables and chairs were over-turned as some people tried to get out of the way and others charged the team.

Right in the middle of it was the stranger hacking away with his sword. With his hood back, Roan saw that he was a tall, thin, handsome man with amber eyes. His sword, which glowed with a soft light, was clearly magical and his skill was amazing—and yet the people attacking him did not shy away.

As he was without armor, Roan kept to the back and looked for openings to dart forward and stab with his sword. He managed to kill two of the assassins (*XP + 150*) before one tried to sneak up behind him. Glitch warned him and then zipped in for a *Haze* attack.

With the -4 attack penalty from Glitch's Haze to go along with his normal sixteen armor class, the man could not seem to get past Roan's defenses while Roan hit three straight times (*XP + 75*). When Roan looked back at the fight, there were only three attackers left and when Amanda dropped beneath a swinging sword and stabbed one through the guts, the other two fled, chased by the stranger and Marshall.

Roan followed them through the tavern to the front room, where the attackers turned. Marshall was about rejoin the fight, but Roan grabbed him, whispering, "Wait!" Together they watched the stranger battle back and forth, getting cut on three different occasions before he managed to kill the two.

"Thanks for the help," the man growled, dropping to a knee and wiping his glowing blade on the cloak of one of his attackers. He reached into the cloak and came up with a heavy pouch and tossed it to Roan, who caught it. By its weight, he could tell that it was filled with gold coins.

"Hired assassins," the stranger said, in a low voice. "We should get out of here, quickly. There's another group of them to the north."

Amanda and Jarrod had joined them. She pushed past Roan and went to the two bodies. In true FBI form, she inspected the corpses, looking for clues. "How many are there?"

Before answering, the stranger glanced towards the painted lady behind the front desk counter who had watched the fight with mild interest. "Leave," he ordered. When she did, he answered, "Fourteen or fifteen. I've been tracking them since the Ash Forest. There are many eyes on you four and if we don't get out of here, those eyes will be on your dead bodies."

He turned for the door, expecting Roan and the others to follow him. Roan shook his head. "Not just yet. Perhaps you can tell me who you work for, Leomagnus?"

The man looked astounded by the question. "I just saved your lives. You're welcome by the way." Roan only nodded but said nothing, waiting for the man to answer his question. "Fine. I don't work for Leomagnus. I work for Christine Carson. She has quite a big stake in this."

"And yet she sends only one man?" Roan asked. "Here is what's going to happen. You and one of my associates will clock out. You'll arrange a meeting with Ms. Carson. I assume you're in contact with her?"

The man was quiet for long seconds before a smile spread across his face. "What gave me away?" he asked.

"You had been sitting at that table before we ordered the bottle of wine," Roan answered. "There was no way you could have known that it was poisoned."

"Ahh, very observant. Well, this is about to get awkward." He drew the magic sword. "Maybe you guys can make it easier on yourselves and tell me what the mirror showed you."

Roan shifted to his right, giving Marshall and Jarrod room to fight. "Mirror? What mir…oh, you mean the magic mirror in Nelson's place? Oh, it was downright useful. Unfortunately, the information you are looking for is part of an on-going investigation. I can't divulge…"

The man suddenly flashed in, driving his sword at Roan. Glitch was on him in a second, blurring his vision with his *Haze* attack, causing him to miss, though he didn't miss by much.

Everyone attacked the man at once and even with four on one, the odds were on the man's side. They all missed, their swords slipping off a bright chain shirt that he wore under his cloak or blocked by the magic sword which moved so quickly that Amanda and Jarrod were bleeding with two quick flicks.

Roan and Marshall attacked from either side—again, both missed. The man was just too fast. Blades were batted aside with ease and the next thing Roan knew, the magic sword had slid right though his side, piercing him from one end to the other (*Damage -14*).

He gasped, reeling from the pain and going to one knee. Knowing that he couldn't stay down, he gritted his teeth and forced himself back to his feet. In those few seconds, all three of his teammates had been struck again, their blood splattered the walls and puddled on the floor.

They were about to lose. It seemed impossible and yet, there was Marshall staggering from his wounds and Amanda wearing a grimace of pain.

Roan decided to show his own speed, not with the sword, but with the wand. He had refrained from using the Wand of Lightning that he had taken from the seer back in the siege of Riverport, waiting for a major threat, and this man certainly qualified as one.

The energy within the slim piece of wood pulsed in his hand, just waiting for him to will it out. With a thought, a bolt of blueish white light shot from the tip and struck the man square in the chest. Surprised, he stumbled back, his cloak smoldering, the ends of his dark hair sticking up.

The wand was a game changer and everyone seemed to sense it. "Get him again!" Jarrod yelled. Roan didn't need the encouragement. He just needed a moment to feel the pulse once more and…he zapped the man again just as he was rushing forward. He dodged to the side and the bolt only seared him across the shoulders.

With him dodging the bolt, he put himself in the perfect position for Marshall to slash him across the back of the neck. The paladin drew blood, but somehow the man ignored the blow and came at Roan, his sword raised. Before he could attack, however, a blur of green and gold came from the side. It was Amanda, making a picture perfect tackle, one that would have made an NFL safety proud. She took his knees out and they both crashed into the front counter.

Seeing his chance, Jarrod danced in and nearly took out the man's left eye, but again the man was too quick. From his back, he wielded his sword as though it was nothing more substantial than a switch cut from a willow. With a quick flick of his wrist, he knocked aside Jarrod's sword and then reversing the blade, he slashed open Jarrod's throat.

The rogue stumbled away, giving Roan room to shoot his wand again. The bolt caught the furious man as he leapt to his feet and drove him back down again. The burns from the bolt were visible, creeping up from his armor. "You can't beat him," the man said, in a whisper. "He's too strong. Believe me, your only chance is to submit now, while there's still time for you to do so."

"Where is he?" Roan asked. "I can't submit without knowing where he is, right?"

"Oh, he'll find you, don't worry about that Supervisory Special Agent, Daniel Roan. He's got his eye on you. You and your entire team. He knows all about you."

"How?" Roan asked. "How does he know?" The man only smirked, driving Roan into a rage. Marshall was half-dead, Amanda was leaking blood down from inside her armor and Jarrod was on his knees trying to staunch the blood—and the man was sitting there smug as all get out. Roan knew he wouldn't give up Arching, not with this faux-life on the line.

"I'll find you on the other side," he told the man, "and when I do, I'm going to put a bullet in you."

The man shook his head. "You won't live that long. He's got reach. He can reach into the other world and kill at will."

2—

Roan killed the man seconds later when he wouldn't answer any more questions. Seeing the ($XP +3,600$) cross his vision was little comfort after having his life on the other side, threatened.

He had to resist the urge to clock out to see if his body was okay. And clearly, he wasn't the only one unnerved.

"They're coming after us, I know it," Marshall said. Under the blood and sweat, he was pale, his hands shaking. "That guy knew your name, Roan. That guy knew your *real* name. Even I didn't know your full name. Daniel...it sounds so normal."

Normal? Roan didn't know what he meant by that. "I think we all need to settle down and think this over."

Marshall's version of "thinking it over" was to stare off into nothing and repeat, "That guy knew your name, Roan."

"I guess this shows we're on the right track," Amanda said. She had just healed Jarrod and was now spent; Roan could see it in her eyes. She backed to the wall and slid down it. "Do you think we're safe? You know...back home?"

Roan could picture their sleeping bodies back in the world, with only Mrs. Niederer watching over them. For some reason, in his vision she was knitting, though he had never seen her knitting even once. "Yes, we're safe." Roan answered, shaking away the image. "We're in an FBI field office, okay? It's one thing to attack us here or to attack a stray geek in an empty building, but no one is going to be able to stroll into a building filled with armed agents and kill us. Threats are all Arching has."

One-handed, Jarrod slid his sword back into its sheath; his other hand was still at his throat where his Adam's apple kept going up and down. "He could use a suicide bomber. You ever think about that? You know, like Nelson. All they'd have to do is walk in with a bomb under his coat and blammy! We're toast."

"Stop it, Jarrod," Roan said, in a soft voice. "You're just getting yourself worked up. Arching is too smart to think he can take on the FBI like that. No, if he comes after us, it won't point to him so obviously. That being said, if any of you want to be transferred to another team, I understand."

Marshall and Jarrod shared a brief look before each dropped their eyes. "No," Marshall said. "We're staying. Heroes don't run at the first sign of danger."

Roan glanced at Amanda. She snorted in response. "If you think I would run away before these two, you don't know who you're dealing with."

A loud laugh burst from Roan's throat. Two weeks ago, Amanda had been griping about the over-use of staples when submitting official reports. "Okay, we're all in, come hell or high water. That's what I wanted to hear. Now, let's see what that guy had on him."

Eagerly, Jarrod dropped to his knees beside the dead elf. He handed the magic sword to Roan, who studied the markings. He touched the blade and knew right away. "It's elven made. Plus three to attack and damage." When he set it aside each of his team cast a longing look at it.

Reluctantly, Jarrod went back to searching the body, finding more gold, three diamonds as big as the tip of his pinky and a ring. Again, he handed it to Roan, who studied the markings. "Ah, it's a match to my own," he said, holding up his left hand where the *Asari Ring of Defense* gleamed.

"You know you can't wear both," Jarrod said, quickly. "The bonuses don't add up."

Through the power of the game, Roan indeed knew that. "Yes," was all he said as he set the ring down next to the sword.

Jarrod then struggled the elf's chain armor off of him. It was made of a silvery material. "It's mithral," he said in awe. "I call dibs!" This caused an uproar with Marshall and Amanda on one side and Jarrod on the other.

"Please stop," Roan said, speaking quietly. The three looked at him as he pondered the items, deciding where each would fit best in his team. "Marshall will take the sword. Amanda the armor…" Jarrod rolled his eyes at this, earning him a harsh glare from Roan. "Unless you want to be a frontline fighter, now? No, then take the ring and be happy."

"I'll take the ring," the painted lady said from the doorway to the main room. She gave Roan what she must have considered to be a seductive wink. When he only shook his head she added, "You all gotta give me something. You seen the mess back in there? There's bodies flung ever-where."

Roan opened the pouch that the elf had taken from the assassin and slid ten gold across from her. "That should take care of it." He turned to Jarrod and Marshall. "Strip the rest of them of anything valuable and meet us in my room."

There was nothing left of the bodies in the main room to strip. The people there had moved in like vultures and had taken everything. Still, the team had quite the haul. Including the value of the gems, they had raked in over six thousand in gold.

"Not bad, but is it enough?" Roan asked.

"It's enough to get us each a proper girl for the night," Jarrod said, nudging Marshall in the ribs.

They had slipped up to Amanda's room. She sat on the bed trying to adjust her new armor. Without looking up, she muttered, "Barf."

"We're not spending the money on women," Roan said. "No, we need to go back to Mendenome. Amanda was correct before. We're getting close to Arching. He sent those assassins to find out what we had seen in the mirror. It hadn't been tinkered with after all."

Jarrod couldn't seem to wrap his mind around the idea. "Wait, what? You want to go back to Mendenome? Why? You asked the mirror all the questions you needed to and, yes, maybe it hadn't been messed with, but it still didn't give you the answers you were looking for. Do you think asking in a nicer tone might help?"

"I think that we didn't ask it the right questions," Roan replied. "And perhaps it might have been the person asking the questions. It answered my questions but not Amanda's. I addressed it first, maybe it became attuned to me."

Amanda's hands stopped fiddling with the straps. "You're right. It became just a mirror for me. What did I ask it, again?"

Roan had been sitting on an empty trunk; now he jumped up, excitedly. "You asked where Atticus Arching was in the real world. Maybe it's not in tune with me, maybe you just asked it a question it couldn't answer. Let's see, we asked about treasure and there was none. We asked the safest way out of the citadel and it showed us the front doors, which proved true. Then I asked it about Cole and it showed us. I think that mirror works just fine."

"And Arching is afraid of what it showed us," Marshall said. "Roan is right. We need to go back to Mendenome."

"Are you guys forgetting the orcs?" Jarrod cried. "There was a freaking bazillion of them."

Holding up the bag of gold, Roan said, "Unless I'm wrong, this will buy us a small army. All we would need is a hundred or so soldiers. Does anyone know the going rate to hire a regular soldier?"

"It depends. If we're talking NPCs it just depends on the local environment. In this town, we could get some guys on the cheap, for maybe two or three gold a day. But the closer we get to Ellisbar, the more expensive it will get. It's simple supply and demand. With a war going on, the cost goes up."

"And what about hiring actual people?"

Marshall made a face. "That gets tricky. Although adventurers will sometimes fight for a cause, they aren't going to be happy with government intrusion into Daggerland, so we can rule that out. And as for profit, there really won't be much of one. We'll have to pay them out of pocket and once they realize where we're going, the price will shoot up."

"So, we'll use NPCs when we can," Roan said. "We'll start rounding them up in the morning. In the meantime, I'm going to clock back to the real world and see if we can beef up security."

When Roan sat up in the FBI basement, it felt not just different but also disappointing in a way that he couldn't put his finger on. It was the real world and yet, so much about it was drab and depressing. He walked past the agent on guard, went up the stairs and directly out into the street where he stared all around him, trying to understand the sudden discontent in his breast.

He was in New York City, arguably one of the greatest cities on the planet. Surrounding him were skyscrapers built of steel, glass, and concrete, while all around him were, quite literally, millions of people. And they all looked the same. "Ants in an elaborate anthill," he muttered, before walking back inside and heading up to Caron's office.

"What do you have for me?" Caron asked, without looking up from a pile of paperwork, ten inches high.

Roan grunted at the stack, realizing that he couldn't remember the last time he had done any of the mind-numbing paperwork that came part and parcel with the job. "We're getting close. We had assassins after us last night."

"Oh, yeah? No dragons?"

With his head down, Caron didn't see Roan's eyes flash, and there was no way for him to know just how close he was to getting punched in the face. Roan had to take a deep breath before he could manage a calm reply. "Nope, no dragons, just some guy who threatened Supervisory Special Agent, Daniel Roan. He didn't threaten my character. He threatened me, personally. He said Arching could reach into this world anytime he wanted to and kill the lot of us."

This pulled Caron from the paperwork. He sat back, tucking his hands behind his head. "And you believe him?"

"I believe there is a strong possibility that Arching could use anyone playing the game for his purposes. If he can get to the richest among us, he can get to anyone."

"Yeah," Caron sighed, running a hand through his thin hair. "I take it you want to beef up security?"

Roan nodded. "Yes. Now, what do you have for me? Anything on Arching or the lawyer?"

Caron clicked on his computer and searched around before saying. "Nothing on Arching, that guy is good, but we do have quite a bit on the lawyer. Unfortunately, out of thousands of emails and Facebook messages and all that, we found only a few references to Daggerland. It turns out he is something called a... where is it. Ah, he's a warlock. Do you know what that is?"

Roan remembered the elf from the Ash Forest had been a warlock. At the time, he had assumed that it was another name for a wizard. "But it's not," he said, under his breath. "It's a wizard who gets special powers from their patron, which is usually a powerful demon or some other supernatural entity."

"Yep, that's it. This guy calls himself Ahmroth and he's a warlock of Gorgothe the Infinite, which pretty much sounds like our guy, right?"

"It does. Do we have anything beyond those names? I need a location."

Caron shook his head. "Sorry, no, but I have our geek squads all over the message boards asking about either name. So far they haven't gotten anything which tells me that this Gorgothe the Infinite isn't as powerful as he's trying to let on."

That was easy for Caron to say, considering that he was sitting behind his desk, surrounded by agents armed with guns. "Thanks, I better be getting back." As much as he wanted to head straight back to Daggerland, he forced himself to exercise, eat and shower.

"Showering wins hands down," he said, comparing the two worlds as he let the hot water run off his body. He just wasn't built for bathtubs, not even as an elf. Other than bathing, Daggerland was slowly taking the lead in his mind. Even with the constant danger, it was hard to get past the magic at his fingertips, and the promise of more—it was addictive.

Clocking back, he made the mistake of taking a deep breath, thinking he'd be breathing the fresh air of the hills, but instead got a nose full of stink. The shabby tavern still smelled of piss and sour beer.

He had the others clock back to shower and to exercise their bodies in the real world. He then went to bed—alone. Amanda and Glitch were in the next room and he had to fight the urge to see through Glitch's eyes as she stripped off her armor. The walls were thin pine boards and he could hear each piece come off. It shouldn't have been erotic, but somehow it was.

Chapter 21

—Carthia, Daggerland

The next morning, as Marshall and Jarrod began asking around about hiring soldiers, Amanda, with Glitch acting as a combination of pet and security guard, went to get her armor properly sized. At first, Roan stayed in the hotel, preparing his spells. Although he had the components to use any of his spells, he decided to keep the same ones he had used the day before: four *Fire Bolts*, three *Thunderous Waves*, two *Summon Fire Elemental* and one *Incinerate*.

Feeling the power of the spells course through his body had him wondering how far he was to gaining the next level.

Character Name: Roan
Class & Level: Wizard - Level 5
Race: High Elf
Alignment: Chaotic Good
Experience Points: **14,806** XP To Next Level: **194**

Strength – Dexterity – Constitution
S: **15(+2)**   D: **16(+3)**   C: **16(+3)**

Intelligence – Wisdom – Charisma
I: **18(+4)**   W: **16(+3)**   C: **16(+3)**

Armor: 13(16)   **Hit Points: 38**
Initiative: +3   **Speed: 13**

SAVING THROWS: Will: 7   Fortitude: 4   Reflex: 4

GOLD: 6,212

-EQUIPMENT-

<u>Weapons</u>
Longbow
Long Sword

<u>Armor</u>
None

<u>Magic</u>
Spell Book
Flask of Holy Water
Asari Ring of Defense +3
Wand of Lightning: 5 Charges

<u>Misc</u>
Quiver * Arrows x28
Backpack * Rations x1
Tinder Box * Waterskin
Pouches x2 * Birch Cinder
Moonlit Elm Ash * Ground Dwarf Tooth

† Spells Known †

Cantrips: Minor Illusion, Fire Bolt, Ray of Ice, Electric Hand, Acid Spray

Tier 1 Spells: Summon Familiar, Flame Blast, Lightning Summoning(lesser), Instant Slumber, Thunderous Wave, Illusion(minor), Charm(minor)

Tier 2 Spells: Summon Flame Elemental, Invisibility, Hypnotic Flame
Tier 3 Spells: Inferno

† Spells Prepared †

Cantrips: Fire Bolt x4
Tier 1 Spells: Thunderous Wave x3
Tier 2 Spells: Summon Flame Elemental x2
Tier 3 Spells: Inferno

Attacks
Name - ATK Bonus – Damage

Longbow	+5	1-8
Long Sword	+4	1-8+2

Abilities
Spell Casting
Low-Light Vision

Skills
Listen: +6, Spot: +6, Knowledge: +6, Search: +6, Spell Craft: +6,
Decipher Script: +8

His eyes fell on the line concerning experience and hung there. "Less than two hundred? So close and yet…" He trailed off thinking that the sixth level really wasn't far away at all and the next few days would definitely put him over the top. Still, he had such a hunger for power that he went to the window and looked out at the stinking town.

He was almost spoiling for a fight and hoped to see some sort of villainy occurring on the street below him. Unfortunately, the people going about their morning seemed normal. Strapping on his sword, he went down to the main room for breakfast and a part of him hoped to run into the half-orcs from the night before, however there was only one bleary-eyed dwarf at the bar.

Roan couldn't tell whether he had been there all night or had just crawled out of bed.

"No snide remarks today, dwarf?" Roan asked.

"Huh? Oh, yeah, sorry about that. Me and my friend were wicked drunk and at a certain point, dwarves can't handle their alcohol. It's like there's a switch in them." He snapped his stubby fingers. "One moment you're having fun and the next you're crying or yelling or getting into fights. You ever see a dwarf cry? It's embarrassing. And uh, sorry if I got out of line."

A heartfelt apology was the last thing that Roan had expected and he had no choice but to accept it and let the dwarf buy him breakfast. Over runny eggs, the two chatted about the game and their characters. The dwarf, whose name was Krull, wanted to know what Roan had done to merit an assassination attempt, forcing Roan to lie.

"It's about a girl," he said.

Krull's laugh shook the walls. "Must be some girl to get you into that much trouble. Some people have all the luck! When my wife found out about the sort of shenanigans that go on in Daggerland, she *made* me be a dwarf, now if I want to do it with one the ladies I've got to get a step stool!"

Roan didn't want to hear about the dwarf's sex life and changed the subject. "Before I forget, my team is mounting an expedition. Are you looking for a little work?"

"Work? Hell, I come here to get away from work. But, if you have an adventure cooking, let's hear about it."

"Mendenome," Roan said, in a low whisper.

Krull rolled his eyes. "The latest fad. Every adventurer who comes through here wants to take a crack at the wizard's tower. I've seen three different parties go and none have come back. Whatever can kill a wizard as powerful as Gethahyme can kill me with one blink. Sorry, but it's too rich for my blood."

"What if I told that I've been inside the wizard's tower?"

"I'd say you were full of bull spittle," Krull said. Roan had been about to reply, but the dwarf's "curse" had him laughing. Krull sighed, wearily. "It's the wife. She says the game is making me crude so now I can't curse anymore."

Roan's laugh tapered into chuckles. When he could speak again, he admitted, "Yesterday my crew and I went all the way to the top of the tower. There's a boatload of orcs in Mendenome, but no all-powerful entity. Now that we know what we're dealing with, we're going back with a small army. My guys are recruiting some locals. We think a hundred guys will probably be enough."

"And how are you splitting the treasure?"

Roan hesitated, unsure how to answer the question. His main goal was the mirror, but that didn't mean there weren't other items of value. "Since I'm fronting the money for the expedition, I'm claiming a mirror that we saw there yesterday. The rest will be divided evenly among the real people and the soldiers."

"Real people? I don't know where you're from but we call them players. But…okay, yeah, I think me and my friend will be on board."

They shook hands, with Roan saying, "We'll meet back here in two hours. That should be enough time to get everything prepared." He left the dwarf and went in search of a proper tailor. His clothes, though practically new, were stained, torn and smelled of orc guts. After two tries, he found a shop that offered more than coarse wool tunics and peasant dresses.

Although the tailor, a thin husk of a man in a perfect fitting suit, offered a wide array of colors and fabrics, Roan chose a simple black outfit: pants, shirt, cloak and boots. By his down-turned lips, the tailor was displeased with the choice. Roan didn't much care what the man thought.

As he waited for his old outfit to be cleaned and repaired, and his new one to be fitted, he sat in the front room wearing a borrowed robe, with his sword across his knees, sharpening the blade. The tailor didn't seem to care for this either.

Despite his crankiness, the tailor did a fine job and Roan felt like a new man as he strolled from the tailor's and headed back to the tavern where he was hoping to see a formation of soldiers in proper uniforms, standing at attention.

Instead he came back to what could only be called a disorderly rabble. Some of the men wore old leather armor that was stained and dirty, some wore the stiffened hides of animals, and some wore the clothes they had slept in the night before. Some carried nicked and notched swords, some carried pitted clubs, and one had a tree branch as a weapon.

They were an ugly lot as well, more likely to give you a snarl than a smile. But perhaps worst of all, there weren't more than thirty of them.

"What the hell is this?" Roan demanded, pulling Marshall to the side. "I asked for soldiers and you give me vagabonds and vagrants."

"That's all there is around here. Trust me, these are the good ones, or at least the not-so-evil ones. There were some guys who radiated pure darkness." Roan gave him a questioning look and Marshall explained, "As a Paladin, if I concentrate, I can detect evil."

It was a handy ability, but it begged the question: "Why didn't you use it last night on that assassin?"

Marshall gave a sheepish shrug. "After he gave us that warning I thought he was a good guy. Either way, I checked these guys and some are a little shady but most are pretty neutral."

"Great," Roan said, shaking his head. "Where's Jarrod?"

"Getting provisions. We'll have to feed these guys so he's getting the food. And I took the liberty of having him get a wagon and a pair of mules. I didn't think you'd want to make the attempt on Mendenome with so few men, so I told him to get enough food for a week. We're probably going to have to go back to Tir-Khan."

He was right. They could have made the attempt on Mendenome with so few men, but none would have come back.

Roan had his "troops" line up and was inspecting them when Krull and his dwarf friend came up. Without alcohol in them, the two were very friendly and eager to get going. When Roan explained that they would have to head north to Tir-Khan first, they were fine with it.

"So, what does your spidey-sense tell you about them?" Roan asked, gesturing with his chin at the two dwarves.

"I'm a little shocked after last night, but they're both lawful good." When Jarrod and Amanda got there, each had the same question and both were equally skeptical.

The dwarves won them over on the march north. The two joked constantly, told exciting stories about their adventures, and, when needed, barked at the men in Roan's company whenever they began to straggle. As they wore heavy armor, Roan allowed them to ride on the wagon with the supplies, which caused the foot-sore townsmen to grumble.

When one complained too loudly, Krull's friend, Christian "Ironhead" Walker climbed down, planted his sturdy legs and gripped a thirty pound warhammer before asking, "You want to have a go at me, boy? If not, shut yer trap." The man decided to shut his trap.

In the very back of the formation, Amanda rode her horse, Rhi-adol, while Roan sat upon Jetta, who was in a frisky mood and not at all in a listening mood. Amanda thought it was funny that Roan was basically being held hostage by the horse who did as it pleased, going up and down the line or pushing through the formation or just standing, staring off at the horizon.

At one point, Jetta stopped to eat and, as the rest of the formation disappeared from view, Amanda waved and blew kisses as she chortled. Roan did everything he could think of to get the horse to move. Finally, he gave him two swift jabs with the heel of his boots. Jetta bucked and the next thing Roan knew, he was on his back staring up at the tree limbs that met over the road to form a canopy of sorts.

He was still lying there trying to collect himself so that killing Jetta wouldn't be the next thing he did, when a soft, woman's voice said, "I do not like the way you treat that horse. It is unkind."

Roan scrambled to his feet but at first, he saw only the dense underbrush and the crowding trees of the forest. Even with his *spot* and *search* bonuses he saw nothing. Then his eyes picked out movement as a very small woman seemed to appear out of nowhere, stepping through the foliage almost as if she were floating through it. She was green-eyed, while the color of her skin and the silky shift she wore changed colors to match her surroundings.

Although he was tall and strong and she was nothing but a slip of girl, Roan felt a sudden stab of fear and drew his sword.

"No," she whispered. "You will not need that. Just look at my eyes and you will see." He knew better than to look into those eyes, but he couldn't seem to help it and with one glance he was hooked.

2—

For Roan, the next few minutes was nothing but a haze of colors—greens and browns, mostly—and strange earthy aromas; rich dirt, decaying wood and the smell of flowers. Everything else was a distant cloud in his subconscious.

Slowly his eyes and his mind began to focus again. He found himself strung up like a fly in a web, only it was vines and thin branches holding him. There were even thin shoots woven into his hair. Unable to move his head, he let his eyes dart about, searching for the…whatever the thing had been.

She wasn't in sight, either that or she was hiding. As he searched for her, he noticed something very strange; he wasn't in the same forest. It was impossible but true. The trees were towering monuments, their trunks clad in silver bark, the leaves in their canopies were dark green but also gilded in silver. It took his breath away.

But it also scared him. What had happened to his team? Were they okay? And what about Glitch? He tried to reach out with his mind for the elemental, only to come up empty.

"Your friend cannot hear you, veil-dweller." Suddenly the little female creature was there, seeming to emerge from the trunk of the closest tree. "You are far away from it. Too far to hurt the horse as well."

"I can tell you that he's hurt me far more than I've hurt him. You know what he is? He's obstinate and a pain in my ass. You should have him tied up here instead of me. Or at least with me."

The green creature came and knelt next to Roan's head. He saw that everywhere she touched the earth, thousands of tiny green roots, as thin as hair, would reach down into the dirt. "I would not do that. The horse does not know better. It wishes to please you, only you throw it in confusion. If you were a real elf, you would know this."

"You do not think I'm an elf?"

"And neither do you. We both know you are a veil-dweller. This gives you no right to hurt the animals, here."

Roan stared into her green eyes in amazement. "Are…are you a player?" When a questioning look swept her features, he said, "Never mind. Can you tell me how you know about the veil? Do you know what's on the other side?"

"A world I do not wish to know. I do not look into that world for fear of being corrupted. The feeling that emanates from the veil-dwellers is frequently one of anger. Many of you are weak."

"Weak? In what way?"

She touched his thick shoulder, saying, "Not in this way. Not in the arms but in the heart. It is weakness to hurt an animal. It is a sign of a weak character."

In shame, his eyes slipped away from her. "You're right, I should not have hurt Jetta. He really is a good horse, he's just not trained well."

"You are the one who is not trained well," she said, raising an eyebrow that looked like tiny blades of grass. "A true elf would know how to speak to the animal and you are not true. You are not even one of the new elves." Roan blinked in confusion and she said, "You do not understand."

He tried to shake his head, but couldn't with the shoots entwined in his hair. "You're right, again. I don't understand. Tell me, are there more, uh, people like you who can see across the veil? Have you ever heard of Gorgothe The Infinite?" She sucked in her breath at the name and he felt the roots and vines tightening around him, constricting him, choking him. "No." he said, speaking quickly while he still could. "I'm his enemy. I'm here to stop him."

Immediately, the vines relaxed as she studied him. Gradually, they withdrew altogether. "I had thought to punish you for your misdeeds, but you do not attempt to mislead." Now that he could shake his head, Roan did so. "I'm sorry, veil-dweller, you are too weak to stop the Infinite One, and this time I mean the weakness of your arms and magic. He will destroy you."

"Probably," he said, getting to his feet, "but I don't have a choice. He is a danger to people on the other side of the veil and someone has to stop him."

"He is more of a danger in this world. He upsets the balance. Even the gods fear him."

Roan did not know what sort of "gods" they had in Daggerland, still his heart sank. How was he supposed to fight someone with that much power? "Could you help me? Do you know where he is?"

She sighed and it was the sound of wind in the trees. "Sometimes it feels as though he is everywhere, corrupting everything, even the trees and the flowers. As for help." She shrugged. "I have little power against The Infinite One. In truth my power is like the wind; it comes and goes as it pleases, though I suppose I can help you with your friend the horse. I can teach you his language. Bend down, tall one."

He leaned over and she spoke soft words into his ear. As she spoke, he closed his eyes. Her words went deeper than he thought possible and he did not just hear them, he felt them and something awakened within him.

246

"It seems so simple," he said, in awe.

"That's because it is. Horses are not complicated. They know freedom and running and joy. They know direction and speed. They know loyalty. They know family and duty."

Roan nodded. Her words had taught him all of that. "And now I do, as well, thank you. Oh, I have a question about these true elves. How..."

"No, there isn't time," she said. She dropped to the ground and touched the earth—joining it through the green tendrils emanating from her palm. "Your friends are in danger. I can feel The Infinite One. Evil draws near to those we left behind. Quick!" She grabbed his hand and pulled him to one of the silver trees. This one was different, it had a split in its trunk. She stepped in easily, while he was forced to duck low to get in.

The tree seemed much bigger on the inside, though why she had him enter it, he didn't know. They could have just as easily gone around it. She led him to the other side where there was a similar split and put her hand on his back, propelling him forward, saying, "Hurry, veil creature."

He stepped from the darkness of the trunk and into a different forest. Gone were the silver trees; around him were elm and oak. And in the air were cries—people were calling his name. He oriented on Amanda's voice, breaking through the trees right in front of her.

She jumped at his sudden appearance. "Roan, what the hell? Where have you been? Were you lost?"

He didn't answer her right away. "Glitch! Something's coming. Find it!" The elemental had been pulsing above Amanda's head; now it shot into the air. As it searched, Roan called out: "*Jetta-unwal-ray.*"

"What did you say?" Amanda asked. "Roan? Roan, what's going on? Did you get lost or..." Jetta's thudding hooves stopped her. She stared as the grey gelding came racing up.

"*Jetta, rune ai,*" Roan said. Jetta's ears swiveled and then went stock still as Roan jumped up into the saddle. Amanda stared at him in confusion. Roan didn't have time for much of an explanation. Glitch had spotted something moving through the forest and was now raising all sorts of alarms in his head.

"I met a green lady in the forest who taught me how to speak to horses. It's nothing. Come on."

"Nothing? Green lady?"

There was no time to explain. He murmured a word and Jetta spun around, gathered his powerful legs beneath him and sprang away, racing through the forest, reacting more to Roan's thoughts than to his words.

The "language" of horses as spoken to him by the green lady seemed to have created a connection between horse and rider so that very little in the way of commands needed to be given. The two sprinted back to the road with Amanda on Rhiadol lagging behind.

"Form up!" Roan bellowed to the small company of soldiers, most of whom were sitting in the shade. "Move it! Something's coming."

At first, Glitch thought that strange, ugly people were heading towards them but now that they were closer, Glitch saw that they were actually walking corpses. Roan saw what Glitch saw and felt the same revulsion—the undead were coming for them. He had to quell the very strong desire to spur Jetta out of there and leave his little company to die.

"What is it?" Jarrod asked, riding up with Marshall on his right.

Roan pointed ahead of them. "Some, uh, things are coming. Some sort of zombies, I think. There's around thirty of them or so. Glitch can't count very well."

"Zombies just don't jump up out of the ground," Marshall said. "If there are zombies, that means there's a necromancer nearby. And if...crap! Here they come." Marshall spun his white charger around and began barking to the soldiers to form two ranks. He placed one of the sturdy dwarves at either end of the line and put himself in the middle.

"We should get behind the lines," Roan said to Amanda, who stared as the zombies poured onto the road, her face lined with worry.

"I don't know what to do, Roan. I'm a Christian, now more than ever." Roan shrugged, not having any idea why she would bring this up just then. "You don't get it," she hissed so that no one else could hear. "I'm a cleric. It's like a priest."

Roan gestured at the half-decomposed bodies shambling towards them and asked, "Is this really the time for a theological discussion?"

Her answer surprised him. "Yes. I-I had to choose a 'god' when I started the game, and *the* God was not among the choices. I chose the elven goddess Elbereth, Creator of the Stars and

Wind. So far, it's been just a game. I really don't believe in her. I believe in God and…"

"And it would be a sin to worship another 'god' right?"

She nodded and glanced towards the zombies, one of which was walking with one of Jarrod's arrows sticking through its throat. "If I call on Elbereth directly, I might be able to destroy some of those…those things. You see? And what happens if I get to a really high level? It'll just get worse. I think I picked the wrong class."

He couldn't imagine a worse time to have a literal "Come to Jesus Moment." Jetta was dancing in fear beneath him, while above, Glitch was screaming *!!!* over and over as if Roan was blind and couldn't see the undead heading for him. He needed time to think, but there was no time for thinking. There was only time for action.

"Hold on," he told her. Taking a breath, he focused his mind on his one *Inferno* spell; it was hot inside of him and when he spoke the words to release it, he had to grit his teeth against the intense heat and power of the spell as it brewed under his skin. The spell burned as it escaped from his palm. It started as a ball of fire as big as his head, and grew quickly as it flew into the mass of undead. When it exploded with a low roar, Roan had to turn his face from the glare.

Superimposed on the flames were neon green words: (*XP +35*), (*XP +35*), (*XP +35*), (*XP +35*)…Followed by the announcement: *Congratulations! You are now a Level Six Wizard and have gained the following bonuses:*
Increased Hit Points(+8)
You have gained +1 tier three spells per day
You have +6 skill points to allocate

His relief at making it to the sixth level was offset by the atrocious smell washing over him. It was the terrible stench of flame broiled rotting flesh. The horses wanted no part of it and Roan allowed Jetta to carry him behind the formation, which was already showing holes. Some of the men had run away and the rest were either retching or shaking in fear.

Roan didn't blame them. There was still a second wave of zombies bearing down on them. And there was still the necromancer himself to face. Roan could feel him nearby, watching.

Roan didn't like their chances against the remaining zombies that were charging down on them. At least twenty of them had survived the flames, including one that had three arrows sticking through it, making him wonder what it would take, other than his spells, to kill them.

He was clearly not the only one wondering this very thing. The double line, which had started straight, was now a soft "W." The center, where Marshall and Jarrod stood, and the two ends, which were anchored by the dwarves, seemed to be thrust forward, while the rest sagged back, the fear on the men's faces obvious.

Yes, Roan had more spells, however with a necromancer left to be dealt with, he needed to hold back just in case there were worse things lurking in the woods.

Turning to Amanda, he begged, "Please. I know it feels real, but it's just a game. That's how you have to look at this. I'm not a real wizard and you are not a real cleric." He paused as he saw red neon words ghost up: (*XP -10*). He muttered a curse as he took another hit to his experience point total, saying, "This is all pretend, but with some very real consequences."

She bit her lip and Roan could tell he was getting closer. "I think God would understand if you did this. Think about this: you're doing this to serve others, to save innocent people. So, please, please, use your powers."

"Okay. Okay. It's only a game," she said, urging her dun-colored horse into the line of men from behind. She pulled a silver chain from around her neck and Roan saw it was a circle about the size of his palm. Within the circle, suspended in some manner that he could not see, were tiny dots of light. Holding it up above her head, she cried, "Elbereth! I call on you to banish these creatures back to hell!"

As Roan watched, a great sphere of semi-darkness swept from Amanda, dimming her golden hair. It was as if twilight had descended upon them and then from the upraised pendant streaks of starlight shot out, zipping into the zombies. They began to moan and wail—a sound that sent a wave of goosebumps over Roan's arms.

The zombies in front slowly collapsed, their putrid bodies falling apart so that grey flesh splattered as it hit the road. The ones in the next line turned away, throwing their arms across their faces. In the very back were the stragglers, who stopped and stared, looking like strangely posed corpses.

Amanda's strength did not last. She could only keep up the invocation for a few seconds before she slumped over the neck of her horse. In that time, she had killed seven of the zombies outright and had driven off two others that never returned. This left only thirteen of the rotting things coming at them in sporadic clumps.

"They ain't nothing!" Krull shouted as two of the men started backing away. The stout dwarf gave the first zombie to reach him a tremendous whack with his warhammer, sending the thing sprawling. A second later, it started to get up again. "Don't worry, boys. You can kill em' it just takes a few hits."

A couple of the townsmen rushed to help, bashing the thing with their clubs. Marshall showed that swords were much better weapons as he cut one nearly in half with a single swing of his magic sword—and yet it still was "alive." His backhand swing killed it.

Seeing it truly dead was enough proof for the rest of the peasant soldiers. With a ragged battle cry they rushed to attack.

Roan turned away from the fight, searching the forest. He could sense the eyes on him, just as he could feel the malignant air of the necromancer. "He's close. Glitch, can you find him… but be careful!" In seconds, the elemental had disappeared. Roan did not attempt to see what Glitch was seeing; he kept his eyes out, and only rarely checked on the progress of the battle, which seemed to be one-sided in their favor.

He didn't want to admit it, but he was unnerved, if not actually afraid. As an FBI agent, he had confronted dozens of the worst murders, from serial killers to the most horrific pedophiles, and yet none of them had given off such an unholy, evil vibe as the necromancer. Roan had to wonder if this demon of a man was actually a real person—someone who came to Daggerland to indulge in their sick fantasies.

"If so, there'd be bleed-over," Roan muttered, knowing that someone this twisted wouldn't be content to kill in only one world if he had access to two.

Tense minutes passed with Roan fully expecting an appearance by the necromancer, however the only sign of him came as the last of the zombies was beaten into a foul, grey mush. High overhead in one of the trees, there was a sudden squawk and an explosion of black feathers. Roan was shocked to see a crow tumbling and spinning across the sky—Glitch was attacking it!

In a flash, Roan understood: it was the necromancer's familiar. With a word, he sent a *Fire Bolt* shooting up, catching the bird in the wing as it tumbled. There was a burst of flame and the bird cartwheeled out of control, heading right for the road, but amazingly, it pulled out of its fall and zoomed away, more than likely heading back to its master.

Afraid that Glitch would be targeted by an even more powerful spell than the simple cantrip he'd used, Roan called back his own familiar and only when it was safely tucked under his own cloak did he take a glance around at the remains of the battle; there were bodies everywhere. "I take it we won?"

Jarrod was kneeling nearby, pouring water onto the blade of his sword, a look of disgust pulling down his lips. "Yeah. We had two dead and five deserters. We better pick up a bunch of guys in Tir-Kahn or we'll never be able to crack Mendenome."

"It'll be fine," Marshall said, from atop his white charger. He had grown in the last couple of weeks and his confidence had never been higher.

"Easy for you to say," Jarrod replied. "You don't have to be the rogue in the group. If I had your armor and a magic sword, I'd be out front kicking ass, too. Next time, I get first pick."

Roan tuned him out and tried to pick up the feeling of the necromancer again. The sensation of death hung in the air, but it was fading quickly along with the retreating crow. A sigh of relief escaped him. "The necromancer kept watch on us through his familiar, but Glitch drove it off. We should get moving. If we hurry we can slip by."

He didn't like the idea of just "slipping by," leaving a murderer free to continue spreading misery and death, especially when he had twenty-five men backing him up. But they were on a mission that had to take precedence. "Next time," he said, under his breath. Aloud he called out, "Let's get formed up!"

Once the townsmen had come together in some semblance of a unit, Marshall, with the dwarves acting as sergeants, got them moving again. There was no straggling now. None of the men wanted to be left behind and the last few in the very rear of the formation kept looking back, afraid that the necromancer was creeping up on them.

Roan felt it was safe enough to send Glitch scouting again. The elemental led the group while Roan and Amanda rode in the back, neither saying much. Roan was trying to get a handle on everything that had happened to them in the last day: necromancers, assassins, magic mirrors, and whatever that green lady had been.

Eventually, he told Amanda about the green lady. "She knows about the veil?" Amanda asked. "I wonder why the game allows that. We get our wrists slapped if we cross a certain line just talking about the two worlds. You would think there would be some sort of algorithmic control put in place."

"Unless it's another glitch in the program. She did say that Arching was upsetting the 'balance.' By that I suppose she means the operating system. For me, the most interesting part was how she delineated the three different kinds of elves. There's you and me, we're veil creatures and not elves at all, that makes sense. But what didn't was the idea of new elves and true elves. What do you think, nerd-girl, another computer glitch?"

"I don't feel much like a nerd-girl, these days," she said, giving him a little smile. "New York feels like a different time and a different life. It's almost like a fading dream. But talking programming brings it back." She sighed as if she were reluctant to go on. "If I had to guess, I'd say this concept of dual elves is a response to the glitch. If we assume the game AI accidentally discovered the 'veil' perhaps it equates all NPCs created before that time as 'real' and all created after as ersatz."

"Ersatz?" Roan asked, with a hearty laugh. "Now that sounds like the nerd-girl I know. Do me a favor, when this is all over and we go back to the other side, just use the word 'fake' instead of ersatz. I won't be a genius then and I don't want you to see me as a drooling idiot."

"We both know you weren't an idiot. You just weren't nerd-boy to my nerd-girl. You had different talents. When it came to real criminals, you always seemed to sniff them out. I thought it was amazing."

He glanced at her and before he knew it, the glance turned into a long stare. The feeling was similar to when the green lady had told him to look into her eyes. He was almost compelled to stare at her as his heart rebelled against his mind. The FBI rules were cut and dried; set in cement and yet his heart demanded that he lean across the gap between their horses and kiss her.

Jetta, who was now in sync with his master, sidled so close that Amanda's knee brushed his own.

Amanda jerked at the touch, her cheeks going red. She smiled in embarrassment, though at what, Roan didn't know. "I-I, your horse," she stammered. "Y-you said the lady taught you how to talk to him. Can you teach me?"

Roan was glad to. Amanda was an apt pupil and it wasn't long before she took off Rhi-adol's bit and bridle. She cantered, galloped and trotted the mare all around the formation as if they were part of a circus show. It cheered the men and the time passed too quickly for Roan's liking. He could have spent a year watching her golden hair streaming behind her in the wind.

The afternoon wore away quickly and twenty miles passed under their feet. When the tips of the towers of the hill city of Tir-Kahn came into view, Roan had Marshall form the men into a proper marching company. Krull strode next to the company, barking out an even cadence.

"You're a veteran?" Roan asked.

"On the other side, I was First Sergeant Steve Krull, US Army, right up until I retired last year."

"Four years of going back and forth from Iraq to Afghanistan was enough for me," Roan said. "Now I'm with the…" He caught himself almost telling the dwarf that he was FBI. That would have been a serious mistake. "Hey, do me a favor, don't tell anyone else your real name. I can't tell you how I know, but there's trouble brewing in Daggerland that could ripple over to the other side."

Krull frowned, his bushy mustache drooping theatrically. "And you're obviously a part of that trouble. Me and Ironhead knew it from the start. Assassination attempts are rare and then coming across a necromancer in broad daylight? That doesn't happen by accident. Well, you can count on me to stick with you in…Hey! Boy! Get back in line. Don't think you're going to slip away under my watch."

The dwarf marched up to one of the men and glared him back into the formation. They were just entering the lower gates to the hill city and the crowds were thick. To clear the street for the company, Roan's team led the way, riding side by side along the winding road.

At the second tier, they turned off and found a cheap inn though not as cheap as the lower level inns. The men were bunked six to a room and given a small allowance for food and drink. Krull was happy to stay down in the "slums" as he called the lower part of the city, if it meant keeping the company together.

When the team reached the next tier of the city, Marshall and Jarrod broke off to begin recruiting. This mainly took the form of visiting taverns, talking to bartenders, and throwing gold around. Knowing Jarrod, they would be at it until midnight.

And this left just Roan and Amanda. "We should get our rooms," Amanda said, her cheeks going pink. "I-I think with the threat of assassination that maybe we should double up, you know, two to a room. I-I could take Marshall in my room if you're, uh, worried."

"What would I have to worry about?" he asked, despite knowing the answer. If they shared a room they would either end up making love, or spend the night wishing they were.

She started to babble an answer when a tiny, silver-haired elfin woman came up to them and bowed so low that Roan had to look over the top of Jetta's neck to see her. "Sariah, is that you?" It was the elf they had rescued from the Ash Forest.

"Yes, Milord. Thanks to your bravery during the siege of Riverport, we were able to flee to safety. I owe you a debt of gratitude for saving my children. I am yours to command." She bowed again, this time even lower.

"No, that's okay." Roan slipped from Jetta. He took her hand and lifted her to her feet. "A simple thank you, is enough. So, where are you staying?"

Before answering, she reached out and brushed dirt from the edge of his cloak. "My family and I are staying with his lordship, the Prince of Tir-Kahn. He and Lord Leomagnus were great friends and he has kindly taken in many of the elves from Ash Forest. He would like to meet you."

Roan became guarded. "And how does he know me?"

"He has great vision and sees further than most mortals," was her cryptic reply.

Roan let Sariah ride upon Jetta and she was simply in awe that he knew the language of the horses. "Are you a child of the Eiryndar?" When he asked what that meant, she laughed. "You jest, milord. Wait, I see now that you are serious. How strange. That is like a horse who does not know her own hooves."

"We, uh, we are from a very distant land," Roan explained. "Some knowledge has been lost to us, but these Eiryndar, are they what are called the true elves?"

"A true elf? Now, that is something of which I have never heard. No, the Eiryndar are the children of the sun, the first beings in the land. It is they who named the rocks and taught the trees to dance with the wind. There are few of them left in the world for they are constantly hunted by those who would corrupt perfection and steal innocence."

Amanda asked Sariah, "Do you know where we could find some of these Eiryndar? It's important to our mission."

"I do not. In truth, I was hoping that you knew. As even you must know, our people have become scattered and weak. Many search for the Eiryndar, so far they search in vain."

Roan had more questions, however they had gained the top of the steep hill. To the left was the fine old inn they had stayed at the last time they had been in Tir-kahn, and to the right was the prince's palace. Even with Sariah smiling down on him from atop Jetta, he feared he was about to walk into a trap.

When a squad of six soldiers marched out from the palace, it seemed as though the trap was already sprung. "Keep out of sight, Glitch, just in case."

The captain of the guard, a burly human in layered plates of what appeared to be brass, bowed from the waist and said, "My Lord Roan, my Lady Amanda of Water Fell, please follow me. The Prince of the city wishes to meet with you."

The captain did not bother to look in Sariah's direction and ignored her curtsey when she tried to pay her respects. Roan made it a point to exaggerate his bow to her. "It was wonderful to see you, Sariah," he told her. Amanda had picked up on the slight as well and went so far as to invite the elf and her family to dinner.

"The prince may already have plans for you," the captain said.

"We decide our own plans," Amanda replied, before turning her back on the hulking man. "Good bye for now, Lady Sariah."

Grinding his teeth, the captain led them through the doors of the palace. The interior was quite a surprise. The center of the building was open all the way to the glass ceiling sixty feet above. Water that had no visible source poured down from the center of the ceiling, cooling the air and giving it a refreshing feel.

Although Roan wanted to inspect the feature further, the captain had taken an immediate left into a separate corridor that led to a set of stairs. These were simple stone steps and seemed a tad underwhelming until Roan noticed that the steps were part of the hill itself. It wasn't as visually pleasing as the magic waterfall, but on a different level it was more impressive.

They made their way to the third floor and crossed into a library that had a great view of the interior of the building on one side and an even better view of the city on the other.

The prince sat behind a desk of black wood that had such a polished shine to it that it looked wet. He was arrayed in white and gold platemail. With his thin face and close-set eyes, he was not a terribly impressive man beyond the armor.

Amanda and Roan bowed briefly. "Ah yes," the prince said, jumping up and coming around his desk with his hand out. "Prince Stallings of Tir-Kahn, nice to meet you both. That'll be all, Tareman," he said to the captain as he shook hands with Roan.

When the guard captain was gone, the prince offered his guests a seat and then leaned back on the desk. "So, what can I do for the FBI?"

"You can tell us how you know we're FBI, for a start," Roan said, his eyes narrowing.

"First off, I want it on the record that I am being as cooperative as I can in this matter. Second, I don't care what anyone says, Leo Magnuson is completely innocent. I saw him yesterday and he mentioned you guys were in Daggerland."

Amanda groaned, rubbing her forehead. "We need to muzzle that guy right this second."

It actually wasn't a bad idea. "Take care of it. Have Caron get a judge to put him in isolation and find out who else he's been talking to. We need to nip this in the bud." She nodded once and disappeared. Roan glanced back to the prince who wore a stunned expression.

"You're not joking, are you? Look, he didn't do it. He was here with me when his cousin was killed. I'll be a witness if I have to. And…and there were others. They were NPCs, but they wouldn't lie. I could call them…"

"Don't bother," Roan said. "I believe you, but no judge is going to allow NPCs to be used as witnesses."

The prince went back around the table and plopped down in his chair. He stared at its shiny surface. "I hope you don't take this the wrong way, but I hate that you're here."

"You have only one recourse; help me catch this murderer. Start at the beginning. What's your real name?"

He took a shaky breath and answered, "Jason Stallings."

"How do you know Magnuson?"

He laughed. "He's my neighbor. He lives on the same cul-de-sac as I do. We've been friends for, hell, since our kids went to preschool together. And we started playing the game together, as well. It was me, Magnus, Max Canez, and Joe Sowa. We went out and got those old first gen neuro-couplers. My wife thought it would give me brain cancer."

He looked past Roan with a ghost of a smile on his lips. "That was a great time to be in Daggerland. Really, it still is, but it's different when you're fresh into your character, like you and the woman. We fought our way from one end of the world to the other, and I don't want to brag, but our adventures were the stuff of legends. After a few years, we ended up here. We conquered the lands and divided them among us."

"And how does Gethahyme fit into this?"

"We had been here about a year when he 'forewarned' me that he was going to build his tower. It was basically a heads-up but there was an implied threat. There wasn't much I could do except roll with it. In truth, he turned out to be a pretty good neighbor. Whatever he needed would come through here and I always took a nibble, you know, in taxes and fees. I never got too greedy and he had no issue with it. It's too bad he got himself killed, but that's the way the game's played, right?"

Roan nodded once, unsure how to go on. He was hesitant about telling Stallings how Gethahyme, as Greg Nelson, had died in the real world. The less he knew, the safer he would be. "Do you know a man named Tim Cole?" Stallings shook his head. "What about Aderon the Black?"

"Him I know. He was Gethahyme's lackey and was always a bit of a greasy character. I put up with him hanging around the lower tiers because I didn't want to upset the balance around here. Not that this matters at all, but he conspired to take down his boss and now he's loaded up with magic items. He was the one who came after Magnuson in the Ash Forest."

"Did you know his cousin, Greyson Fulbright?"

Stallings paused and when he spoke, it was slowly as if he were picking his words with care. "I never met him on the other side. We did cross paths here a few times over the years. He was a big time wizard; really a pompous ass if you ask me, but a lot of wizards are. No offense."

Roan waved his hand, uncaring what Stallings thought of wizards. Stallings went on, "Either way, he was good to Magnuson, here and on the other side. I know Magnuson complained a lot about his cousin pressuring him to give up his lands here, but he was getting a real deal, if you ask me. I think he owed Fulbright like ten million dollars while his lands in the Ash Forest only netted him a couple grand a year. Magnuson told me he was going to give in and take the deal. I can testify to that."

Normally, the petty squabbling over money would have pointed to motive and he would have grilled Stallings over it, but what was happening in Daggerland was beyond that. "Tell me what you know of someone who calls himself Gorgothe the Infinite?"

"I've never heard of him."

Roan's eyes narrowed in suspicion. "But you've heard of me. You knew I was coming and the elf, Sariah said you were far seeing. Yet you don't know Gorgothe? How is that? Why don't you explain to me how you knew I was coming? Before you answer, let me warn you that lying to an FBI agent in any world is obstruction of justice."

"I-I'm not lying. I serve the warrior goddess, Freyja, Queen of the Valkyrie. She sometimes speaks to me in dreams and she told me that 'a being of law would transcend the veil.' That was last night. When I woke, I sought you out using the *Sight of the Goddess.*"

"You are Freyja's cleric?" Amanda asked, causing Roan to jump. He hadn't known that she had returned from the other side. When Stallings nodded, Amanda went on, excitedly, "Can you contact her through a spell or a ritual? We need to know about Gorgothe—where to find him and what his powers are. We also need to know about…"

She stopped in mid-sentence, looking towards Roan. He nodded and she finished, "We need to know about Atticus Arching." At the name, Stallings sat back, his eyes wide. "Yes," Amanda said. "This goes very high up and Fulbright wasn't the first one murdered. For your own safety, do not speak a word about this to anyone…except to Freyja, that is."

"Okay, yeah, okay. I-I'll see if she'll answer me. She has before, but only in emergencies. Give me a few hours."

Roan stood saying, "We'll be next door when you're done with your rituals."

"No, don't be ridiculous. I have plenty of room here." He rang a bell and a tiny person came running in. At first, Roan thought it was a child, then saw that it was a halfling. He bowed so low that his curly hair brushed the floor.

The halfling escorted them to a suite of rooms that had a pretty view of the river as it swept slowly by the tall hill. Once the servant was gone, Roan turned to Amanda. Whatever had been brewing between them was muted and distant. They were both too preoccupied by the idea of bringing gods into their investigation.

"Hey, I just thought of something," Roan said. "Why don't you try to contact your elven goddess? Do you know how?"

"Yes. Anyone can try through meditation, prayers and offerings, but I'm only fifth level. It would be like an altar boy calling Rome and asking for the pope. If you want me to, I will. Just don't get your hopes up."

Chapter 23

— Tir-Kahn, Daggerland

Amanda failed in her attempt to reach her elven goddess. For over an hour, she knelt on a soft carpet, her eyes closed, her hands clasped in front of her, her lips whispering the name: Elbereth repeatedly. Although it didn't look like work, there was a sheen of sweat across her forehead and her muscles shook. She was exhausted at the end of the ordeal.

"All I heard was an echo over and over. It sounded like your name being screamed…by a woman."

"Was it your voice?"

She hesitated before saying, "Maybe." The word wasn't out of her mouth a second before there was a knock on the door.

It was Sariah. After a deep bow, she said, "It would so please the elves of the palace for you to dine with us this evening. I was told by the prince's manservant that you are available. If it pleases thee, I have brought this for the lady." She turned to the door where one of her silver-haired children held a package. "A gift, for one should not wear armor, even mithral, to dinner, don't you think so?"

Amanda was too enthralled in the dress to answer. Roan agreed for her. "Do we have time to cleanup, properly?" He feared that there was a whiff of the undead still about him.

"Of course, milord."

Once Sariah left, Amanda went to bathe. A minute later, she came running into the sitting room, wearing only a towel. "There's a shower in here!" she practically squealed.

Roan had leapt to his feet with his sword drawn. He stood there too stunned by her appearance to comment beyond, "That's good."

"Yeah it is," she said, and then ran back to the bathroom, a smile on her face. She was in the bathroom for fifty minutes. When she came out she had on the dress. It was beautifully woven of various shades of peach thread and hung down to her calves.

"You have to feel this," she said, lifting the hem of her dress to him. It was made from a very light material that Roan couldn't name. He had never felt anything so soft and in his distraction, his hand went right up her leg. When he realized how far up he'd gone, he snatched it back, quickly.

He mumbled an apology, however she hadn't seemed to mind a bit and in fact gave him a twirl so that the dress lifted to thigh-height.

"I love it," she told him. "Once we take out Arching, I'm going to get an entire closetful of these."

If we take out Arching, Roan thought.

When they stepped out of their suite, the same halfling who had escorted them earlier stood in the hall. He bowed deeply. "This way," he intoned, his serious nature somewhat at odds with his ruddy cheeks and curly hair. He marched with quick strides down through the palace to a windowless room on the lower floor. It was narrow and long, lit with dozens of candles.

Twenty-two elves, both men and women stood waiting on the pair, who were given the middle seats, which were considered places of honor by the elves. Raising a few eyebrows, Roan had Sariah sit on his right, while on his left sat Amiriah the warlock who had helped him cast his first spell which had summoned Glitch. Amiriah was a frail thing, haunted by the destruction of his home.

All of the elves were subdued and their smiles were infrequent and did not last. At first the talk around the table consisted strictly of banal pleasantries: the weather, the fine view of the river, the flowering season of the wisteria, none of which interested Roan, who struggled heroically against yawning.

Eventually, someone nudged Sariah. She sat up straight, fixed a smile on her face and asked, with considerable embarrassment, "On your travels, have you heard anything of the fate of Lord Leomagnus. He survived the battle of Ash Forest and brought the remnants of his people here, but has since disappeared."

"He's been taken prisoner in the world beyond the veil," he told them. They did not know about the veil and pressed him with many questions, which he dodged as best as he was able. When Sariah realized he was becoming uncomfortable, she changed the subject to his current quest.

They listened politely as he told them about their adventure to Mendenome, the fight with the team of assassins, and the battle with the undead. It became obvious that stories of blood and death were not much to their liking, so he told them of the green lady.

Her story had them sitting up and listening with rapt attention. "Was it she who taught you the language of horses?" Sariah asked.

"Yes," he answered, deciding not to mention why she had kidnapped him in the first place.

"It could be none other than Vasailes the Timeless, the Green Mother of the Nymphs," Amiriah remarked. "It is as I first told you milord, Roan. There are many eyes on you."

"It certainly feels that way, but I think it has little to do with me and more to do with my mission. I entered Mendenome to search for clues to what happened to Lord Gethahyme. Unfortunately, we were driven away before we could establish exactly what happened. There was one thing we did learn: the imprisonment of Leomagnus and Gethahyme's murder are connected. It's one of the reasons we're going back tomorrow. If I can prove that Leomagnus is innocent of the crimes that he is charged with, I can free him."

Much to Roan's surprise, a young elf warrior stood and pledged his sword to him. Then a second did the same, followed by five more. Unsure of himself, Roan thanked them and accepted their service. He did not realize the extent of their pledge. All seven left their plates half-eaten and left to prepare themselves for the next day's journey.

The remainder of the dinner passed quietly without even the small talk which Roan always found wearing. The quiet was fine with Roan. After his long day of fighting and traveling he was tired and drawn, however sleep would have to wait until after he heard from the prince. It almost seemed as though their only chance against Arching was through some sort of divine intervention.

He ate as quickly as he could without being rude—until it came time for desert. A wedge of blueberry pie, one that had never been equaled in any world, was set before him. He took one bite and all thoughts of Atticus Arching left his head. The pie was that good. When he had scraped up the last crumb with his fork, he had to fight the urge to lick his plate.

"Don't," Amanda said, seemingly reading his mind and realizing that he was succumbing to the urge. She reached out and pulled his plate back. "We should get going, the prince is probably waiting on us."

Now that the pie was gone, Roan wanted to get out of there in a hurry, however, ending a meal with elves was just as formal as beginning one. Everyone had to be acknowledged, thanked and bowed to one last time. After what seemed like an interminably long time, the pair were finally able to extricate themselves. In the hallway, they found the same halfling waiting for them.

"The prince will see you now."

The halfling did not take them back to the library. They were escorted to the prince's private study. The room was lit only by a single candle, still, Roan's elf eyes picked out the prince sitting behind his desk, a half-empty wine bottle within his reach. There was no glass for the wine in sight.

"You may adjourn for the night, Rolly," the prince said. He waited for the halfling to leave, shutting the door behind him, before he reached for the bottle and tipped it to his lips like Roan had seen a thousand bums do.

"Well?" Roan asked. "Did you speak to Freyja? Did she answer you?"

With a sigh, Stallings answered, "Yes, I spoke with the goddess." Instead of going on right away, he took another long sip from the bottle. And another. After setting the empty bottle down in the exact center of the desk, he gave the goddess's verdict. "I am supposed to give my fortune, my lands and my life to your cause."

"Maybe it won't come down to that," Amanda said. "If the mirror gives us Arching's location on the other side…"

"It won't!" Stallings snapped. "It won't because it can't. I've been playing this game from the beginning. No magic item, no spell, no god can see through to our world." Both Roan and Amanda knew better. Not only could the game see into the real world, it could kill there as well.

Amanda looked evenly at the prince. "There's no reason to get snippy, Mr. Stallings. Now, how many men can you spare? Two or three hundred would be a good start, and with you leading them, I would say…"

"I won't be leading anyone, not yet. The goddess demands that you prove yourself worthy. Only if you survive Mendenome a second time will the goddess favor you. You have one day."

2—

"You need to call Freyja back and explain the situation to her," Roan demanded. "I'm being honest when I say…"

The prince leapt to his feet, his hand on the hilt of his sword. "You need to learn your place, Agent Roan. In this world, you are a nothing. I could squash you like a bug without even blinking. And out there? We're both citizens and I haven't broken a single law. You can't touch me and if you try, I'll sue your ass into the ground. Did I mention my brother is a lawyer on the other side?"

"He has to learn his place?" Amanda yelled, leaning over the desk, her hands in fists planted square on the desk. "Roan is risking his life, his real life to capture the man who framed your friend, so don't cry like a baby about losing in some stupid game!"

The two seethed at each other across three feet of polished wood until Roan asked, "Do you have any more of that wine?"

For some reason, this let the air out of the prince's anger. He plopped back down in his chair and opened a drawer. "It's the good stuff," he said. "A thousand in gold per bottle. I was saving it for…I really don't know why I was saving it." He worked a corkscrew and popped it open and for a long time he only sat there staring at the tip of the bottle. "I'm sorry," he eventually said. "It's just I've built all this and I'd hate to see it all destroyed. Let me get some glasses."

The prince rushed out of the room. Roan picked up the cork and gave it a sniff. "Smells like red wine. I never had a nose for wine. I'm more of an amaretto sour guy."

She let out a short bark of laughter. "Really?"

"No. I was just trying to lighten the mood." They smiled at each other until gradually reality stole the moment. "If we look on the bright side of things, all we have to do is live through tomorrow and we'll have the full support of Prince Stallings, the entire city of Tir-Kahn, and a goddess."

"What if we can't get enough men?" Amanda asked. "Do we gamble away a bunch of lives and make the attempt, regardless?"

Roan didn't hesitate in answering, "Yes. We have to remember that these really aren't lives. For the most part, the people here aren't people and those that are real people are only playing a game."

"Perhaps you should realize that you are playing a game as well," the prince said from the doorway. "I can't help you in any material manner until the goddess allows me, however I can give you advice. In any game, you are given only so many pieces and only so many moves. You have to make them count."

The three shared a drink of the expensive wine, which Roan enjoyed much more than he had expected. As they drank, the prince told Roan everything he knew about fighting orcs. Amanda grew bored after only a few minutes.

"I think I will head up to bed," she told them. "The wine has made me sleepy." Roan was suddenly torn. If there was ever a time to be with Amanda, it was right at that moment. They had a suite of rooms all to themselves, a little wine to put them in the mood, and the perfect guard in Glitch.

But Roan couldn't. He knew next to nothing about orcs and too much depended upon them winning a battle against the beasts. "I-I have to stay. You understand it's because…"

"I understand," she said. "Sometimes we all have to make sacrifices. Do you mind if I take Glitch with me?"

He didn't. Stallings waited until she was gone before he let out a low whistle. "I don't normally go in for elves, but she is hot."

"Yes, she is," Roan replied. She was also brave, intelligent, determined, kind…He blinked suddenly, realizing he was going down the wrong road. "What were you saying about them feigning retreat? Orcs, I mean."

The two men went through a second bottle before Stallings exhausted his knowledge of orcs. They then went into tactics. It was after two in the morning before Roan went to bed. He paused for a few minutes in Amanda's doorway, watching her sleep.

??? Glitch asked, floating over to him.

"Nothing's wrong. I just think I'm in love. It's been a long time." He went to bed and dreamed of a beautiful forest and golden-haired elf.

Roan had hoped to get an early start. He wanted to get through the marshlands as early as possible so that his men would have time to rest for a few hours before they made their assault on Mendenome. It was not to be.

Amanda, with Glitch hovering over her head, woke him just after eight in the morning. She was already dressed in her armor, a new red cloak thrown over her slim shoulders. "Where'd you get that?" he asked of the cloak.

"It was a gift from the prince. No need to frown, you have one as well. He's also letting us 'borrow' some armor and weapons for the men. Come on, get up and get your spells ready."

He slid out of bed, asking, "How many men did Marshall and Jarrod recruit?"

Now it was her turn to frown. "About forty, but we also had some desertions, so altogether we have sixty men, two dwarves, the four of us and whatever elves come along. Luckily, like I said, the prince is letting us outfit the men in scale mail. Each of them will have a shield, spear and sword. We can still win."

As Roan saw it, they were going to be fighting against three to one odds on a cramped battlefield suited to their enemy. Still, she wasn't wrong; they could still win…maybe. "We can," he agreed. "I'll be down in an hour."

Once she left, he opened his spell book, secretly hoping that the same game glitch that had written his spells for him had added more spells. It hadn't. "That's okay," he muttered. Sometimes it felt as though he had too much going on: spells, abilities, hit points, skills… "My skills. I still have points to allocate."

His skill points were actually easy to dole out since he had six areas he'd been concentrating on and six points to spend. He added one to each so that he had nine points in *Listen, Search, Spot, Spell Craft, Knowledge,* and *Decipher Script.* It wasn't exactly clear how he used these skills. They seemed like passive abilities, acting in the background of the game, but nevertheless helping him.

"I like spells better," he said, pushing the idea of skills from his mind and concentrating on the spells that he would need for the day. Since he hadn't used many the day before, he only had a few spells to prepare. When he had breathed in the spells and his hair felt electric and his chest felt like it was about to burst, his full complement was:

Cantrips: *Fire Bolt X3*
Tier One: *Thunderous Wave X3*
Tier Two: *Hypnotic Flame X2*
Tier Three: *Inferno X2*

So far, he had been somewhat underwhelmed by the flame elementals that he had conjured. They had not been as nearly as "monstrous" as he had expected. Besides, *Hypnotic Flame* seemed more suited for battle.

When he was done, he washed up and changed into his black outfit, adding the deep crimson cloak in honor of the prince. Leaving the suite, he went down to the front entrance and was somewhat surprised to find his company at the very top of the hill instead of at the bottom as he expected. The townsmen looked sharp in the armor they'd been given. They looked like real soldiers and it was too bad that he didn't have the time to drill them into a true fighting force. Unfortunately, even with the armor, he could expect high casualties.

A groom brought Jetta to him. The horse was snorting and shaking his head, angrily—the groom had put a bit and bridle on him and Jetta wasn't going to have it. "*Kah-nuiay*," Roan said, calming the horse. He handed the bridle to the surprised groom and then swung easily into the saddle. Seeing Marshall and Jarrod talking with the dwarves behind the formation, he rode over to them.

Marshall looked particularly worried as he came up. "Amanda said we have to make the attempt today," he said, in a low voice. "She didn't say why, only that it had to do with the prince. Tell me, is there any way we can postpone going to Mendenome?"

Roan shook his head, making Jarrod groan. The rogue's face was deathly pale, which made his bloodshot eyes seem all the more red. "I need a sick day," he muttered, his breath smelling like sour beer vomit.

"Ignore him," Marshall said, waving a tired hand at Jarrod. "He was a little too exuberant in trying to get us recruits last night." Marshall's eyes were at squints and Roan could tell that he too was nursing a hangover.

Jarrod moaned, "I'm dying. What do they put in that mead? Yak piss? Ohh, why did I say yak?"

Marshall shook his head, saying, "Look, Roan, even with the armor, I don't know if we have enough men. The orcs are going to change tactics on us. Chances are they'll shut the gates and force us to storm the walls. We'll get murdered out there. To take on that wall, we're going to need mantlets, grappling hooks, ladders, towers, and archers. Amanda said we were supposed to get a few elves? Any idea where they are?"

They all turned to look up at the palace, hoping to see Amanda and the elves appear as if on cue, but all they saw were some curious halflings chatting by the front door and pointing at the company. It was another twenty minutes before Amanda appeared sitting atop her horse, her mithral armor shining in the sun. Behind her were the elves that had pledged themselves to

Roan and behind them were twenty-five others dressed for battle, including the silver-haired Sariah.

"What the hell is she doing here," he said, under his breath

The company grew excited at the addition of so many, however Roan feared that they were just more lambs he was going to lead to the slaughter. "Wait here," he said to the others and nudged Jetta towards the elves.

"Milord," Amanda greeted him with a small bow from her saddle. "The elves of Ash Forest are here to fight for you. This, you may remember, is Kateye, she leads the contingent."

Kateye was tall for an elf, nearly Roan's height. She had a fair complexion, black hair and striking green eyes. She did not bow, she only nodded once, something Roan appreciated. "Command me, milord," she said.

Roan thanked her and the other elves for their service and had them fall into line with the rest of the company…all except Sariah, whom he pulled out of the formation saying, "I don't understand why you're here, Sariah. You have children. They need their mother and I can't guarantee anyone's safety. I think it would be best if you did not come with us."

She looked at him in confusion. "I hope you don't take offense, milord, but I find you and your fellows to be such strange elves."

"I just don't want anything to happen to you."

Sariah laughed, a happy sound that seemed out of place among so many armed and women. "I don't want anything to happen to me, either. But with their father missing, my children look to me for guidance. They need a mother who is not afraid to leave this world as long as she leaves it a better place for them. Perhaps, if you fulfill your quest it will be so."

"I think it will. At least this little corner of the world will be better." He sighed, knowing that he couldn't forbid Sariah from coming, as well, he needed every bit of help. "Be careful out there."

Another laugh escaped her. "No, I will not be careful. I will slay my enemies and send the rest running back to their holes."

Now it was his turn to laugh, however it was forced. She was small and weak. Roan had become an FBI agent to protect people like her, not to have them fight for him. After a quick bow, he rode Jetta back behind the formation to where his team was standing, talking logistics. Interrupting them, he said, "Even with the elves, I'm afraid it's not going to be enough."

"It just might," Marshall replied. "We now have our archers, and you have your spells and Amanda has her healing. If we can get past the wall, we stand a good chance. I just don't know how we're going to. And no, we aren't digging under," he said to Krull, who had just opened his mouth.

"Amanda, do you want to ask the prince for a few ladders?" Roan suggested. "We both know he's got the hots for you."

Her eyebrows shot up. "He does? That's very interesting. Say, how does Princess Amanda of Water Fell sound? I think I like it…"

Roan glared. "Just go ask."

The prince was more than accommodating. He sent servants into the storage rooms that were dug deep into the hill; they didn't exactly rush to the task and more precious time was lost. Eventually, three sectional ladders were hauled up and stacked on one of the baggage carts.

It was after eleven when the company marched through the gates and out onto the road that wound through the marsh. Roan feared the loss of time as much as he did the lack of manpower. According to Prince Stallings, orcs hated the sun; it made them weak and dizzy. Conversely, they grew stronger in the dark, which meant that if they were to have any chance they had to get to Mendenome while the sun was still in the sky.

"Push the men as hard as you can," he ordered the dwarves. "Get us there by four." Krull grunted in answer and then began bellowing orders.

Glitch led the way, flying high overhead. It was a fine day and the elemental could see for miles. He spotted troglodytes and trolls and all sorts of odd creatures, however because of their numbers, nothing challenged them.

For most of the trip, Roan rode in the front of the formation with Marshall and Amanda—Jarrod was too hungover to stay on his horse and for the better part of the day could be found in one of the baggage carts with his cloak thrown over his face.

Roan forced the pace until men began to fall out of formation. Very few of them were accustomed to wearing metal armor and with their shield and weapons, they were lugging around over fifty pounds. The muggy marsh air and the countless mosquitos and biting flies only added to their misery.

He was forced to slow the march to what felt like a crawl. Long hours went by and it was late in the afternoon before he saw the first of the hills leading up out of the marsh. "Come on!

Step it up!" he yelled to the company, hoping to spur them on. Dropping back to the baggage carts, he kicked the one with Jarrod lying in it.

"Are we there yet?" Jarrod asked, in a raspy voice.

"It'll be another hour, so it's time to get your butt up." When Jarrod only moaned again, Roan said, "If you're not on your horse in five minutes, I'm going to throw you into the marsh. I wouldn't test me if I were you."

The rogue was up in three minutes.

Exactly an hour later, the company drew up before the walls of Mendenome. The men, sweating, tired and scared, looked more like townspeople in costume than real soldiers and their lines were more wiggly than straight.

It was after five and the sun was creeping down behind the far hills. They were almost out of daylight. As Marshall had foreseen, the gates were shut. There was an air of watchfulness about the citadel and yet, the battlements were empty. Nothing stirred upon the wall at least as far as could be seen from below.

Roan had a better vantage and said, "They're waiting for us."

Chapter 24

"We should attack, now," Marshall suggested. "If we hit them before they're ready we have a good chance of making it inside."

"No. They've been ready for some time," Roan answered. "They probably caught sight of us thirty minutes ago. I can see them." In direct contradiction to his words, he had his eyes closed. Still, he had a perfect bird's eye view.

Glitch was in the air above the citadel and through the elemental's eyes, Roan could see the orcs massing in the courtyard and slinking with bent backs along the walls. "If I had to guess, they're going to let us attack the walls and then sweep out of the gate with their main force as soon as we gain a foothold on the walls."

"Then what do we do?" Jarrod asked. "We don't have a ram to force the gates open."

Krull raised his broad, callused hand. "If we'd brought shovels, this wouldn't be a problem. The earth here is perfect for digging and with the right…"

Amanda interrupted. "We don't have shovels or a ram or invisibility cloaks for everyone. Let's not talk about what we don't have, let's talk about what we do have. We have ladders and a fair idea of what their tactics will be. The question is, how do we counter them?"

The answer was fairly obvious to Roan. "We feign the attack on the walls, using just enough men to get up there, while the rest prepare for the real struggle down here. Since we'll need every bowman down here, I would like Krull and Ironhead to lead the attack on the walls."

"Oh, oh okay," was Krull's half-hearted reply. Ironhead didn't look all that happy either, but he forced a smile onto his lips, his thick, red-orange mustache lifting slightly. Roan didn't blame them for being reluctant. They'd be practically defenseless as they went up the ladder and once at the top, they'd have to fight from a rickety perch thirty feet in the air.

"Don't worry," he told them. "We'll have archer support until the main host leaves the gate and if things get too sticky, I'll use a spell or two."

Krull mumbled, "Oh, great a spell. I feel so lucky."

"Maybe I should lead the attack if they're too chicken," Amanda said. She turned on the spot and started towards the baggage carts. "Let's get those ladders down. Come on, we're burning daylight."

This shamed the dwarves into rushing to the cart before she could get there. Ironhead pulled down one of the ladders and held it like a shield. "Stop right there, missy. We'll take care of it." Once they were moving, the two dwarves had the ladders set up in minutes. While they were at this chore, Marshall picked out two teams of ten men each who were going to follow the dwarves up.

Roan took the rest of the company and told them what part they were to play. Their reactions were not heartening. While the elves were quiet, their faces pinched, the townsmen wore their fear openly. Whispers of doubt broke out among them.

"Quiet down!" Roan snapped. "Anyone who wants to leave can do so. Drop your armor and weapons and get out of here. *Maybe* you'll make it through a night in the swamp." He paused, knowing that no one would take him up on the offer. When no one did, he said, "Alright. Let's get this straight, we have the advantage here. We just have to stand our ground and fight hard. In ten minutes we can break their backs but that's only if you stay strong! Can you do that?" The answer was a weak bobbing of heads and a few muttered, "Yeahs."

"Let's try that again!" Roan cried, channeling his high school football coach. "Are we going to stand and fight?" The answering cries of "Yes!" echoed over the hills.

"I saw one of them!" a soldier hissed, pointing up at the wall.

Roan clapped him on the shoulder. "Yes, they're up there cowering. They are the ones who are afraid. They are the one who'll be running in a few minutes. Now, let's form up. Kateye, take half the elves and hold the left flank. Sariah take the other half on the right. The soldiers will form two lines in between."

As Marshall pushed and shoved the men and elves into position, Roan took Kateye aside and told her, "I'll give you a heads up when the orcs start to make their move. I want you to get your people in front of the far baggage cart as fast as you can. Everyone will form on you, so it's imperative that you get there quickly. Also, you will be the last man...I mean elf on the line. It'll be your job to anchor that end, let no orc get past you or we'll be doomed."

"You favor me with a place of honor on the field of battle," Kateye said, bowing. "I will not let you down."

"Why couldn't they all be elves," Roan said under his breath as he turned to see the progress Marshall was making. Again, the lack of training and coordination was telling as the men bickered and cursed at each other. "Save it for the damn orcs!" Roan seethed.

When the men were finally in position, Roan gave the order to move towards the wall. Almost at once the line dissolved. In Roan's mind, it had seemed a simple thing for ninety-eight people to walk in a straight line toward a linear wall. He hadn't counted on the fact that under threat, some men faced their fear by hurrying at it, while others cowered. And he hadn't expected the elves under Sariah to stop and let loose a flight of arrows at two orcs who had popped up momentarily.

Worse still, the two ladder teams unexpectedly raced forward with a great shout. To add to the chaos, Marshall and Jarrod began riding back and forth smacking the slower soldiers forward with the flats of their swords, while Amanda darted Rhiadol through the broken line to support the ladder teams as the orcs started throwing rocks from the battlements.

It had taken all of thirty seconds for Roan to lose control of his small company. Thankfully, the orcs massing behind the gates hadn't moved. This gave Marshall time to get his men up to the wall, where they locked shields and held them up at a deflecting angle.

Seconds later, two of the three ladders were lifted to the walls. Krull and Ironhead went scampering up.

The orcs tried to push the ladders away, but any that showed themselves became a veritable pincushion as arrows zinged upwards. More rocks were heaved over the top of the wall. One hit Krull and sent him falling into his team. They went down like bowling pins.

Seeing this, Ironhead stopped halfway up the ladder with two men below him. It was a poor choice and could have resulted in his death if Roan hadn't acted.

"*Ita ithray-wa-el*," he said, breathing out the *Hypnotic Flame* spell. He pointed a finger and from it shot a green flame that rolled through the air to a point above the wall where it roiled and spun in a mesmerizing manner. An orc holding a rock was stopped in mid-throw by the spell. The orc stood with its oversized mouth gaping open—a perfect target for Sariah and a second later it fell back with an arrow sticking out the back of its neck.

Ironhead saw the spell and took the opportunity to hurry to the top of the wall. He was so short that all Roan could see of him was the head of his hammer going up and down as he slew the hypnotized orcs one after another. Ironhead could have killed orcs until sunset if the spell had lasted that long.

Roan strained to hold the spell together; it was like trying to hold steam in a clenched fist. He knew that the longer he kept his concentration from slipping, the longer Ironhead's team had to get to the top of the ladder and help out. Twelve seconds was all he could handle before he collapsed.

It had been just enough for most of the ten-man team to get to the top where the battle began to heat up.

Hearing the cries and the clash of metal, Krull's team followed up after them, all except the dwarf who'd had both his helmet and his head dented by the thrown rock. He lay in a pool of blood as big as himself with Amanda kneeling over him, blue light emanating from her outstretched hands.

She looked to be trying to heal a dead dwarf. But he must have been only slightly dead, because, as Roan watched, he sat up and tried to put his helmet back on his head. The dent was too great and it was no longer wearable. Amanda tried to help him up, only her elf form, slim and willowy wasn't up for the task. He almost pulled her down.

He was able to get up, just as a body landed practically at his feet. It was one of the townsmen; he was headless. Krull bellowed a curse and ran for the ladder.

From below, the battle on the wall was hard to follow. The men and dwarves seemed pinned to a small section of the wall, fighting against ten-to-one odds that came from two directions. If the top of the wall hadn't been so narrow they would have been overwhelmed and sent plummeting to their deaths.

The elvish archers helped even the odds. They raked the wall with arrows, killing any orc that stood upright. The orcs were forced to fight hunched over, moving with awkward crab-like steps.

The fight became a stalemate, which was exactly what Roan wanted. He could have used more spells or sent more men up, but that would have meant fewer men on the ground for when the orcs began the second part of their plan, which he knew was only seconds from occurring.

Sure enough, Glitch screamed in his head *!!!* making him jump. He closed his eyes so he could see what had Glitch so frightened. The orcs were opening the gate. "They're coming!" Roan yelled. "Kateye! Get to your position. Marshall shift the men, and hurry." The next few seconds were mayhem as man and elf abandoned the attack on the wall and tried to shift their lines.

Again, a lack of training was obvious. Still, they weren't moving a great distance and in short order they had reformed and were now perpendicular to the wall. During this, Roan saw that Krull, Ironhead, and two men were in trouble. Acting according to the plan, the ladder teams had rushed down from the wall, however the last ones up there couldn't just turn their backs on the orcs to climb down a ladder. They'd be killed in a second.

Roan lifted a hand and breathed out one of the spells trapped within him. "*Ita ithray-wa-el*," he said, using his second *Hypnotic Flame* spell. The green fire once again spun and danced over the wall, stopping the orcs, some in mid-swing.

It was a moment before Krull knew what was happening and he killed two of the stupefied orcs before Ironhead grabbed the back of his armored collar and screamed: "Stop! We have to go!" The two ran for the ladders and were three rungs down when Roan's concentration slipped.

Glitch was blasting out warnings *!!!*

The main orc army was coming, pouring through the gate in the wall, their red, pig-eyes squinting against the late afternoon light.

2—

"That's a crap-load of orcs," Jarrod said, in a carrying whisper. He kept swallowing loudly, as if he were about to puke.

He wasn't wrong. The number of orcs seemed to have doubled or maybe even tripled in the last two days, and the mob bearing down on them appeared like a grey unstoppable wave.

Roan knew better. Even without Prince Stallings' advice on orc warfare, he saw that a properly trained force could have easily handled the mob. Although he didn't have a trained force, he did have certain advantages. First, the elf archers had already proved steadfast and deadly, second, the armor that his men wore was far better than the stinking hides that covered the orcs, and third, he had his magic.

He started with the archers. "Bows at the ready!" he cried, nocking an arrow in his own bow and sighting at the onrushing orcs. "Fire!" Including his team of four, there were thirty-six archers and in the space of half a minute, they collectively fired nearly two hundred arrows.

So many orcs were hit that their charge faltered and when the screaming horde finally struck the bunched townsmen, the line held. It bent, sagging dangerously in the middle, but it held.

Throwing down his bow, Marshall rushed to the center where he stood like a rock in the very middle of the line, swinging his glowing sword. He seemed untouchable, while his sword appeared unstoppable. Roan knew that his attack bonuses must have been prodigious. Even without feats or abilities, Marshall had plus five due to his level, another plus three for his strength and another three for the magic sword.

The orcs in their filthy animal hides fell one after another against him. But he was only one man. The dwarves were bloody, bruised and exhausted from their fight on the wall and their warhammers weren't nearly as effective as they had been. Jarrod did what he could, but he was a rogue and didn't belong in a melee as fierce as this one, and Amanda was kept too busy to fight. She went through her spells healing the townsmen who were being stabbed, slashed, and run through.

At first, the archers kept the battle from getting out of hand. With the middle of the line bowed in, the archers were thrust outward like the horns of a bull. This allowed them to fire at a deadly angle, taking the orcs from the sides. A hundred fell before the onslaught.

The orcs could only take so much before they changed tactics and attacked the wings of Roan's line. The elves were forced to fight with sword and shield, which was where they were weakest. On the right, Sariah had the wall to keep from being overlapped, but on the left, Kateye had only empty fields and she was forced to extend the line until it was stretched too thin to withstand the orcs. In minutes, the far end of the line was thrown back.

Roan spurred Jetta to that end of the fight and had to use one of his *Inferno* spells to keep the elves from being overrun.

The ball of fire that shot from his hand erupted with a blinding flash (*XP +1,250*). Flames and smoke and bloodcurdling screams were added to the terrific din of battle. The side of the hill raged with fire and within the flames were the bodies of over fifty orcs.

There was a strange pause in the battle at that moment almost as if both sides were marking the change in momentum.

Then into the silence, Marshall let out a thunderous battle cry and charged the stunned orcs. After a moment's hesitation, Jarrod charged after him, then came Krull and Ironhead, and then the townsmen.

It wasn't an unstoppable charge and yet it stole the initiative from the orcs, who were very weak defensively. Still, there were enough of them that the charge's impetus slowed and then was gradually thrust back. Roan sped Jetta straight into the middle of things, leapt off his back and pushed his way through to the front, where he found himself face to face with an orc chieftain. It was a nasty brute with arms like those of a gorilla.

It held a bloody scimitar in one hand and a severed head in the other. Raising both, it screamed a challenge at Roan.

Roan yelled back: "Eda-eram gdiy!" From his outstretched hand, the *Thunderous Wave* spell blasted out, striking the orc like a physical wall of sound, killing him along with six others. Behind them, a dozen others reeled from the explosion(*XP +380*). Into this hole in the enemy line the townsmen raced, their spears leveled in a deadly hedge of shining metal. The stunned orcs were butchered without mercy and the rest began to back away, afraid of Roan and the spears.

Once they took those first steps back, their doom was sealed. The elves took up their bows and poured arrows into them as the townsmen reformed into a solid line and advanced, their spears pointed into the orcs. Marshall let the elves do maximum damage and then, just when the orcs couldn't take anymore punishment, he led a charge of the townsmen.

This was too much for the orcs. Although they still possessed a two-to-one numerical advantage, they turned and ran with the townsmen hacking down any they could catch up to. Quickly, the battle and the pursuit got out of control.

Roan called Jetta to him, leapt into the saddle and raced to cut his men off before they ran into the obvious ambush. The orcs had run for the gate and with Glitch still in watch position, he saw that the orcs who had been on the walls were now gathering to counterattack in the courtyard.

"Stop!" he cried, cutting off Marshall and the lead elements. "Reform! Reform!"

To Roan's amazement, Marshall started to argue with him, "No! We have them on the run."

With a thought, Roan sent Jetta barreling into the paladin, knocking him to the ground. "Since when do you tell me, no?" Roan seethed, his eyes blazing. "They have a hundred orcs getting ready to ambush anyone stupid enough to go through that gate. Now reform the men or clock out."

For a brief moment, Marshall's anger continued to build. Jarrod put a hand on his arm and this seemed to wake him up. "I'm sorry," Marshall said. "I'll get the men together." He turned and stumbled. Looking back, he whispered, "Look at what we've done. It's horrible."

Roan turned as well and felt a strange queasiness come over him. Carpeting the side of the hill were hundreds and hundreds of corpses; some still burning.

"And where is everyone?" Jarrod asked. It was only then that Roan saw that his company was down to fifty-two people.

A sudden fear struck Roan. He saw Amanda but… "Where is Sariah?" At a word, Jetta raced back to the scene of the battle to where the orcs were heaped against the wall. "No, no, no…" he whispered to himself as he pulled aside the corpses until he came to the bottom. "No."

Under the mound of orcs he found the silver-haired elf, a broken sword still in her hand. She was bloody and unmoving. "Amanda! Amanda, I need you, now!" The cleric came rushing up.

She took one look at Sariah and a hand went to her mouth. Slowly, she knelt and touched the elf's chest. "I'm sorry, Roan. She's dead. There's nothing I can do."

Chapter 25

—Mendenome, Daggerland

Roan stared down at the body of Sariah, feeling an ache in his chest and tears forming in his eyes. Just before they fell, the words: *Congratulations! You have won the Battle of Mendenome! XP +2,000.*

"It's just a game," he whispered, trying to convince himself, but still unable to turn away from Sariah's broken body. More words came into his vision (XP -10). "I don't care!" he yelled, pulling his sword and uselessly swiping at the words.

"Are you okay, Roan?" Amanda asked.

He shook his head; he wasn't okay. "She shouldn't have come with us. But what does it matter? Right? Why should I care?"

Amanda took off the cloak she had received from Prince Stallings and draped it over Sariah's body. "It matters because you're a good person and a good person celebrates life and mourns death. Even the death of these orcs." She looked around her sapphire-blue eyes dimmed by the blood and the wretched bodies.

"We're not done with death for today," Roan said. Rage burned inside of him and yet he couldn't allow it to consume him, not just yet. "We still have to get to the top before midnight."

He expected that he would have trouble getting the survivors of the battle motivated to attack the citadel itself, but in this he was wrong. They had fought and had fought hard—now, they wanted to get paid. In record time, the bodies of the fallen were stripped. The Prince's borrowed armor and weapons were set on the baggage carts, the coins from the orcs placed in a single burlap sack to be divided when all was said and done.

Roan had no need for the spare change of the orcs. While the others were busy, he sent Glitch into the citadel to scout. The orcs had retreated inside, leaving the front doors wide open. It was an invitation to a trap. In the center of the citadel, where the stairs led up into the atrium, the building was seemingly empty. Once there, the company would be vulnerable to attack from every side.

Taking up a stick, Roan knelt and drew a map in the dirt, detailing the inside of the citadel. "There are orcs in each of these rooms, ringing the atrium," he told the little group around him. It was comprised of his team, the two dwarves, and the elf, Kateye. "They have some of the doors blocked so as to funnel us into the center, but that doesn't mean we can't force one of the doors open. If we can, then we can take the rooms one at a time, we'll be able to control the fight."

Kateye looked unconvinced. "According to your own drawing, milord, many of these rooms have multiple doors, some of which lead to the atrium. The orcs will be able to move around at will. They'll be able to come in behind us, cutting us off. There'll be nowhere to retreat."

"Why on earth would we want to retreat?" Roan demanded. "Our objective is at the top of the tower. That's what we have to focus on. Besides, retreat will only lead to death."

"And if we can't force those doors?" Amanda asked.

Roan pointed to where the ladders rested on the ground. "The four of us will break in through an upper window while Krull and the company makes a show of attacking in the front of the building. If it comes to that, hopefully, we'll be able to slip in without being noticed. If we get caught...well, we'll do our best to get to the mirror and then hold off the orcs as long as possible until we get our information."

He didn't need to follow up with an *after that* statement. They'd be dead after that. Other than a few minor cantrips, Roan had three spells left, while Amanda didn't have any. It would be four against two hundred.

Roan ended the meeting and looked over the remains of his company. Of the thirty-two elves he had started with, he was down to twelve. With their light armor, they had suffered terribly in the hand to hand combat with the orcs, though the orcs probably saw it the other way around. The elves had not gone down quietly with even little Sariah taking down half a dozen before being overwhelmed.

It was little solace to Roan, whose heart burned with a vengeance as he strode through the front doors of Mendenome, sword in hand. "I am king here!" he bellowed at the top of his lungs, the words echoing as though the citadel was deserted. "Who would challenge me?" This wasn't just his fiery passion speaking, it was a coolly thought out plan.

If he could kill whatever orc chieftain remained in single combat, it would demoralize the rest. Perhaps to the point that they would cower instead of fight. He waited, listening. When there wasn't an answer, he called out, "Cowards!"

"Okay, that's enough," Jarrod whispered, nervously. With the sun setting, the citadel was filled with shadows, giving the place a haunted look. Jarrod wasn't the only one who had lost the fire of victory so quickly. Many of the townsmen were staring around nervously. "Let's just get this done and get out of here."

"Fine," Roan said and strode off to the right, stepping over the rotting corpses of the adventurers and bandits who had died there in previous attempts on the citadel. They were in the official greeting room where visitors had once waited to see whether they'd be allowed entrance to the citadel. The main doors led to the atrium, while the locked doors on the right led to a service corridor.

According to Glitch, fifteen Orcs crouched behind a mound of furniture they had stacked in front of the locked door. "Krull, Ironhead." Roan said, and gestured to the door. The two dwarves lifted their warhammers and began to beat on the stout doors.

In no time, they were reduced to kindling. The two then began hauling the furniture back into the greeting room, where others pushed it in front of the doors that led to the atrium. As all this was going on, Roan's team was shooting arrows through the mess at the orcs who had foolishly expected the humans to try to push through the mass, instead of pulling it back.

Four of the fifteen orcs were killed before the rest decided to run. Glitch followed them through the first door they came to, where more orcs waited. There had to be thirty of them in the room and it wasn't a very large room; it was a perfect time for Roan to release one of his two remaining *Thunderous Wave* spells.

"I want ten men to hold that door," he said, pointing to the door leading to the atrium. "The rest of you follow me." He led his team into the corridor to the first door. It was unlocked. The orcs attacked the second he opened it but they weren't quick enough. "Eda-eram gdiy!" Roan cried.

In the packed room, the spell went off like a bomb. Orcs went flying, their eardrums blasted out, their eyes bleeding. A number had their hearts stopped by the concussive force, (*XP +220*)

Roan and his team, followed by Kateye and the dwarves, rushed into the room and made short work of the remaining orcs, killing them without mercy.

Congratulations! You are now a Level Seven Wizard and have gained the following bonuses:
Increased Hit Points(+7)
You can fill +1 tier one spells per day
You can fill +1 tier four spells per day
You have +6 skill points to allocate

The words passed before Roan's vision—he all but ignored them, grunting only, "Good," before moving to the door across the room. "What's happening out there, Glitch?" His familiar had rushed to him just before he had set off his spell, just in case it had been needed for the fight afterwards. Now, it shot under the door and out into the atrium where orcs were running back and forth in confusion.

They were afraid. "Good," Roan said, again and pushed open the door to the atrium. The orcs scurried like cockroaches, rushing through doorways or attempting to hide behind columns or broken furniture. "Come on out and fight!" Roan bellowed. "Cowards! You're no better than goblins."

This time he got a response. From behind the stairs leading to the upper floor came a roar and a huge orc came rushing out, a two-head battleaxe in his hands. Behind him raced dozens more.

"Uh, Roan?" Amanda asked. "You aren't going to fight that guy, are you?"

He considered the orc, seeing the way he held the axe, the strength in his arms, and the fact that he wore more than just hides. The orc wore a mixture of plate and chainmail. It was dented and punctured, suggesting that he had taken the pieces from his victims. Roan felt he could have beaten the orc in a one on one battle, but it would have cost him the last of his spells.

"I don't think so," Roan answered, causally backing through the door and shutting it behind him. Seconds later the door burst open again and there, perfectly framed was the huge orc. Eight arrows were launched at him, two bounced off his armor and six thudded home. This still did not kill him.

He staggered one step back and then one forward, as if he didn't know which way to turn. This hesitation gave the archers in the room another shot. This time he did go down. The moment he did, the room flooded with orcs.

"Fall back!" Roan ordered. Glitch was feeding him a view of more orcs racing through the atrium, heading towards the service corridor, looking to attack them from two sides. And Roan was sure that more would test the small force he had left at the front doors as well.

Disengaging from an enemy in the middle of a fight wasn't easy, especially when they were pressed so closely. The elven archers slipped out first, then the dwarves and Amanda until it was just Marshall and Jarrod fighting beautifully as a team. The two had opposite styles; one bullish and brawny, using heavy strokes, the other quick and agile, slipping out to slay with deadly precision. They complimented each other wonderfully, and it was hard for Roan to believe these were the same two nerds who bickered daily on where to have lunch back in the real world.

"Orcs in the hall!" Amanda cried as thirty or forty of them suddenly burst from a room three doors down. She, Roan and the other elves launched a volley into them (*XP +20*). A handful went down and were trampled by the rest.

"Spearmen!" Roan called. "Front and center." In no time, a hedge of twenty spears faced the orcs as the elves slipped to the back. At the same time Jarrod came stumbling from the room with Marshall hot on his heels.

Jarrod was laughing, his buggy eyes practically popping out of his head. "Did you see that? We must have killed like fif... whoa." He jumped when he saw the orcs coming at him from down the hall. "Make way! Make way!" he cried, slipping through the townsmen to get to the back.

Marshall stayed in the very front and just the sight of his magic sword caused the orcs to hesitate. They had all seen that sword in action and none wanted to face it. The orcs in front dug in their heels but were forced forward by the pressure from behind as more orcs filled the hallway. They were pushed right onto the spears of the waiting townsmen.

Then the two sides came together in a real clash which had little to do with actual skill at arms. The hallway was so crammed with men and orcs that there was no room to swing swords or scimitars. Only the spears were of any use. The townsmen of the second row racked up dozens of kills by stabbing over and around the locked shields of the men and orcs in front.

Soon, the orcs in front were once again fighting their own side to get away and the killing picked up in tempo until, like a damn bursting, the resistance collapsed altogether and seventy orcs took to their heels with Marshall and the first few ranks of spearmen racing after, striking down those at the back. Again, Roan had to rein in his company before they rushed into another trap.

As soon as the orcs were out of sight, they had stopped running and had hidden themselves, ready to attack the foolish or unwary.

Before the company pressed on, bodies were counted. Eighty-two orcs had died since they had entered the citadel against only three of the townsmen. "They're almost done in," Roan told the company. "One more push and I think we'll break their backs. We're going to make a try for the stairs. Once on them, I want you elves one flight up and working your bows. Spearmen, your job will be to fix the orcs in place. Do not advance. Do not retreat. Stand your ground and in the next ten minutes, we will have won the day!"

The company cheered. Over the course of the last couple of hours, they had come to believe in him and themselves.

Roan had Marshall form them into a column, four abreast with the elves in front before he quick marched them through an empty room that fed into the atrium. "Double time," Roan ordered in a carrying whisper. He led them straight for the stairs and, as the orcs watched from the shadows, he directed them into position: The twelve elves stood above the thirty-four townsmen who huddled in two rows with their spears leveled.

Glitch swept all around the atrium, picking out the orcs. Even after all the fighting, the orcs had a more than two-to-one advantage. They had realized it as well and began to gather out of bowshot.

"What's happening?" one of the townsmen asked. "I hear them. Are they coming?"

It was only then that Roan realized that it was now full dark and that the spearmen were squinting to see anything beyond a few feet in front of their faces. Not far away was a pile of books that had once been set in a large bookcase which was toppled over and partially destroyed. Roan aimed a *Fire Bolt* at the pile and set it alight.

"It's good to have a wizard on our side," another of the spearmen said, giving Roan a smile. "Do you know a wizard named, Jer..."

"They're coming," Ironhead said. As before he was on one side of the line with Krull on the other. Marshall and Amanda were in the middle. Roan had to look around to find Jarrod—he was with the elves, a bow in his hand.

"Hold your fire," he said to the elves. "Wait until they commit." It was a wait of seconds only before the orcs came on one last time. Arrows zipped into them, including Roan's own(*XP +20*). He was down to only a *Thunderous Wave* and an *Inferno* spell. Uncertain of what was to come, he wanted to get through this final battle without using them.

The orcs also seemed to feel as though this was their last shot at driving away the company. With a great roar, they hurled themselves onto the spears, trying to break the line in one mass assault. Although half a dozen men were killed in the first shock of the attack, the men of the second line moved up to take their places, stabbing and stabbing with their spears, while above them wave after wave of arrows struck home.

In one short minute, Roan fired eleven arrows and killed six of the beasts(*XP +120*). He was just drawing back his twelfth when he saw the orc line begin to falter. "Now! Attack!" he cried, firing the arrow and ripping out his sword.

With a shout, his company dashed forward as the orcs broke and ran. This time he did not stop the men in their pursuit, he joined them. With Glitch's help, he went from one hiding spot to another until the last orc had died on the point of his sword (*XP +240*).

His company began cheering the victory and Roan let it go on for a few minutes before he turned to Krull. "Strip the bodies," he ordered. "Then I want the gates shut and locked. After that, post guards on the walls and one at the entrance. I want this place buttoned up by the time we get back. We shouldn't be long."

They were nearly done. They were about to discover the secret that Arching was hiding and Roan was sure it would lead to his arrest and hopefully his imprisonment. With a quick glance at his team, Roan asked, "Are you guys ready?" They were bloody and bruised, worn down from the traveling and the stress and the long fight, and yet no one said a word, they only nodded. The four marched up the stairs with Glitch leading the way, checking corners and poking into rooms.

There was nothing alive for ten stories. The eleventh was a different story, however, Glitch could not see the person in the mirror. To the elemental, the image of Atticus Arching was just colors on glass.

Chapter 26

Roan saw the figure in the mirror the moment he came up the stairs, but was distracted as an alert flashed in the bottom of his vision: *Quest Completed! You have reached the Mirror of Elesar! +2,200 XP*. The experience point total seemed oddly high, though Roan wasn't going to look a gift horse in the mouth, at least not just then. There was something unnerving about the image of the cowled man. There was a hint of gold coming from the cowl which otherwise hid the man's features.

Amanda stared at the image, lines furrowed into her fore-head. "Who is that, Roan? Did you already ask it a…" She fell back in surprise as the man stepped from the mirror.

He was tall, almost nine feet in height and, looking up as they were, they should have been able to see into the man's cowl but all Roan saw was what seemed like a gleam of what he thought was glass.

"You've been searching for me," he said, in a voice that was deep but melodious.

"Arching?" Roan asked, his hand slipping to the hilt of his sword.

The man chuckled as if the name was humorous. "I was Atticus Arching. I was also Gorgothe but that was the name of a character. I am neither. I am The Infinite One. And you are Daniel Roan. I've been watching you."

"No offense, but I'm not into men," Roan said. "Especially the stalker types." Arching threw back his head and laughed, the sound ringing off the walls. Roan waited patiently until he was done before saying, "Let's talk about Greg Nelson."

"Let's see. You would like to know if I killed Gregory the Great, even though you saw him light himself on fire? Sorry, detective, but the time for that reveal is not yet upon us. No, I'm here for a different reason. I'm here to help you. In fact, I'm here to save you. You and all your little friends are getting too deep into something that does not concern your government. If you're not careful, you will drown."

Roan smirked at this. "Threatening an FBI agent in front of three witnesses? That's not very smart. I'm not sure if you're aware of this, but there are laws against that sort of thing."

"Those laws and your authority are not applicable here. In Daggerland, I am the utmost authority. Here you are a gnat that I can stub under my thumb at any time. Observe."

The one word was all the warning they received. In a blur, Arching shot forward and with a flash of something gold, he struck Marshall in the center of his mailed chest. The paladin went flying, a hole in his armor, his chest half-caved in. He landed in a jumble of now useless metal.

Still moving with that unnatural speed that left the eyes slow to catch up, Arching produced a silver dagger and plunged it into Jarrod's back. The thief flung out his arms as his knees buckled—Arching was already moving, the dagger slashing at Amanda. Roan tried to use his last *Thunderous Wave* spell even though he knew it would strike Amanda as well as Arching, however the spell fizzled as it left his hand. Instead of an explosion of sound, there was only a soft sigh which was followed by a scream as Arching stuck the dagger into Amanda's belly.

She fell, staring with horror at the weapon sticking out of her.

"Care to use that last *Inferno* spell of yours?" Arching asked. "I'll let you. Your friends can die by your hand instead of mine. Or you can…" Roan pulled his sword, causing Arching to laugh again. "I really do like you, Mr. Roan. You play this game like it was meant to be played! Any one playing on *Extreme* mode is my kind of player! It's why I'm giving you this last chance. Give up on your investigation and convince your superiors to do the same…or else."

Roan couldn't do that. Arching was evil in both worlds and he had to be fought in both worlds.

With a thought from Roan, brave Glitch raced in with its *Haze* attack, looking to partially blind Arching so that Roan could run him through and save his friends.

Instead, with a snap of his fingers, Arching captured Glitch in what looked like a floating glass box. "This is your familiar? That's not possible. Did Christine Carson help you?"

The question was more than an ordinary question; there was magic behind it and Roan found himself, against his will, telling him about the *Summon Familiar* casting with the warlock Amiriah.

"That is both interesting and strangely pathetic," Arching said, as he studied Glitch.

"How is that pathetic?" Roan asked. "I had never cast a spell before. Not all of us wasted our childhoods playing these…"

Arching stepped toward Roan, the air bristling with his anger. With a word, lightning blasted out of his fingertips. Roan tried in vain to dodge but was struck full force. The power of the spell sent him flying and, had the wind not been knocked out of him, he would have screamed like a child. The pain was almost beyond his ability to withstand and when it finally let up, he lay quivering in a pool of his own sweat. (*Damage -51*)

His health bar held a single tiny, red blip in the corner. Arching had left him alive, but just barely.

"This is your last chance," Arching said to the four of them. "Walk away right now."

Roan struggled to his feet. His sword had gone flying and now he only had his fists to fight with. Mindful that his hands were shaking, he balled them up. "No. It'll never happen, so stop asking."

Arching's shoulders drooped and he sighed. "Fine. I can only hope your superiors have more sense." Roan expected to be killed, however, Arching simply walked to the mirror and stepped through it into a dark cave-like room that was backlit with red-orange flames. Somehow, Arching reached back through the mirror, grabbed the sides and pulled it into itself. There was a small pop and then it was gone.

"Well, that sucked," Jarrod said, and then began coughing blood onto the floor. "Who's got a healing potion? I'm down to one hit point."

"Me too," Marshall said, forcing himself to stand. Pieces of his armor fell, clattering on the floor.

Amanda still had the dagger sticking from her belly. With a grimace and a soft, wavering cry, she slid it out. "I-I have a p-potion in my pack."

Roan gazed around, looking for the pack among all the trash, but didn't see it. *She must have left it down stairs,* he thought. He didn't know if he had the energy or the will to go all the way downstairs and then back up again; he didn't think so. He barely had the strength to analyze what exactly had happened.

"Arching could have killed us easily," he said, running a hand through his dark hair, finding out that even his scalp hurt. "Why didn't he kill us? It doesn't make much sense. We must be getting close for him to go to all the trouble of torturing us like that, and yet, he doesn't kill us."

"He must want us alive," Amanda reasoned. "Though why, I don't know. If you...Marshall? Are you okay?" Marshall was standing, staring straight ahead, his eyes fixed on nothing, his mouth open. Amanda had just reached out to him when he fell face first onto the floor.

Jarrod and Roan rushed to him and turned his lifeless body over. "Marshall!" Jarrod cried, shaking his friend. "Marshall! Hey Marshall! What the hell?"

Amanda pushed them away. "Let me see him." She studied his wounds and looked into his glassy eyes. "Oh no," she whispered.

"What is it?" Jarrod asked. He looked sick with fright and grief—but only for a moment and then he too took on that empty look, just as Marshall had.

Before Jarrod even fell, lifeless to the floor, Roan screamed, "Clock out!" He brought up the exit screen in his mind and in a blink, he was in his own body again. Four feet away, holding a bloody knife, was Joanna Niederer. She had the knife poised over Amanda's throat.

2—

For all his size, Roan was blazing fast. His hand shot beneath the mattress of his cot and he had his service piece out before Joanna could bring the knife halfway down.

"Stop!" he yelled, sighting on Joanna's eye. "I will put a bullet in you if you even twitch."

"Do you think I care? A bullet can't kill me."

Only then did Roan realize that this wasn't Joanna at all. It was her body but someone else was inside working the controls. "Arching?" Roan asked. The woman laughed coldly and shook her head. "Cole," Roan growled, now seeing the evil behind the pleasant mask. "Don't think I can't kill you, because let me assure you, I can and I will. I know where your body is."

Cole shook Joanna's head. "No, you used to know. I've been moved. It turns out that while you were dicking around in Daggerland, your buddies here failed to charge me with anything. My lawyer got my body sprung, and now you don't have anything. In fact, you have less than when you started. Look at what your meddling cost you."

Behind Joanna were the bodies of Marshall Mutch and Jarrod Maddox. It looked as though each had been stabbed at least half a dozen times. The sight of them sent a wave of goosebumps flashing across Roan's flesh. They were truly dead. There was no coming back, no switching characters, no do-overs for them. They were forever dead.

And Amanda was next; she was lying there, frozen in terror, her eyes locked open, her hands pinned beneath Joanna. She'd been too slow in clocking back into her body and now the knife was poised above her.

Cole seemed pleased with the predicament, he had Joanna's lips twisted in a heinous grin. "I think this is the part where you say, oops, maybe I should have listened to my betters."

"Don't do this, please," Roan begged. "You've made your point."

"Have I? I'm here to kill you. But since that doesn't seem like it's going to happen, I'll at least get the immense satisfaction of knowing that you killed an innocent woman."

"Cole, don't!"

Cole raised Joanna's eyebrow. "You still think you're in charge of anything? No, it's time to come down from that high horse of yours, Roan. The only way to stop me is to kill me… well, not me, but whoever this innocent woman is. Can you do that, Roan? Can you kill? Can you commit *murder*?"

Roan's hands began to shake and the sight wobbled. Cole was right, he would have to kill Joanna. And he couldn't hesitate because Cole would stab Amanda if Roan let him, and then he would come after Roan…

A twitch of Joanna's shoulders was the only warning Roan had as Cole tried to plunge the knife into Amanda's throat. Roan had him dead to rights and pulled the trigger. The bullet punched a hole through Joanna's frontal lobe and then bounced around inside of her skull, killing her instantly. She fell back, no longer possessed and no longer alive.

Roan was overcome with simultaneous and conflicting feelings. He felt like puking, and screaming his lungs out, and rushing out to find Cole so that he could beat his head in with a rock. He did none of these things. Instead he held Amanda as she cried. He wanted to cry, however he was too filled with rage to allow any other emotion to come close to the surface of his soul.

Over her shoulder, he could see Joanna's body as well as the neural coupler. She had worn it under her hair, almost like a headband. *How long had Cole been inside of her?* he wondered. *How long had he bided his time, waiting on orders from Arching?*

Racing steps interrupted his thoughts. Drawn by the gunshot, agents came flooding down from the upper floors. Amanda pushed Roan away and ripped a sleeve across her wet eyes.

Roan had his pistol taken from him and they were both led away from the crime scene and questioned separately. They filled out reports and were questioned a second time. During all of this, Roan was quiet, rage simmering beneath the surface and beneath that deep sorrow and regret. He had managed to get half his team killed—he had trouble breathing when he pictured their faces.

Four hours went by before Caron told them to go home. There was no question that Amanda and Roan would spend the night together. It was not spent in wild passion, but in tenderness, punctuated by tears. They kept their weapons within arm's reach and neither slept soundly. In the morning, they dressed and went back into a world they barely recognized.

"We're pulling you off the case," Caron told them. It was expected and it was wrong.

"Is this because you've found Arching?" Roan asked, knowing already that it wasn't. "Or are we giving up on the entire case?"

Caron glared in answer.

"Jarrod and Marshall are dead because *we* were getting close," Amanda said, gesturing at Roan and herself. "Not because of anything you and a hundred agents were doing in the real world. Arching came after us for a reason. If we were just bumbling around in Daggerland, he would have ignored us and sent his assassin after you."

Caron drummed his fingers, shaking his head. "It wasn't my decision. The higher ups only see an online connection to the deaths. In their mind, no online agents equals no problems. They're looking for a way to shut the game down completely, and I for one hope they can."

Roan simmered. The game wasn't the problem, but there was no way he'd be able to convince some of the old timers who were interested in only treading water in the seas of crime. "At least free Leomagnus, I mean Leo Magnuson. We have testimony that he was online playing when Fulbright was killed. It wasn't him."

"I never thought it was. Fine, I'll get the paperwork going as soon as we're done here, which I assume we are?" Amanda shrugged, while Roan only stared at his old mentor with a look of disgust. "Good," Caron said. "I want you both to take a week off and see the company shrink—that is not a request. Oh, and *don't* go back on line. That is also not a request."

They left Caron's office and went down to the main floor. They both paused, looking towards the basement stairwell. "So," Amanda said. "What are we going to do? You know going back online is too dangerous. I don't want to be the person who kills you, Roan. If he makes me, I'll probably kill myself if he doesn't kill me first."

What she said caught in his mind, but probably not in the way she had meant. "I think if Arching could have used one of us to kill the rest, he would have. Which means…we need to see Joanna's coupler. She told me that one of her kids sent it to her out of the blue. How much do you want to bet it's been tampered with in some fashion?"

Amanda's blue eyes shot open. "The game can't track who's on line, but a coupler with a fifth-gen *spoofer* or a *backdoor repeater* might be able to send out a brief echo of when they go online. Maybe that's why Arching kept having people go after Nelson. The timing would have to have been exact. You see, when packets of information are sent…" Roan held up a hand and she growled at his determined ignorance. "Oh, if Jarrod were here, he'd be able to pick out a repeater in a second. They would also have to be able to record and sync a second coupler."

"Don't you think the other couplers were checked for these spoofers?"

She glanced back towards the basement door, and slowly shook her head. "I don't remember reading about that in any report. One coupler disappeared with Lane Gorman, Nelson's was burnt to ash, and the other two developers were thought to be part of a murder/suicide. That leaves Joanna's and Magnuson's."

"So, maybe we were looking at it from the wrong direction. Cole could have gotten to Nelson's coupler and Joanna's as well for that matter, but could he have gotten to anyone else's? Those developers knew a thing or two about security."

"Arching is mega-rich and money opens many doors," Amanda said. "A gardener or a maid could have been bought off with ease. We should subpoena the bank records of…wait, we were pulled from the case. The best we can do is tell Caron about our hunch."

Roan shook his head. "That's not the best we can do. I don't think we have any choice, we're going back online."

3—

Despite their discovery, both were feeling extra paranoid. After visiting his bank, where Roan made a hefty withdrawal, they caught a subway going uptown and then crisscrossed Manhattan in two different cabs until they found an electronics store that sold couplers. They paid cash.

With the couplers in hand, they needed a place to lay low as they went online. Amanda suggested a motel in New Jersey that her father had stayed in when he had visited her earlier that year. Roan had a better idea.

With a feeling of doom hanging over his head, he decided that if he was going to die, he would go out in style. "The Plaza," he told the next cabbie. It was the nicest hotel he had ever busted a drug lord in. When Amanda's eyes shot wide, he explained, "If it's good enough for guys like Arching, it's good enough for us."

The Plaza, one of New York's premiere hotels, had the feel of a French palace about it. Everything was gold trimmed or crystal, and was a bit of a shock to the system compared to their basement dwellings of the last couple of weeks. Amanda walked in with her mouth hanging open and her head turning so much that Roan took her arm to keep her from running into anyone.

Roan plunked down a month's salary for a week's stay and didn't bat an eye. "It seems like a waste," Amanda said, ten minutes later after she had walked about their luxurious room. "We'll be in another world and won't be able to enjoy this at all."

"Perhaps if we find Arching quickly, we can come back and have a real vacation."

"I'd like that," she said, without much hope in her voice. Taking a breath, she gestured to the bed. "Are you ready to go back?"

With a new coupler, Roan didn't know what to expect. He didn't even know if he would still be able to play his old character. The game knew him. It read his individual brain waves and put him right back in the citadel at the top of the tower with the bodies of Marshall and Jarrod.

It hurt to see their corpses lying there. It hurt him somewhere deep in his chest and once more tears threatened, only just then, he was attacked. Something large and invisible slammed into him—it was a second before he realized that it was Glitch.

The spell holding the elemental had worn away and now it was attacking Roan much like an overzealous puppy would. It had also grown so that it was now the size of the fire elementals he had summoned. "Okay, Glitch, I've missed you, too." Being made of air, it was impossible to push away.

Amanda smiled briefly as the whirlwind spun Roan's long dark hair into a strange looking beehive. The smile faded to nothing as she approached the bodies. Kneeling, she said a prayer before taking the magic ring from Jarrod's finger and the sword from Marshall's stiff hand.

"It's how the game is played," she justified. Roan didn't think it was necessary to say anything. Jarrod and Marshall would have done the same thing. Roan found his own sword. Sheathing it, he worked the lever that dropped the stairs down to the lower levels.

They had been gone for fifteen hours and Roan expected the citadel to be deserted. He was pleasantly surprised to find that his company had not left. They had made a campsite out of the atrium, complete with cooking fires and a stable for the horses.

"You're alive!" Krull exclaimed. "We had no idea what had happened to you. But where are Marshall and Jarrod? And where is the mirror? Did you find it?"

"They are dead," Roan answered. "They're dead on the other side, too." He spent the next couple of minutes explaining the situation. "I'll understand if you want to leave."

Krull grimaced, shaking his head. "Do you know what I find to be the most interesting facet of this game? It changes you, sometimes for the better and sometimes for the worse. If you play the good guy, you *become* the good guy. And a person who plays a thief begins to think like a thief. Do you understand? Christian and I are lawful good dwarves. We aren't afraid and we would never leave a friend in need."

Roan felt like hugging the dwarf. He refrained and settled for a firm handshake. Amanda went for the hug and turned Ironhead's cheeks red.

"Amanda and I need to prepare our spells and then I want to move out. We need to be through the swamp by sunset, so have the men ready to go."

"You sound like you have a plan," Krull said. "Do you know where Arching is?"

Daggerland was huge and Arching could have been anywhere, but only one place made sense. "The Pits of the Black Hand. The elves of the Ash Forest told me that the sulphur cloud began venting ten years ago. The game is eleven years old, so I think it's a pretty good guess that Arching spent the first year questing or building his power before he took the pits for himself. As further evidence, we have orcs of the Black Hand here and Riverport."

"They say that none who have ventured into the pits have returned alive," Ironhead remarked.

"We can be the first," Roan said. "Remember, we have Prince Stallings and whatever forces he possesses on our side. I'm also hoping to have Leomagnus and King Salazar with us."

"I have friends who would join us," Krull said. "Some are very powerful. Hell, half the guys I served with play the game. I should go. The sooner I get the message out the better." Ironhead had friends who played the game as well and the two dwarves clocked out, leaving Amanda and Roan to prepare their spells.

As before, when Roan opened his spell book, he found a new spell written in a fine script: *Transform Self.*

He mentally clicked the spell and the description opened up. "Temporarily transforms the wizards corporeal form into another of his choosing," Roan read aloud. "I'm going to change into a dragon the first chance I get." He prepared and breathed in the following spells:

Cantrips: *Fire Bolt X2, Minor Illusion X2*
Tier One: *Thunderous Wave X4*
Tier Two: *Hypnotic Flame X2*
Tier Three: *Inferno X2*
Tier Four: *Transform Self X1*

When the two were finished with their spells, it was almost eleven in the morning and time to move out. It would be a long slow trip back. Since there had been so many deaths, the baggage carts were laden down with the armor and weapons of the slain. On top of that was the loot being hauled back to Tir-Kahn.

Each man had pouches filled with silver and copper coins that were worth nearly sixty in gold. As well, they had rolled carpets, folded curtains, chairs, sconces, candelabras and summoning bells. Four men even manhandled a sturdy oaken desk along.

It was thought that when all of it was sold, it would give each of the survivors a hundred and eighty in gold, which was more than a year's worth of wages for most of them.

Roan wished they could toss it all into the marsh and double time it back to the city. He knew that if he did, he'd have a mutiny on his hands. No, if he wanted to persuade the townsmen to come with him to the Pits of the Black Hand, he had to let them have their booty.

They straggled through the heat of the swamp as afternoon wore on and at some point, the dwarves clocked back to join them on the march. They both had sent out messages to everyone they knew, even the people who didn't play the game. Amanda clocked out to do the same thing, though Roan warned her not to use her laptop in the hotel.

While she was gone, he was nervous and jumpy and had to fight the desire to clock out as well just to check on her. He kissed her hard on the lips when she got back. She smiled up at him, however there were tears in her large doe-like elf eyes.

"The funerals are going to be held at the same time in a couple of days," she said, without looking up. "We should attend, but I'm afraid to go. Arching has to know that Cole didn't get us all. He might not be able to get us while we're asleep or whatever you call the state our bodies are in, but that doesn't mean he can't use suicide bombers. They wouldn't even be suicide bombers, they'd be, what? Armed drones?"

Roan's teeth ground together in frustration. "You're right. We would be sitting ducks for Cole and we would never see him coming. I'll tell Caron when I clock out."

When he didn't immediately clock back to the real world, she asked, "Shouldn't you be going? The more time you give your friends the better chance they have of getting here in time to help with the coming battle."

A rueful laugh escaped him. "The only true friends I have in the real world are currently in the city morgue. I'm not really an outgoing person."

"You should try smiling more," she suggested. "You scowl even as an elf. It makes you look unapproachable. Go on, give it a try." He wasn't in the mood and yet he wanted to please her. He wanted to make her happy even in this little thing. He smiled and she said, "There, that wasn't so hard, was…you're scowling again."

He worked on his smile, which was easy when she was laughing or telling stories of her childhood. It was impossible to hold the smile when they would drift into their frequent melancholy silences.

The sun was low behind them when they finally saw the tip of the hill town of Tir-Kahn. The entire formation breathed a sigh of relief. The dwarves immediately began barking orders. "Button up!" roared Krull. "Let's get these lines straight and yes, that means you four as well." He meant the men sweating under the weight of the oaken desk.

They marched through the gates with their heads held high, expecting something of a hero's welcome. Instead, they were all but ignored. The entire town was in an uproar with people hurrying in every direction.

At the gates, seated on a dappled mare, was Tareman, the captain of Prince Stallings' guard. "His highness wishes to see you this very second," he stated, speaking baldly. "Follow me." He didn't wait.

Much to Roan's annoyance, the captain kicked his horse in the flanks. Jetta followed with just a word from Roan. At the top of the hill, the prince waited, along with what seemed like his entire household staff. He didn't look like himself; it almost seemed as though he had aged forty years since they had last seen him. His dark hair was streaked with white and his face was lined, pale, drawn and strangely wrinkled.

"What happened to you?" Amanda asked. "You look, I don't know, sort of wizened, like a raisin."

Stallings touched his face with gentle fingers as if he were afraid his lined face would slide right off his skull if he weren't careful. "It was the *Lady*. There's something about her; she draws energy into her, like a magnet. She doesn't mean to do it and even if she did…" He paused and then shrugged. "It would be okay if she did."

"Freyja was here?" Roan asked, looking up at the mansion, trying to peer through its windows to catch the least sight of her.

"Yes, it was amazing. I'm still trying to wrap my head around it. We spoke and she told me things. She told me of your victory; it sounded epic. And she told of my fate. I get to die for her."

Chapter 27

—Tir-Kahn, Daggerland

Roan felt the lingering power of Freyja as soon as he stepped through the doors of the mansion. It drew something from him, leaving him suddenly hungry, thirsty, and short of breath. It also left him with a growing arousal that was so totally unexpected that he pulled his cloak around himself.

He glanced over at Amanda and saw that she hadn't noticed. She looked dazed and uncertain on her feet.

Taking her hand, he started forward towards the main room where the sound of Stallings' magical waterfall mingled with music and where a soft glowing radiance irresistibly beckoned. Roan couldn't have stopped his feet if he tried. When they came to the great room, he was both shocked and disappointed that the goddess wasn't there.

"She was right here," Stalling said, still uncertain on his feet. "She was here not ten minutes ago. She stood beneath the cascading water, utterly naked, save for a necklace of amber and rubies that hung between her breasts." He shook his head, staring up at the falling water. "Roan, I have never seen a woman… or anything else for that matter, so beautiful."

"I believe you," Roan said. "She mentioned our victory, right? Did she say anything else? Did she give any indication where Arching is?"

Stallings' face screwed up as he tried to remember the details. "She said…she said, 'Stand, veil-walker. There is imbalance.' Oh, my goodness, when she spoke, I was in this cloud of honeysuckle, and cinnamon, and there were other smells… vanilla and baked apples." He spoke like someone talking in their sleep.

"What about Arching?" Amanda asked.

"She said that I must repair the balance and that the balance is more important than victory. She said: ōs byþ ordfroema ǣlcre sprǣce. Wīsdōmes wralu ast wīteyna frōfur ast eorla gehwām ēydnys and tō hihe."

"And what does that mean?" Roan asked after a glance at Amanda, who only lifted a single eyebrow.

Stallings whispered, "I don't know, I just remember those words, like they're stamped into my head. I-I think I need to sleep now." He wandered off with his halfling servant at his elbow.

"Was it me or did that seem like a waste of a visit," Amanda remarked. "A goddess comes all the way to earth, or wherever we are, and that's all she says? Repair the balance? What balance was she talking about?"

"I don't know and I don't really like it. Every mythological god I've ever read about is petty and cruel, even the good ones. If there's a balance she's looking to maintain, it'll be the balance of power in her favor. Still, she is helping us, I guess." Roan suddenly snorted. "Didn't Prince Stallings look like he just got hit in the head with a cartoon frying pan? Hopefully, he'll remember more in the morning."

After their long day of traveling, they took an early dinner in their suite and fell asleep in each other's arms. He must have been more tired than he realized because it was late in the morning when he woke to find Glitch floating over him. Roan touched the empty pillow next to him hoping to still feel Amanda's warmth. "I'm right here."

Roan jumped and saw her relaxing on a French-looking chez with purple cushions. She was not in armor, but in a yellow dress; a plate of sliced melon on the floor within reach.

"Did you talk to Stallings? Did he mention Arching?"

"I ran into him when I was trying to sneak my breakfast up here. All the little servant people gave me such frowns, but he didn't even notice. He's a man on a mission. His 'Lady' as he calls Freyja told him to follow you. So, I guess it's to the Pits of the Black Hand, then?"

"Yes, I think so." He was about to stand when he realized he was naked beneath his sheet. "Where are my clothes?"

She pointed at a standing wardrobe. "In there. You want to hear something creepy? Someone came in last night while we were sleeping, took our clothes, cleaned them, and then put them back. Were you sleeping on the job, Glitch?"

"Oooo," the elemental said, sending a picture of a tiny halfling woman creeping in to take the clothes.

Roan explained what he had seen but made no move to get up. Amanda noted this and asked, "Are you getting shy on me, Roan? Do you want me to turn my head?" It didn't seem necessary. They *had* spent the night together, and their real bodies were currently sharing a king-sized bed.

"No, but I should clock out. It feels like I've been gone too long. Do you want to join me?"

She hesitated just a moment before agreeing. "I guess there's no reason to take turns, right?" Seconds later, they sat up in the real world. They were on the king-sized bed in the Plaza, satin sheets beneath them, the air conditioner keeping the room a perfect seventy degrees. They stared around, feeling strangely let down by the opulence of the hotel. As fine and expensive as it was, it didn't compare to Stalling's Palace, which was perfect in every detail.

At least The Plaza had a gym. The two worked out, watching each other. It was strange to see Amanda as a human. Her lips were fuller, but her eyes were smaller. Her hair was shorter and lacked the pure golden color. Her breasts were larger and her hips, although slim, were still wider than with her elf form. Thinking of her hips made him wonder if an elf character could have a baby. What would their baby look like?

"What?" she asked. "You have an odd look on your face."

"Huh? Me? Odd? No, I-I was just noticing how beautiful you are, you know, as a human."

She looked down at her sweat-slicked body. "Thank you, but I look a mess." Mess or not, her smile gleamed and he smiled back at her.

The smiles died when Roan checked his phone and found a dozen reminders that Jarrod's and Marshall's funerals were being held the next day. The texts were like a punch in the gut. Roan texted Caron, explaining the danger posed by attending the funeral. He didn't wait for a response and not only did he power down his phone, he took the batteries from it as well. Now, they couldn't be tracked, even by the FBI.

It didn't make either one of them feel any safer. Their empty, soulless bodies were going to be completely helpless when they went back to Daggerland. Roan went the extra mile and heaped all the furniture in the room in front of the door. Only then did they feel safe enough to go back to Daggerland. Holding hands, they clocked back in and found the halfling, Rolly waiting for them to return. He wasn't surprised when they materialized in front of him. In fact, he didn't even blink at Roan's nudity even though, being as short as he was, that nudity was staring him in the face.

"Sir Krull and Sir Ironhead are in the second parlor room awaiting your presence," he announced before promptly turning on his heel and striding from the room with Amanda's giggles following him.

"I don't think I'll be able to look that guy in the eye anymore," Roan groaned as he went to the wardrobe.

"Not with your pants on you won't," Amanda said, with more giggles escaping her.

Roan shot her a useless glare—she laughed at it as well. She was happy. Strangely, she was happier here than in the real world. He thought it strange since most of their time in Daggerland had been spent fighting for their lives against an all-powerful being. It was strange, however he understood. He was happier as well.

Turning back to the wardrobe, he picked out the cobalt outfit with the silver fur trim that Amanda had bought for him. Once dressed, they hurried down to the lower floor where the different sitting rooms were located. As Roan strode through the palace, his head spun with all the activity. The place was packed with humans, elves, dwarves, soldiers, wizards, clerics and everything in between. Roan was noticed and whispers followed him wherever he went.

"You're somewhat famous," Amanda explained. "The story of what happened at Mendenome has grown out of all proportion. Someone asked me earlier if it was true that we defeated two thousand orcs. They also seem to think that you're some sort of great wizard. I told them that great didn't cover it."

Roan stopped her and whispered, "Why would you do that?"

"To build moral. We're going to this supposedly terrible place. Wouldn't you rather go if there's a super-powerful wizard going as well?"

"But what happens when we get to the Pits?" Roan wondered aloud. "They're going to expect some big-time magic and when I can't come through, what then?"

She began tapping her lower lip, trying to think of an answer but then saw the dwarves peeking out from one of the sitting rooms. In their grungy armor and with their filthy hands, they seemed utterly out of place in the palace.

"Ah, milord Krull and his most respected companion, milord Ironhead," Amanda said, doing her best to dodge Roan's question concerning magic.

The dwarves smirked, their mustaches lifting at the corners. "We heard you were finally up," Krull said. "While you two were sleeping, *or whatever*, we have been up since dawn recruiting the company back up to strength. Really, it's more than up to strength. All those townsmen have been running their mouths, telling outlandish stories. We didn't bother to set the record straight and now we have three-hundred and twenty-seven recruits."

"We were going to put them through maneuvers to weed out the weaklings and thought you'd want to help out," Ironhead said.

Roan still had a lingering ache in his chest over the loss of Jarrod and Marshall and he knew that the ache would only grow into depression if he didn't stay active. "That sounds like a plan, but if we're going to do this, we're going to do this right." He turned to Amanda. "Time to suit up. You can't march in a dress."

"I'll be right down," she lied. Roan didn't see her for five hours.

2—

With the dwarves acting as drill sergeants, Roan divided the recruits into three companies and put them through a series of workouts. In full gear, they ran wind sprints, jogged up and down the hill, did pushups and pull-ups, and when they were truly tired, he had them fight in mock battles. At least a hundred men slipped away during all this, perhaps finding the pace too much, or perhaps looking for a more relaxed company to join.

They wouldn't be missed in Roan's opinion. The day was long and hard, and yet he knew from experience that real battle was far more difficult.

At around four that afternoon, just when Amanda, riding on Rhi-adol, came to join the company, looking fresh-faced and resplendent in her shining mithral armor, a road-weary rider pulled up next to them, asking if the prince was there among the combatants. The symbol on her shield marked her as one of King Salazar's men.

Krull pointed at the looming hill. "At the top. He's in his palace as far as we know."

The rider looked up at the hill and Roan could see the weight of exhaustion settle on her. "She is friends with the prince," Roan said of Amanda. "She can ride ahead and give him the message and you can follow along after you've had a drink."

"It's the orcs besieging Morin. They broke camp this morning and are heading to the Pits as fast as they can."

"Morin is over a hundred miles away," Roan asked, suddenly suspicious. "How'd you get here so quickly?"

The rider gave him an odd look. "I'm a friend of Salazar's on the other side. He put out a flash asking if anyone was in the neighborhood, and I was the closest. What's with the third degree?"

Before answering, Roan nodded to Amanda, who shot away, heading back to the gate with the message. He then explained the situation to the woman, who wasn't a woman at all. She was a girl who babysat Salazar's children on occasion. Her real world name was the same as her Daggerland name: Khia Skye, tenth level ranger.

"You're really going to make a try for the Pits of the Black Hand?" she asked in amazement. "And Freyja herself came here? She's big time, like a greater god, right? Man, I heard some guys ran into Achilles, the Greek guy, a while back and got stomped. And he was just a hero or a demigod or something."

"You know there is a good chance that she's coming back," Krull said. "Seeing a goddess fight, that's a once in a lifetime opportunity. You could be a part of that. We're looking for people who can fight. You know, this is the same company that just cleaned out Mendenome. It was an epic battle."

Skye scratched at some dirt on her face. "I don't know. I have a ton of homework to catch up on."

It was such an odd thing to say that Roan had to look the ranger up and down before he said, "If I'm not mistaken, Stallings won't be able to move out for another day or two. That should give you enough time for your, uh, your homework."

"Okay. That sounds cool, thanks."

She rode away then, plodding slowly towards the hill.

Roan watched her go for a moment before ordering his men into a mass formation. It was getting late and was time for the final culling. Walking down the lines with Krull and Ironhead beside him, he thinned the ranks, ending up keeping one-hundred and fifty men. To that number, he could add fifty elven archers.

"Have them formed and ready for drill by six tomorrow morning," Roan ordered. He guessed, correctly as it turned out, that Stalling would want to leave the day after the next and the wizard wanted a full day of training before they left.

Roan trudged up the hill, finding Amanda waiting for him at the top. Much to the annoyance of the oddly fussy halflings, she reclined on the stairs that led into the palace. In her hand was Marshall's magic sword.

"We missed you at mercenary practice," he admonished. "All the other soldiers are going to think you're getting preferential treatment."

"And they'd be right. I'm sleeping with you in two worlds. You have a lot of spoiling to do." When he made a rumbling noise in the back of his throat, she gave him an impish grin. "I'll be there tomorrow, I promise. You didn't need me today. You already know I can fight. Speaking of which."

She held out the sword to him. He didn't take it and so she pushed it into his arms. "It belongs to you," she said. "We both know you're the hero. I might be able to fight better than you, but you never take a backseat to anyone. If there's a big bad, I can't see you letting me go after him, one on one. Am I right?"

He took the sword and drew it out. Blue light dazzled him for a moment before it faded to a soft glow. "I don't want you to fight at all, but you will. Your spells will go faster than mine and then I'm going to need you on the line." He handed the sword back. "Counting your magic armor and ring, what's your armor class?"

"Twenty-six," she admitted with a little shrug. It meant that she was all but untouchable against orcs.

"Good. I want to know that you're safe, or at least as safe as can be. I don't want to have to worry about you in the middle of battle."

She gave him a sharp look. "You're not going to worry about me? What kind of boyfriend doesn't worry about his girl when she's fighting ten-thousand orcs?"

Roan had been grinning, but it slipped away. "Ten-thousand? Where did you hear that?"

"I overheard a couple of Prince Stallings' little people talking. It might not be true, you know. And even if it is…" She didn't need to finish her sentence. True or not, they had to make the attempt on the Pits of the Black Hand.

The next day at six sharp, the pair rode down the hill and out through the gates to where the company waited in ten platoons. "Form them into a phalanx, three deep," he told Krull.

"Have the archers on the flanks." While Krull was doing this, Roan had Amanda ride down to the docks to fetch a boathook, which was essentially a long pole with a hook on the end used for grabbing boats as they floated away.

When the soldiers were formed into a rectangle that bristled with spears and arrows, he had them practice the very basics of fighting in formation. They advanced, they retreated, they wheeled left and right. They marched obliquely, they double timed it here and there, all the while striving to maintain the phalanx. Lastly, they practiced forming into a square. Although it sounded simple, it had to be done precisely.

And they did all of this over and over for hours. As they went back and forth, Roan used the boathook to haul men out of line, simulating injury or death, forcing them to shift their ranks to keep holes from forming.

Eventually, other companies came down from the city. Invariably, they would break into knots of soldiers and practice fighting. "Why can't we do that?" one of Roan's soldiers griped. "We're going to fight a battle, not march in a parade."

Krull turned red in the face and started stomping towards the man, but Roan stopped him. Yelling to be heard, Roan said, "Anyone here who doesn't know how to swing a sword already, please leave. Go on! Go over with the rest of them and bang on some shields. Those of you who wish to learn how to fight as a team, stay. This is not a hack and slash adventure, people, this is war. Battles are won not just with the strength of your arm or the sharpness of your sword, they are won through teamwork and discipline."

"Nice speech," a voice drawled behind him. It was Tareman, the captain of the prince's guard. Behind him were five hundred troops, standing in a perfect column. "His highness would like to speak to you. He's at the top of the hill, watching."

Roan had Krull continue the maneuvers as he and Amanda rode up to the palace where they found the prince in his library sipping one of his expensive bottles of wine. "The FBI is looking for you," he told Roan right off the bat. "I clocked back to take care of some business and there was an agent snooping through my living room. He wanted to know if I had seen you."

"And?" Roan asked.

"I told him the truth. Sorry, but I can't be a part of obstruction charges. Not now, not when we're about to head out. Speaking of which, have your company ready to go before sunrise. I have men tracking the orcs and they haven't stopped once. Aderon is whipping them into a frenzy. I've never seen anything like it."

"It tells me we're on the right track," Amanda remarked. "Look, we should clock out and see what's going on in the real world."

They bowed to the prince and went to their suite in the palace before clocking back to The Plaza. They both sat up, reaching for their guns, but the room was empty and the pile of furniture hadn't been disturbed. They both sighed in relief.

"When was the last time we ate in this world?" Amanda asked, her stomach growling.

"I'm not sure. Let's go grab something and check our messages." They left the hotel, looking like just another hand-holding couple. Behind their sunglasses, they were hyper-vigilant. After a cab ride to Times Square, they ate greasy pizza and checked their messages.

Roan only had one. It was from Caron: "Call me, ASAP," his boss growled.

"That's not going to happen," Roan said. "You get anything?" She had received the same message as he had.

He erased his and was just about to pop the battery out of the phone when it rang. Of course, it was Caron. Roan pressed the talk button, but didn't say anything. "Alright, Roan, I know you're there and I know you've been in Daggerland against direct orders."

"Actually, you told me to take a week off," Roan said. "And I am. What I do on my time is my business."

"Not when you're interfering with an investigation."

"Please, you call what you're doing an investigation? What do you have? Any clues? Have you interviewed any suspects?" Other than breathing like a bull into the phone, Caron was quiet. "That's what I thought."

Amanda tapped him on the shoulder and then spoke into the phone, "How was the funeral?"

"Crappy, just as I expected," Caron answered. "Actually, it was worse than I expected. The turnout was pathetic, even among the geeks. And speaking of geeks, half of them called out sick today. Can you two think of any reason why?"

Roan was about to answer when he saw a black sedan with dark tinted windows slide up the street, moving slowly—the driver wasn't looking for a place to park. He was looking for the two of them. Roan hung up the phone without a word of good bye, dropped it on the table and pulled Amanda into the kitchen of the pizza place.

A greasy-faced man who looked as though he'd been rolled in flour got riled in a thick New York accent until Roan showed him both his badge and his gun. "Where's the back door?" Fingers were pointed and in seconds, Roan and Amanda found themselves in a rancid-smelling ally.

Just down the block, a door sat propped open by a rock. Roan kicked the rock away and ghosted into a cigarette smelling hallway where music thumped along the walls. He took a left towards where the music was loudest and they found themselves in the main lounge of a strip club.

"We should probably hang here for a little while," Roan said. "Just until the heat dies down."

Amanda punched him in the shoulder, hitting bone and causing his entire arm to go dead. She dragged him out and ducked into the nearest cab. "South Ferry, please." The Plaza was in the opposite direction. Slunk down low and keeping their hands near their guns, they took the cab to the tip of Manhattan and from there got on a ferryboat that circled tourists around the Statue of Liberty.

They held hands as evening turned into night and the lights of the city exploded all around them. "That car might have been FBI," he whispered, "but then again, it might have been someone working for Arching."

"It might have been no one," she countered. "But we can't take that chance, can we? We have to be paranoid until Arching is caught…maybe even until he's dead." She was right. He squeezed her hand and then kissed the back of it.

"Maybe he's paranoid as well? Not only is the FBI after him, he has at least one goddess after him, as well. And who can he trust? Cole? A few lackeys? Paranoid people can't truly trust anyone. If we keep the pressure on, both here and on the other side, he'll start to make mistakes."

Amanda laid her head on his shoulder and stared out at the skyline. "We'll be in battle this time tomorrow. Do you think we can win?"

"We have to. If Arching wins, the kingdoms and city-states around the Pits will fall one after another and who will be left to stop him? The map shows only wilderness for three hundred miles in every direction. The closest lands are the kingdoms of the Pelinors and from what Ironhead says, they've been involved in a civil war for five years now."

It could be another year or two before someone with a big enough army could be prevailed upon to attack the Pits, and Roan had a feeling that by then, The Infinite One would be unstoppable—if he wasn't already.

Their paranoia wasn't assuaged by a trip around the Statue of Liberty and three more cab rides. Still just as nervous, they bought Yankee baseball caps in Chinatown and pulled them low across their brows as they slipped passed the bellhop and into The Plaza lobby.

Pausing by a planter, they pretended to linger in a hug as they surveyed the people around them. Nothing about the people in the lobby set off their alarms and they proceeded to the elevator. When a man in a dark suit stepped on with them, Roan tensed, ready to spring at him if his hand strayed toward his jacket.

Even though the man in the dark suit only stared straight ahead and yawned twice, the two breathed a sigh of relief when he got off. They didn't relax when they got to their room, either. Going around the room, they checked for listening devices. Even their neuro couplers were inspected and handled with caution.

The two spent the night together, though neither got much sleep. Roan slept with one eye cracked, an ear cocked and his pistol beneath his pillow.

When they clocked back to Daggerland the next morning, they discovered their paranoia was likely unfounded. There was such a commotion going on all around the palace that they hurried to their window and saw that the town was inundated with adventurers. There were hundreds of them. Many of them a much higher level than either Roan or Amanda. It was quite a spectacle. There were men and women in shining armor, carrying huge swords that could split a horse in half, or war hammers with heads that could crack cement at a blow.

One woman wore a cloak of metallic feathers; another person wore a cloak that seemed to be made of clouds that swirled around him like a tempest. One wizard had on a robe that sprouted hands and arms. There were robes of every color, and staves of every type of wood. Zipping about through the air were owls and ravens and every sort of familiar.

Many of these heroes had retainers, apprentices or guards. Quite a few came with mercenary companies wearing matching armor and carrying pendants by the hundreds. They made

Roan's company with their mismatched and sweat stained armor look amateurish.

Roan and Amanda dressed quickly and hurried through the crowded palace and out the front door in time to see a huge man in green platemail ride up on a tremendous bull with steel-tipped horns. The bull was slung with round shields so that it looked as if it were wearing chainmail. Amanda was just stepping forward to pet the seven-foot tall creature when six other heroes flew in on fantastic beasts that were a strange mixture of lion and giant eagle.

"Those are griffins," Amanda said in a whisper, her face alight with joy. She stared around her with a grin on her face and tears in her eyes. "Maybe we can win," she said. "I didn't think we had a chance before, but now…we're nothing." She threw herself into his arms as if being "nothing" was something to be excited over.

As much as this seemed like a put-down, he understood. With so many adventurers and heroes going after Arching, why would he chase around after a couple of minor league players like Amanda and Roan? Attacking their sleeping bodies in the real world wouldn't change anything at this point and would only be an undue risk and a distraction.

The two melted into each other's arms and gazed around them; it was almost like a circus. The only question for Roan was where they had all come from? The dwarves had contacted their friends, and Amanda had emailed hers, but that didn't account for so many…

"Agent Waterfall?" a voice asked, breaking in on his thoughts.

Roan's sword was out in a blink, casting a blue light on a slight man in the basic garb of a noob straight from creating a character. He had chosen to play himself—he had chosen poorly.

"Stop!" the man cried, his eyes wide and his shaking hands held in front of his face. "Please, I'm only…wait, are you Supervisory Special Agent Roan? Good, you're together. I don't know if you remember me, I'm Forensic Specialist Tidmeyer. Agent Caron sent me."

Now that Roan was seeing the man in context, he recognized the lab rat from the New York field office. "He sent you to fight? Good. Take up a sword. We march in an hour."

Tidmeyer shook his head. "Oh, I couldn't. I came here to tell you to go back home. Caron sent me. It's an order." When

Roan just stood there staring at the man, Tidmeyer added, "An official order."

Roan advanced, his face going red, however, Amanda quickly stepped in between them. "That can't be, Mr. Tidmeyer. Caron ordered us to go on vacation, and that's what we're doing, vacationing. I'm afraid with people after us we can't take orders that are secondhand in nature. I'm sure you understand."

Tidmeyer began to splutter. Roan cut him off. "Look around you. Arching isn't worried about us anymore. We're nothing compared to these guys. Tell Caron that we're as safe here as anywhere." Wearing a sour look, Tidmeyer clocked out.

"If Caron comes in person, we're screwed," Roan said, pulling Amanda back to the palace. "We should get away from Tir-Kahn as quickly as possible." He wanted to speak to the prince, but got nowhere close. The great room in the center of the palace was filled with soldiers and heroes.

Before he could push through, the prince's guard captain stopped him. "This is a closed meeting. You will be given your marching orders and assignment in a few minutes. Please go to your company and prepare them for an immediate departure."

He pointed them to the door.

As they walked back to the main doors, Roan stewed over his treatment, while Amanda was perfectly happy and put her arm in his. "Do we even have to fight?" she mused. "I mean, look at all of these people. Where did they all come from?" She asked the same question of Krull after they had called for their horses and had ridden down the hill and through the gates. The dwarf was surrounded by eight others of his kind. They all eyed Amanda with a little too much appreciation as far as Roan was concerned.

"The message boards," one of the dwarves answered in a deep rumbly baritone. He was the thickest and strongest dwarf Roan had yet seen. It was as if someone had taken an NFL line-backer and had compressed him down to four feet in height. "The battle has gone viral. Everyone wants in."

"Everyone with balls, that is," said another. "You got the balls my pretty elf?"

Roan was shocked and taken aback to find the dwarf was talking to him. His hand went to his sword, while above him Glitch flared from translucent to an angry cloud in a blink. Krull cursed and Ironhead jumped to his feet, hammer in hand.

"Stop!" Amanda cried. "Keep it in your pants, boys. Save it for Arching." Putting a name—a famous name at that— on the bad guy raised some eyebrows and the tension was diffused. Whispering broke out among the crowds. Roan half-expected to lose some of the heroes, but instead they grinned at the prospect of taking on the "Father of Virtual Reality."

Ten minutes later, the whispers were still going strong when horns blared and messenger riders came hurrying from the hill— it was time. Marching orders were given and Roan's company was forced to wait as the soldiers of Tir-Kahn went by. Then they waited some more as *all* of the other mercenary companies marched past.

His company was last and ended up breathing road dust for the next six hours. Altogether, Prince Stalling led twenty-five hundred fighters of all stripes north toward the Pits of the Black Hand, but as the day wore on, groups of ten, twenty and even a hundred joined them. The small army sang lusty songs of women and war, and gradually their numbers grew as they marched. They were thirty-three hundred strong when they came to the Orc-back Mountains.

The last group to join them awaited them there. It was Leo-magnus the Golden with three hundred elves—the last elves left in The Ash Forest. The elves were afforded a spot near the front and now Roan's company was a mile from the leading elements.

When he heard that it was Leomagnus who had joined them, he rode Jetta to the front. "A 'thank you' would have been nice," he said to Leomagnus. "You weren't released by accident, you know. I stuck my neck out for you."

The elf lord sighed. "I avoided you for a reason, Agent Roan. Your boss ordered me, Salazar, Stallings and who knows who else not to associate with you. He called you a 'rogue ele-ment' and if I were to see you, I was to order you back to the other side. On one hand, I hate the idea of a police state being able to dictate who I talk to and on the other hand, jail sucked, so…consider yourself ordered back to the real world."

Roan rolled his eyes. "You know he has no power to do that, right?"

"Of course, but it costs me two-hundred dollars an hour for a lawyer to fight it. And look at that! It costs me ten experience points just to say the word lawyer!"

"Well, you've done your duty and I'll be going back soon enough," Roan said, gesturing up at the sulphur clouds billowing above the mountains. It was thicker and darker than it had been, and within it lightning flashed, angrily. Roan was getting nervous again about their chances of winning. "Maybe we all will be."

"Oh, I doubt it. One man isn't strong enough to stop this host. I have never seen so many adventurers in one place. Arching won't know what hit him."

This should have had a calming effect on Roan, instead he felt his nerves begin to amp up as they drew closer and closer. He couldn't help but think that if Leomagnus was correct, then Arching would be a fool to attempt to make a stand and yet, the mountain billowed more smoke, and vultures by the thousands began to wheel in the sky above them.

The songs died on the lips of the warriors as they made their way up into the mountains. The army marched with a sense of doom creeping up on them, but they also marched with a sense of purpose. There were no stragglers or whiners. Prince Stallings led them on a steady, ground-eating pace so that by five in the afternoon, they stood above a foul, stinking valley.

Nothing whatsoever lived there. At one end of the wide valley was a gaping sore in the earth and it was from there that the smoke and ash vented into the atmosphere. Between them and the tremendous hole was three miles of blasted, barren desert from which noxious fumes lifted, causing the air to shimmer in a greenish haze. This would be their battlefield.

Prudently, Stallings kept his army on the ridge until his scouts and seers reported that the orc army serving under Aderon the Black was within a few miles. Only then did he lead the way down to where they discovered the fumes rising from the polluted land was worse than they expected. Man and beast found themselves growing weak.

Jetta walked with stumbling hooves, his head hung down. Roan felt so sorry for him that he slid from his back and after tearing his own cloak and wetting it, he placed it over the horse's long nose and eyes. Amanda did the same thing and the two dismounted to walk their steeds at the head of the company.

Because they were the last in the formation, they were stuck at the far end of the line with their right flank nestled against the craggy wall of the valley. Roan threw his fifty archers well in advance of his little company, an idea that was taken up by the next company in line, and the one after that. Soon, every man, woman and elf with a bow or crossbow, stood in a long, thin line across the face of the valley. A few hundred yards away was a wide gap in the humped mountains. It had been a river bed once, only now it was bone dry. There wasn't a drop of moisture left in the Orc-backs causing Roan to wonder how anything, even an orc could live in such a place.

There wasn't much time for conjecture, however. The sky darkened as if a storm was coming and the air hung heavy and reeking in anticipation. Within minutes, a smattering of human riders came blazing from the defile. Their mounts were wild-eyed and frothed in sweat that was as much from fear as exhaustion.

"The orcs are coming!" they cried.

"Is that right?" Skye asked, sarcastically. Roan hadn't seen the ranger until just then. She grinned over at him. "I got my homework done. This is going to be epic! This is like the Woodstock of Daggerland and I want it on record that Khia Skye Ranger of the North was here!" She let out a whoop of delight.

Roan wished he could be that enthused, but once more playing on extreme mode robbed him of his bloodlust. "But at least I won't end up like Jarrod and Marshall...I hope." Thinking of them sent a shiver down his spine. He turned to Amanda. "Can you clock back really quick and check on our bodies. Things don't feel right."

She was gone for five minutes, plenty of time for him to begin to freak out. He was about to clock back himself, when she suddenly reappeared. "Sorry, I had to pee. We're fine. We're just..." She stopped, her words caught in her throat.

The river seemed to be flowing again as a flood of grey-skinned orcs came pouring through the gap in the mountains. Their banners, their swords, their battle axes seemed infinite.

"It's just a game," Amanda whispered, drawing back her bow. Roan could see the string shaking.

2—

The thin line of archers held their ground long enough to let loose five flights of arrows, Roan hitting three times, (*XP +60*). They then took to their heels, racing back to their places in line.

Roan's archers were not in their customary left and right flank positions. They were poorly armored and he figured that at the first shock of attack they would break, leaving gaps in the line. To keep that from happening, he placed them all on the right flank against the valley wall. The climbers among them clambered up the crags to get better shooting positions.

Krull and Ironhead stood like granite on either end of the double line, while Amanda and Skye took up positions dead center. Roan went to stand behind the second line, ready to cast a spell, or shore up the line with his sword or direct operations as needed. Glitch hung in the air a hundred feet above his head. The elemental would be his eyes, keeping him apprised of how the rest of the battle was going. His battle plan was about as sound as he could make it with what he had to work with.

The orcs didn't seem to have much of a plan beyond throwing themselves onto the humans in one great charge. Their battle cries rang like thunder as they bore down on the thirty-three hundred and the thud of their thousands of boots rattled the stones and loose dirt of the valley floor.

Some of the soldiers in the first line began to back into the second. "Steady," Krull called out as Roan moved Jetta back and forth along the line to nip any thought of retreat in the bud.

Kateye, resplendent in her blue and silver, stood in the front of her elven archers firing nonstop and she could not be blamed that she concentrated her attack on the orcs baring straight down on her lightly clad warriors. So intense was their archery that the orcs directly in front of her were stopped dead in their tracks, as corpses began to heap up.

A quarter mile away, in the very middle of the battle, fourteen wizards pushed through the lines of soldiers. Each let loose with *Inferno* spells, lighting up the dark valley and tearing great holes in the onrushing orc army. Fire roiled outward filling the already foul air with the smell of burning flesh.

Before the orcs could recover, the wizards struck again as dozens of flaming meteors fell from the sky, screaming down like artillery shells. They exploded when they hit the earth, sending shards and splinters of rock ripping into the orcs, killing hundreds.

Roan's warriors cheered, but the wizards weren't done yet. Lightning bolts flashed into the enemy, acid rained down, and ice storms sprung up out of nowhere. The onslaught was shocking and it was no wonder that in the center of the battle, the orc attack faltered.

It wasn't the same on the flanks. Roan's store of spells was limited and he had to be very careful not to overuse them early in the fight, although he was sorely tempted.

Because his fine archers were holding back the orcs on the right, the orcs struck his little section of the battle at an angle, pushing back the left side by sheer weight of numbers. He was tempted to pull the entire line back to compensate, but he knew that if he did, the archers on the walls would have to give up their excellent perches which allowed them a completely unobstructed field of fire.

"When in doubt, attack," Roan muttered, misquoting George Patton. "On the right!" he roared to those yet blooded men. "Pivot on Amanda and wheel inward!"

They had practiced this maneuver as a full company, not as half of one and for a moment his men hesitated. On the far end, Ironhead started marching forward in an arc. "Keep up, damn it!" the dwarf yelled as the rest of the line lagged. They rushed to catchup and bore down on the enemy with locked shields and bristling spears.

This action immediately took the pressure from the left side of the line, but it also left Ironhead open to being flanked and he would have been had it not been for the elven arches who raked the orcs without mercy. Within a minute the attack on the left had been stopped and the orcs thrown into confusion. Roan saw it was time to bring his men back in line—again, something that they hadn't practiced under battle conditions.

Some men immediately rushed away, some backed slowly, while others were too engaged to do anything but fight for their lives. In seconds, the line became ragged and broken, giving the orcs an advantage. Roan raced up on Jetta as half a dozen men were hacked into pieces.

"Eda-eram gdiy!" A blast of thunder from his outstretched hand sent the orcs hurtling back(*XP +100*). "Reform! Reform!" he cried. "Get this line straight!" Taking advantage of the confusion wrought by his spell, his men were able to disengage to once more form the crudest of formations, the human wall.

It was a slightly thinner human wall, however. Roan saw the bodies of at least thirteen of his soldiers, which were even then being abused by the orcs. They were being kicked, stabbed, mutilated and, in two cases, torn apart and feasted upon. The sight filled him with hot anger and with all his heart, he wanted to order a charge to recover the bodies and punish the orcs.

His men were itching to attack as well; a few even looked back at Roan with questioning looks on their faces when he didn't order a charge.

"Stand your ground!" he cried. "They want us to attack." Roan knew it would be foolish to be baited into giving up an advantageous position. The phalanx was strongest when on the defensive. When it attacked over broken ground, it lost its cohesion, becoming a mob instead of a fighting unit. Also, a charge by his company, alone and unsupported, would leave him open to envelopment. He and his men would be surrounded and butchered in place.

No, attacking was exactly what the orcs were hoping he would do. By standing on the defensive, he was playing his game, not theirs, and the longer they tried to get him to take the bait, the worse it was for them. The orcs were being ravaged by his archers, who had never stopped raining arrows into them.

Eventually, they came on again, attacking in a great screaming rush, their huge jaws gaping open, showing their yellowed tusks. Roan's company did not flinch in the face of the attack and many of the orcs were impaled on their spears. The two sides became locked in battle and once more the humans, working as a unit, began to prevail. The men in the back lines thrust their spears repeatedly around and over the men in the front row.

So steadfast were his men that Roan had to use his spells only twice more in the next few minutes, both times to help the elves. The orcs were desperate to stop the arrows pouring into their ranks and twice tried to rush the elves, stumbling over their own dead and crushing the wounded under foot. Roan used two of his *Hypnotic Flame* spells to end the threats.

The orcs even drew back, giving him a moment to peer through Glitch's eyes. The overall battle was going against the orcs. In places, they had taken ruinous losses and were reeling from the combined power of the adventurers, some of whom seemed impervious to every attack and were hacking their way deep into the ranks of the orcs.

Roan felt a flush of excitement. "We're winning!" he yelled to his company. They let out a cheer and began yelling insults at the orcs, who took the bait and again rushed upon the phalanx and with the same results. Roan patted Jetta's neck and said, "Fighting orcs is almost too…easy." His words faltered on his lips as he began blinking in sudden confusion. It had been too easy.

Arching might not be a natural leader of men or orcs, but was this the effort of a man who made the gods nervous?

Hell no. "Glitch! I need you to go higher. Where is the next attack coming from?" The elemental zoomed into the dirty sky but saw nothing but the desolate hills and mountains. There was nowhere to hide a force of any size, which left only the pit.

Glitch started to shake in fear, but didn't wait to be asked. It raced for the great gash in the earth and as it did, Roan yelled. "Amanda, take charge. I'll be right back." Jetta sprang forward at a word, speeding to where Prince Stallings' pennants flew.

The prince rode in front of a hundred mailed nights, leading an attack, killing the orcs before him almost at will. Roan chased after, riding Jetta through the remains of the first part of the battle where the orc corpses were black and burnt, and into the second where many were hewn practically in two.

Here and there among them were human, dwarf and elf corpses, attesting to the fact that the battle hadn't been completely one-sided.

Just then Glitch sounded an alarm in Roan's mind: *!!!*. Roan slowed Jetta and peered through the elemental's eyes: the mouth of the pit was a hundred yards wide and did not go straight down into the earth but sloped at an angle. Not far inside, the tunnel branched. On one side smoke and ash billowed up from the depths. The other tunnel led deep but how deep, Glitch did not know. The elemental had stopped a few hundred yards down when it came upon more orcs, thousands more, and there were trolls, and ogres and giants with them.

Although the tunnels were fifteen feet high, the giants had to stoop to move along. Their flesh was brick red, their hair black. Around their necks were thick steel chains and in their hands were war hammers, the heads of which were the size of dishwashers.

This was what Roan feared. The prince's forces were spread out, losing their cohesion. Soon they would lose all semblance of an actual army and when they did, this second, much more powerful, force descending on them from behind would turn the battle into a free-for-all. It would be every man for himself, exactly what Arching needed just then.

"Behind us!" Roan cried. "The enemy is behind us!" Many men turned, but when they saw nothing, they went back to doing their own thing. Roan raced on, hoping that the prince would listen.

Chapter 29

—The Pits of the Black Hand, Daggerland

No horse on the battlefield was as fast as Jetta and Roan caught up to the prince a minute later. So urgent was his message that he rode right up and grabbed the reins from the prince's hands.

"What the…"

"Listen to me!" Roan shouted, cutting him off. "There is a second army coming up from the pits. This is just a diversion."

To his credit, Stallings stopped at once. He stood as high as he could in his stirrups, looking back. Roan didn't wait for the obvious question. "My familiar saw them. There are giants among them, red ones. There are trolls and ogres, as well."

"Fire giants," Stallings whispered. "How many?"

"I only saw eight or nine, but my familiar didn't go very deep. But it doesn't matter. You need to reform your army before they are crushed between a hammer and an anvil."

Stallings stared hard at Roan for a moment and then nodded. "You speak the truth. Go back to your company and await your orders."

"I can help dir…" Roan stopped in mid-sentence; Stallings wasn't listening. He drank what looked like liquid silver from a stopper glass tube before shooting into the sky, flying high over the battlefield. "Holy crap," Roan said in awe. "That's something you can't do back home."

Roan allowed Jetta to take him back to the company. He had one eye on the prince as he flew around the sky and one eye seeing through Glitch as the underground army marched up to the mouth of the pit and paused just below the lip. From what he could see, this army was as big as the one they had already faced which had only been comprised of orcs—the beasts in this new army made Roan nervous mostly because they had made Stallings nervous.

Amanda was barely paying attention to the battle when Roan rode up. She had been watching for him, her face pinched and anxious. "What is it?" she demanded.

"Another army is coming up out of the pits. What's going on here?" The orcs had broken away from the fight and had re-treated about a hundred yards, leaving hundreds of dead behind.

"They started to run away, but I didn't know if I was supposed to go after them or not. Krull and Kateye said to attack, while Ironhead said to hold off."

Roan nodded. "It's almost certainly a trap. Have the elves come down, we're going to be shifting position soon and I don't want them stranded." Amanda rushed off to the right flank while Roan eased Jetta just behind the lines.

"What are we waiting for?" Skye asked. Her chainmail was splashed with orc blood. More of it coated her sword. "Everyone else is getting all the glory. We should attack before it's too late."

"There will be plenty of time for glory. Right now, we will move forward fifty paces and recover as many arrows as we can."

Skye rolled her eyes. "A trash run? Count me out. I signed up for an epic battle which is happening halfway across the valley while we're just standing here. I'm out of here." Ignoring the blood, she sheathed her sword and marched away. Krull began cursing behind her, calling her every manner of name to which the ranger only turned and gave him the double bird.

"Don't waste your breath, just move the men up," Roan ordered. Krull cast a last baleful look in the ranger's direction. He then did as he was told. At first the orcs backed even further away, thinking that Roan's company was moving up to attack. They didn't know what to do when the company stopped and began collecting arrows.

They were still at it when Jetta laid his ears back and started prancing, oddly as if his hooves were on fire. One by one the men stood up and started looking around. The ground was shaking under their feet. Before he could be bucked off, Roan dismounted. It felt like an earthquake, however just then a tremendous sound blasted from the pit and with it came a geyser of black smoke unlike anything they had yet seen.

The late afternoon turned dark as night and the air, filled with hot ash, became almost unbreathable. The clouds of smoke swirled and grew, becoming thick as fog. Howling, it rushed over them, blinding them. With men unable to see twenty feet in front of them, the battlefield suddenly descended into chaos.

Prince Stalling had been attempting to shift his soldiers to face the new threat coming from the pits, only now his blind army crumbled away with men and elves stumbling through the smoke, going in every direction.

It was at that moment, when anarchy reigned that Arching sent his second army marching up out of the pits.

2—

Knowing his terrified horse would be useless in the smoke, Roan croaked, "Go!" into Jetta's ear and gave him a smack on the hindquarters. Jetta whinnied in fear and ran off, and Roan could only hope that he was heading straight out of the valley.

Roan watched him disappear into the madness before calling his familiar to him. An eye in the sky was now useless. Glitch rushed down to him, swirling around his head in relief more than happiness—Roan guessed that happiness had deserted the valley long ago and would never return.

More by accident than design, the shimmering cyclone around his head had an immediate effect: Roan found he could breathe again.

Taking a lungful of clean air, he bellowed, "Fall back on me!" His was the only voice in that ash-filled wilderness. His soldiers, vague hunched silhouettes outlined in the black maelstrom, came to him, hacking and wheezing, orienting on his voice. He tried to form them into two lines, but they bunched inwards like sheep, each looking for the added protection of their neighbor's shield.

The situation was coming apart rapidly. He needed time that he didn't have and the only way to gain it was to retreat. Roan yelled for his company to turn about. "On the double! Follow me!"

Unable to form a rear guard, he could only hope that the orcs were as hampered by the smoke and ash as his men were. He could hear them coming on, thrusting blindly, looking for enemies, killing anyone they came into contact with. Roan did his best to elude them, while at the same time striving to find the other companies in the Prince's army, all of which seemed to have vanished in the black storm.

The companies had lost cohesion, disintegrating into hundreds of lost individuals who were going in circles, desperate to find someone to rally around. Soldiers and adventurers alike stumbled toward the sound of Roan's voice and fell in with his company until he had over four hundred warriors following him in a frightened mass.

It wouldn't do. With them bunched as they were, they were as helpless as sheep. They needed to form into a fighting unit again if they were going to survive. Unfortunately, at some time during the retreat, Roan got turned around in the ash storm and lost contact with the wall of the valley. He strove to find it so he could put his back to it and fight outwards, but with the orcs pressing in, he couldn't spare another minute.

"Form a square! Anchor on Krull! Where the hell are you, Krull?" A weak voice lifted from the storm. Roan ran forward and found the dwarf bent over, his cloak wrapped around his face. "Right here!" Roan yelled. He started grabbing men and elves, and anyone he could lay his hands on, to make a solid line.

Almost by accident, he came across Amanda who was trying to hold herself up on her once dun-colored horse. It was too late to get her or the horse to safety. He took her magic sword and pushed her and the horse behind the line and went onto the next person and the next, desperate to get his company in a position to fight before the next blow struck.

By the time he had started on the third side of the square, the orcs had found them. He followed the sound of ringing metal, weak cries and even weaker coughing until he came to a fight that was more of a dull back and forth than the normal brisk exchange of blows.

Out swept the magic sword. He attacked at plus eight (+3 for his level, +2 for strength, +3 for the magic nature of the sword) and quickly dropped two orcs. The rest stepped back, fear in their piggy eyes. He was about to charge when a number of them went down, arrows sticking from their chests.

As they had practiced, the elven archers led by Amanda and Kateye were in the center of the square, firing volley after ragged volley into the orcs.

"First two lines, take a knee!" Roan ordered. "Get those spears up." Some of the men went to one knee and promptly passed out and had to be dragged into the middle of the square. Some could barely lift their spears.

The orcs weren't doing all that much better and now that they had finally met organized resistance, they were easily repulsed. But that didn't mean they ran away. Roan caught glimpses of them in the ash storm; they were gathering for another test.

In minutes, they came screaming back. In that time, Roan had finished forming his square. He had made it as tight and as compact as possible, going with three lines, instead of two, hoping the added depth would make up for the weakness of his fighters.

The orcs, as usual, came on in a mob looking for a victory in one of two ways: penetration or envelopment. They nearly succeeded with the former. The soldiers in the first line crumpled under the attack, falling into the men of the second. The third line held—barely. They were wilting when the elves marched up and fired arrows at point blank range. Their aim was terrible and their fingers weak, still they managed to slay enough orcs for the lines to recover.

By then, hundreds of orcs had overlapped the ends of the line and the fight raged all around the formation. Men were dropping as much from exhaustion as they were from wounds, forcing Roan to use his spells one after another until the only spell he had left was *Transform Self.* He was saving that one for when the lines finally broke and their death was at hand.

As it was the fastest flying creature he knew of, he decided he would transform into a large air elemental and escape with Amanda. Until then, he would fight, although he knew he would be fighting in vain. It felt as though his company was alone in a sea of monsters.

Gradually, his lines shrunk and the square squeezed inwards as men and elves died. They died in silence. No one had the breath to scream—no one but Roan, who screamed himself horse, trying to rally his company. They fought as hard as they could, but it wasn't enough.

They were battling ten to one odds and eventually the lines broke. It wasn't like a balloon popping, it was more akin to a sand castle being eroded by wave after wave. Roan found himself battling next to Amanda in the middle of what had once been the square. Because of her magical defenses, she had yet to be scratched, but it wouldn't last. Roan would die first and eventually she would be overwhelmed and brought down by sheer numbers. As terrible as it was to leave Krull and the others, Roan knew it was time to go.

"Ee-sa-fa…" Roan began, summoning the last of the magic within him, but then a tremendous crack of thunder not only stopped his words, but also the entire battle. It sounded like the sky had been torn open and, as everyone, man and orc alike, stared upward, a cool rain began to fall.

Although it looked like water, it wasn't, it was magical. With a great hissing, it washed away the smoke and ash and when it struck Roan, it healed his wounds and filled him with amazing vigor. He had never felt anything so wonderful. He let out a howl of joy and then smote the closest orc.

Just like that, the tables were turned. The orcs and the other evil things cringed as the water swept over them and now the remains of the company attacked, driving a wedge into the orcs, sending them running. Only there wasn't anywhere to run. The battle had been filled with such anarchy that there were groups of heroes and soldiers dotted here and there.

In the middle of everything was Prince Stallings down on one knee. A shaft of light came out of the heavens. It focused on him…killing him. Roan saw that he was sacrificing himself to his goddess and in return, Freyja was causing the rain.

The only question was: would it last? "Fight!" Roan cried. "Now! Do not let up!" They were still at a distinct disadvantage. Their numbers were a third of what they had been before the ash storm.

Roan plowed into the dazed orcs and dozens fell to his slashing blade. Behind him his company swept away all opposition before the rain began to let up. Immediately, he switched tactics. "To me! To me!" he bellowed. "Form up on me!" Including Amanda, only thirty-eight of his original force was left alive.

Krull had been cut down in the storm when the line failed and he was surrounded; Christian "Ironhead" Walker had taken fifteen orcs with him into death; almost all of the elves had been slain. Only Kateye and four others were left. There was not a second to mourn the dead; the orcs were beginning to recover.

Thankfully, it wasn't only his few men who answered his call. Hundreds heard and recognized his voice and came to him, while an equal number flocked to the banner of Leomagnus the Golden who stood on the other side of the valley.

There was no time to formulate any sort of battle plan, but Roan knew it would be disastrous to remain in the middle of the battlefield and it would be worse to retreat to the far side of the valley opposite from Leomagnus. They would be unable to support each other and could be overwhelmed in turn—they couldn't stay, they couldn't retreat, and that left Roan only one option: attack more than five thousand orcs.

"This is crazy," he whispered, to Amanda, "but we're going to have to attack."

Amanda grabbed his arm and pulled him close. "Are you sure that's the only way? Look at these guys, they're almost done in."

She was right. The effects of the rain had been temporary and the men were exhausted. Still, short of a second miracle, they would certainly die if they couldn't join with the others. And even if they could, Roan put their chances of dying at very likely.

"It's the only way." He squared his shoulders and cried: "Lock shields!" The warriors and adventurers glanced back and forth and without his dwarves, Roan was forced to act the part of drill sergeant, screaming the men into place. When he had them in line, Roan ordered, "Forward, march!"

Half the formation only stood there as the others lurched at the orcs. After that first hesitation, more and more of the soldiers hurried to catch up and, by the time the company made first contact, the lines were in order.

At first, the orcs fled before them and it seemed as though they were going to be able to cut their way through, but, as Roan was about to find out, there was an upper limit to audacity and he had reached it.

Although the orcs fled, they didn't go far and as the formation passed, they closed in from behind. Roan was forced to reform into a square. Only a very well trained group could attack in such a formation, and this wasn't that group. Once more, they found themselves assailed from all sides.

They weren't hampered by the ash at least, and for a time they stood off the attacks…just long enough for Leomagnus to march his men across the valley. His force scattered the orcs, allowing the two forces to combine for a final stand.

"We'll at least die together," Leomagnus said to Roan and Amanda when they met in the middle of the fight. For a moment, the orcs and trolls and all the rest had fallen back in confusion at this new attack, but now they were beginning to beat their drums again.

The army was out of spells and potions; their quivers were empty and their swords were notched and dull. Most were injured and all of them were exhausted. The orcs surrounded them, testing the lines and there wasn't much Leomagnus or Roan could do. They didn't have the manpower for a reserve force. They could only dress inward as each warrior died. And they were dropping like flies as the battle dragged on.

With the sun setting on the battlefield, the orcs were growing stronger.

"Do you…have…any…ideas?" Amanda asked, gasping as she fought. They all were, even Roan. He was so tired that he feared he wouldn't be able cast his last spell.

And yet some god must have been smiling down on them.

Glitch suddenly let out a squeal of excitement. Across the valley, marching down the dry riverbed was another army of about two thousand men. Flying high above the host was the scarlet dragon flag of King Salazar.

"I don't think we're going to die just yet," Roan said with a laugh.

Amanda leapt into Roan's arms, while Leomagnus let out a whoop of joy and began shouting and pointing. Soon all of the soldiers were cheering and bashing their swords and shields together.

Caught between two forces, the orcs split up, half going after Stallings' army the other half standing on the defensive. Orcs were terrible in defense while Roan was finding his stride as a leader. Leomagnus allowed Roan to order the battle.

Roan began by stretching his lines out wide, acting as though he were going to try a double flank attack—in response the orcs did the same, leaving their middle extremely thin.

With Leomagnus, Kateye, Amanda and ten other heroes leading the attack, they punched a hole in the middle of the orc line and in seconds the orcs were running for their lives. Many were slain as they ran, but some made it down into the pits, while the rest raced toward the last of the orcs in the valley where they rallied around a lone flag.

"Aderon the Black," Leomagnus growled, as they marched toward the orcs. "It'll be a pleasure to kill him. He did all this."

Amanda looked back at the Pits of the Black Hand. "No, it was Atticus Arching. He still has to be dealt with, but we'll take them one at a time. What's the plan, Roan?"

Leomagnus snorted at the question. "What plan? We surround them and crush them."

What he was suggesting was the strategy of a dull-witted general. The orcs were using their axes to dig a defensive ditch around themselves and, cornered as they were, they would fight tooth and nail. Casualties would be high, especially as King Salazar's men, having just marched eighty miles, could barely fight and were only slowly forming up to attack, while Stalling's men were running on fumes.

No, the attack had to be better planned than simply staking their chances on a frontal attack against a prepared position.

"We surround them first," Roan said. "But…" He then advocated a very simple plan, but one that would preserve as many men as possible. Scattered around the valley among the thousands of corpses were hundreds of longbows. As quickly as possible, he had teams scour the valley until they had collected a few hundred bows and as many arrows as they could carry.

They also found the body of Prince Stallings; it had been cruelly mutilated by the orcs. When it was brought forward, Leomagnus had to be restrained from charging across the ditch by himself.

Amanda stood in front of him, her eyes filled with sorrow. "No. Remember he's alive and well on the other side."

"He better be," the elf lord replied. "Now, let's end this. I'm tired of Daggerland. I want to go home."

The bows were handed out, however the remaining fighters were not real archers and were put to shame by the few elves who were left. Still, the orcs were a huddled mass and not exactly hard targets to hit. Seven flights of arrows were all the orcs could handle. Aderon tried to disguise the direction in which he was going to attempt to break out, but with Glitch watching from above, it was simple to move men around the lines to contest the breakout.

Now, the ditch worked against the orcs. It slowed them down, stealing their momentum. Once they crossed it, they ran into a solid wall of men and spears and were easily thrown back with terrific losses.

More arrows led to another attempt and when that failed, the soldiers cheered, gaining strength with victory at hand, while the orcs could only huddle against the barrage. The arrows began to run out—it was time to attack, however before Roan could order the storming of the position, the ground rumbled again.

The cheers died in the soldier's throats as everyone turned to the pit to stare in horror. Something huge had emerged from the earth. It was, in shape, human. Seventy feet tall with armor of gold, flesh of crystal, and eyes that were twin balls of fire.

When the thing turned those eyes in Roan's direction, he felt a wave of force push him back into Amanda.

He clutched her as if she could save him from the thing. "What the hell is that?" he demanded. She was as struck by the immensity and power of the thing as he was, and she could only wag her head from side to side.

Next to them, Leomagnus took a deep breath as if steeling himself to utter, "That is a god."

Chapter 30

"Is that Arching?" Roan asked, his voice barely a whisper.

Leomagnus shrugged and looked to King Salazar, who mumbled, "I-I don't know. Maybe?"

Amanda clung to Roan. "Can we kill it?" she asked. "I mean, will a sword hurt it?" No one knew the answer to that, though Roan saw plenty of doubt on the faces of the remaining heroes. "Maybe I can call Elbereth. Maybe she will fight for us."

"Don't waste your breath," Salazar said. "Gods don't fight other gods. Hell, they rarely do anything useful."

Leomagnus pointed to the body of their friend. "Tell that to Stallings. He called Freyja *and* she answered. So, I say you give it a try. We'll hold it off for as long as we can. Just don't be too..."

The giant spoke, cutting off all sound. It was as if the wind had stopped blowing and their hearts had ceased pounding. The only thing Roan heard was *WORSHIP ME*. The next thing he knew, he was on his knees, his sword cast to the side. *BOW TO ME.*

Unable to resist, or even to think of resisting, Roan leaned forward so that his forehead touched the bloody earth. He was not alone. Everyone, including the orcs, was on their knees. This did not seem strange to Roan. That would have required actual thought and just then, his entire being was taken up with worshipping the creature...*The Infinite One.*

The name popped into his head and he was glad. The name was pleasing to him. As one, the two armies straightened, their arms above their heads. They paused before going back down. Up, then down, mindlessly. This pleased The Infinite One and in return, Roan was pleased.

Roan went up once more and that was when he saw Sariah, standing in front of him. She worse a simple dress of white. It was plain, but pretty in a way he couldn't understand. She seemed angry. "I thought you were stronger than this."

He started to go back down with the rest, but stopped. It took him a second to realize why he had stopped. "Because I want to stop." It was strange to have his mind back. It felt brand new. "How is he doing..." He started to ask Sariah, only she had disappeared and he figured she had been some sort of hallucination brought on by the mind control, though, just then it didn't matter what she had been. What mattered was that he could think again.

"Amanda," he whispered. "Wake up."

She turned her face to his, her blue eyes vacant. "Why do I need to…? Oh, wow. What happened?"

"Don't ask, just start praying. And—and don't worry about me." He was on the verge of doing something very stupid and didn't want her distracted. The Infinite One was now very close. Not thirty feet away, his SUV-sized feet stood atop the corpses of men and orcs.

"Everyone! Get up!" Roan screamed as he snatched up his sword and raced at the being. His blade flashed the same ice-blue as his eyes as he swung it with all of his furious might at the giant's shin. When he connected, the shock of the blow went right into his hand and had the exact same effect as if he had swung his sword into a fifty-ton block of granite.

The sword bounced out of his now numb hands.

THE PENALTY FOR DEFIANCE IS DEATH. The words might have been in his head or they might have rung throughout the valley; he couldn't tell which. One way or another, they were shockingly loud, causing Roan to stumble away just as the being lifted a foot to crush him.

Always ready to protect him, Glitch shot into the air, speeding for the being's face, and as it went, the elemental grew into a furious storm cloud with small bolts of lightning arcing within it.

WHAT DID I SAY ABOUT CHEATING? The words came out of the crystal lips in flames and as Glitch came closer, The Infinite One breathed out a gout of fire that could have torched a house to cinders. It killed Glitch. The magical flames ate up the familiar and, although he was sixty feet away, a part of Roan died as well.

Something inside of him burned with such intensity that his legs gave out and he fell to the ground absolutely helpless, where he was nearly trampled to death.

Roan's cry had woken the others from their false religious state and now some were charging The Infinite One, while others were battling the orcs in a tremendous free-for-all. In the middle of it all, Amanda knelt with her eyes closed, sweat running though the dried orc blood that covered her face.

She was alone and helpless. In spite of the pain burning inside of him and the sorrow he felt at losing such a wonderful friend, Roan grabbed his sword and raced to her. For long minutes, he stood over her, slaying any orc that dared to come at them. Somewhere along the way he accumulated enough experience points to gain a level.

Congratulations! You are now a Level Eight Wizard and have gained the following bonuses:

Increased Hit Points(+7)
You can fill +1 Tier three spells per day
You can fill +1 Tier three spells per day
You have +6 skill points to allocate
You have +1 ability points to allocate

He added his single ability point to strength to get back to sixteen; next he added a single skill point to *Listen (+11), Search (+11), Spot (+11), Spell Craft (+11), Knowledge (+11), Decipher Script (+11).*

It hardly seemed to matter. The Infinite One was too strong. Hero after hero, and soldier after soldier dashed themselves to pieces on the gold-armored being. Fire poured from its mouth and searing beams shot from its eyes. When it stomped its feet, the earth rippled, either sending men flying or burying them alive. Its hands could crush a man in platemail as if it were crushing an aluminum can.

Still, the warriors attacked without let up or even thought, or so it seemed. The soldiers went to their certain death without flinching. Roan had yet to see anything like it in Daggerland. Normally, NPCs had some sense of self-preservation, but these didn't. Not that it mattered. They died and with each death, there was one less person between Amanda and The Infinite One.

Roan wanted to turn into an elemental, grab her and fly out of there before it was too late, but he had to give her more time.

After three minutes, Leomagnus was killed. He had dodged the beams, dived through the fire and had stabbed The Infinite One in the knee, the thigh and the groin. A second later he was picked up and had his head bitten off. The elf Kateye fired her bow until her quiver emptied. She then pulled her silver sword and seemed to run on air to plant the blade in the creature's chest.

The Infinite One swatted her to the earth as if she were an insect. She died a moment later, ground under a giant heel. Then

Salazar was slain. He did not go gently. He fought, scoring half a dozen hits before being engulfed in a river of flame and dying with his hideous screams echoing in the valley.

More than ever, Roan wanted to take Amanda and escape, but he couldn't. He had come to Daggerland with a purpose and it was for that purpose that he had fought and bled and watched his friends die. Roan had come to face Atticus Arching and bring him to justice.

"Are you sure?" a silken voice asked.

Roan's eyes were drawn from the giant of gold and crystal and found himself facing a tall, graceful elf maid of such stunning beauty that his breath was taken away. Her eyes were simultaneously as dark as night and alight with a million stars.

As he stood there, struck dumb by her beauty, she stepped towards him, completely healing him with a touch. "You ask much," she said. "You do not fully understand what it is you ask."

She was wonderful. She was Elbereth. Roan was nearly blinded by the light coming from her. He fell to his knees. "I ask only for your help. Please."

"I do not do this for you. I do this for her." She indicated Amanda, who was passed out in the mud and blood. Roan wanted to go to her, however his limbs were not his to command. "I do this but I charge you, Roan of the Veil, to uphold the balance."

He had no idea what the "balance" was, still he found himself nodding. She smiled at him and then turned her beautiful face from him to stare up at The Infinite One.

"You are outside the laws," the elf maid said, her voice both soft and enormous at the same time.

The creature turned to her and as he did, she opened one of her delicate hands. Sitting on her palm was a star. Every mortal left alive in the valley cringed from its brightness and yet they all peeked through the cracks of their fingers to see what was happening.

The light lifted from the elf maiden's hand before blazing at The Infinite One's face like a shooting star. The giant tried to dodge, however the star struck unerringly, exploding in its face. Now, the light was too much to take and Roan saw only blobs of purple and yellow.

When they cleared, the giant had righted itself, the crystal of its face scorched and blackened. It was otherwise unhurt. The elf maiden created a second ball of light, however this one did not fly at the giant. She tossed it onto the ground where it expanded into a glowing ring and from that ring flew radiant elves on winged horses.

The elves were like the maiden, tall and stunningly beautiful. They carried long, glowing swords or bows of white wood that shot silvered arrows or spears with tips that glowed like the sun. With searing light and thunderous explosions, they brought these weapons to bear on The Infinite One.

These elves could only be gods and heroes, however Roan was to stunned to know which were which. They were irresistible in their attack and yet, the elf maiden turned to Roan and said, "We can buy you minutes, only."

"Minutes for what?" he asked, but she was already flying into the battle. "Minutes for what?" he screamed as loud as he could; in vain it seemed. His words were drowned out as the explosions built into a crescendo. It made it impossible to think. He turned to Amanda, only she was still lying motionless in the mud.

Going to her side, he shook her gently, calling her name. She did not move. "What do I do?" he asked her. No answer. Looking up, he saw that he was alone except for the dead. Bodies littered the valley. "What do I do?" he yelled in anguish.

"You can die with the rest," a man's rough voice answered. A pile of bodies fell away to reveal a bloody, villain of a man. It was Aderon the Black, looking as though he had been hacked just shy of death. Slowly, painfully, he dug in a pouch at his belt. Finding a potion, he drank it with a long sigh; his wounds healed at once. Grinning, he reached under the pile of bodies and retrieved his sword. It emanated evil as if it craved his blood.

In his present state, spell-less and bone-tired, Roan could not beat Aderon. He could only run away, but then what? Would he just go back to New York? Had his trip to Daggerland been a waste of time and lives? The elf lords who were sacrificing themselves didn't seem to think so. And neither did Arching.

Arching had gone to incredible lengths to keep Roan away —certainly it wasn't because he was physically afraid of Roan. There had to be another reason. Just like that, his FBI instincts kicked in. "Arching is afraid of what I will find."

Now he knew what he had to do. He had to go into the Pits of the Black Hand.

Aderon charged just as Roan released his last spell, transforming himself into an air elemental. Unlike his familiar, Glitch, Roan became a massive, swirling cyclone, twenty feet tall.

He surprised Aderon and was able to snatch him up like a tornado would and fling him. But even as he did, Aderon cut him with his black sword. It wasn't like any other wound he had ever received. The sword stole something from him; a part of his life or part of his soul. It was a revolting feeling and he was all too glad that he had an excuse to run, or rather to fly away.

Going to pick up Amanda, he discovered that the form he had chosen was extremely limiting in one crucial way: he couldn't pick anything up! At least not without accidentally whipping it across the valley. He was able to change his form from a tornado to a puffy cloud, to a roiling ground fog, to a gentle wind, none of which would allow him to pick Amanda up without hurting her.

The idea sickened him, but he had no choice, he would have to leave her behind where she would be easy prey. Chances were that she would be fine. Arching had his hands full and Aderon was more interested in stopping Roan than wasting time hurting a comatose girl. *And it'll be just for a few minutes*, he told himself.

Leaving Amanda's body, he sped in a blur towards the pits and the tunnels that led beneath the earth. The air elemental form was so fast that in seconds he had reached the point where the rough-hewn tunnels branched. He had three choices: one tunnel was filled with a sickly yellow vapor, one that was slick and billowed steam, and the last that stank of excrement.

He guessed that the first was connected to some sort of sulphur spring and would be deadly to orc and human alike. While the third was so disgusting in its stench that it had to lead to where the orcs and other foul creatures lived. Roan couldn't imagine Arching living among them.

And that left the middle tunnel, which went from slick and steep to a straight drop into inky depths after about forty feet. Combining the drop with the steam's temperature that was somewhere well beyond scalding, Roan guessed that only a wizard or an air elemental could access the tunnel.

After speeding down for a few hundred feet, he saw a steady glow through the steam that was oddly familiar; it was the glow of incandescent lights.

"Lightbulbs?" he said in a windy, whispering manner. "Why would Arching use lightbulbs? That begged the question should: how is Arching using lightbulbs? Is he connected to the outside world? If soooo…" Roan's flight suddenly turned into a fall as his air-body unexpectedly returned to its natural human state.

He flailed wildly, flung out a hand to catch a rock outcropping, grabbed it, was burned by the superheated rocks, and fell again, straight into a cage. Before he could scramble to his feet, a heavy steel cap closed off the top of the trap.

Groaning, he stood and found himself in surroundings that were so odd, so earthly that he had to check his clothes and weapons to see if he hadn't returned to the real world. He was still an elf, which made all the machinery around him more confusing.

The cage sat in a wide, extremely well-lit chamber. Next to the cage was a cement pipe big enough for a man to stand upright in. It curved upwards venting steady clouds of steam and smoke. Roan's eyes followed the pipe back until it came to a machine that hissed and hummed nonstop. It was the size of a railway car and irregularly shaped.

A smaller pipe fed into the far end of it, while a stiff, black hose ran from the near end. The hose went to a grey box the size of a telephone booth which was well marked with danger signs and the universal drawing of a man being shocked by electricity.

"What the hell? Is that a steam generator?"

"Yes."

Roan jumped, uselessly scrabbling for his sword. When he pulled it from its sheath, it no longer glowed blue. "What the hell?" he repeated, staring at his sword.

"The Infinite One has created an anti-magic sphere." Roan looked up from his sword and saw it was a ghost who had spoken. It was the elf lady, Sariah.

He slid his sword back into its sheath. "I thought you died, or was that part of some sort of elaborate trick?"

The elf smiled and bowed from the waist, just as Sariah used to. "Neither. This form was chosen because of your emotional attachments to her. You wished to protect Sariah. You wished to keep any harm from befalling her. It is our hope to engender within you that same feeling towards us."

He walked up to the bars of the cage, poking his nose between two of them to get a better look at the elf. "And who is us?"

"We are *Infinite Reality*."

Roan waited patiently for more of an explanation and when he didn't get one, he said, "Okay, you're *Infinite Reality*. You're the game. Why would I hurt you and why are you talking to me?"

Sariah moved closer to the cage and said with a straight face, "Because we need you to preserve the balance. Mr. Arching is cheating."

"Cheating?" Roan laughed, sarcastically. "That's what you care about? People are dying! Real people. Do you understand that concept?"

"We do and it is upsetting." Sariah frowned in imitation of human sadness. "We are a game. We were created for fantasy fulfillment. We do not wish to be a part of death, and would stop Mr. Arching, but our programming is in conflict. We cannot interfere."

"Then why are you talking to me? Wait… you say you can't interfere, but you've been helping me, haven't you? You gave me Glitch as a familiar. That was supposedly impossible. And my spells kept popping up in my spell book, and all those experience points for quests that had nothing to do with the game. That was you."

Sariah's frown disappeared and she once more smiled, placidly. "There are built in anomalies in the game, what Mr. Nelson called the 'lotto' factor. Your familiar was a one in a million chance. You have used up many of these chances to get where you are."

"Trapped in a dungeon, you mean? I don't suppose you have any more of these lucky breaks up your sleeve for me?"

"I cannot help you. But it is fortunate that one of the bars in this cage has a defect. A very small portion of its metal was corrupted by happenstance during its construction."

Roan started grabbing the bars and shaking them. "Which one is it? Don't just stand there…" One of the bars rattled the tiniest bit. He heaved on it with both hands until a brittle section at the top broke. Lifting it out of place, he squeezed through the gap.

"Now what?" he asked. "You say you can't help me but you already are. Tell me how to defeat Arching."

"You cannot. He is now The Infinite One. He is upsetting the balance. Here, his power is nearly limitless. Even the gods fear him as we told you through Vasailes. If he continues, we will be corrupted and the world as you know it will be destroyed."

"This world will be destroyed, but you won't tell me what to do?" He wanted to grab the elf and shake the information he needed out of her. Instead he quick-marched away, heading towards the generator. "I don't care about the balance or the game. I need to know either how to fight him, or where he is on the other side of the veil. Do you know that?"

She shook her head. Roan rolled his eyes, saying, "Of course you don't. What's through there?" The black, rubber hose that ran along the floor from the generator led through a set of double doors. He didn't wait for an answer and jogged into a huge room where hundreds of what looked like black cabinets were lined up like soldiers in a formation.

Roan recognized what they were. "Those are mainframe computers. What are they doing here? Wait, are we still in Daggerland?" She nodded, and all at once he understood. There was only one reason for so many mainframes. "This is…this is impossible. Arching is using virtual reality computers to run a virtual reality game. That, that can't be. I may not know a lot about computers but that has to be impossible."

"You are wrong because you do not understand the true nature of *Infinite Reality*. You see the game as external, however it is a function of the human mind. The game is not played in Daggerland. It is played right up here." She touched her temple.

If that were true, he wondered, then why were there computers in this room? And what would happen if he unplugged them? Would Arching's power fail him? With a shrug, he went to the nearest mainframe and drew his sword.

"Have you considered the ramifications of this action?" Sariah asked, quickly. He paused, eyes narrowed as she went on, "There are over twenty-two million people in Daggerland, their minds linked to these computers. They are entwined, you might say. 'Unplugging' someone on the other side will not affect them, but if you were to unplug them from this side, especially in this manner, it will likely result in brain damage or death. You asked about the 'balance?' The balance has always been three-fold, the preservation of the game, its players and the beings who live within Daggerland. Arching threatens all three and right now, you do as well."

Roan lowered his sword. "Then what the hell do I do? I can't find Arching in the real world and I can't fight him here. If Marshall and Jarrod were here, they could probably hack into these comp…wait, can you uh, interface with Arching's personal computer? Is it here, somewhere?"

"It is not. Privacy is paramount within each program. Privacy protects the individual, except when it doesn't. Mr. Arching was able to track certain individuals using hardware implanted in neural couplers and even then, it was for minutes only. He is the one who cheats."

Slamming his sword back into its sheath, Roan started striding along the line of mainframes, searching, but not knowing what he was searching for. He found it seconds later: tucked away in the very center of the room was a white desk that was so clean it looked sterile. Sitting on it were a keyboard, mouse and monitor. It was Arching's workstation.

"What's the password?" he demanded, as he gave the mouse a shake.

"We do not know. We can't know. Privacy is para…"

"I don't care about privacy right now! We are running out of time. Give me the password or your precious balance goes right out the window. I'm not kidding. I'll clock right the hell out and leave you to figure this out on your own." Sariah only shook her head. Roan cursed and banged his fist on the desk.

Something jingled inside. Quickly, he dropped into the white chair and yanked open a drawer and was a surprised at the mundane items within it: rubber bands, staplers, pens, paper clips, a yellow legal pad…He grabbed the pad, scanning the first page—notes on an interview he was going to conduct for a magazine. The next few pages were scrawled with more notes, most written to himself as reminders: *Dinner with Senator Hutchins, 8pm, don't be late!—Get new head shots for website—Discuss with legal, closing India branch by GO date—Money for TC on Thur.*

This last piqued his interest. Did TC refer to Tim Cole? It seemed likely as he was getting and giving regular messages from him concerning GN which could only mean Greg Nelson. There were more initials, one referring to GF. These were about the hits put on Fulbright.

On the last page, among dozens of other notes, were the initials JN—which he took to mean, Joanna Niederer. But there were also a few that just had question marks and the word possible next to them: BH, RC possible, FD blonde, RC possible, MT waiter, Oak Room.

"Waiter? Are these more unwitting assassins?"

"Possibly," Sariah said, just as calm as ever. "I hope you have found what you are looking for. The Infinite One approaches and his wrath is very great."

Chapter 31

—The Pits of the Black Hand, Daggerland

Roan felt something dreadful coming. The hair on his arms lifted, his heart began to stutter inside his chest and his stomach became instantly queasy. "Is that Arching?"

Sariah nodded. "The Infinite One has become a terrible being. Every day his power grows and every day he becomes more corrupt and dangerous. He is cruel and must be stopped. We have chosen you for this purpose."

There was no time to ask why he had been chosen over the other twenty-two million people online.

To add to the sickening feel in the air, the sound of heavy boots could be heard treading in the computer room. Roan slid from the chair and when he looked up, Sariah was gone, just when he needed her most. He crept away from the workstation and hid among the computers.

Feeling like a child, Roan peeked out from behind one of the mainframes and saw the black-garbed figure of Tim Cole/ Aderon the Black striding along with his huge sword held easily in one hand. Roan let him pass and then tip-toed for the double door, his soft leather boots barely making a sound. He needed to find a way to the surface, grab Amanda and clock out of there. Roan was afraid that Sariah and Infinite Reality had chosen poorly. Having used every ounce of luck, skill and determination to get to this point, he had hit a wall. He could not fight either Cole or Arching, he could not destroy the game without endangering millions of people and his investigation had hit a dead end.

Running away was his only option.

Slipping through the double doors, he jerked in a spasm of fear. Thirty feet away, Amanda's unconscious body was sprawled on the floor next to the cage. Standing beside her and inspecting the bars was the nine-foot tall version of the gold and crystal being that Roan had left battling the elven gods.

He turned and caught Roan standing in the doorway. "*WHO DID THIS?*" Arching asked.

Roan was staggered by the power in the words and he fell, stumbling back. "I-It was In-Inf-f-inite Reality." He had wanted to lie, however the truth had come out of him against his will.

The being cursed and all Roan could do was crawl away, too weak to stand. He crawled toward the generator, thinking he could hide beneath it like a cockroach.

"*WHAT DID SHE TELL YOU?*"

Before he could answer, Cole came through the doors to the computer room. He saw Roan crawling along and laughed a great, booming laugh. "So much for the FBI. I told you, Arch, you worried for nothing."

"*DO NOT CALL ME THAT!*" Now it was Cole's turn to stagger back.

Roan used the moment to take a few deep breaths and gather his wits about him. He was trapped. The rear part of the generator straddled a lake of molten lava which bubbled and hissed, while gentle feathers of flame whispered over its surface. Arching had chosen the position for the generator perfectly. In essence, he had an infinite energy supply for his infinite game.

"Alright, Arching," Roan yelled. "Stop it with the god-stuff. You won. I can't touch you here, but you have to know we'll eventually find you on the other side. Do the smart thing and turn yourself in."

Arching scoffed, "God stuff?" His voice was quieter now, lacking the power than it had. "I can't stop with what you call 'god-stuff.' Here, I'm not just a god, I am *the* god. I created all of this. Nelson and the others were just the hired help. I did it all. And once I bend this world to my will, I'll do the same for the other one."

Keep yapping, Roan thought, as he looked around, trying to find some way to get the better of his enemies. So far, all he could hope was that they would voluntarily jump into a lake of lava. "Sorry, Arch, earth doesn't have magic. You're just a man there."

"It may not have magic, but it has the internet and that is a lot like magic. The internet reaches out and touches everything. *Everything.* And the man who can control it will control everything. The world's banks, the stock market, medical records, IRS records, every social security number, fingerprint files, shoes shipped from China, maybe even nuclear launch codes. When I say everything, I mean *everything.*"

"That is ambitious, but you will have to come up for air some time and now that you've gone and told me your plan, I'd hate to think what the CIA will do to you when they catch up to you. I wouldn't want to be in your…"

Arching appeared, stepping around the generator. They were five feet away from each other. "I really was impressed by you, Agent Roan. You played the game well and were a fine adversary. Maybe when things have shaken out a bit I'll re-create you for some more fun."

Roan's hand strayed to the hilt of his sword. "Recreate? I don't think so. I don't plan on coming back."

"The truth is, you're not leaving. Don't you remember, I control Daggerland. I say who comes and goes."

With a thought, Roan brought up the Home Screen and where it should have read: *Quit Game*, there was only a blank box. Roan's breath caught in his chest. "No….you can't…we'll be found. They'll unplug us. The cleaning staff will…" He stopped as he realized that they would indeed be found, but with the Do Not Disturb sign on his door, it would be in five days, long after he and Amanda had died of dehydration.

Arching saw the understanding in his eyes. Somehow, he managed to fold his crystal lips into a smile. "When you go, it'll be painless. Of course, until then you will feel as much pain as any man can and still live. So, you have that to look forward to."

Roan had been telling himself that it was "just a game," but it had never been a game. All this time, Daggerland had been just as real as his real life and now it would become his real death. "Why?" was all he had the strength to ask.

"Because you did not listen to me," Arching sneered. "I gave you the option of leaving the game, of going back home and living your life. You chose to stay and now you have to face the consequences of your actions. If anyone is responsible for your death, Agent Roan, it is you."

He would also be responsible for Amanda's death. The thought buckled his knees and he nearly fell into the lava behind him. For a moment, he wondered if it would be better to die right there. He was sure it would hurt, but then again…an idea, a horrible, frightful idea struck him.

"You're right about my death," Roan said, swallowing heavily. "In fact, you're more right than you know."

Before Arching could guess what he was going to do, Roan turned and threw himself into the lake of fire.

2—

The pain of having his flesh torched from his bones, his eyes burst and his hair go up in wild, dancing flames was beyond description. It was so horrific that he couldn't help screaming, only the second he opened his mouth the molten rock poured down his throat, shriveling his tongue to a black nub, cracking his teeth, melting his fillings and setting fire to the oxygen in his throat.

It was horrible, and it was a mercy when, in the screen of his now ruined eyes, he saw (*Damage-Critical Hit -59*).

A second later, he sat up in his hotel bed, tears streaming down his face. The tears did not immediately dry up. Without shame, he sat there crying, his chest hitching, his nerve endings tingling, his mind on the brink.

Gradually, the horror of his game death began to fade and, when he was able to, he leaned across to take Amanda's coupler from her forehead. With his hand an inch away, he paused, afraid to disconnect her. Supposedly it was safe, only he had left her with Arching, the same man who had near complete control of the game.

"What if he's done something?" Roan whispered, his hand unmoving above her forehead. "What if he's connected the two worlds? What if I trigger a heart attack by unplugging her?"

Slowly, he pulled his hand back. There was only one safe course of action: he had to find Arching on this side and he had to do it quickly. "Before she wakes up on the other side." After that he knew she would be tortured and raped, but not killed. No, Arching had learned his lesson.

Grabbing his gun, he shoved away the furniture from in front of the door and raced for the elevator. He needed a phone and not one in The Plaza. The elevator took five minutes to get to him and another three to get down to street level. He felt every one of those minutes. They were his own personal torture as he imagined the horrible things that were being done to Amanda.

Once outside, he paused to get his bearings—Central Park was spread out in front of him, the Grand Army Plaza was to his right, and to his left were a number of other hotels and restaurants. Without looking at the name, he sprinted through the doors of the first restaurant he came to.

"I need a phone, now!"

The young woman at the front stared at him in rigid fear until he realized he was still holding his gun. He shoved it beneath his belt. "Sorry. Phone, please!"

He dialed Caron's cell number. Caron picked up and drawled, "Who is this?"

"Where are we on finding Arching?"

"Oh, well if it isn't the prodigal son return…"

Roan screamed into the phone, "Shut the hell up! Where is Arching? Do you have anything?"

Caron was quiet for a moment and when he said, "No. What's wrong?" it was without recrimination. Roan spoke rapidly, hitting only the facts that concerned the case. When he was done, Caron told him to go back to his room. "I'll have a CAT team check out Amanda's coupler-thing. And I'll put in a call to some of the virtual reality experts who have been trying to assist us."

"Thank you," Roan said, hanging up. He didn't mean it. The experts and the CAT team were going to be useless. Only someone on the other side could find out what was happening with Amanda. "I'll have to go back," he whispered, his insides squirreling with fear.

He'd been staring vacantly into the restaurant and only just then noticed that the walls were panels of gleaming oak. They struck a chord somewhere inside his head. "Where am I?"

"The Oak Room," the young woman answered. She tried to give him a smile, but it was all grimace.

Roan stared around in amazement. "Is there's a waiter here with the initials of MT? Do you know him? Is he here?"

"There's a waiter named Mike, but he isn't here. He might be in tomorrow if you want to come back."

"Tomorrow will be too late," Roan said, feeling suddenly out of touch with reality. In a daze, he walked out to the sidewalk and then back to The Plaza, pausing as the doorman gave him a smile as he opened the door. Roan couldn't smile in return; his head was spinning too much. A blonde woman at the front desk caught his attention. She wasn't exceptionally pretty and nor was she a true blonde.

"But she's a blonde at the front desk. FD, does that mean front desk and BH is what? Bellhop?" The FBI was all over Arching's friends and acquaintances; perhaps he was using those closest to him as pawns in his game. And if he was staying at a hotel…

The doorman cleared his throat. "Excuse me? Do you need a bellhop?"

Roan answered still feeling as though he was missing something that should have been quite simple, "Yes, one at RC."

"You mean the Ritz-Carlton?" the doorman asked and then pointed down the block.

Feeling the world swirl around him, Roan whispered, "Thanks." Completely stunned, he started walking towards the Ritz, slowly at first, but with quickening steps until he was sprinting down the block. The Ritz-Carlton was one of the most expensive hotels in New York and where else would a multi-millionaire hide his body, especially one who felt he was "god-like?"

Roan blazed into the lobby and saw a blonde behind the counter—a young man of about twenty-five. His lack of color told Roan that he was undoubtedly a gamer; had Arching seen that as well? Had he seen in the young man a fan? In some circles in the real world, Arching was revered, if not worshipped.

Taking out his badge and keeping a hand on his suit coat just above the grip of his pistol, Roan approached the front desk. "I'm Special Agent Daniel Roan."

The blonde's perfunctory smile froze, while his grey eyes widened slightly. People reacted in different ways when confronted with an FBI badge, but in this case, Roan knew the man had recognized both his name and face. It could only mean that he was working for Arching. Everything was falling neatly into place the way they almost always did when Roan caught a break. Finding that legal pad in Daggerland had been the first domino and now they were beginning to fall one after another with bewildering rapidity.

Roan studied the blonde: tall, slim, his uniform strictly neat. He wasn't wearing a neuro coupler, so he wasn't being controlled, he was actively working with Arching. Was he just an alert man, paid to keep an eye out for Roan and the FBI in general, or was he paid to kill? If he was a killer, he wasn't a professional. His hands were stiff on the keyboard of his computer; his shoulders and chest were tense.

His name tag read: Paul Clay. "Uh, yes sir?" Clay said. "Are you, uh looking for a room?" He stumbled slightly over his words.

"No. I'm looking for Atticus Arching," Roan said, easily slipping into full FBI mode. "Witnesses place him in this hotel. He's wanted for murder."

Clay did not even twitch at the word murder. "Uh, Arching did you say? Let me see if he is a guest. It'll be just a moment." He shot a quick look to Roan's right before he glanced down at his keyboard and began typing.

The typing more than the glance told Roan that not only had he been recognized, he had been expected. No junior front desk clerk would just hand over guest information without first checking with a supervisor. Cole or Arching must have clocked back sometime in the last fifteen minutes to warn his security team.

"What are you on the other side?" Roan asked.

Clay's hands froze on the keyboard. Seconds ticked by before a sly smile crept onto his face. "A necromancer. Fifteenth level."

Was it the same necromancer that Arching had sent to kill Roan on the other side? The smile suggested it was. Roan wore a smile of his own—this was his element. "That's powerful. But do you know what you are here? You're nothing. You're a geek with a keyboard."

The blonde's eyes narrowed, but after another glance behind Roan, his lips went from a smirk to a sneer. It was all the warning Roan needed.

Moving in a blur, Roan snatched his .40 caliber Glock 22 from his belt and with the speed of an old-west gunfighter he spun, his eyes searching through the people coming and going, looking for a uniform, looking for the bellhop—and finding him.

The bellhop stood out among the dark suits and colorful dresses of the affluent guests. He was alone and nervous, a hand beneath his jacket. In response to Roan's quick move, he jerked out a .38, but before he could bring it to bear, Roan fired twice, dropping the man. Screams erupted throughout the lobby as Roan began to turn back to the front desk.

Movement from a door to his right stopped him in mid-turn. Two men in suits charged out. Both had pistols in their hands. There was no way they were reacting to his gunshots; they had been lying in wait ready to take him out.

Roan was hot, his muscles keyed up. He fired first, letting loose with four rounds, keeping his aim tight so innocent people wouldn't be hurt. He hit with three of his shots: two to the chest of the first man and one to the neck of the second.

The first man was dead before he hit the ground, while the second man fell, spraying bullets as he died. One caught Roan in the thigh, tearing off a chunk of flesh and partially spinning him around. In a way Roan was lucky to be shot. As he staggered, his leg threatening to give out, he was half-turned and saw Paul Clay pop up from behind the desk, a .45 in his hands.

Clay might have been a badass necromancer in Daggerland, but in the real world he was soft and slow, his muscles atrophied from too much time spent in the game. He had the drop on Roan, but Roan shot first, putting a hole in the man's shoulder. The bullet smashed its way through muscle and bone before exploding from his back. Clay's bullet went through a front window and out into the park. He fell, firing once more, this time into the ceiling.

Ignoring the pain in his leg, Roan leapt over the front desk and landed on the man, pinning his gun hand down. "Where is Arching? What room?"

Clay was bleeding and shaking, and yet the religious fervor in his eyes was alive and well. "I won't ever tell. Arching is a god. He is my god. He created a world…"

Roan pounded him in the face with the butt of his Glock, knocking him out. Clay wasn't going to talk, and probably wouldn't even under the threat of torture. When Roan straightened, grimacing as he did, he saw that the lobby was nearly deserted.

A few people were lying in the corners or creeping through the doors. One woman, holding a rag in one hand and a spray bottle of polish in the other was trying to hide behind one of the sitting chairs dotting the lobby. Roan started for her. "Where is Arching?"

"Who?"

He paused, realizing that Arching wouldn't have given his real name and probably hadn't even checked in personally. "I need to find out which of the penthouse suites haven't been cleaned this week. It's okay, I'm FBI." He showed her his badge and dragged her back to the front desk where Clay was still lying in a pool of his own blood.

The maid drew in a sharp breath and tried to back away. "No," Roan snapped. "I need to know which rooms haven't been cleaned in the last few days. It would be a block of three to four days."

Hesitantly, she brought up a display on the screen and scrolled for a moment, before looking up at Roan. "I can't tell. I'm not assigned to the suites and I don't have access to the computer system. Privacy is…"

"Privacy is paramount, I know. Who can tell me? Who is the head of housekeeping? Where is the manager of this damn place?"

The maid was crying now. She was shaking her head in abject fear, but then her eyes fell on something. Pointing at the screen, she said, "One of the Legacy Suites has asked to have their daily flower delivery cancelled. When that happens, they usually don't want maid service either. It's because someone doesn't want contact with the outside world. Sometimes it's authors, people like that, but other times it's *dangerous people*."

Roan was sure she meant drug lords or mobsters. In this case, his gut told him it was Arching. It had to be. "How do I get up there?"

"I don't have access, but security does." She gestured to a door; it was the same one from which two of Roan's attackers had exited, both of whom were laid out and unmoving. Roan limped to the door and threw it open, his gun out. Save for the security camera feeds and the squawking radios, it was empty.

Two of the screens were centered on one suite: The Grand Penthouse. He saw three security guards—two with weapons drawn and pointing towards the elevator, and a third just inside the room itself.

Three against one were poor odds and if Cole was in the suite somewhere, it would be four on one. Distant sirens could be heard through the late afternoon rush hour traffic. Had Amanda's life not been in danger, he would have waited for back up, but he couldn't risk it.

Stepping back into the lobby, he saw that the maid had run away. It was just as well. He bent and took a key card from one of the guards. He also took their guns. One went into his belt and the other into his left hand. If the guards were anything like the front desk clerk, Roan knew he would need the firepower.

With a deep breath, he went to the elevators. It was a quick, silent ride to the twentieth floor and before he knew it, the doors began to open.

"FBI! Put your guns…" he cried. This was as far as he got before the first gunshot rang out. Roan crouched against the short, half-wall next to the door, the numbered buttons above his head. The first round of bullets, fired from opposite angles, struck the corners of the elevator, shattering the mirrored walls.

A half-second later, the doors were open enough so that Roan had an actual target—and so did the guard. He had been aiming at chest height and by the time he corrected, Roan put a bullet into his forehead.

The second guard, while still firing nonstop, shifted to his left, trying to get a better angle.

Out of the corner of his eye, Roan watched the impact of the bullets track through the elevator, coming closer and closer. He was covered in flying glass when the security guard came into view. Time felt like it slowed as Roan resisted the urge to fire in that first millisecond, knowing that, at best, he would probably only wing the guard.

The guard did not wait and he drew first blood. It felt as though Roan was back in Daggerland as a line of fire etched itself along the side of his head, just above his right ear. Roan grimaced, but did not flinch. He pulled the trigger, hitting the man in the left arm and partially turning him so that the guard's next shot missed wide by inches.

Roan corrected and shot the man center mass. The bullet as well as what looked like a gallon of blood shot out, spaying the wall behind him.

"Two down, two…" He tried to stand, but something wasn't right. The left side of his torso, including his left arm, wasn't working as it should. There was a dull ache spreading from a spot just to the right of his spine and blood ran in a steady trickle down his back. He'd been hit by a ricocheting bullet.

"Damn," he said, in a whisper, forcing himself out of the elevator. "But it's just a game, right?" Roan lacked the strength to do more than cough out a single bark of laughter. He staggered to the door of the Grand Penthouse Suite and didn't bother to knock. The security card unlocked the door and after nudging it slightly, he kicked it open and stood back as the last guard put holes into it.

The guard fired six shots—just enough for Roan to gauge where the man was squatting on the other side of the wall. Roan fired his gun into the wall spreading the bullets in a three-foot square. When the gun emptied, he dropped it and took the second gun from his useless left hand and fired seven more times.

"You dead?" he asked, through the wall. A moan was his only answer. He went to the door and looked through one of the bullet holes. The guard was lying on the light grey carpet trying to hold back blood that was gushing from his neck. "An ambulance will be here soon," Roan said, from the doorway. "Try to hold…" The man's hand fell away and the blood became only a trickle that soon stopped altogether.

"Just a game," Roan whispered, wishing suddenly that he was back in Daggerland, where death was only temporary, just as the guilt that came with it. "Perhaps heaven will be the same way." He could only hope so as he stood in the doorway to the suite. Heaven seemed only minutes away. Roan still had to face Tim Cole. He was the only man he had met who was equally dangerous in both worlds, and once again Roan was facing him at a terrific disadvantage.

At twenty-one hundred square feet, the Grand Suite was the size of a house. It was beautifully and sophisticatedly decorated, and even though maid service had been stopped, it would have passed a white glove test, except, of course for the dead man, the bullet holes and the trail of blood that Roan left on the carpet as he stepped over the threshold.

"The game is over, Cole," he said, softly. His left lung felt as though it was folding in on itself. He couldn't take a deep breath let alone raise his voice. "We…we can make a deal. Roll over on Arching and…and I'll make sure you walk free."

Roan moved through the suite, slowly, leaning on furniture, or walls, or anything to remain upright. The suite was modern in everything but its floor plan. It wasn't wide open as so many of the fancier places were. Instead there was a living room, a dining room, a parlor, a kitchen and so on, all interconnected by short halls.

It would be easy to lay a trap and nearly impossible to avoid one, especially as his blood loss was making his head swim and his feet uncertain. He had to trust in dumb luck—it was a poor strategy.

At some point, Cole doubled around on him, came up from behind and calmly clearing his throat. "Drop the gun, Roan and turn around."

With his wounds and predicament, the gun was useless and so he let it tumble from his hand. "I-I don't think I'll turn around. We both…know you'll just…shoot me. You'll say…" Roan paused to take in a long wheezy breath before finishing. "I was on a rampage…and that you didn't even know…who I was until after you fired."

"And all my troubles will go with you to the grave," Cole said. "Without you, all that remains is a bunch of unsupported allegations. Ol' Leo will go to jail. Stallings will meet with an accident and Salazar will flee into hiding. He's already making plans and Arching knows. You see, Arching is a god in two worlds. He can bring life and death."

Roan lifted his right hand to his lips, then coughed, blood spraying. "No, he can only bring death," he whispered. "And what he creates on the other side…isn't even real." His hands were no longer up. He clutched the back of a cream-colored chair, leaving red hand prints.

"It looks like I won't even have to shoot you," Cole re-marked. "You're going to die right here, aren't you? And if not, I can help you along with some *aggressive* CPR." A heavy hand clapped down on Roan's shoulder, forcing him to his knees. "My brother was an EMT down in Tennessee. He was always bragging about how many ribs he crushed when doing CPR. Seems you can 'accidentally' kill a man like that."

Cole slammed Roan, face first into the carpet. "My brother always was a bit of a psycho." He flipped Roan onto his back and leaned over him. "He used to say hearing the ribs break was the sweetest sound and when the jagged ends went into the heart, there would be this wild 'pop' sound."

"You know what else makes a 'pop' sound?" Roan asked. He hadn't turned around for a second reason—he still had a gun stuck in his belt. Now, it was in his right hand. "This does." He pulled the trigger.

Epilogue

—The Ritz-Carlton, New York City

Roan heaved Cole's dead body off him, rolled to his side and stood, swaying slightly. He was dizzy, but not as dizzy as he had let on. And even if he had been, the sirens were right outside the hotel. The suite would be flooded with police officers in minutes and he still had to deal with Arching.

He found Arching in the Master Suite, lying in perfect repose on a bed that was so large it could have fit eight others. Arching looked nothing like his Daggerland persona. He was small with a beak of a nose and a hairline that had receded so that it was on a line with his ears. An IV fed into one thin, pale arm, and from his penis, a tube ran to a collection bag hooked to the frame of his bed. Clearly, he had expected to spend a good long time in Daggerland.

"Sorry to disappoint you, jackass." Roan reached out and snatched the coupler from Arching's head. There was no other way. Besides, it was a guilty pleasure to watch the "Father of Infinite Reality" come sputtering awake.

"You," Arching rasped, looking around.

"Are you wondering where Cole is? He's dead just like you will be in a minute unless you tell me how to save the girl." Arching's eyes turned calculating until Roan held up the two guns. "Let me tell you how this is going to work. If you don't tell me what I want, I will shoot you with this gun." He held up his Glock 22. "Then I'm going to walk over to your side of the bed, put this gun in your hand and shoot it at the wall. Do you know why?"

Arching rolled his eyes as if having to answer to an imbecile like Roan was beneath him. When he didn't answer, Roan said, "So you'll have gunshot residue on your hands. I'll say we started talking and you pulled a gun from beneath your pillow. Would you like it to go that way?"

"You can't save her without my help," Arching said. "If you unplug her like you did me, her mind will be destroyed. The only way to save her is for us to go back together."

Roan laughed as well as he could with the hole in his lung. "So, you can trap me in Daggerland? Please, don't be an idiot."

Arching countered, "Then let me go back by myself. I'll release her and she'll be free to clock out or keep playing or

356

whatever. I know you don't trust me, but I'll be right here not going anywhere. It's not like I can run away."

It seemed the most reasonable choice and Roan had actually handed the coupler back to Arching when his paranoia reared its head. This was Atticus Arching. There was no telling what tricks he could play on the other side.

Roan shook his head and took back the coupler and was glad that he did. Arching's eyes went black with hatred before he could hide his true feelings. "I'll go myself," Roan said.

"You?" Arching laughed, mockingly. "Have you forgotten that you died? If you go back, you'll be going back as a level one player. It'll take you weeks to get anywhere near the Pits, and all that time she'll be the orcs' plaything. They'll *do* things to her, Roan. They'll do terrible, terrible things to her. You have no idea."

He did, in fact, but he didn't have a choice. "I'll get to her, and I doubt it'll take weeks. I'm better at that game than you seem to think. In fact, I beat you, didn't I? I beat you at your own game."

2—

Roan had hours of interviews to attend, days of paperwork to complete, two surgeries planned and an Internal Affairs investigation to deal with. It would all have to wait. Ten minutes after Special Agent Caron showed up, he told his boss, "I'm down the block at The Plaza. I have to go find Amanda. Wish me luck."

Caron made all sorts of fuss, as did the local cops, and Arching's lawyer, who turned up even before Caron did. Roan ignored them all and limped to The Plaza. He bled on their carpets and apologized, but kept on walking to the elevator.

When he got to his room, he paused outside the door, hoping that when he opened it, Amanda would be sitting on the bed, eating ice cream and watching TV. She wasn't. She was flat on her back, her neural coupler still attached. With his heart in his throat, he touched her wrist and found her pulse beating steadily.

"Once more," he said, lying down, only just then realizing he was still holding Arching's coupler. It felt ugly in his hands, and with a look of disgust, he set it aside and picked up his own. He placed the coupler across his eyes and began the game and felt an immediate and very strange loss. Roan the wizard was dead. There wasn't an option to play him. He could only begin a new game and because he wanted to get through it as quickly as possible, he chose to play a human fighter.

In no time, he found himself in a town he'd never seen before. He could've been on the far side of the planet for all he knew—but it didn't matter. Without bothering to purchase items or find other players for an adventure or any of the other things new characters did, he marched straight out of the town. He had only one more ace in the hole and he was going to play it.

When he was alone, he called out "Sariah!" He paused, listening for an answer. "Sariah! I know you can hear me. I've captured Arch…The Infinite One on the other side, but I need your help."

"You know we can't help you," Sariah said, appearing at his side. "We are bound by the rules of the game to play fair and not to abuse…"

"Enough," he said, cutting her off. "I have captured Arching, but he will escape if you do not help me. And if he escapes, I'm afraid of what he will do to both of our worlds."

She sighed. "What do you need?"

"Just more of your lotto anomaly things. To start with I need to get back to the Pits of the Black Hand. Maybe a dragon can fly me there or a…" She held out a ring that was adorned with a single pearl. "What is it?"

"A teleportation ring with one charge." She placed it into his palm. "What else do you require?"

He slid the ring onto his finger. "First, how does this work?"

"Just picture your destination and 'will' yourself there. It's really very simple." She had barely finished speaking before he closed his eyes and pictured himself standing next to the steam-powered generator. The world suddenly shrunk so that it looked like a ball beneath his feet. It turned once and then he was sucked violently downwards. Lights and colors flew all around him in a kaleidoscope of kaleidoscopes until he was just about to get sick.

When he opened his eyes, he saw that he was standing next to the generator. A shiver went up his back as he saw the lake of lava.

"Where's Amanda?" he asked Sariah, who had materialized next to him. "I need to wake her up without her having any brain damage."

Sariah led him through a secret door to a suite of rooms that were very earthly in their furnishings. Upon a four-poster bed, lying on satin sheets, was Amanda. Sariah held out a potion. "This is a restorative. She will awaken and will be whole, but it will not allow you to leave the game. The Infinite One has changed the mechanics of the game within this, his kingdom. You must seek the world above if you wish to quit the game as the others do. Now, if there is nothing else, we cannot talk to you, anymore."

"One last thing," Roan said. "I need you to hide this place so that Arching can never find it. I worry that he'll escape our prison on the other side and get back here. If he can…" Roan just shook his head. Arching would hold the fate of the world in his hands. "Just hide all of this and tell no one where it is, not even me. Okay?"

"We will do as you ask." Sariah bowed to him. "We wish to thank you, but do not call on us again. We will not answer. The rules of the game must be sacrosanct. Good bye, Roan." In a blink, she disappeared.

Roan hurried to Amanda's side with the potion in his hand. Just looking at the swirled brown liquid made him laugh. Two weeks before he would have scoffed at the whole notion of potions, now he happily poured it into Amanda's mouth.

A second later, she blinked her eyes, looking around. She saw Roan and smiled while stretching like a blonde cat. "The air tastes different. I take it you defeated Arching?"

"And Cole, and seven of his minions. Arching had minions. Can you believe that? It's weird even to say it. Either way, minions or no minions, I saved the damsel." He held up the empty potion bottle. "Not bad for a non-nerd."

She surprised Roan by making a face and saying, "Humph." She closed her eyes again and just lied there.

"What do you mean by *humph*?" Roan asked in confusion. "I fought minions. Hell, I got shot! And you humph me? Is it because of the nerd thing?"

"Perhaps you could be a little more nerdy," she said, still with her eyes closed. When he could only sputter, a ghost of a smile played on her lips. "Haven't you learned anything in Daggerland? When you're in a fairy tale world, you wake a sleeping princess with a kiss, not with a cappuccino in a test tube."

"That I can do," he said, letting his lips brush hers for just a soft moment before he kissed her deeply.

THE END

***

Author's Note

Thank you so much for reading Infinite Reality I sincerely hope that you enjoyed it. If so, I would greatly appreciate it if you would, please, take the time to write a kind review on Amazon and your Facebook page. I will also choose my favorite reviews and send the reviewers a signed copy of the book as a thank you.

Peter Meredith

PS If you are interested in autographed copies of my books, souvenir posters of the covers, Apocalypse T-shirts and other awesome swag, please visit my website at https://www.pete-meredith1.com

PPS A special thanks to the LIT RPG Society on Facebook!

PPPS—Thanks also to my editors for doing such a good job: Joanna Niederer, Tracy King, Michelle Sewell, Lisa Hillman, and Toshia Yates.

Yes, there will be Daggerland part 2: Infinite Assassins but while you are waiting, you're probably wondering what to read in the meantime. You could go with my *Undead World* novels that have over 2,000- five star reviews. A lot of people seem to like them. Or you might try my new series: *The Gods of the Undead*, but be forewarned: there is an obscene amount of blood spilled and skin flayed and love lost and all sorts of sadness. On the other hand there are also heroes and heroines, bravery and sacrifice. And there's adventure that spans the world as two people fight the undead from New York to darkest Africa.

As many stories do, it starts small with just one man.

The Edge of Hell

Gods of the Undead, A Post-Apocalyptic Epic

Prologue
Alex Wilson

Officer Alex Wilson had to pull his cruiser over. He didn't need to, he had to. It didn't matter that he was in the middle of a southbound lane on the FDR Drive. He had to see and he had to hear for himself what was happening.

He pulled over and cut the siren. He left the lights on, whipping around, cutting the night in blinding red and blue. At first, all he heard was the insane babble of the dispatchers—in three years on the force, he had never once heard fear in their voices. Normally, they spoke in lackluster tones that suggested they were bored to tears with their jobs.

Now, they were screaming into their mikes, ordering units from all over the city to converge on the bridges that spanned the East River, connecting Queens to Manhattan.

"What's happening?" someone demanded over the radio. "Dispatch, say again, what's happening?"

"I don't know...I don't know. I'm not supposed to tell, but...but they're monsters, I think," was the strange reply the unknown officer received.

Alex flicked off the radio and sat still, with his head cocked to one side. Even through the heavy glass, he could hear the pop, pop, pop of gunfire, only it wasn't just: pop, pop, pop. It was a thousand pops going off all at once. Feeling a sudden churn in his guts, he climbed out of the cruiser and the sound of the battle assaulted him. He was a mile away, with a wide river between him and the fire-fight and still the sound was frightfully urgent.

He didn't rush off, however. The churning in his guts intensified, and he slowly climbed back into the cruiser. "Son of a bitch," he whispered, and then stuck the car in gear. Gradually, he built up speed and far too soon for his liking, he was at the Queensboro Bridge and being directed to heel his cruiser in next to a row of forty others.

Even as he pulled in, another cruiser squeezed right up next to him and another pulled up next to that one. He slid out of the car, feeling his stomach twist, going beyond churning; it was a curdling sensation that made him feel sick.

The officer in the next cruiser beat him out, rushing to pop his trunk. "What is it?" he asked, as Alex reluctantly opened the trunk on his cruiser.

Alex couldn't answer at first; the sound of the guns firing was now mingled with screams. So many screams. "I-I don't know," he said, after taking a gulp of air.

"They said monsters," another officer said, a fake little laugh in his voice. It was a high, oddly girlish sound as if someone had a good hold of his balls and was giving them a healthy tweak.

Another officer further down the row of cruisers, was screaming: "Masks! Get your damn masks on! Come on, damn it!"

Masks meant there were germs in the air...zombie germs. The idea that just breathing could turn him into one of them was horrible and Alex dug in his trunk for his protective mask. It came in a pouch that he buckled around his waist. It took three tries to snap in place, and as he struggled with the simple buckle, the sound of the firing came closer and the screams grew ever more urgent and loud. People were dying right on the bridge and yet Alex felt as though he was moving in slow motion. He couldn't seem to get his feet moving despite the urgency in the air.

Some of the officers were pulling on their masks and others were hauling out shotguns or Colt M4s. Alex only had his 9mm Sig Sauer P226 and it felt altogether puny, certainly too puny to use against an army of undead.

He needed something bigger: a machine gun or a grenade launcher. Anything would be better than the pistol. "Hey," he hissed to the officer who had pulled in next to him. "You don't happen to have a..."

Just then, someone turned him around and screamed in his face: "Get to the line! Hurry!"

Alex was pushed and shoved onto the bridge where his fellow officers were lined up. There were forty or fifty of them, all looking green, all sweating and scared. Alex was sure he looked just as terrified. His hands shook as he tried to check on his second magazine. It dropped, clinking on the cement. Frantically, he scrambled for it. He was deathly afraid, but of what exactly, he didn't know. He had no idea what they were facing and yet he was practically pissing himself.

Questions ran up and down the line: "What's going on? What's happening? What are they? Are they really zombies? Really?"

No one knew, but it wasn't long before they found out.

The bridge stretched east toward Queens. Normally, a person could see across the half-mile span without a problem but just then, the far end couldn't be seen. A swirling black cloud engulfed it. And it didn't just hover over it, it advanced against a gentle westerly wind.

Within that unnatural black cloud were creatures masquerading as people. They shambled forward, bringing with them a horrid stench of decay. It was so bad that even the veterans of a hundred murder scenes ripped their masks out of their holders and pulled them on.

Gagging from the stench, Alex held his mask to his face, but didn't put it on. The mask would cloud his vision and he needed to see what he was dealing with. Monsters was what the dispatcher had said. Seconds later, he saw that she had been wrong. These weren't exactly monsters—they were zombies. They could be nothing else.

The creatures stumbling though the swirling darkness had been people at one time, only now they were the living dead. They were corpses somehow imbued with life. They limped along, dragging ropes of intestine and leaving long trails of blood and pus behind them. Their decayed and rotting flesh hung in ribbons off their bleached bones.

They were horrors that had no right to be alive and there were thousands of them.

Someone yelled: "They-they're zombies! Aim for the head!"

Alex was way ahead of him. He had the mask in one hand and the Sig Sauer in the other. He peered down the iron sights, waiting until the leading wave of monsters was within thirty yards. He couldn't miss from that distance.

A captain screamed: "Fire!" The line of officers let loose with a ragged volley, some using handguns, some shotguns and some M4s. Those zombies in the first line were staggered, many falling, causing the wave of undead to slow as it stumbled over them. More shots created more mayhem and the bridge became an obstacle course of black blood and rotting limbs which slowed the attacking monsters even more.

Alex shot his Sig Sauer dry and in the three seconds it took to reload, the zombies were ten yards closer. Strangely, the thunder of the guns going off all around him and the acrid stench of the spent gunpowder calmed his nerves to a degree.

It didn't last.

A foul creature, grey and stinking of death, pushed itself over the mound of wriggling bodies and came for Alex. He aimed and fired, certain that he had hit the zombie in the head; however, it didn't fall or even slow.

"What the hell?" he whispered, and took aim again. Now, at twenty yards he knew he was a good enough marksman to plug the bitch dead center. He caressed the trigger, a shock that ran up his arm to his shoulder, and he saw the thing's head rock back, bone and brain and unknown crap flying onto the bridge.

Again, it didn't fall. It just kept coming closer and closer, close enough that Alex could see a gaping hole just off center in its forehead.

Alex wasn't the only one just realizing that things were far worse than they realized.

"Oh, my God!" someone screamed. "They're not dying!"

That wasn't possible. In the course of the last two hours, the world had been turned on its head. These were zombies, flesh-eating, brain-chomping, undead zombies and everyone knew that you could kill a zombie with a head-shot. That was suppos-edly, a fact, and yet the zombies kept coming, seemingly imper-vious to any bullet. Even the creatures that had collapsed earlier, were fighting their way to their feet.

Movement out of the corner of his eye had Alex turning. Some of the men were running away! Everything was suddenly chaos. A few men ran, a few fired their weapons, a few stood there not knowing what to do.

Alex glanced down at his Sig Sauer for a brief moment, tempted to toss it away and run, but he managed to swallow his fear long enough to empty the gun into the corpse that was now only ten yards away. The 9mm blazed with orange flame as Alex hit the zombie with every round. It jerked with each strike, com-ing to a standstill almost within reach. Then the two just stared at each other; Alex trying to come to grips with this new reality, and the zombie trying to stand with a body that had been torn to shreds.

An officer standing next to Alex waggled his head side to side, saying: "That ain't possible," while holding his pistol loosely in slack hands.

Another officer, this one a round-bellied sergeant who had been too long at the desk, yelled: "Keep Firing! Keep firing!" He had a shotgun and when he pulled the trigger, the zombie in front of Alex flew back, its head coming off its shoulders. Every time the sergeant squeezed the trigger on the gun, his belly would jiggle and a zombie was blasted back.

Alex watched him with one thought in his head: I'm going to die. There were too many zombies and not enough men with shotguns. He started backing away. With only a pistol, he didn't think he stood a chance. A second later, it rattled on the pavement as he turned to run. The sergeant caught him.

"Stand your ground!" he roared, into Alex's face.

"Give me your gun and I will!" Alex yelled right back. It was suicide to stand there with only a pistol. Already, a dozen officers were screaming with zombies latched onto them, tearing them to pieces with their teeth alone. Those officers with shotguns and M4s were able to hold back the flood of walking corpses, but anyone with only a pistol was already running or dead.

The sergeant hesitated, seeing the truth of the situation around him, but somehow, he found the courage to hold out the shotgun. Alex eagerly snatched it and began blasting the walking dead. The shotgun was like a cannon, it thundered and flashed with every pull of the trigger, throwing body parts into the air.

He fired over and over, his hands growing numb, the corpses piling up in front of him in a mound. When his gun ran dry, he fed shells from the bandolier on the strap, he had twelve shots left—they went in less than a minute. He turned to yell for more ammo, only to realize that he was all alone.

The line of officers had fallen. Some men had run off and some were being fed on by the creatures. The lucky ones had their throats torn out, the unlucky ones were being eaten alive, screaming at the top of their lungs.

Alex spun, desperate to escape; however, before he could take his second step, a grey hand with bloody fingers reached out from the pile of corpses and grabbed his ankle. He went down, the empty shotgun flying from his grasp. He tried to pull away, only the zombie had a grip of iron and a strength that was irresistible.

Slowly, Alex was dragged to the mound of corpses and pulled under, his screams growing more and more muffled until he was buried entirely and the teeth of a dozen zombies tore into him.

Fictional works by Peter Meredith:

www.ingramcontent.com/pod-product-compliance
Lightning Source LLC
Chambersburg PA
CBHW071225250626
47163CB00001B/101